PRAISE FOR
WORKING THE KILL ZONE

"*Working the Kill Zone* is an enthralling, nonstop, and action-packed adventure. William Craun skillfully writes with evocative detail and transports the reader into the hectic world of being a mercenary in Iraq. A must-read for any thrill-seeker who enjoys exploring the excitement and chaos of war."

—**Christopher Watkins,** Sniper, 3/75 Ranger Regiment, and Author of *Millennial Ranger*

"Great book! *Working the Kill Zone* is a vivid account of life on the cutting edge during the early days of the war in Iraq. The story is skillfully written, captivating, and the ending is unexpected and excellent. How much of the story is real? That's hard to tell. If you've been there, you will recognize that these events happen. If you've never been there, you will feel like you are right there in the middle of all the insanity."

—**Major General James Joseph,** US Army

"If you thought you understood the war in Iraq, think again. William Craun's debut novel tells the story of America's forgotten warriors, the private military contractors who laid down their lives for their friends in battles the US government was too cowardly to fight."

—**Kenneth R. Timmerman,** *NY Times* best-selling Author of *The French Betrayal of America*, and other books.

"A fantastic collection of vignettes depicting the range of combat operations in Iraq. The tone is as real as it can get on the bonds of brotherhood challenged by fog of war, the dynamic tension between organizations, and the enemy always has a vote."

—Brigadier General Marianne Watson, US Army

"Thrilling book, difficult to put down. Written by one who obviously experienced many of the situations encountered by Alex, the main character in the book. The author has been there, done that."

—Bill Bowler, Chief, NYSU Police

Working the Kill Zone: An American Mercenary in Iraq

by William Craun

© Copyright 2021 William Craun

ISBN 978-1-64663-345-6

Published by

3705 Shore Drive
Virginia Beach, VA 23455
800-435-4811
www.koehlerbooks.com

Working
The Kill Zone

AN AMERICAN MERCENARY IN IRAQ

WILLIAM CRAUN

VIRGINIA BEACH
CAPE CHARLES

ABOUT THE AUTHOR

BILL CUT HIS TEETH in the US Army as an Airborne Ranger. He began contracting security early in 2004. He survived the better part of fifteen years in and out of Iraq and Afghanistan, working government agency contracts for five different private military companies—some good, some not so good.

The tactics, techniques, and procedures described in this book, and maps, illustrations, and quotes, are either in the public domain or a creation of my own. If names, places, and events resemble any person, place, or thing, it is purely coincidental. The CIA and NSA can pound sand; none of this has anything to do with you.

—The Author

CONTENTS

PROLOGUE

IN MARCH 2003, AMERICA launched a crushing ground assault on the Iraqi Armed Forces of Saddam Hussein. Within twenty-one days, Hussein's government was out of business, and all the major cities in Iraq were under the control of American allied forces. By May, President George W. Bush declared an end of major combat operations with his "mission accomplished" speech, and then he proceeded to withdraw the bulk of the American forces from Iraq. The expectation, according to Donald Rumsfeld, the US secretary of defense, was that "hopefully, the Iraqi people will throw down their weapons and greet us with open arms."

They were both wrong.

Initial Iraqi euphoria wore off as expected jobs and basic life necessities were not forthcoming to the Iraqi people. The former military, the Sunni Muslim Fedayeen and Ba'ath Party loyalists, were disenfranchised by the "coalition" government. Shi'ite

Muslims saw the opportunity to assert themselves after decades of repression. Most ominously, Islamic doctrine demanded that the invader be expelled: "Slay the unbelievers wherever you find them and drive them out of the places whence they drove you, for such a test of your Islamic faith is worse than death and killing. . . . Kill them. Such is the penalty for those who deny the true faith" (Koran 2:191).

Occasional acts of violent resistance by indigenous insurgents gradually turned into swirling chaos. Foreign jihadists flooded into the country; Shi'ites and Sunnis viciously tore into one another, seeking revenge and vying for control; both sects targeted the Iraqi and coalition security forces; criminal elements took advantage of the lack of security; neighborhoods invaded each other . . . and everybody blamed America for all of their problems.

Mortars, missiles, rocket-propelled grenades, small-arms fire, suicide bombers, car bombs, roadside bombs, ambushes, raids, snipers, assassinations, kidnappings, beheadings, and more insanity all became part of daily life in Iraq. The American military had too few troops on the ground to secure even its own lines of communications, let alone stem the rising tide of violence throughout the country. Supply convoys from Turkey and Kuwait were attacked numerous times on a single trip, car bombs repeatedly hit practically every entry point to every compound, terrorists controlled much of the countryside and many of the cities, and the twenty-minute drive from the Baghdad airport to the US Embassy was impossible to make without casualties. The country was burning out of control, and death was the order of the day.

Into the void stepped private military companies and an army of independent security contractors. If you had the training, the guts, and were willing to pull a trigger when needed, there was good money to be made in the deadliest place on earth . . . *working the kill zone.*

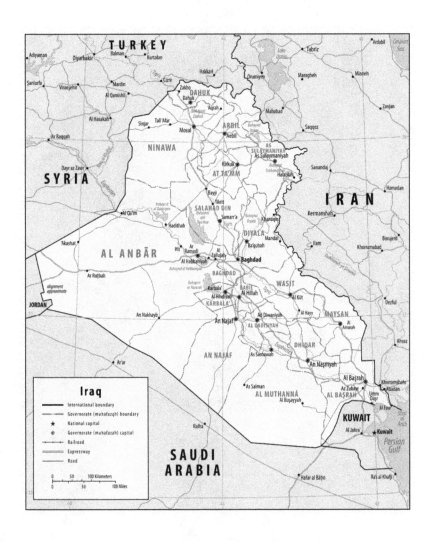

Map of Iraq

CHAPTER 1

Gun Runners in the Triangle of Death

Baghdad, Iraq 2004

ALEX DREAMED OF BEING a soldier from his earliest recollections. His father, his hero, was a veteran of three foreign wars, and Alex wanted more than anything to follow in his giant footsteps. When Alex was a young man his father asked him if he wanted to be a Ranger.

Alex replied, "What do *they* do?"

His father looked at him like he knew all the secrets of life and said, "They run around in the woods and do all the really cool stuff."

"Yeah, Dad, I'd like that" was probably the most naïve thing he ever said.

A month into Ranger School, Alex thought about his father as he poured the blood from his blisters out of his boots and peeled the loose meat off his feet and toes. He quickly pasted strips of moleskin on the new blisters that had developed on top of the old ones, pulled on his driest socks, and tugged the boots painfully back onto his feet.

In the darkness, someone whispered, "Ruck up," and the Ranger patrol rose to move out again. Alex heaved the heavy rucksack onto his aching shoulders and grabbed his rifle. His legs trembled under the weight of all the extra ammunition, water, and special equipment they made him carry. He had not eaten for over two days because they had missed their resupply, and it had been weeks since he had a proper meal. It had also been weeks since he had slept more than a few precious minutes at a time. Every exhausted fiber in his body screamed out for nourishment and rest.

Suddenly an RI, or Ranger instructor, pushed past Alex and inadvertently stepped on a Ranger candidate who had fallen asleep and failed to get up. When the RI realized what was going on, he kicked the man in the stomach with a combat boot and yelled, "You worthless fucking piece of shit! You'll get *all* your Ranger Buddies killed!"

The man tried to get up, and the RI pushed him to the ground again.

"Now you can get all the sleep you want 'cuz you're done here! Work your way downhill to the road and wait there for the slug truck to pick you up and take your sorry ass back to the crib!" Alex heard rather than saw the former Ranger candidate as he stumbled away from the patrol and went crashing and sliding down the side of the mountain; the ordeal was over for him.

Alex struggled to keep up in the dark. *Thanks, Dad. You really hooked me up. I'll bet you're laughing your ass off right about now.*

Ten years later Alex was himself a grizzled veteran of violent conflicts and war across the globe. Along the way he had become an officer, a captain, and distinguished himself as a warrior and a leader.

He had also married. Initially his wife was okay with his constant and often unannounced deployments, but when she gave birth to their daughter, Jackie, she began pestering him to get a normal job and to be a proper father. With feelings of guilt and fatherly responsibilities, Alex left the Army and accepted an offer to make some serious money with an investment brokerage firm.

At first the money and lifestyle were rewarding, but Alex had issues with "normal" life and civilians in general. He didn't suffer from PTSD or anything like that, but he found most conversations with people shallow and meaningless. Moreover, he had little interest in making friends with anyone who had not sacrificed for their liberty in some way.

His wife intensified her henpecking.

When the US invaded Iraq and the call went out for former special operations men who would work in the combat zone for good pay, he jumped at the opportunity. Alex blasted his resume out to several private military companies (PMCs) that he knew were doing business in Iraq, and he signed up with the first one that said yes.

His wife left him.

From his window seat on the left side of the Boeing 707, Alex surveyed the lunar landscape 30,000 feet below. Along their flight path, for hundreds of miles from Beirut to Baghdad, the only distinguishing features were gigantic ripples in the sun-scorched earth that spoke of long-dead rivers and ancient flash floods cutting through the sand to be swallowed up by the thirsty desert.

Alex wondered how many armies had marched through this desolate land. He looked south and imagined swarms of Egyptian chariots making a dark smudge on the earth below as they attacked the Kadesh in the first recorded battle in human history. He could see the land through which Alexander the Great led his Greek army against the vastly superior Persian Empire. How many Roman and Byzantine legions had marched down the dusty trails below? How many empires had been made and broken in this land? Mohammed himself, Crusaders, the Mongols, the Turks, the Germans, the English, and many more. How many people had died here for the imperial ambitions of others? He wondered if his bones would join those of the adventurers of millennia past.

As the plane passed over the Euphrates River and neared Baghdad, Alex had second thoughts. This was his first foray into the cauldron without being part of the US Army and all its assets.

The assessment program his new company had put him through was sketchy at best. At first, he thought that it was just a short refresher course for experienced operators, but in the end, he realized that many of the men invited lacked any significant operational experience. The criteria for acceptance seemed to be if a man was breathing, walking, and willing to pull a trigger, he was good to go. However, the company had presented a picture of professionalism and operational competence on the ground in Iraq, and Alex had accepted their offer—yet another monumentally naïve decision.

The company was created by and staffed with ex-Special Forces and Ranger operators. They explained their US government contracts as a mix of static security, mobile bodyguard (or personal security detail, i.e. PSD), and convoy security. They told Alex's class that they were selected for PSD and would be equipped with state-of-the-art equipment—from weapons, communications, and medical, to fully armored vehicles, air assets, Big Army support, etc.

During the training, Alex had naturally gravitated toward a couple of experienced operators, one of whom sat next to him now and went by the call sign Predator. They struck up a friendship after selection while they waited at home for the call to deploy that seemed as if it would never come. Predator was an extra-large all-American from the Midwest with a shock of blond hair and a short, well-trimmed beard. He cut his teeth in

10th Special Forces Group in the Pacific, hunting down Philippine jihadists and Southeast Asian drug cartels. Over countless beers, he and Alex determined that they had supported each other on operations from time to time without ever coming into direct contact with one another.

Alex's four-year-old daughter, Jackie, absolutely doted on Predator. When she saw him, she would fling herself into the air, fully trusting him to catch her, and then wrap her arms around his neck and smother his face with kisses. He played with her and chased her around and made her squeal with delight. One night he woke up with a flashlight shining in his eyes. Little Jackie told him, "I thought there was a gwizzly bear in your room! I came to help you!"

Alex felt the plane descending as they neared the outskirts of the city of Baghdad. The pilot put on the fasten-seatbelts sign, and his Australian accent boomed over the intercom: "Buckle up and hang on, mates! Barf bags are in the pocket in front of you. I suggest you pull one out and keep it in your hand!" Alex noticed that the crew fastened themselves into their seats not with seat belts but with shoulder harnesses. He looked out the window again and thought he could see the Baghdad International Airport almost directly below them.

Suddenly the plane lost power and began dropping fast. Alex felt his stomach lift to his mouth and barely kept it down. He gripped the armrests and tensed his legs as his whole body tried to lift out of the seat. Then he felt the pilot give the bird some juice, and his stomach settled down a bit. Suddenly, the pilot cut the power again and tilted the plane hard left. All manner of conflicting feelings and physical reactions coursed through Alex's body as the pilot spiraled the plane down toward the ground. The engines revved with tremendous noise as the pilot gave them fuel to stabilize his descent, and then he cut the power again. He repeated the process over and over as the plane plummeted to earth.

Alex looked around the cabin and saw big, strong men unnaturally pale with death grips on their armrests and some with their faces buried in their little paper bags. He recognized that this was an evasive measure to avoid getting shot from the ground, but nobody had warned them. He looked at the interior structure of the commercial plane and said to Predator, "Surely this thing isn't made for this kind of stress. I wonder how many times this lunatic pilot has done this."

No answer. Alex looked at Predator; his eyes were bulging and fixed directly on the seat to his front, and his knuckles were white from gripping the armrests. Alex snickered.

"Hey, man, are you still alive? You might want to breathe a little. I'll bet you're not real keen on rollercoasters either, are you?"

Predator gasped for air. "Fuck you, man. This ain't natural. It's not right. I can't fight back. I'm at someone else's mercy."

Alex laughed and mimicked a small voice while wiggling his fingers at Predator: "And we're all gonna die."

Predator snapped his head around and glared at Alex for a moment, and then his eyes darted back to the seat in front of him and he gripped his chair tighter. "And if we don't die, I'm gonna beat your ass."

With that thought, Alex braved looking out his window again. He saw the tarmac clearly as the plane spiraled to the left toward the ground at a dizzying speed; everything else was a blur as his senses went into overdrive. He glanced out the windows on the right side and saw only the sky. With his stomach objecting, he looked back at the rapidly approaching tarmac and then could not tear his eyes away. He muttered to himself, "I wonder if this is what it feels like when your parachute doesn't open, and you burn in."

This time Predator answered him: "Asshole."

Alex watched, mesmerized by his impending doom and helpless to do anything about it. He felt no panic or apprehension, only resignation and morbid fascination that he was able to watch it so clearly. Right at the point where Alex thought he was going to actually see the left wing impact the runway and shear away, a heartbeat before the plane slammed into the ground and burst into flames, the pilot applied power, jerked the plane to the right, level with the runway, and touched down like a feather.

Alex emerged from the plane at Baghdad International Airport into an oppressive heat magnified by the black tarmac. He looked around and saw a twenty-foot wall made of giant concrete Jersey barriers, called T-walls, encircling the entire airport. The plane had parked away from the terminal, which between the invasion and neglect had clearly seen better days. Burmese contractors—Gurkhas sporting AK-47s and wearing blue polo shirts and boonie caps emblazoned with their company logo—herded the passengers along the boiling-hot tarmac and into the terminal.

After they finished with their bags, customs, and immigration, they were met by a company man who introduced himself as "Alien." Alien was a former Force Recon Marine who said he came over purely for the money, but Alex would soon find out that he was a selfless operator who was a consummate professional and naturally thought of others first. He was from New York and looked and moved like an NFL middle linebacker. He was a wealth of information and promised to help them get settled.

The company compound was just off the airport tarmac but still inside the big wall that surrounded the airport. It looked like a run-down trailer park. Lacking a perimeter wall of its own, the outer ring of the compound was a junkyard of vehicles and a few garage-size buildings made from scrap plywood and tin. Several mechanics in greasy coveralls labored in the sweltering heat to fix the company vehicles. Alex pointed at them and said, "I wonder how much *they* get paid."

Alien offered, "Not enough, for sure. I met a guy who told me he drives supply semis from here to the Green Zone on Route

Irish for three grand a month. I said, 'You do *what*? For *how much*? Are you *crazy*?' I just wanted to get away from him; I hate talking to dead people."

Most of the trashed vehicles appeared to be unarmored, and many displayed the telltale signs of aggressive driving, roadside bombs or IEDs, and small-arms fire. A few were just twisted and charred remains speaking of a particularly violent and fiery demise.

He craned his neck back to see two mechanics welding a steel box with no top into the back of a Ford F350 pickup truck.

As they pulled into the center of the compound, Alex found himself surrounded by a maze of forty-foot-long sea-land, or Conex, boxes converted into living and workspaces. Iraqis milled about everywhere. Alien saw him eyeballing the Iraqis and nodded toward them as he parked the vehicle.

"They're Kurdish Peshmerga. The name means 'One who confronts death.' Their ancestors have been fighting for autonomy here for thousands of years." No one attempted to exit the vehicle. This was new to all of them. "Over time, and depending on who has ruled over them, they've oscillated between being a guerilla group to something like the Mafia, to the official military of Kurdistan, and back to being guerillas. The Turks call them terrorists, and we call them allies.

"We kind of screwed them after the First Gulf War by letting Saddam fly aircraft and gas the hell out of their cities. But we helped them in the end, and they appreciate that and are more than willing to fight for us. They understand that without our help they'll be alone again, and the Arabs and Turks will try to kill them all, down to the last child. One thing's for sure: after thirty-five years of persecution under Saddam, they would work for us for free just for some payback. There are no better men to have with you in a firefight; they'll be there with you when you need them."

With that, he stepped out of the truck, and they followed him into a trailer with *Operations Center* stenciled on the door.

★ ★ ★

The next morning found Alex in the back seat of an unarmored Ford F350 pickup truck with Kurdish mercenaries, wondering if he hadn't made a huge mistake. *This is not what they told me I'd be doing when we were in the States.*

The last words of the operations manager at the mission brief this morning had been "Don't expect any help from Big Army, probably not even medevac. If anyone gets within a hundred meters of the convoy, shoot them. And remember!" He raised his hand. "What happens on the road stays on the road! Good luck."

The four gun trucks made their way around the tarmac of the Baghdad International Airport, or BIAP, toward the compound exit and the "Red Zone."

The mission sounded simple enough. The team of four gun trucks and nineteen men would move from their base compound at BIAP to Abu-Ghraib where they were to pick up four bobtails—the tractor part of a tractor trailer—and escort them some forty miles north to Balad. There they would receive four 40-foot trailers full of weapons and ammunition. The team would then escort the convoy south and west to a compound near Fallujah and turn it all over to the Iraqi Army.

Alex choked on the dust billowing through the open window, and the early-morning sun already burned his skin. The trucks had no armor except for the square metal box for the rear gunner, so they would run with the windows down to keep shards of glass from raining in on their faces and to allow them to fire their weapons out the window to confront whatever threat came at them. He felt the door of the truck with his hand and knew that it would not stop any bullets or shrapnel. He twisted his body to the right so his body armor faced the side of the truck, and he sat on the edge of the seat, hoping to gain some small protection against attack. Sitting wedged against the front seat and sideways like this also enabled him to better cover his sector, which was basically everything to the right of the vehicle. With a glance he saw the Kurdish fighter, who sported the call sign and sideburns of Elvis, do the same in the back seat on the driver's side.

In the bed of the truck, inside his steel box, another Kurdish fighter, call sign "Grim Reaper," charged his Russian PKM machine gun, pulled a black ski mask over his face, and topped it off with a black Kevlar helmet. Alex looked along the rest of the motorcade and noted that the visual effect was very intimidating. It was clear for all to see that this was an extremely dangerous collection of vehicles and men. Since the gun trucks were unarmored and the tractor trailers would make the convoy slow and vulnerable, the men would show off their firepower and try to scare everyone away from the convoy. They called it high profile. As soon as they left the compound, guns would bristle from the windows like a porcupine.

Alex pulled back slightly on the charging handle of his M4 and checked to make sure he had a round seated in the chamber. He checked his Glock 17 pistol by feeling the loaded chamber indicator on the right side of the pistol, then thought better of it and took it out of the holster. He pulled back slightly on the slide and eyeballed the rim of a bullet sitting ready in the chamber and holstered the weapon again.

The T-walls began to crowd close, and the trucks were forced to weave through the serpentine barricades that blocked any car from just zooming past the guards. Just before the exit, the T-walls opened up, and Alex found himself looking into the barrel of a 25-millimeter chain gun mounted on the turret of a Bradley Infantry Fighting Vehicle. The turret swung around and trained its guns back on the exit. Alex never saw the soldiers manning the big tracked vehicle; they were buttoned up and feeling snug inside with all that armor wrapped around them. He thought, *Too bad we're not doing this in one of those.*

The trucks accelerated into the Red Zone, and guns came up to the windows. Alex leaned against the front seat and brought his M4 to his shoulder. Resting the barrel on the door just inside the window, he scanned back and forth.

The radio came alive with the lead truck calling warnings back to the others. "Parked vehicle right side . . . three walkers coming our way, left side . . . two men sitting on the curb . . . pile of trash, right side one hundred meters . . . white bongo truck coming up from behind . . . hadj with a cell phone standing by doorway, right side one hundred meters." Pedestrians could be part of an ambush and pull out weapons and start shooting; anything could disguise an improvised explosive device, or IED; vehicles approaching from behind might be car bombs, or VBIEDs; and cell phones were often used in surveillance or to initiate IEDs. Anything that might be a threat was relayed over the radio.

The first leg of the trip they could travel as fast as the trucks and roads would allow. Speed might help disrupt the timing of an IED attack or spoil the aim of someone with an AK-47. They kept about 100 meters distance between each truck and raced along the airport perimeter road for close to a mile before they turned hard right into "Shooters' Alley." They had two choices of roads on first leaving BIAP. Shooters' Alley was a narrow street through a small town with two-story buildings from which the locals enjoyed taking potshots at passersby. The other route went through what they called the "Gauntlet." The team chose the seemingly least dangerous of the two and accelerated into Shooters' Alley.

From the corners of his eyes, Alex saw everyone covering their assigned sectors. Skeeter, the operations manager, was also sitting sideways in the front passenger seat with his M4 at the ready. Alex stole a glance at the Kurd on the seat next to him. The Kurd had his back to Alex, scanning his sector behind the driver. Dutchy, the team leader and driver, was driving fast and very aggressively. Vehicles peeled out of the way, and people scurried to get off the street.

Alex was in the second truck of the small, fast-moving

motorcade. Scanning his sector, he could see the truck in front of his and the one behind. Dog was driving the lead vehicle with three Kurds in the cab. In the truck directly behind Alex, Outlaw was in the driver's seat with Predator riding shotgun and two more Kurds in the back seat and one in the bed. The last truck was driven by Alien with a full contingent of Kurds.

As they raced through the narrow streets, the Kurds in the first truck leaned way out the windows, brandishing their AK-47s to warn off pedestrians and traffic. Early-morning traffic was light, and they managed to get through the town without major incident. Alex relaxed a little.

OK, that wasn't too bad, he told himself. Then he noticed a hole about the size of a bullet in the window frame, or B pillar, of the truck. He was certain it had not been there when they started. He shifted his rifle to his left hand and felt the back of his seat with his right until he stuck his finger into the other hole the bullet had made. He never even heard the gunshot that would have hit him in the chest if he'd been sitting back. As it was, for it to impact the doorframe and strike the seat, the round must have been fired from such an angle that it flew within an inch or two of his face without him even noticing. *Daaamn!* he thought

Alex settled into place and scanned his sector, trying hard to see everything at once. They sped past small buildings, compounds, and rubbled open spaces in the suburban sprawl of Baghdad. Everything appeared dilapidated, with trash and debris and ruins everywhere. People were out and about to get their business done before the oppressive heat arrived later in the day. His eyes darted from one possible threat to another until he started to get a headache. As if on cue, Skeeter said over his shoulder, "Don't try to focus on detail; it'll give you a headache. Just try to take it all in at once and focus on what seems out of place."

Alex fixed his sights on a car driving toward them from the right. It looked to him like it would intersect with his truck in less than thirty seconds. As he readied himself, he saw the Kurd in the lead truck lean way out the back window, waving his AK-47. Then, bracing himself with his thighs on the window frame, the Kurd leveled the rifle and fired a burst of several 7.62 rounds, stitching a line of holes across the hood of the approaching car. The car slowed, smoke billowing from the hood as Alex and the rest of the gun trucks motored past.

The roads began to narrow and crowd with cars and carts and people, and the convoy slowed. The Kurds were all hanging out of the windows now and brandishing their weapons to scare the people away. The men in the truck beds peered ominously over the steel lips of their baskets, ready to unleash their belt-fed machine guns.

This can't be real, Alex thought. *Mad Max, eat your heart out.*

Then they were again free of traffic and racing forward. Skeeter pointed toward their front. Alex quickly took in that the on-ramp to the highway ahead of them was blocked with traffic several cars wide and up to the top of the overpass, where he saw US Army armored vehicles passing. Alex smacked Skeeter on the shoulder and pointed off the shoulder of the road to the hard-packed sand and back up onto the highway past the traffic jam.

Skeeter shook his head. "Nope, we stay on the hardball—company orders."

The Kurds came out the windows again as the convoy slowed and the gun trucks were forced to close their gaps almost to bumper to bumper.

Boom! Suddenly Alex was jolted by the loud crack of an AK-47! One of the Kurds in the lead truck hung his entire body down to his thighs out of the window as he held on to the doorjamb with his left hand and brandished an AK-47 with his right. They were side by side with a civilian car. The Kurd fired the assault rifle into the trunk of the car and then swung it up and smashed the driver's-side window with the barrel and jabbed it at the driver's face as the truck crunched the side of the car and pushed it aside. The Iraqi jerked his steering wheel to the right and slammed into another car next to him.

Alex started madly checking his sector. Now that they had upset the locals, they probably would not have to wait for insurgents to kill them. Images of the Blackwater security team's naked, charred bodies being dragged through the streets and hung from a bridge in Fallujah by angry locals a few months earlier came to his mind.

As they pushed past the car, Alex saw that it was full of people, and the driver was bleeding from his face and shocked. From within arm's reach, the driver looked at Alex with a complete lack of understanding. Holding the side of his face where the Kurd had smacked him with the rifle, he leaned forward as if to protest. Alex took his left hand off the barrel of his weapon and motioned with his palm down. At least he was still alive. The Iraqi man sat back incredulously, blood flowing freely between his fingers. Alex started to feel uneasy about what they were doing.

✯ ✯ ✯

"Jihad is ordained for you, though you may dislike it. It may be that you dislike a thing which is good for you and that you like a thing which is bad for you. Allah knows but you do not know."

Koran 2:216

Haider Shawkat was a mechanical engineer before the Americans came. Now he struggled to make a living in a small rural shop with his extended family on the outskirts of Baghdad. He was driving his small car slowly in heavy traffic, listening to the idle chatter of his wife and children and focusing on the road and cars to his front. Suddenly, he was startled by the sound of a gunshot from behind his car. He looked in his rearview mirror and saw a blur of something coming up behind him. He spun and looked over his left shoulder to see huge trucks closing in on him fast with men in black masks hanging out the windows, screaming and waving rifles.

They weren't wearing uniforms. He did not recognize the vehicles, and he was not sure what they were screaming about. Without waiting for him to move out of the way, the first truck crunched into the side of his car as one of the armed men leaned out and fired a rifle into his trunk and then smashed in his window, sending glass all over Haider and his family. Then the barrel of the AK-47 struck him in the side of the face, splitting it open and splashing his blood across the windshield. He tried to veer away and crunched into another car; he slammed on the brakes and came to a grinding stop. Holding the left side of his face with his hand, he looked up at the next truck to see the barrel of an American assault rifle staring back at him. He sat back in his seat and looked at his hand to find it covered with blood.

> *"O you who believe! What is the matter with you, that, when you are asked to go forth in the Cause of Allah, you cling heavily to the earth? Do you prefer the life of this world to the Hereafter? But little is the comfort of this life, as compared with the Hereafter. Unless you go forth, He will punish you with a grievous penalty and put others in your place. . . . Allah has power over all things."*

Koran 9:38–39

More shots rang out from somewhere behind Alex, but he resisted the urge to look back that far out of fear that he would miss a threat coming at them from his sector.

Dog tried to pick his way through the traffic, and the Kurds frantically tried to get people to move away. Finally, there was no room to move, and the trucks came to a complete stop.

It seemed to Alex that all noise stopped, and his heart pounded in his ears as he scanned his sector in what felt like slow motion. He focused in on a van a few cars over. Several men got out of the vehicle and walked briskly between cars toward the convoy. Alex keyed his mic with his left hand: "Three o'clock, several dismounts—"

He never had the chance to finish because one of the men raised his AK-47 and Alex shot him twice in the chest: game on! Alex swung his rifle toward the next closest target and fired just as the man ducked out of the way. Bullets ripped into the vehicle, and dust blasted Alex's face, blurring his vision while shards of metal tore his shirt and nicked his ear. He searched for another target. Grim Reaper opened up with his belt-fed PKM raking back and forth along all the cars in front of Alex. Alex could not believe what he was seeing.

Holy shit! We're sitting ducks. If we stay here, we're all going to die. Gotta do something . . . anything! he thought as he reached for the door handle with his left hand. Just then, another attacker exposed himself, and Alex shot at him as rounds from Grim Reaper's machine gun peppered his body.

"Push through! Push through! Get us out of here! Push through!" Dutchy yelled over the radio. Alex resisted the urge to un-ass the truck and looked for more targets. Another face popped up from behind a car and dropped down before Alex could aim. Then two hands with an AK-47 came up and sprayed thirty rounds in the general direction of the truck, hitting everything but the truck. In the next heartbeat, the face appeared again to assess the effect of his volley, and Alex shot him in the head.

Gunfire erupted again from the truck behind Alex, and then from the left side of the convoy as Dog crunched his truck into the cars to his front, trying to split the seam between them and push his way through. As the cars were pushed into one another, their combined weight soon brought the big truck to a stop. Dog must have put it in four-wheel drive because all four tires screamed and billowed smoke until one of them bit into a small sedan and launched the truck over the car. The big truck went up and then down hard. From only several feet away Alex saw the small faces of two children in the rear seat of the car looking through the window at the truck's undercarriage as it came back down and crushed them. The tires bit into the wreckage, and spinning glass, debris, and blood in a rooster tail, the truck broke free and shot forward. Alex looked away and tasted bile in his mouth.

Then they were racing down the road again.

"Anyone hurt?" Dutchy called over the radio. Alex wiped blood from the side of his face, feeling the sting of small cuts from the shrapnel. He looked at Elvis next to him, who looked back and grinned, shaking his head. He slapped Alex's leg and gave him a thumbs-up. He pounded on the rear window, and just a gloved hand rose above the steel box with a thumb extended toward the sky. The other trucks all reported no casualties. Alex said to Dutchy, "We're OK," and he went back to pulling security.

The B pillar now looked like swiss cheese, and Alex shook his head, again wondering what he had gotten himself into. *This is crazy. How many people just died so we could stay on the road and have the right of way? Were all of them a threat? Did we need to be there?*

The trucks could easily have driven off the road and around all this traffic. This wouldn't have happened if they'd had armored vehicles like they'd been told they would when they signed up. *If they can't secure their lines of communication, the Army should do this with helicopters,* Alex thought. *If they can't do that, maybe it shouldn't be done. We aren't doing anyone any good out here. What's going to happen when soldiers come to these neighborhoods trying to "win hearts and minds"?* It dawned on

Alex. *It won't matter . . . too much money to be made by people who don't risk being here, and nobody questions the methods or dead bodies because "war is hell."*

With Kurds once again hanging out the windows, they motored west on the highway connecting Baghdad to Fallujah, toward a town called Abu Ghraib.

The convoy slowed. "Big Army convoy up ahead," Dog called over the radio.

Dutchy responded, "Make sure your PVS panels are displayed, and get the Kurds back in the truck." The Army saw the bright-orange panels and allowed the four gun trucks to pass. The convoy carefully passed the Army vehicles, with their .50-caliber machine guns and MK 19 belt-fed grenade launchers. Alex figured they were taking supplies to Fallujah where American forces had surrounded the city and were slugging it out in brutal house-to-house fighting.

Once past the Army, the convoy accelerated, and the Kurds came back out the windows, brandishing their weapons again.

Within a minute Alien called, "Silver Mercedes traveling east just crossed over the median and fell in behind us."

Before Dutchy had a chance to respond, Alex heard the *tac-tac-tac-tac-tac* of a belt-fed machine gun some distance behind him. "What's going on?" came Dutchy's voice.

Then the deep *whump* of an explosion. Alex looked back just in time to see a huge fireball engulf a bridge they had just passed. Then the concussion from the explosion passed and sucked the air out the windows of the truck. His ears started ringing.

"What's happening?" Dutchy hollered into the mic.

Predator's voice sounded like it came out of a long, hollow log. "It's OK; they're still with us."

After a short pause Alien came up on the radio again. "Roger that. We're OK. My rear gunner hit the car and it ran off the road into the bridge pylon and went up like a nuclear explosion!"

Alex wondered how much explosives the car was carrying to make such a large detonation and how much damage it would have caused him and his team if the driver had managed to pull alongside their motorcade.

They motored on.

As they neared Abu Ghraib, traffic slowed again. Skeeter hollered back to Alex, "We're gonna turn right up here, and the MMC compound is about three blocks down." The MMC was the materiel maintenance command.

"Nice" was all Alex could muster.

Skeeter was serious as he said, "I'm gonna need you to meet the contracting officer. Tomorrow I need you to come back with a new team and make this run again."

Alex thought, *Did I just hear what I heard? Did the last sixty minutes qualify me as a veteran ready to lead a team on this suicide mission?* He said, "Sure."

Traffic was thick now but moving. The trucks closed ranks. Alex was scanning to the front when an explosion detonated perhaps fifty meters in front of Dog's truck. *Boom!* Alex threw up his left arm in reflex as another shock wave passed through the truck. Traffic came to a stop.

Everyone was craning to see what had happened when several men with AK-47s appeared and poured fire into the vehicles they had just crippled with the explosion.

"Push through!" Dutchy screamed into the mic. Skeeter and Alex simultaneously fired into the flank of the attackers and were soon joined by all their firepower facing that side of the road. With several assault rifles and three belt-fed machine guns blazing away, the convoy pushed through what traffic remained and past two mangled and burning SUVs. With a glance Alex spotted bodies roasting inside the vehicles.

Alex put a fresh magazine in his M4.

Pulling past the T-walls and into the MMC warehouse

compound was a bit surreal for Alex. Suddenly there was no stress. He looked at his watch. It was 9 a.m.

Then it was time to go again.

The four bobtail tractors, driven by local Iraqis, fell into the middle of the formation with two of the gun trucks up front and two in the back. The next leg of the trip would take them some sixty miles north to Balad to pick up trailers for the semis. The cargo was ammunition and weapons bound for the Iraqi Army in Fallujah.

As the team pulled out, Alex saw a group of men standing by the compound exit. They avoided his eyes, but when the Iraqi drivers passed them, they drew their fingers across their necks like a knife. Alex understood the locals resented them for having jobs and helping Americans.

Due to the lack of paved roads, for several miles their route took them east back along the same road they came in on. In short order, Alex realized that all the insurgent action was on the westbound side of the divided highway. Insurgents were trying to disrupt the flow of supplies being pushed into the battle at Fallujah. *It's clear that we have failed to secure our lines of communication, like Napoleon and Hitler in Russia, the French in Vietnam, or countless other military failures in history. After we get the cargo, we have to come back this way again today. Not good.*

They rolled without event back to the outskirts of Baghdad and then north on Highway 1, or MSR Tampa. As Alex scanned his sector, he marveled at the amount of filth everywhere. Trash was simply pushed aside along the road and into huge piles between buildings that in some cases extended for hundreds of yards beyond the road. People rummaged through it for whatever might be useful. The skeletons of vehicles blown up, burned out, and left behind were also scattered alongside the road.

From behind every pile of trash and abandoned car, Alex and his team expected an IED or ambush. Alex noted numerous holes blasted out of the asphalt from IEDs. Some obviously came from the side of the road, presumably from under a pile of trash or some other camouflage, but others clearly exploded from beneath the road. To Alex this indicated people were digging holes in the asphalt and planting the explosive and covering it up again so it would blow directly up, creating maximum damage to a vehicle. It was unlikely that this could be done without notice, which in turn meant that the locals were complicit.

Not surprised, Alex mused.

At the city of Taji, they were forced to pick their way through an entire convoy of burning tractor trailers and security vehicles. Big Army was on-site, but they had been too late to help with the fight.

The convoy turned off the highway onto secondary roads that would take them to LSA, or Logistical Support Area, Anaconda. Almost immediately, Dog said over the radio, "IP checkpoint comin' up, one hundred yards."

Dutchy responded, "Slow down but don't stop. Whatever you do, push through; don't stop! Tighten it up, everybody. Be ready for anything!"

Everyone pointed their weapons directly at the police. Alex heard Grim Reaper's machine gun clunk on the roof as he leveled it. The Iraqi Police were heavily infiltrated and known for killing large numbers of people at roadblocks. Somehow, Alex had not expected this. The IPs stood very still and stared at the convoy while keeping their hands away from their weapons to avoid any threatening gesture. They were outgunned and in a vulnerable spot, and they knew it. The convoy eased through the roadblock without incident.

Skeeter turned to Alex and said, "Those motherfuckers will wait for a softer target to rob, kidnap, or murder."

Alex nodded but thought, *That should have been in the mission brief.* Then it occurred to him. *Of course! "Contractors don't fall under Iraqi law." Still, it would have been nice if someone had warned me.*

The road narrowed and twisted through the countryside, significantly slowing the convoy. The palm trees, brush, and reeds crowded close, obscuring vision. At each bend in the road, Alex expected an ambush. People walking along the road watched the convoy with vacant expressions. As they passed a house, or rather a family compound surrounded by brick walls, Alex saw a man step through the gateway, dialing his cellphone and then talking like he had some exciting news for the listener. Alex keyed his mic and called it over the radio. Dutchy leaned over and said, "Yeah, we'll probably see his cousin down the road. I'm sure all the bad guys in the sector know we're here already; they're just keeping tabs on our progress until they can set up an ambush for us."

Dog announced that they were approaching another roadblock. "Looks like ING this time." Iraqi National Guard, or Iraqi Army, was generally viewed as less infiltrated and, while "green-on-blue" incidents happened often, more reliable. The Kurds came off their window perches and held their weapons in a nonthreatening way as the convoy eased by again without stopping. One of the ING soldiers waved, and the Kurds waved back. Alex watched as the soldiers searched a car on the side of the road and paid little attention to the convoy.

The road continued to twist and turn, and the foliage became thicker until Alex caught only glimpses of walled houses and activity beyond the brush. Dog called, "River ahead, and Big Army is there."

"Roger, VS-17 panels out. Make sure they can see them," Dutchy responded, and Skeeter took the orange marking panel and waved it out the window.

As they emerged from the dense brush, Alex saw that the "river" was little more than a wide creek or a man-made canal. A rickety little pontoon bridge spanned the water, and on the other bank he saw the turret and main gun of an American M1

Abrams main battle tank. Alex was familiar with the tank, and he knew that for almost two miles the crew would not miss a target.

The convoy slowly crossed the bridge one at a time. While his truck waited for the rest, Alex noted several things about the Army security that told him they knew they were not safe. The commander was observing from his hatch, but he was very low, and the rest of the crew was buttoned up inside. He picked out a couple of odd shapes in the brush and realized that there was at least a squad of well-camouflaged infantry soldiers pulling security for the big tank. Alex relaxed for a moment.

A short distance from the river, the convoy turned right onto a four-lane divided highway, and the LSA came into view. It was set a few hundred meters off the road and stretched for miles. The land around the compound had been bulldozed, creating hundreds of intermittent berms. *Probably to keep car bombs away, but a ground assault could use them as cover*, Alex thought. But then beyond the wall he spotted row after row of armored vehicles and tanks all parked dress-right-dress. *Who in their right mind would attack this place?*

An Army major escorted them to an enormous field of bunkers, each the size of a large house and presumably filled with ammunition and weapons that had belonged to the army of Saddam Hussein. Some of the bunkers had been blown apart during the invasion, leaving huge craters. The US Department of Defense used the cache to supply the new Iraqi Army, but, lacking the manpower and confidence in the Iraqis, they hired PMCs to secure the cargo during movement.

Four 45-foot trailers stood alone in a field between two bunkers. The security trucks pulled off to the side as the bobtails maneuvered to hook up the trailers.

Alex watched the drivers hook up and saw that the trailers had no tops. Predator sidled up to Alex. "I'm not really down going back the same route we came in on."

Alex nodded. "Yeah, but . . . don't have a choice." Alex absently watched a driver walking around his semi, checking the wheels by smacking them with a tire iron.

Predator said, "This isn't what they told us we'd be doing."

Alex nodded again. "No, it's not." The driver climbed up the side of the trailer to see what was inside.

"What are we going to do?" Predator asked.

As Alex shook his head and said, "I don't know," the driver fell several feet off the truck, rolled over onto his hands and knees, and started vomiting.

Alex headed over there and keyed his mic. "Check this out."

"Yeah, he probably ate one of the little packets in the MREs that says, 'Do Not Eat,'" Dog laughed over the net.

With his Glock in his right hand, Alex climbed up to see what was so disturbing. To Alex's amazement, the trailer was full to the brim with RPG warheads—no crates, no launchers, just warheads thrown in and piled up, thousands of them. Alex had seen a number of these sailing across the battlefield, and one of them made a considerable explosion. *An IED in the side of this truck would be spectacular.*

Predator came up on the other side of the trailer. His eyes got wide and he muttered, "Oh my God."

Alex looked over to the other trucks, each had crates of weapons and boxes of ammunition piled to the top.

Predator said, "Didn't we pass under a bunch of bridges on our way here?"

Alex nodded. "Yes, we did."

"Jesus. Everybody and their brother's gonna know what we're carryin'."

"Yes, they will." Alex jumped off the truck.

The Iraqi driver refused to drive the truck, so Dog took the wheel. The conversation went something like "Are you nuts?"

"No, man, I've driven these before. Piece'a cake."

Skeeter took over the wheel in the lead gun truck, and Alex moved to the front, riding shotgun in Dutchy's truck. With the trailers now attached, Predator's truck moved into the middle of the formation, and Alien's truck took up the rear.

On leaving the compound, Skeeter stopped broadside across the first two lanes to stop traffic from the left and allow the convoy to pass behind him. As Dutchy raced across the median, he pointed at two large sedans barreling down the road in their direction.

"Stop them."

Alex came out the window to his thighs, waving his rifle at the cars. Dutchy stopped broadside over both lanes with Alex's side facing oncoming traffic. The cars did not slow. Alex brought his weapon to his shoulder and pointed it at the first car. If anything, they seemed to accelerate, and then it was too late. The first car was careening down the shoulder past the gun truck. Alex expected them to detonate as they sailed past. He brought his rifle back up and pointed it at the road in front of the second car and squeezed off several rounds. That driver laid on the brakes hard and brought the heavy sedan to a deep-throated-screeching, tire-boiling stop.

Dutchy chortled, "They must be in a hurry to get to work."

Keeping his eyes on the ominous-looking Mercedes with tinted windshield and smoking tires, Alex thought, *A hurry to die, maybe. Why would anyone ignore the warnings? Surely we just disrupted someone's motorcade.* The convoy passed behind him and headed west.

Then they were racing ahead again to resume their position at the number two spot in the convoy. The convoy speed was significantly slower now as the semis strained under their heavy cargo. Dog's semi kept right up with them. *Man, look at him handle that rig.*

Dog's voice came over the radio. "Hey, I got no brakes!"

Great. They kept going.

They turned off the road again, past the tank position, and

across the little bridge. Dutchy pulled over and waited for the semis to carefully cross. He keyed his mic. "If one of those goes in the drink, we'll have to circle the wagons and wait for Big Army to fish it out." They crossed safely.

Around the first bend and just out of sight from the soldiers, Skeeter called, "We just foiled an ambush. They knew we were coming; we were just too fast for them, fuckers!"

Alex's truck rounded the bend. Just feet from the road, a scrawny old cow lay on her back with her groin cut open wide enough to stuff a considerable amount of explosives inside. Two young men in black man-jammies were darting away. Looking back over their shoulders, they disappeared into the tall brush.

The convoy made it through the country roads again, back out onto the highway, and headed south. At their first underpass, Alex watched a man up on the bridge talking on his cell phone as the convoy rolled by under him. He keyed his mic and let everyone know.

Rounding a bend, they came to a traffic jam behind a Big Army roadblock. Dutchy said, "It looks like they've blocked off the other side too, somewhere down there out of sight." There was no traffic going the other way.

Waiting as Skeeter contacted the soldiers, Alex kept his eyes on the cars and people around the convoy. He noted an IED crater, moist with fresh asphalt strewn across the road, and wondered what had happened since they passed through here earlier. He saw the American soldiers scanning from their HMMWVs with .50-caliber machine guns and automatic grenade launchers. Still, he felt uneasy.

Skeeter came over the radio. "Big Army's clearing an IED in the road just ahead. They have the other side of the highway blocked off about a mile or so down, but they're gonna let us pass through."

Skeeter drove his vehicle into the median, and the rest of

the convoy followed around the last of the civilian cars and the Army Humvees. A short distance past the roadblock a crew of Army engineers were assessing a large white plastic sack with the nose cone of a 152-millimeter Russian artillery round sticking out. It was just sitting in the middle of the road like someone had accidentally dropped it and had not wanted to hang around long enough to retrieve it. Alex wondered if it was dropped out of a moving vehicle or if it was being planted as an IED right here when the Army showed up. Was this intended for his convoy also? Alex thought again of those children. *If that had happened to my family, I'd be out for blood, for sure.*

Another hundred meters past the IED, the convoy pulled out of the median onto the road again and for a minute or two had peaceful sailing. Tall reeds swaying in the breeze crowded the right side of the road, completely obstructing Alex's view. The other side of the road was more open, with country dwellings and assorted shack-like buildings and businesses. For the first time on their trip, there were no pedestrians present, and the bustle of Iraqi life was absent. The hair stood up on the back of his neck.

They slowed as they neared the far-side roadblock, and then Alex saw people crowded along the road like something exciting was happening. He suddenly felt like he was in a fishbowl.

WHOOMP! Alex was jolted by the sound of a not-too-distant explosion. He looked at Dutchy and said, "Was that us?"

Predator hollered over the radio, "Alien's been hit! Contact six o'clock! Alien's down!"

"Hang on!" Dutchy yelled as he cranked the steering wheel hard left and floored the accelerator. The big truck chewed up the median and shot up onto the northbound lane with tires boiling. In kind of a vacuum, the last thing Alex saw of the roadblock was everyone, including the soldiers, standing stock still with their mouths agape, suspended in time.

As Alex came out the window as far as he dared, with both

hands on his M4, he heard Dutchy already calling for a medevac. Elvis mirrored his position from the back seat.

Predator called, "Contact right!" The truck in front of Alex's fired at a squat building with adjacent walls. Alex and the two Kurds opened up in the same direction as the trucks raced back into the kill zone. Alex was trying to find targets when he felt the truck grind to a stop. A fresh surge of gunfire erupted from behind the wall, and Alex emptied his rifle in return. Not wanting to get shot in the back, he changed mags and continued firing with his right hand as he opened the door and stepped out. Suppressing the urge to assault the ambush, he ran to the other side of the truck and fired a few rounds over the hood. Predator and his Kurds in the next truck, along with Elvis and Grim Reaper, were all laying down hate, so Alex looked around.

Alien's truck had taken the IED in the right side from the tall reeds along the road. The truck had apparently flipped and rolled down the road; it was a mangled, burning heap. The small-arms fire started from the other side of the road. Alien was crawling in the road, trying to drag one of his Kurds with him. Another Kurd, Sweets, sat slumped over in the middle of the road with bullets kicking up dirt and asphalt all around him. Alex sprinted over to him and grabbed the backstrap of his body armor, dragging him back to the truck. He sat Sweets with his back to the wheel to give him as much cover from the incoming fire as possible. As he let go of Sweets, Alex saw two neat holes in the center of his forehead with black blood bubbling out. Sweets looked at him like he was trying to figure out what was happening.

Alex looked again to the others and ran back into the maelstrom again. He grabbed the Kurd known as Viper from Alien and started pulling him. A bullet hit the buttstock of his rifle and splashed plastic into his face, and he dropped to a belly crawl, dragging Viper to where he had left Sweets. Skeeter was there now, trying to render aid as rounds kicked up dirt in his face. Alex swung his M4 back over the hood of the truck and fired back to spoil their aim. A head popped up from behind the wall and directly into Alex's sight picture. He pulled the trigger and saw the man's headdress go red before he disappeared below the wall again.

Alex searched for targets. The Kurds to his right concentrated on the little shop, ripping it to shreds while Predator and his men poured fire around the wall. Alex knew that if the insurgents were ready to assault the kill zone, things would get uglier fast, but all he could see in the chaos were fleeting figures and muzzle flashes. He went low behind the truck and pulled a grenade from his kit. With his rifle dangling from its strap, he unwound the tape on the grenade, pulled the pin, and heaved it over the wall into the courtyard, yelling, "Grenade!" As it exploded, he said to himself, *That changes things, doesn't it?* He went back up, looking for targets.

Skeeter, pointing at the prone Viper, hollered at Alex, "See if you can do anything for him." Alex kneeled and rolled Viper on his back and checked for bleeding, then any holes in his chest, but found nothing. Skeeter came back and leaned over Viper.

"Yeah, he's fucking gone. Look at his eyes. Musta been the concussion, scrambled his brains."

Alex went back up with his rifle to look for targets when he heard, or felt, the *thump-thump-thump* of incoming helicopters. Then a shadow quickly crossed over him, and the wall erupted in thousands of pieces as a minigun opened up on the insurgents. Alex saw men running toward a minivan behind the courtyard in a vain attempt to escape the little UH-58 Blackbird's second pass. Hundreds of rounds from the minigun shredded the van and everything in it. Doors fell off and bodies fell out. The rotor wash from a much bigger Blackhawk medevac blew over Alex as it landed behind him in the middle of the highway, and medics jumped out with their kits.

Alex looked back to the smoldering shop. A blue Bongo truck

had gotten caught in the crossfire and was cut to pieces. Elvis ran over, firing his AK-47 at the car. He wrenched the driver's door open and reached inside. He pulled out a man who had miraculously survived the onslaught and threw him to the ground, screaming, "Ali-Baba! Ali-Baba!" The driver rose to his knees with his hands outstretched, and the Kurd smashed him in the side of his head with his rifle. The man collapsed back against the car, and Elvis grabbed him and threw him to the ground again. The man raised his hand again, and the Kurd shot him through his hand and into his face. Blood and brain splashed over the car.

★★★

"Not equal are those believers who sit at home in safety and receive no hurt, and those who strive and fight in the Cause of Allah with their wealth and their lives. Allah hath granted a grade higher to those who strive and fight with their wealth and their lives over those who sit at home or in safety. Unto all of the faithful hath Allah promised good things: But those who strive and fight for Him shall receive far greater reward over those who have not."

Koran 4:95

Haider's face throbbed under the bandage as he polished the brass plate he had found in the rubbish heap next to his village. He was wondering if he would be able to sell it when the IED exploded. The windows shattered, and the shock caused him to fall back off his chair, and he and his family sprawled to the floor.

Then a burst of gunfire came from the courtyard next to his shop. His brother ran to the back of the shop in which they lived to check on the rest of the family, and Haider told his wife, "Stay here, and stay down."

He rushed through the shop to the side window that faced the large courtyard. From the door of the room he could just make out several figures shooting Kalashnikovs over the wall toward the highway. Then bullets started ripping through his walls and windows, showering his home with what remained of the glass and shards of wood and plaster. His wife and children screamed, and he frantically tried to crawl back to them. As he moved toward his family, he stole a glance out a new hole in the wall and saw his uncle's blue truck being decimated in front of the shop. He had thought that his uncle was away. He crawled back to the shop and huddled with his wife and children as what was left of his world was destroyed.

Haider began reciting Koranic verses that had been drilled into his head since his earliest childhood memories.

"The punishment for those who wage war against Allah and His messenger and strive to make mischief in the land is only this, that they should be murdered or crucified or their hands and their feet should be cut off on opposite sides or they should be imprisoned; this shall be as a disgrace for them in this world, and in the Hereafter they shall suffer a grievous chastisement."

Koran 5:33

Alex held his position as the gunfire died away. He knew his job was now to secure the area until the medevac was finished and gone. Several of the Kurds moved in an assault line across the dirt lot toward the shop and burst through the front door. In moments, they dragged a man out by his hair, followed by a woman being pushed and thrown to the ground and then some children. Then several more people were herded out and forced to the ground. One of the Kurds shouted, "Ali-Baba," and leveled his assault rifle at them in a stance designed to absorb the recoil as the gun fired on automatic. Alex knew they would have a massacre on their hands, but Predator grabbed the man's rifle and jerked the barrel toward the ground.

The Kurd yelled, "Ali-Baba," and pointed at the house: "Bomb! Bomb!"

Predator shook his head and angrily said, "No!"

The Kurd took a deep breath, and then everyone turned to see a Big Army HMMWV with a .50-caliber mounted on the top roll into the lot.

Alex glanced back at the road. The medics had several men stretched out alongside each other, and they were trying to jam a laryngoscope down Viper's throat to force air into his lungs.

He looked back at the shop, where an Army lieutenant and an ING officer were confronting the Kurds, trying to convince them not to kill the prisoners.

Back on the road, the medics were stuffing Viper into a body bag. There were two others next to him already zipped up.

Alex rubbed blood and grime from his eyes and thought, *What the fuck am I doing here?*

Medevac took the dead and most serious casualties with them. Alien painfully climbed into the back seat of Alex's truck.

The semis fell in behind Alex's truck as they picked their way through the roadblock and throngs of gawking onlookers. *I'm sure you found that entertaining,* Alex thought.

Before they were out of sight of Big Army, the Kurds were out the windows again, brandishing their AKs. Only now they had lost some of their brothers and cousins and were bent on brutality. Alex was not sure who did it, but a shot rang out, and a man riding his bicycle on the shoulder of the road fell in a dusty, tangled heap as Alex's truck passed him. Then, as they tried to push through a traffic jam, the back-seat Kurd in Skeeter's truck stuck his rifle out with one hand and fired a burst into a taxi that was too slow getting out of the way. As Alex passed the car, he saw the driver slumped over the steering wheel with a big, red, wet stain spreading over the back of his white shirt. To Alex's relief, they fell in behind a Big Army convoy that would not let them pass. Alex breathed deep, and the Kurds settled down.

They followed the Army convoy almost to Fallujah and then turned off into an Iraqi Army compound. The same Army major was there waiting for them. He made no mention of the fact that the security team had lost a gun truck and taken serious casualties. Alex wondered if he had taken a helicopter to get here.

As they loaded up to leave, the Iraqi semi drivers came to Dutchy and asked him for an escort back to Abu Ghraib. They reported that locals who had seen them arrive had jeered at them with threats.

"O you who believe! Do not take the Jews and the Christians for friends; they are friends of each other; and whoever amongst you takes them for a friend, then surely he is one of them; surely Allah does not guide the unjust people."

Koran 5:51

Of course, the answer was no. Alex never discovered their fate.

The team hit the road again as the sun was setting. Without the semis to slow them down, they were able to take a different route, and with little traffic at this late hour, they were able to maintain high speed. The big Fords raced through the night and made it back to BIAP without further *major* incident.

Medics at the Army aid station plucked shrapnel out of Alien until he looked like he had the measles. They stuffed cotton in his ears to help with the loud ringing that wouldn't stop; they told him it was to keep his brains from leaking out.

Back at the company compound, the first thing Alex did was clean his M4. Predator joined him, saying, "Y'know, I had a jam in that fight today and had to pick up an AK-47 that was just lying there." Then he looked at Alex's buttstock and asked, "What happened there?"

Alex snorted. "I got hit tryin' to pull Viper off the X."

Predator snorted back. "Crazy."

"Yeah, we should both go draw new rifles."

Predator nodded. "My jam was in the barrel. I think it was substandard bullets—not enough powder to push it all the way out the barrel. I'm lucky I stopped pulling the trigger. Eventually it might have blown up in my face."

They wandered over to the supply trailer. As they waited to draw new rifles, Alex studied the team chart hanging on the wall. There were slots for twenty-six teams, but only six were filled in. Alex asked the supply clerk, "Tony, what's this about?"

Tony handed Alex an M4 and wrote the serial number down on the team chart next to Alex's name. "It's how I keep track of who has what."

"No, I mean, there's space for a lot more teams."

Tony shrugged. "The contract calls for twenty-six teams."

Alex asked, "Where's the rest?"

Tony grunted. "You're it."

"How long have you been here?" Alex didn't want to be too direct with someone he didn't know.

Tony didn't seem too concerned as he handed Predator a rifle. "Company's had the contract for six months now." He pointed at the guns. "You can shoot them in the morning out back to make sure they work. Just don't aim at the tarmac."

With Predator, subtlety went right out the window. "How much does the contract pay?"

Tony bit his bottom lip for emphasis: "*Fifty thousand* dollars a day!"

Alex was trying to do the math in his head. "How much do they pay the Kurds?"

Tony bit his lip again. "*Four* hundred."

Alex said, "A day?"

Tony shook his head. "A month!"

"Hm." Alex needed a calculator.

The two checked their weapons and then walked toward the mess hall for dinner.

Alex said to Predator as they walked, "This contract's worth over eighteen million dollars."

Predator whistled. "Not bad for one year, seein' as how they hired Kurds instead of American expats like they told us in the States."

Alex nodded. "Yeah, *and* the government allows a twenty-percent markup for profit on contracts."

"That's three point six million off the top, and whatever they can squeeze out of the rest of the contract." Predator shook his head. "All for two dudes who own the company. You'd think they could afford a few new rifles."

Alex was looking at Predator. "How'd you do that?"

"Do what?"

"The math."

Predator shrugged. "I dunno."

Alex scratched his chin. "Hm. Yeah, or some armored vehicles, or better, a couple Chinooks to move the cargo."

"Amen."

They joined Alien hobbling toward the chow hall.

"How's it goin'? Can I give you a hand?" Alex asked.

Alien reached for the doorknob. "Nah, I'm good. If I don't bend over, I won't throw up. Concussion screwed up my equilibrium. Doctor says I can't fly, or I'll lose my hearing."

Predator asked, "Plannin' on goin' somewhere?"

Alien looked at them. "Thinkin' about it. You?"

"Thinkin' about it."

They entered the chow hall just as the program manager stood up and called for everyone's attention. He had obviously waited for them. The three took a seat at the nearest table.

Alex asked Alien, "Is this the AAR?"

"What's that?" Alien said sarcastically. "This is the 'get back up on your horse' pep talk. I've heard it before."

"Really, when's the after action? There's a hundred things to go over to avoid making the same mistakes again."

Alien shook his head. "Nope, all they're interested in is filling up seats for tomorrow's run. The team leaders will hook up with the teams over massive amounts of booze after dinner. We'll get our assignments then. Nothing will change."

When the PM was done rallying the troops, Alex, Predator, and Alien ate in silence.

On the way back to their hootches, Alex said to Alien, "So, this is as good as it gets, huh?"

"Yup."

Men gathered around a cluster of picnic tables with bottles of liquor and cases of beer. Dog toasted himself and announced he only had three more months of this until all his bills were paid. Skeeter looked deeper into his glass and said nothing. Outlaw was arguing with Predator. "Well, ya gotta die sometime!" The rest of the men seemed to be a collection of everything from zombies counting the minutes they had left to live to meth tweakers ready to get back out on the road and kill something.

Dutchy appeared with a notepad and pen and plopped down next to Alex and said, "OK, which one of you wants to drive tomorrow?"

Alex and Predator looked at each other and together they said, "You're joking?"

Dutchy's eyes narrowed.

Then Alex said, "You know, I'm not altogether comfortable with what we're doing here. I'm not sure I want to do this again."

"Me too. This isn't what I signed up for," Predator said.

Dutchy did not press the issue; he seemed to accept their

decision. He pursed his lips, drew in a deep breath, and left to inform the company.

Right away, Alex got on the phone and started making calls.

Within thirty minutes someone tugged on his shirt and told Alex, "The PM wants to see you."

Great.

★ ★ ★

Alex looked at the PM, who obviously forced a smile and said, "Have a seat." He shuffled some papers and said, "The company wants me to offer you a job in Mosul."

This surprised Alex. "Doing what?"

"Standing up a new operations center."

"Really?"

The PM nodded. "Yes, you'll have several Kurds working for you to help you get things up and running."

"I don't speak Kurdish, or Arabic."

"We'll get you an interpreter."

"Aren't the Kurds out of their element in Mosul?" Alex asked.

The PM shrugged. "Sort of, but they're resourceful."

Alex was already finished with this conversation. "Resourceful like they were on the road today?"

The PM furrowed his brow and looked over his reading glasses at Alex. "I'm afraid I don't know what you mean."

Alex said casually, "You wouldn't know, would you? You weren't there, and you can't be bothered with a debriefing."

The PM stiffened and sat up, but before he could say anything Alex went on, "Let me get this straight. You and the company don't care about your operators here where you're safe, and you want me to go hundreds of miles into 'Indian country' and expect me to rely on you for support?"

The PM angered quickly. "You have no reason to talk to me like that, and yes, that's exactly what I expect you to do."

"Let me tell *you* something, *Colonel.*" Alex reached out and tipped over his nameplate on his desk, which was obviously a memento from his time in the Army. "You know full well that if we were in the Army, someone would be court-martialed for what happened on the road today. You may not care, but the locals are not likely to forget who we are by the time we roll out again tomorrow, down the *same* roads. For me to do it again or to accept your offer would, for starters, be to condone what happens and become part of it."

The PM started to rise, and Alex pushed the table into his lap, pinning him back against the wall. "You need to sit your ass back down. I'm not finished. Your company promised us fully armored vehicles crewed by American expats, state-of-the-art equipment, and PSD work. Not unarmored trucks, weapons that don't work, untrained Kurdish gangsters, tactics that would get you a no-go in basic training, and certainly not suicidal convoys." The PM started to protest again, but Alex shoved at the table again and raised a finger. "You gotta learn how to *listen, Colonel.*"

He continued, "We both know what's going on here. Where are your twenty-six teams required for the contract? I understand risk, and reasonable risk for something worthwhile is acceptable, but I'm not willing to go on your suicide missions so you and your two bosses can stuff your Cayman Island bank accounts."

Alex let go of the table, and the PM stood and moved to the side to avoid another crush. He snarled, "I could have you killed for this."

Alex turned and headed for the door. "Bring it on. Or let me save you the trouble. I'm leaving here tomorrow."

The PM saw a Glock tucked in Alex's waistband and grabbed it, pointed it at his back, and pulled the trigger. *Click.*

Alex turned as the PM looked at the pistol. "Empty chamber. Don't know what to do with it, do you?" The PM looked up just in time to see Alex's fist contact his nose. Lights out.

"Or maybe I'll be leaving tonight."

CHAPTER 2

Valhalla, the Great Hall of Dead Warriors

THE TRIP TO TIKRIT was an entirely different experience. Two fully armored Suburbans with thick ballistic windows and running at top speed the entire way was a much more sensible method of travel.

The compound, however, was less comforting. West of the city, it was an isolated two-story, flat-roofed house surrounded by twelve-foot-tall T-walls. Inside the T-walls was another six-foot-high wall crafted of mud bricks and mortar that was an original part of the house compound. Two Iraqi locals with AK-47s sat in the shade on folding chairs, "guarding" the only entrance that had no gate or door. The trio and their escort pulled off the main dirt road into the compound.

"Check this out. Man, we got some work ahead of us," Predator groaned, shaking his head. Alex was already making a list of what they needed to do to secure the compound.

"Wrong," said Alien. "You guys have a lot of work to do. My contract doesn't start for another two weeks, and I'm going to rest and catch some rays."

"What for? You're already black as the ace of spades, man. Take my duty and let my pasty white ass get a tan." They both laughed.

Alex's mind raced as three extra-large men came out from the inner compound to greet them. "Welcome to Valhalla!" bellowed one of the men, sporting a company baseball cap and a big award-winning moustache that any Viking would have been proud of. Holding his huge arms out and up to the sky, he bellowed again. "I'm Odin, and this is my great hall where brave warriors may live forever!" Alex instantly took a liking to him.

Predator howled with laughter. "I'm home, Father!" They hugged like two angry grizzly bears.

"This is my son, Thor, and my nephew Wolfman." Of course, all the colorful names were their call signs, but the relationships turned out to be accurate. Thor was almost as big as his father, but with a far more serious nature. It was clear how Wolfman earned his call sign, with eyebrows and ear hair merging with a beard that hung halfway down his chest, thick fur obscuring his arms and covering the backs of his hands to his knuckles, and long, thick hairs pushing their way up and out the back of his T-shirt.

It turned out that Predator did know Odin and had served under him in 1st Special Forces Group in Eastern Asia. Now, Odin had himself set up nicely with a contract to provide security for a company trying to work the oil fields nearby.

Alex held out his hand and said, "I'm Cap, this is Alien, and apparently you know Predator."

Odin crunched Alex's hand in a vise grip. "Yeah, captain *and* Airborne Ranger!" He rolled his eyes. "Don't you worry; we won't hold any of that against you. We're one big happy family here." He turned to Alien. "How you doin', *Jarhead*? You healin' OK?

You just take it easy for a while and we'll get you on your toes in no time!"

After the introductions and insults of endearment, they got right down to business.

"This is a sweet gig here." Odin's booming joviality took on a more serious tone as he showed the trio around. "But things have been getting hotter 'n hotter with the fight in Fallujah going on. It seems all the hardcore foreign terrorists left the fight to the locals down there and spread out here in the countryside. If we keep giving work to the locals here, the sheikh in this neighborhood lets us be, but I'm worried about out-of-towners messin' up a good thing.

"We have three compounds like this one between here and our headquarters in Erbil; mostly we use them like safe houses for the PSD teams so they don't have to travel at night. Cap, you and Predator need to make this place tight for us, and when Alien's ready he can join the PSD teams. Now, all you have for personnel is the two guards out front who do eight-hour shifts, and a cook who'll take care of all your culinary needs. These guys come from the sheikh, who I pay myself, so you can feel safe with them. They'll die for you rather than let him down."

Odin showed them where the weapons and ammunition were stored: M4s, Glocks, German MP5s, and Russian AKs and RPKs, a crate of hand grenades, and crates and crates of ammunition and pyrotechnics.

"Help yourself to whatever you need, and resupply the PSDs as they pass through." He had a radio room set up as a relay station. One room was entirely full of bottled water and a pallet of Meals, Ready-to-Eat, or MREs. Behind the house were building supplies, tools, a huge pile of empty sandbags, a generator—"Just in case I forget to pay your utility bill"—and an assortment of other useful items. There were also two armored SUVs, a small tractor with a backhoe and front-end loader, and several fifty-gallon drums of fuel. Odin finished up by orienting them on a map and showing them where the other company assets were located.

About two hours before sundown, Odin and his entourage said their farewells. "Alien, you sure you don't want to go with us now?"

"No sir, I'll just hang out with these guys for a few days. Thanks."

"OK, if you need anything, just call us, and if we can't deliver it, we'll arrange for the locals to get it for you."

They drove away, and everything got freakishly quiet.

After a minute of staring at their dust trail, Predator mumbled, "This is gonna suck."

"Any of you guys speak any Arabic?" asked Alex, looking at the guards.

"No."

"You're right; this *is* gonna suck."

"What do we do, Cap?"

Alex looked over at them and realized that they were both expecting him to take the lead. He took a deep breath and said, "Well, it's gonna get dark soon, so let's break out those RPKs and find some good fighting positions. You guys want to look on top of the house? Maybe we can take turns on watch tonight, so we don't get any nasty surprises. I'm gonna look around the perimeter and set up some early warning and create us a back door in case we need to bug out. Tomorrow we can start with some serious improvements."

They stopped by the radio room, and each picked out a handheld Motorola and made a communications check. Then they went to the arms room, chose their personal weapons, and Alien and Predator grabbed two machine guns, some cans of ammunition, and headed to the roof. Alex grabbed several ground flares, a roll of duct tape, and a spool of trip wire and went outside.

As he approached the front entrance, he saw a third man

with the two guards. He was a grizzled, skinny old man carrying a cloth-covered basket that he held up to Alex, saying something Alex did not understand. One of the guards said in broken English, "He brings you food."

Alex nodded to the old man and touched his right hand to his chest, saying, "Thank you." The man gave Alex a toothless smile, cackled something unintelligible, waved his hand up in the air, and took off down the dirt road. Alex set the basket in the shade and used hand and arm signals to let the guards know he was going to look around.

He walked outside the perimeter, taking it all in. They had good fields of fire for the most part, but there were a few places where the scraggly trees crowded near the compound. From the roof, they would not be able to see anything close to the wall on the outside. As he walked, he felt like he was being watched, so he decided to wait until dark to come back out and set up some trip flares. He went back into the compound and found two ladders. He laid them on the ground at two different spots against the T-walls where he thought he and his team could get up and over the walls without being seen from the front of the compound. Then he set up several flares between the T-walls and the inner wall. He grabbed the food basket and then a crate of grenades and went up to the roof. He told the others what he had seen and done.

The roof was ringed with a three-foot parapet almost two feet thick, and someone had reinforced it with additional sandbags, which would give them some protection against small-arms fire and RPGs. They were on the highest point around, which gave them a tactical advantage but made them stick out like a sore thumb. While staying low to avoid prying eyes, they built up individual fighting positions with sandbags on the corners and in the center of the roof to protect them from the shrapnel of grenades being tossed onto the building. They kept improving their position as much as they could.

When the sun went down, Alex went back outside the perimeter and set up several trip flares, concentrating on likely avenues of approach. As he returned, the guards were friendly and seemed not the least bit curious about what he was doing. He went back into the house, grabbed a few blankets, a case of water, and MREs. He had seen Iraqis cook with dried fecal matter for fuel and thought, *The last thing I need is to get dysentery from the local food.* He set a couple of trip flares in the stairwell and then went up to the roof.

The night was mostly quiet, only broken by occasional sounds of distant gunfire and the change of their guard. When he slept, he dreamt of his daughter, Jackie, and her mother. He did not blame his wife for leaving him because he was always gone anyway, but he missed them both.

The three men were at work again by sunrise. Alien took radio watch and worked on range cards, or sketches of the surrounding area, while Alex and Predator set about improving their defenses. They found a pallet of collapsed Hesco barriers behind the house and constructed an obstacle course beyond the front gate. They would work on a door later.

At around ten o'clock Alien called to them from the top of the house, "PSD comin' our way, ten mikes, four SUVs and thirteen pax," using the shorthand for *minutes* and *passengers.* Alex let the guards know, and Predator joined Alien to make sure no unwelcome guests followed the convoy. Shortly, four SUVs pulled into the compound.

Thor dismounted from the second vehicle and said that they were just stopping to drop off "Valkyrie." They'd pick her up on their way back later that day. Alex thought, *Her?* Three vehicles unloaded the expected menagerie of motley security operators and their clients, but then a woman stepped out of the fourth. Predator walked up and jabbed Alex in the arm with his elbow.

"Check *that* out."

Alex mumbled, "Dude, put your tongue back in your mouth

and wipe the drool off your chin." But while he was trying not to be crude or too obvious, Alex was immediately quite taken with her as well. She had her dark-brown hair pulled back in a ponytail and wore sunglasses that highlighted her sharp features and full lips. She wore a white blouse with khaki pants and desert boots, but it was the tactical holster with a big Sig Sauer .357 magnum pistol strapped to her thigh and accentuating all her perfect curves that did it for Alex. His knees weakened. He tried to act nonchalant as she strode up to them, but all he could think was, *Wow, what a stunning woman.*

"Hi, I'm Linda, or you can call me Valkyrie. I'm a medic, and I came to take a look at Alien," she announced as she held out her hand to them. Predator grabbed it and introduced himself, trying to make his best impression. Alex looked down at his hand and saw how dirty it was, and then he thought how grubby he must look.

She smiled at him and laughed. "It's OK, I have hand sanitizer with me." As he shook her perfect hand, he thought, *Holy shit, she knew what I was thinking.*

All Alex managed to choke out was, "Alien's upstairs."

"Thanks," she said as she resumed her gait toward the house. It was all he could do not to stare at her as she walked away.

Predator was not as reserved. "Oh my God, I'm in love," he said as soon as she disappeared into the house. "She's a Stateside ten for sure"—a desert ten of course being any female in Iraq not wearing a burka, no matter how ugly she was.

"Yeah, you and the rest of the Neanderthals in Iraq," said Thor, "but I'd be careful with my little sister. If she doesn't cut your balls off, my father will."

"Your *sister*?"

"Yeah, and she's not just a pretty face either. She's used that cannon she carries, and her call sign means 'the chooser of the dead.' In Norse mythology the Valkyrie are goddesses who decide who dies heroically in battle, and then they take them to Asgard and Valhalla for Odin as his slaves." Thor snickered like he knew he did not have to watch after his little sister.

Alex said, "Daaamn! So, is she here to help Alien or to whisk him off to the afterlife?"

Thor laughed and threw his map on the hood of the vehicle. He showed them where the team was going and told them he expected to be back here with enough time to return to Erbil for a poker game that night. They saddled up again and took off toward the west in a cloud of dust at a high rate of speed.

Alex and Predator went back to work. The Iraqi guards helped them build a fighting position for the guards. Throughout the day they heard distant explosions and gunfire.

"Somebody's having a really bad day." Predator shook his head.

"Yeah, I just hope they don't figure out we're sitting out here all by ourselves anytime soon," Alex responded, wiping the sweat from his face. By noon they were fairly satisfied with their progress and took a break for lunch. They washed off the top layers of dirt before they went upstairs.

Alien and Linda had set up a camouflage net for shade, furnished with some chairs, a table, and a fan, and were cleaning weapons when Alex and Predator joined them. Linda had taken off her sunglasses, and Alex found it hard to look directly at her, thinking, *God, thank you for bringing her here today. She's the most beautiful woman I've ever seen.* He asked, "So, what's the prognosis, Doc?"

"He's doing OK, but he's a bit unsteady. I'm thinking if he wants to be on the payroll, he should probably go back with us to Erbil and work in the office for a while."

Predator ripped open an MRE and chuckled. "*Him* in an office?"

Linda handed Alex a cold Coke and said, "My dad told me you were an officer."

"Yeah, well, we all make mistakes. If I'd stayed enlisted, I'd probably still be in the Army," Alex told her as he stole a glance at her eyes. *Beautiful, warm, almond-shaped, amber-colored eyes . . .* He looked away quickly. *Stop it; you'll make a fool of yourself.*

"Why'd you get out?" she enquired.

Alex shrugged. "I don't really have a good answer for that. Another mistake? It seemed like the thing to do at the time. I was on the verge of being promoted, which would have taken me out of the field. I figured if I was going to be an admin puke, I might as well get paid for it, so I became a stockbroker."

She raised her eyebrows. "Really? Why did you come over here?"

Telling himself that she could not possibly be interested in him, he thought, *She's only making conversation.* He snickered and said, "At least here I can shoot back when someone tries to destroy me." She laughed. He continued, "Really, I suppose there were a lot of reasons. I couldn't just sit and watch this on TV like other people. I wanted to be here. This is the kind of environment that I feel most comfortable. Anyway, I'm better at this kind of stuff than I am dealing with people back home."

He shook his head.

"People back home don't have a clue about what's really important. Their greatest concerns are figuring out what movie they're going to see or what restaurant they'll eat at tonight. They stress over nothing, and they all think they have the answers to everything. Over here things are simple, and people rely on you for what you are and what you do. There's no sales pitch here; it's all about what action you take."

"Are you married?"

Holy shit, she is interested. His head started to swim, and his vision blurred. "No," he choked and looked down at his food, "but I have a little girl and I miss her very much."

WHOOMP! A large explosion much closer than the others brought them all to their feet. They saw the pillar of smoke as it rose to their east over the nearest buildings, about a half a mile away.

"Come on, dude," Alex said to Predator, "let's get back to work." They both grabbed their weapons and hurried down the stairs with a new sense of urgency.

They spent the rest of the afternoon fashioning a metal door at the entrance, placing tar and broken glass along the top of the T-wall, and jerry-rigging some floodlights along the perimeter that they could flash on any unwelcome nighttime visitors. They worked quickly and without wasted motion. It was nearing sunset before Thor checked in to report that they were on their way back.

Alex's radio crackled. "Valhalla, this is Thor. We have three victors and twelve pax. Be advised, we are being followed. We have one victor, a white bongo truck, about a mile behind us. I say again, we are being followed."

Alien responded, "This is Valhalla. Roger that; I copy three friendly victors with twelve pax and one unwelcome guest following you."

Thor came back, "Roger that. I think we're about ten mikes out."

The three men took their positions to overwatch the convoy's approach. Alex told the Iraqi guards at the gate as best he could—by drawing a picture in the dirt, using hand and arm gestures, and with smiles and frowns—that the convoy was being followed. They understood and took their place in their new fighting positions.

The convoy careened through the entrance and came to a grinding halt in the courtyard. Alex could see that they were all tense as he approached Thor.

"Y'all gonna try to make it back to Erbil tonight?"

Thor said, "Yeah, if we hurry, we should be alright."

"Hey, you don't have any extra NODs, do you?" Alex asked

Thor as he watched Linda climb into her vehicle. Two of the PSD operators got in with her.

"No, but Dad has some on order. I'll bring you some as soon as I can. We'll be back tomorrow about the same time." Some night observation devices would definitely help with security.

Predator ran up to the vehicle. "That bongo truck stopped back on the road. He's just sitting there. It looks like he's waiting for you."

Thor's eyes narrowed. "Thanks, we should be OK once we hit the hardball. He won't be able to keep up." He fired up the engine, and the motorcade pulled out of the compound. Linda waved as she passed Alex.

Alex and Predator went to the top of the building. Alien was looking through his binoculars at the mysterious bongo truck. He said, "Check this out. The guy's not following the motorcade. He's just sitting there."

Alex said, "Great, that means he's sizing up *us*."

"Not good," agreed Predator.

"He's talking on a cell phone," Alien said.

Alex nodded. "Probably telling his buddies he's found some likely victims. We better be on our toes tonight."

"Wanna take him out now?" Predator smiled.

Alex snickered. "Cat's outta the bag now anyway. Why spoil the fun? Let's wait for the party to start. Really, if we do him now, we'll be murderers in the eyes of the locals. If we do him later, nobody will care."

About twenty minutes later the sun went down, and the bongo truck drove slowly past the front of the compound. The Americans stayed out of sight, and the Iraqi guards gestured to the driver with their palms to their hearts. When he was gone, Alex went to the front gate. The demeanor of the Iraqi guards had changed. They were clearly tense and walked about nervously. Alex pulled them into the compound and closed the gate. He placed their chairs by the inner wall and gestured to them to listen closely for any noises outside and to raise the alarm if they heard anything suspicious. They seemed relieved. Then Alex went back to the house and reset the trip flares and placed some boxes and chairs in the stairwell to slow any would-be attacker's ascent.

The hours dragged by painfully as the men were first alert and then fatigued. Around midnight the guards changed. Alex heard their anxiety as the old guards told the new ones of the mysterious bongo truck and their suspicions. In the eyes of Muslims who truly followed the sacred texts, Iraqis who helped the Americans were marked for certain death.

> *"They but wish that you should reject your Faith, as they do, and thus be on the same footing: But take not friends from their ranks until they flee in the way of Allah. But if they turn renegades, seize them and slay them wherever you find them; and take no friends or helpers from their ranks."*
>
> Koran 4:89

The old guards left quietly, but quickly. It seemed to Alex that the new men were equally anxious.

With Predator on watch, Alex lay on his back and gazed up at the stars, amazed at their number and their brightness. The night was a bit nippy. He pulled his poncho liner up to his chin and was soon fast asleep.

★★★

"Cap, wake up." Predator hovered over his head, poking him in the shoulder. "There's something out there."

Disoriented, Alex sat up with his Glock in hand and rolled over to follow Predator at a high crawl to the edge of the roof. "What is it?"

"I don't know, but I heard metal on metal, and I think it came from that direction," he whispered and pointed toward a wadi on the other side of the dirt road in front of the compound.

Alien was already at the other corner in the fighting position they had erected. Alex picked up a pebble and tossed it at the Iraqi guards to make sure they were awake. They were. Then he filled his pockets with grenades, grabbed his M4, and moved cautiously to the rear of the roof to watch and listen.

Suddenly there was a flash of light from the wadi, followed by a dull *thump*. Alien hollered, "Incoming!" and opened fire with his RPK toward the wadi. Predator cut loose with his machine gun a heartbeat later. Three mortar rounds exploded in quick succession about 200 meters behind the compound. Alien and Predator kept up their fire for another minute, raking back and forth along the wadi. Then they stopped and all was still.

Alex called the tactical operations center, or TOC, on the radio; no answer. He pulled out his cell phone; no signal. He thought, *Great, here we go again, way the hell out in the middle of nowhere with no hope for help.*

As dawn broke, the men began to relax. Alex was stiff from the morning chill and cramped from sitting in one position and gripping his weapon and straining to hear. He moved back to the front of the building and looked over to see the guards huddled and pressed up against the inner wall. He wondered if they'd fight or hide when the shit hit the fan. He slid down with his back against the wall and breathed a deep sigh.

Predator came up to him at a low crouch with three steaming cups of instant coffee, and Alex said, "Man, I knew there was a good reason to hang out with you." Alien joined them, and they sat together for several minutes, saying nothing, just relishing the sunrise, the coffee, and life.

Finally, Alex said, "You know they'll be back. Now that they know what they're up against, they'll bring more friends."

Since the sun was up now and the PSDs were ready to hit the road, the TOC finally responded and took their report of the night's contact and a request for supplies. The men then again set about working to improve their defenses.

About midmorning, Thor and his entourage showed up again. This time they brought some of the requested supplies, but no Linda. Thor said to Alien, "If you're ready to go on the payroll, we'll pick you up on the way back this afternoon."

Alien looked at Alex and Predator. Alex said, "Don't worry about us. We'll be fine. Besides, if you get killed out here, the company won't pay you. This gig called for two expats. Go ahead." The matter was settled, and Alien would return to Erbil with Thor later that day. The PSD departed to the west, and the trio went back to work.

At midday, Alex and Predator walked over to the wadi to see if there was any sign of the mortar attack from the previous night. The ground and scrub were chewed up from their machine-gun fire, but they found no sign of blood or dead bodies. They found some tire tracks.

"Probably little white bongo truck tire tracks," muttered Predator.

Alex observed, "That could be. Anyway, they set up way too close, which is encouraging because they clearly don't know what they're doing."

Later that afternoon the radio began to crackle, but no intelligible transmissions came through. Minutes later, the TOC called and told the men that Thor's PSD had made contact.

"They called us on a cell phone, but we lost contact. We think they have casualties, but we're not sure. We're trying to get an Army QRF to check on them," he said, referring to a quick reaction force.

"What do you want us to do?" Alex asked.

"Nothing, just sit tight and be ready to help if they need it."

"Roger that," responded Alex.

Alien tried to reach Thor on the radio. The only response was an occasional burst of static. Then Thor's voice came clearly over the radio: "Can you hear me?"

Alien keyed the mic and said, "Roger, this is Valhalla. What's going on?"

"We need help! We have casualties; we need QRF and a medevac!"

"Where are you?"

"I think we're about five miles west of you! Two of our vehicles are down and I made it to high ground so I could get through to someone!" He gave Alien the grid coordinate from his GPS.

"OK, give me a minute and I'll try to get you a medevac."

"Be advised, we are still in contact!"

"Roger that, stand by."

Alien called the TOC, who in turn tried to get a response from the Army. After several minutes they called back. "The Army says they're busy. It may take some time."

Without another word, Alex and Predator put on their body armor and headed for the SUVs. Alex grabbed a medic bag on the way out.

"Maybe we should each take a vehicle," Alex told Predator.

"Got it." They fired up the vehicles and pulled out of the gate.

They covered the five miles in only a few minutes, coming to where they could see smoke trails from burning trucks. They tried to raise Thor on the radio but made no contact. Alien let them know that he had also lost contact with Thor.

They topped a rise, and the bloody scene came into view. The dirt road was flanked by two high sand dunes, and two smoldering vehicles were on the road about a hundred meters apart, one on its side and the other standing upright. Several bodies lay motionless in the road.

"What do you want to do?" Predator asked Alex over the radio.

"Well, if they're still here, they'll be on the high ground next to the road, and we'll be killed if we just drive down there. Let's dismount and move on either side of the road just off the crest of the hills to see if we can make contact or clear the area."

Predator jumped into action. "Roger that; you take the left and I'll go right."

Alex plugged the ear jack into his Motorola, stuffed a bottle of water in his pocket, slung a bandoleer of extra magazines over his shoulder, grabbed his M4, and stepped out of the vehicle. It was blazing hot now, and everything felt surreal as he moved up the embankment. The mix of powdery sand and gravel made it hard to move, his breathing seemed amplified in his ears, and his heart pounded.

What the hell am I doing? This is crazy. He glanced over at Predator, who poked his head over the top of the berm to take a look. He looked back at Alex and shook his head.

Alex did the same, but his reaction was different. He dropped down quickly and tried to make sense out of what he had just seen. He frantically waved to Predator and pointed his rifle upside down, indicating the enemy was on the other side of the hill from where he was lying. Predator moved quickly toward Alex. Alex whispered into his radio, "There's at least a dozen of them and they have prisoners."

His chest heaving from the effort, Predator made it to Alex.

"This berm goes down again on the other side and about a hundred meters further over that way." Alex pointed in the direction they had been moving. "There's a bunch of them in a circle around some of our guys on their knees. I bet we don't have any time at all before they kill 'em. Let's get a little closer, and then pop up over the top. You lay down fire and I'll rush them. Keep an eye out behind us. We don't know who else is still around."

"Sounds good. Let's go."

They scrambled below the crest of the berm for another fifty meters. Alex looked at Predator, who nodded. The two men rose and moved to the top of the crest. As soon as the men below came into sight, they began to fire. Predator dove to his stomach and fired into the crowd below as fast as he could. Alex charged screaming like a madman with his M4 tucked to his shoulder, aiming as he fired, one, two, three . . .

He stumbled and went head over heels, cartwheeling down the slope. Without missing a beat, he was back on his feet in a cloud of dust and still firing. Then, *click*, his weapon was empty. Still screaming, he ejected the empty magazine with a flick of his trigger finger as he reached for another mag with his left hand; he jammed the new mag into place, slapped the bolt-release button, and was firing again within another heartbeat. On solid ground now, he charged forward firing, firing, firing. Then it was over and there was no one left to shoot at.

He changed his magazine again and checked to make sure none of the enemy would stand back up to shoot him. Then he looked up to Predator, who gave Alex a thumbs-up and turned to check behind him.

Alex looked at the Americans lying flat on the ground and said, "Which one o' y'all called for a taxi?"

"Holy shit, man! That was freakin' incredible," Thor exclaimed as he got to his feet. "I thought we were dead for sure. Let's get the hell out of here."

Sudden gunfire erupted from Predator's position on top of the ridge; he was firing back toward the road. Alex and the others scrambled back up the berm.

"It was that white bongo truck. He got away." Predator was furious. "I knew I should have killed that son of a bitch the first time I saw him."

Alex asked Thor if there were any more.

"I don't think so. I think they all came together to gloat over us and get a piece of our flesh."

"OK." Alex pointed to two of the men. "Go get our vehicles and pull up to the kill zone so we can load up the casualties."

One of the men said, "They're all dead."

Thor said, "Yeah, they hit our trail vehicles with an IED and RPGs. By the time I got my vehicle turned around, the bastards were already in the road, shooting everyone that moved. We went to high ground but stayed too long. They hit our engine with an RPG, and we bailed out. They were having fun scaring us, but I'm sure they were going to kill us too until you showed up."

At the top of the berm they were able to contact Alien, who told them that a medevac was finally on the way.

Alex said, "OK, well, let's secure the area." He pointed at the two men holding AK-47s they had picked up from their former captors. "You two go to the crest of the berms on both sides of the road so we don't get any more surprises." They moved out quickly.

Alex, Predator, and Thor moved down to the kill zone as the two vehicles pulled up. Alex told them to join their buddies at the top of the hills, and they moved out quickly also. Alex and the other two checked the bodies to make sure no one was still alive. None were.

"What about your clients?" Alex asked Thor.

Thor said, "They're fine. You just ordered them all to the top of the hill. They wanted to talk on the way back, so they all piled in my vehicle."

Alex raised his eyebrows. "No kidding? I guess you earned your pay today."

"So did you, my friend. So did you," said Thor as the *thump-thump-thump* of the medevac helicopter drew closer. Alex popped a green smoke grenade to guide the birds to them.

✩✩✩

"Allah has purchased from the faithful their lives and worldly goods, and in return has promised them the Garden. The Believers will fight in Allah's Cause, they slay and are slain, kill and are killed. Such is the promise he has made them. Rejoice in the bargain you have made."

Koran 9:111

Haider was bleeding badly from the wound in his side as he pulled his white bongo truck into the hospital at Tikrit. He would have to trade the truck for another vehicle. His carefully planned glorious victory against the Americans went bad when those other Americans showed up out of nowhere. He had gone back to his truck to get his video recorder so he could tape the deaths of the last five Americans when he heard the shooting. He knew from the sound of the gunfire that none of the holy warriors were returning fire, so it must have turned for the worst. He tried to run when the Americans fired on him, and a bullet struck him in his side as he drove away. He hoped his new friends from the mosque would not hold this against him. After all, he had caused the death of several of the *kafirs*, and he knew where the others were staying; that should be worth something.

"Fight those who believe not in Allah nor in the Last Day, nor hold that forbidden which hath been forbidden by Allah and His Messenger, nor acknowledge the Religion of Truth, though they be of the People of the Book, until they pay the Jizya with willing submission, and feel themselves humbled."

Koran 9:29

★★★

Thor and the clients stayed the night at Valhalla. After Alex showed them where all the booby traps were, Thor broke out a bottle of whiskey, and they all began to settle down. Alex felt good about what they did, and Predator was euphoric. A clear victory in a firefight was like no other feeling. The only things that kept them from lighting a bonfire and dancing a war dance were their fear of attracting more mortar fire and their respect for the men who had died that day.

Thor was less enthusiastic. He was visibly shaken by the loss of so many of his friends and worried about how he was going to replace them. Alien told him not to worry about the last part; there were men lining up back home for the chance to come over.

"I'm sure your father has it covered."

Thor said, "Yeah, lots of people want to come, but getting some that are really good is tough, and getting them to stay after their first contact is another issue altogether. It's tough driving down these roads, waiting for something unseen to blow you away."

Predator settled down next to Alex and offered him a fist, to which Alex responded by knocking his knuckles against Predator's. "Man, I wish I'd had a camera today. I'd be a winner for sure on *America's Funniest Home Videos* if I coulda caught Cap here goin' ass over teakettle down that hill."

Alex smiled. "Very funny. I forgot to tie my shoelaces. What about you, shootin' at ghosts?"

"That was no ghost. That dude in the white bongo truck has our number. He's probably their ringleader, and he's after us. He'll be back, and I'm gonna kill him next time for sure."

They bantered back and forth, sipping their whiskey for a while longer until exhaustion overcame them and, one by one, they drifted off to sleep. Alien took the first watch, and the night grew quiet again. Alex hoped their impressive display of firepower the night before would discourage any would-be mortar men from disturbing his sleep again tonight.

★★★

At first light, Predator was heating water for coffee and the compound began to stir. Alex rubbed his hands together and wrapped his poncho liner around him to ward off the chill as Predator handed him a cup of steaming-hot coffee.

Alex said, "Did I say thanks yesterday for standin' tall with me?"

Predator laughed, "No, you're just an ungrateful bastard like that. Anyway, I wouldn't have missed that show for the world. Man, we did good!"

Alex was more sarcastic. "Yeah, and today's another day. I wonder who's gonna try to kill us today."

"What's it matter? Let 'em come; we're ready. I've never felt better at my game, and you're just friggin' crazy. Anyway, it sure beats the hell outta runnin' convoys or ridin' a desk back home."

"You got that right, brother. OK, I feel better now. Let's get to work."

Within an hour, Alien hollered at Alex and Predator, "PSD inbound ten mikes, five victors, fifteen pax." The men took their positions. Thor came outside to greet the motorcade.

Odin and his entourage entered the compound. He was not his normal jovial self; he was concerned for his son and his men. Linda stepped out of one of the vehicles, and Alex's heart missed a beat. Odin said to Thor, "Well, boy, let's go inside and you can tell me all about it."

Predator looked at Alex and Alex said, "No, I'll pass. You go ahead. Someone's got to keep an eye on things out here." He went back to work as Predator bounded up the steps after Odin and Thor.

Alex was building scaffolding at the corners of the compound that would get them up high enough to lean over the wall to look down the base of the T-walls outside the compound. He figured if they were here long enough, he might eventually make them into machine-gun nests so they could get interlocking fire all the way around the compound. Of course, this would be tricky if there were to be only four of them there on a regular basis, and he still wondered if the Iraqi guards would fight. They might turn their weapons on the Americans with the hope of getting a pass from the insurgents. *After all*, Alex thought, *the sheikh may scare them, but he probably won't be around during a fight.*

After a while Alex sensed he was being watched. He looked over his shoulder to see Linda standing there. He started to get lightheaded again, much like he did when he was moving up the hill the day before. His movements became difficult, and he felt clumsy. She said in a light voice, "Thank you for what you did for my brother yesterday."

Alex felt tongue tied, and through the ringing in his ears he heard a weak "Sure" croak out of his throat.

She said, "I can't think of anybody else who would have done what you did."

"Predator didn't hesitate," Alex said.

"Yes, and he told us he followed your lead the whole way. He's a good man to have with you."

"The best. I'd surely be dead if it weren't for him, and this wasn't the first time."

"My father would like you to come inside so he can thank you also."

Alex shook his head. "I'm not sure that I feel comfortable with that. I'm not good with an audience." His legs felt like spaghetti, and he was afraid he would fall if he tried to walk.

She smiled. "Don't be so modest. C'mon, let's go inside." She took him by the arm and walked with him to the house. Electricity coursed through him as her breast pressed against his arm. He caught a whiff of her fragrance and felt intoxicated. Then he snapped out of it when he thought, *Oh my God, I must smell like a goat.*

When he walked into the room, all the men stood and clapped. Alex turned beet red. Odin came to him and lifted him off the ground in a bear hug that took his breath away. With fire in his eyes and a voice that shook the windows Odin declared, "Son, you are a man among men, and I wish I could be half the warrior that you are! You've delivered my boy and our clients from the jaws of death! Though we mourn the loss of our other brothers, we rejoice at the lives that you saved through your strength, your courage, and your action!"

He simmered down a bit.

"I wish I could give you a Silver Star for your valor, but since I can't, I hope you'll accept this small token of our appreciation." He handed Alex a check for 25,000 dollars.

Alex looked at the check and said, "Sure, why not?" They all cheered and slapped him on the back and shook his hand. Predator came up to him grinning, and Alex said to him, "What the hell did you tell these people? I shouldn't have left you alone with them."

Predator howled, "Nothin' but the truth, brother, and don't worry, they gave me one too." Alex smiled at him; he knew that solved all of Predator's personal problems with a single day's work. After he couldn't stand it anymore, he eased on out the door again and went back to work.

Linda followed him with a couple of cold Cokes. She asked him to sit with her in the shade for a few minutes. "So, why so humble?" she asked.

"Oh, I don't know. I suppose I feel bad for the guys who died," he said.

"Yeah, me too, but I always have to tell myself that they knew what they were getting into when they came over here. It wasn't the first time in combat for any of them," she said, trying to lighten the weight of something that would bother her for the rest of her life.

He said, "I think about the men that we killed too. I always think of what I would do if I were in their shoes, or sandals."

"Then why do you do this?"

"Again, I don't really know. I just can't stay away. Don't get me wrong about the Iraqis that we killed. I figure the same way you do that when they picked up their guns, they knew what they were doing too; the gloves come off and they're fair game. I've seen the insanely cruel things they do to other people, and I've read the Koran, the Sira, and enough of the Hadiths to understand that they'll never stop until we're all converted to Islam or dead. Then there's the action. It's really a strange sensation. When it's beginning to happen, I feel this dread leading up to it, and I think I can't possibly do this. Then at the moment of truth everything becomes clear and slow motion, and I just do it." She started to ask another question and he headed her off at the pass. "What about you? Why are you here?"

She laughed like she'd been caught. She had figured that if she kept asking the questions, she wouldn't have to answer any. Most guys never tired of talking about themselves. She said, "This is a family business now. Even my mother's here. She works in our admin office. My father's brothers run the show back in the States."

"Where?"

"Tennessee."

"Really? Go Volls! You don't sound like a Southern belle."

She laughed, "Very funny. I'm an Army brat. We lived all over the world while I was growing up. Tennessee's just a great place for old soldiers to fade away."

Alex wished this part of the conversation would go on forever. They chatted for some time until the entourage emerged, and Odin walked over to them.

"Well, son, all good things must come to an end. I'm afraid I'm going to have to take my daughter back with me to Erbil. We have work to do." He shook Alex's hand and said, "Thank you again for what you've done. You take care out here for now, but I've got other ideas you might be interested in soon enough. Oh yeah, and we'll get you those NODs as soon as they come in." He turned and headed back to the vehicles as Thor and Predator walked up to them.

Thor said with a somber voice, "Thanks, Cap. I don't know what to say. I owe you my life and I won't forget that." He walked off, shaking his head.

Linda became anxious as she watched her brother, and she said to Alex, "I've got to go. My brother needs me right now. I'll come back to see you as soon as I can." She reached up and kissed him on his stubbly cheek and turned to Predator and gave him a hug, "You guys take care of each other and call me if you need *anything*." She turned and ran off after her brother.

Predator put his arm around Alex's shoulders and grinned like a Cheshire cat as he watched her leave. "Damn, dude. You are a piece of work."

"How's that?"

"Yesterday we were nobodies. In a single day you get us paid what I'd be pressed to earn back home in a year, you have the strongest man in Iraq groveling at your feet, and the hottest babe in Iraq licking your face." He let go of Alex and slapped him so hard on the shoulder he staggered forward. "I hope I'm just like you when I grow up."

Alex laughed and rubbed his shoulder. "It's all your fault. You could have lied to them."

Predator said, "And miss all this fun? I think not. Let's go help Alien with his gear."

The next few days and nights were peaceful at Valhalla—no PSD and no midnight mortar raids, the still air broken only by the distant sounds of IEDs and gunfights from the direction of Route

Tampa, or Highway 1. The two men completed the four towers, or platforms that would raise a shooter high enough to see over the T-wall, one at each corner of the compound, and drilled the Iraqi guards to man them in a firefight.

They took the time to study the ground around the compound and devised routes they could use to bug out if they needed to. Realizing any escape to the west would probably mean death in the desert, they agreed that the best avenue took them east into a shallow wadi covered with scrub trees, reeds, and brush. The wadi roughly paralleled the main dirt road for almost a kilometer until it reached a small village at the outskirts of the city. Then they would skirt around the northern part of the city and make their way to Route Tampa, then north and northeast to Erbil.

On the fourth night after their firefight, Predator again hissed at Alex to wake up. Disoriented, Alex flashed back to the first Gulf War when he awoke to see a man in a gas mask screaming, "Gas, gas, gas!" He reached for his protective mask and could not find it. He panicked and scrambled to his knees, feeling around in the dark for his mask before he realized he didn't have one.

"What the hell are you doing?" Predator whispered.

"Nothing. What's going on?" Alex's confusion started to clear.

"We've got activity out there."

Alex was immediately alert. "What, where?"

"About an hour ago I could see the headlights of several cars pull up into that village over there to the east. Then I saw the glow of more out to the west. A minute ago, I heard noises that don't belong coming from behind the compound. I think we may be surrounded."

Alex looked over the parapet to see if the Iraqi guards were alert. One lay prone on the ground, and the other was sitting in a chair. It appeared that both were asleep. He took a pebble from a collection he had gathered for just such an occasion and tossed it at the man in the chair. The pebble hit him square on top of his head, and he woke with a start. He looked up at Alex, who hand signaled him to be quiet and then signaled that they had visitors. The Iraqi quietly woke the other guard.

Alex sat back and whispered to Predator, "OK, you got the front and I'll take the back. As soon as anything happens, flip on the floodlights and let 'em have it. Use the grenades when they get close to the wall."

"Roger that."

Alex moved quickly in a low crouch to the back of the house. The sand they'd put down on the roof muffled his sound, but his footsteps amplified in his ears, and he felt for sure they'd hear him. He reached the parapet and felt in the dark for the pile of grenades, put two in his pockets, and then picked up the RPK machine gun. He tucked it to his shoulder and slowly pushed the selector switch off safe, which, when it clicked, sounded to him like banging a hammer on a metal door. He looked down the sights as he scanned the ground beyond the compound. He heard faint unnatural noises, but he saw nothing.

A few seconds later one of his trip flares exploded in a shower of eerie, wavering light, illuminating the entire rear of the compound. Square in his sights he saw the silhouette of a man sitting on the T-wall and looking at the palms of his hands like he'd just grabbed a fistful of crushed glass. Alex blew him off the wall with a burst from the machine gun. Another flare went off, and several shadows scurried in different directions. He cut loose with the rest of the hundred-round drum of ammunition.

The floodlights came on as he grabbed for the pile of grenades and started pulling pins and tossing them over the wall as fast as he could. He heard firing coming from the front of the house, and tracers arced up toward the roof from all directions. He managed to get off five grenades before the first one blew up. Trip flares lit up on both sides of the house as the insurgents started to run wildly for cover. Predator was also throwing grenades now.

Alex saw a flash of light from the brush about 200 yards away and a streak of light like a laser coming toward them. He hollered, "RPG!" and fell flat on his stomach as the rocket slammed into the side of the T-wall and flame burst over the top. Alex crawled back to the RPK and slapped in another hundred-round drum of ammunition, racking the charging handle back as another rocket slammed high into the side of the house. Flame and rubble showered the roof. Alex got to his knees and cut loose with the RPK toward the brush. The floodlights were all blown out by now, but the trip flares still cast their spooky glow and shadows all around them.

The fire from the insurgents tapered off as Predator and Alex continued to blast every clump of brush and rock and shadow within range around the compound. Then there was no return fire. The flares dimmed, sputtered, and went out.

Alex pressed himself to the parapet, straining to hear through the ringing in his ears. The only thing he could make out was a low groaning from someone who was obviously hurt very badly. After several minutes, the noise grew louder, and eventually it stopped. The men stayed where they were until dawn.

As visibility increased, Predator shuffled up to Alex with coffee. Alex gave him a wry smile. "You are definitely the *man*. How're you doin'?"

Predator plopped down next to him and said, "I'm alright. I got some fragments in my calf, but they'll just match the ones in my other leg from the Army. I wonder if I'll be able to tell the difference. And my knuckles and elbows are all scratched up too, from hittin' the deck." Alex looked at him weirdly. "What're you lookin' at?"

"The hole in your hat," Alex said matter-of-factly.

Predator snatched his baseball cap off his head and twisted it around. "I'll be damned."

There was a single clean hole in the bill of his cap, just above his left eye. He tried to push his little finger through the hole. "Looks like 7.62. Very cool. I'm gonna have to keep this one for sure." He put the hat back on. The AK-47 round must have passed within an inch of his face to make a hole like that.

Alex asked, "How'd the guards do?"

"They did great, man—just like we practiced. They got up in the towers, and as soon as the lights went on, they poked their AKs over the side and hosed it down. Yeah, they did fine."

They sat there until they finished their coffee.

Predator called the contact report to the TOC and requested resupply. Alex got two more cups of coffee and took them with him as he went down to check on the Iraqi guards. They were sitting in their chairs, wrapped in blankets with their AKs between their legs and leaning toward each other, talking and making gestures like they were going over their heroic exploits. They saw Alex coming and, grinning, they started to rise. Alex gestured to stay seated and handed each a cup of coffee.

He saw blood on one of their sleeves. His eyes narrowed and he pointed to the man's arm. The guard held up his palm and waved it back and forth, then clenched his fist and pounded it to his chest and grunted. Then he grinned like a little kid. Alex understood. He had a man-sized story to tell, and the wound was a badge of honor to prove it. Alex pulled four crisp 100-dollar bills from his wallet and handed two of them to each of the guards. Alex felt a little guilty at the paltry sum, but he knew it was probably as much as a month's wage for them, maybe more. They were clearly pleased, and completely surprised.

Alex put his right palm to his heart and said, "*Shukran.*" They both nodded and put their hands to their chests in a similar manner. One of them said in perfect English, "You are welcome."

Back on top of the house, Alex and Predator were eating their breakfast when a convoy of Iraqi police and several SUVs came into sight. They pulled up in front of the compound, dismounted, and fanned out. Several men came to the gate and pounded on the door.

Predator stayed on top of the house, and Alex went down the steps to face them. He did not know what to expect and mentally prepared himself for the worst. He slung his M4 so it hung at the ready across his chest with the muzzle inoffensively pointed down in a way he could bring it to bear quickly.

The guards had already opened the gate, and several men entered. Three uniformed police with AKs at the ready and one officer standing with his arms folded listened to the guards as they explained what had happened with great animation to three civilian men wearing white dishdashas. They all stopped when Alex stepped into the courtyard, and watched him as he walked toward them. The three police raised the barrels of their weapons ever so slightly, and their eyes narrowed while their officer dropped his hands to his side, closer to his sidearm. Their body language was very threatening, but Alex understood that this did not necessarily mean they were friends with the men who had died here during the night. Alex placed his right hand to his heart, nodded to the man who seemed to be the center of their attention, and introduced himself.

Offering his right hand to Alex to shake, the distinguished-looking man with a shocking white beard and mustache said in perfect English, "Hello, my name is Sheikh Ibrahim Khalaf Ali, and this is my property. I am pleased that you were unhurt in this unfortunate incident. My nephews here tell me they are indebted to your attention and leadership. We thank you and offer you whatever assistance you may need."

Alex exhaled a breath of relief.

They strolled around the outside of the compound and observed the carnage. The old sheikh was not in the least way concerned with the dead, and he spoke with Alex as if they were strolling through a park at Oxford University. He talked about his trips to America, his friendship with American politicians and movie stars, and philosophy and history. He talked about anything and everything except the death and gore that lay in his yard. Alex listened as attentively as he could and responded when he thought appropriate.

However, what really had Alex's attention was the way the men treated the bodies of the dead insurgents. Alex expected them to have some respect, but they did not. They kicked the bodies to make sure they were dead before they grabbed them by the cuffs of their pants and dragged them back to the road. One man picked up a severed arm and scratched his back with the stiff fingers and then offered it to his friend as if to shake hands in greeting. The other man shook it with vigor, and they laughed and tossed the arm onto the stack of bodies they were collecting.

At the road, the police rifled through the pockets of the dead men and stuffed the loot in their own pockets. One man tripped one of Alex's flares, which flamed up and scared him into sprawling face-first in the dirt, to the laughter of his friends. When they were finished and had collected all the weapons and ammunition, they unceremoniously tossed the bodies onto the back of a flatbed truck.

Odin showed up with Linda and an escort. Odin and Sheikh Ali immediately retired into the house together.

Linda came up to Alex and looked at him quizzically. "Are you OK?"

"Yeah, I'm fine. Predator took some shrapnel in his leg. You should look at him," he said, his words short and clipped.

She furrowed her brow and said, "That's not what I mean. I know you had a terrible night and I'm concerned."

"I'm sorry. I've just been watching the way these guys treat the dead. There's not a shred of care in them that people died last night. I won't lose any sleep over them either, but I wouldn't play catch with their body parts either. I can't understand why these people don't stop with all the hate and try to live productively. I just hope we don't ever get to the point back home that we accept death so callously. I want my little girl to grow up feeling safe and secure. Anyway"—he tried his best to smile—"I'll be fine, thanks."

They walked together to the back of the house and up to the roof.

Predator had been watching the cleanup. "Hey, Cap, ya know, there's at least a dozen bodies stacked on that truck. I do believe that's a record for us." They watched as the truck pulled away to the west. Predator said, "Check that out: there's nothin' out that way for miles. They're just gonna dump 'em in the desert somewhere. Prob'ly won't even bother to cover 'em with dirt. Man, what a way to go; the cleanup crew gets to play kickball with your head and then toss you into the desert for the buzzards to chew on."

"Buzzards gotta eat too," Alex snickered.

"Yeah, well, I guess when I'm dead I won't much care what happens to me, but fire would clean things up nicely."

Alex said, "Yeah, I want to be cremated too. I don't want any critters, buzzards or worms, munchin' on my carcass."

"You want a funeral pyre? Or will a thermite grenade stuffed up your butt work OK for ya?"

Linda tried not to laugh. "All right, you guys, stop with the morbid jokes. Let me see your leg."

Predator said, "I thought you'd never ask," and dropped his pants.

Alex howled with laughter, pointing at Predator's Mickey Mouse boxers.

"Hey, man, at least I'm wearin' some."

✦✦✦

"If the hypocrites, and those in whose hearts is a disease, and the alarmists in the city do not cease, we verily shall urge you on against them, then they will be your neighbors for but a little while. Accursed, they will be seized wherever found and slain with a fierce slaughter."

Koran 33:60–62

Haider was just able to get up and move around now. The bullet had broken two of his ribs and traveled down his side to lodge in the top of his hip. He felt lucky. The doctor told him that if the bullet had not ricocheted off his rib, it probably would have entered his lung or some other vital organ. His family would arrive soon to take him home.

There was a knock at the door. He struggled to get up from his chair and opened the door. To his surprise, his new mullah entered the room with two men he did not know, one of whom was the biggest, ugliest, scariest man Haider had ever seen. He greeted them and invited them to sit down. The mullah sat with him, but the other two men stood back and said nothing. Haider stole a glance at them and began to worry.

The mullah began, "Brother, the news is not good. The information you gave us has again caused the death of many of our faithful warriors."

Haider was horrified.

The mullah narrowed his eyes and leaned forward until Haider felt his hot breath on his face. "But there is a way for you to redeem yourself in the eyes of Allah."

Haider's head began to spin. He felt certain now that they would make him strap on a suicide vest and blow himself up. His voice was creaky and uncertain when he responded tentatively, "How may I assist in Allah's Cause?"

The mullah breathed, "You are an engineer, are you not?"

"Then fight in Allah's Cause. Incite the believers to fight with you."

Koran 4:84

⋆⋆⋆

It was Alex's turn on watch, and he sat sipping a cup of coffee. The nights were getting colder now, and the clear sky enabled him to see well. He listened for anything out of the ordinary and peered into the night shadows. He thought of his daughter, Jackie, and wondered if she would like Linda. *Of course she would.*

He wondered too what he would do with himself when he went back to the States. His old business was out of the question; the money was good, but he did not like promising people a great future and then watching their dreams go down with the stock market. Maybe he could get a job with one of the PMC's training facilities out in the woods, but he knew competition for those jobs would be fierce and limited mainly to family and company insiders. Personal security was out of the question. Ex–Secret Service people had a lock on that industry even though most of them never make contact with any real threat. For some fantasy reason, people with money had the impression that Secret Service agents were the experts. Besides, he did not want to wear a suit again—too Hollywood.

No, he figured, *this is where I belong. Some cesspool in the anus of the world where the entire population wants to kill me.*

He heard a commotion coming from the east: voices yelling, and then a burst of gunfire. Predator materialized next to him. "What's goin' on?"

"I don't know. It's coming from that little village over there." Alex pointed to the east. He poked his head over the parapet and saw that the Iraqi guards were alert. They watched as headlights of several vehicles emerged from the village, heading in their direction. Then another long burst of gunfire from the village, and

Alex saw tracers following the vehicles. Then a heavier volume of fire opened up on them as they cleared the last building. As they raced toward the compound and got closer, Alex could see the markings on their white vehicles.

"Iraqi police. What the hell?"

The vehicles came to a skidding halt in front of the compound, and a dozen or so uniformed police bailed out and ran to the front gate. Alex saw the officer from the other day run with his pistol in his hand until he was obscured by the T-wall. They pounded on the gate, yelling. Alex looked over the edge and saw one of the Iraqi guards looking through a gap in the doorframe and yelling back at them. He clearly did not want to let them in. Then a sudden flash of light and a loud bang as his brains exploded out the back of his head. Alex and Predator both instinctively ducked down out of sight.

"Holy shit, what do we do now?" Predator said.

Alex flipped his M4 off safe and, rifles first, they both peeked over the edge just in time to watch the other guard open the gate. The Iraqi police streamed in, and the guard dropped his weapon into the dirt and fell to his knees. Pistol outstretched, the police officer walked up to him and shot him in the head also. Alex and Predator opened fire together, dropping the officer where he stood. The rest of the police fired back. Alex emptied his magazine and dropped down for cover as he ejected the empty one and slammed in another. Then he pulled a grenade from his pocket, yanked the pin, and tossed it into the courtyard as he hollered to Predator, "Grenade!" Predator dropped down next to him and changed his magazine also. When the grenade exploded, they both went up again shooting. The police were running back toward their vehicles, firing at the top of the house as they went.

✬ ✬ ✬

"If thou comest on them in conflict, deal with them so as to strike fear in those who are behind them that haply they may remember."

Koran 8:57

Haider watched as the police opened the gate for his martyr. The sweaty young man in the driver's seat next to him gripped the steering wheel like a vise and mumbled breathlessly over and over, "Allahu Akbar, Allahu Akbar, Allahu Akbar . . ."

They had been able to approach the compound from the west with the driving lights off. It seemed that nobody from the compound noticed them coming. Certainly, all their attention was on the commotion caused by the police. Then there were a couple of gunshots and the compound erupted in gunfire.

He urged his young driver to ease the bongo truck closer. He told the young man that the mullah would honor his promise and take care of his family, reminded him that he was going to paradise, and stepped out of the truck. He urged the young man forward again. The truck had some difficulty moving and strained under the weight of all the explosives they had packed into the bed. Then it began to speed toward the compound.

"That you strive and fight in Allah's Cause, He will forgive you your sins, and admit you to Gardens under which rivers flow, and to beautiful mansions in Eden: that is indeed the Supreme Achievement. And another favor which you love: help from Allah for a speedy victory over your enemies."

Koran 61:12

***

Alex yelled, "We gotta close the gate!"

He jumped to his feet and ran across the roof toward the rear of the house. He was struggling past the junk he had placed in the stairwell when he heard Predator holler, "White bongo truck!" and cut loose with another burst of fire as the truck entered the compound. Alex pitched forward and down the stairs as the concussion from the explosion sucked the air out of his lungs and the building collapsed on top of him. His world went black.

Alex's next sensation was a terrible ringing in his ears. He heard himself breathing but could not see anything. Slowly his vision began to clear, first as a pinprick, and gradually as a small hole. He found himself sitting up on his knees, looking at his hands. He could not feel them, but they were covered with something dark and wet. He told his fingers to move, and they slowly responded, first one and then another, and then he was able to squeeze them together in a fist.

Through the eerie haze he could tell that the house was destroyed. He tried to get up as rubble and dirt fell from his clothing, and his body pitched sideways into the debris. As he lay there, he had a sudden thought: *Predator!* He rolled onto his stomach.

He tried to lift himself up by his hands and knees and felt something hot and wet run down his face and drip off his nose and chin. It tasted salty. He was bleeding. He sat back on his feet and tried to feel for injury. With what little sensation he had in his fingers, he could tell that the back of his head was a mess. He brushed the rubbish off the wound and reached into his cargo pocket for a pressure dressing. He fumbled with the package until he was finally able to rip it open. Then he unraveled it and dropped it on the ground. He struggled to pick it up without falling over again. Then he pushed it to the wound and wrapped the ends around his head a couple of time, tying it off at his forehead.

He tried once more to get up, but his left leg was completely numb and not cooperating. With considerable effort he managed to get to his feet, but with his first step he crashed down into the debris again. He thought, *This isn't working too well. C'mon, you gotta help Predator.* He rolled over and pushed himself to his hands and knees again. He pulled a broken piece of two-by-four to him and used it to steady himself as he rose to his feet. Using the two-by-four as a crutch, he picked his way to the front of the collapsed house.

The front of the building was obliterated. He called out in a hoarse whisper for Predator. Nothing. As he pushed around in the wreckage, the feeling in his leg began to return. It was not a good feeling. Hot, searing pain radiated from below his hip, but at least it was beginning to work. He frantically pushed the rubble aside, but he found no sign of his friend. He picked up one of the AK-47s and shook off the dirt. With bloody and grimy hands, he pulled back slightly on the charging handle to make sure a round was chambered, and then he removed the magazine to find it full of ammunition. Replacing the magazine, he slung the rifle over his shoulder and continued to search for Predator. After several minutes of searching he realized that it was fruitless. He sat down on a pile of debris and buried his face in his bloody hands.

His mouth and lips had turned to a dry paste of crusted blood and sand, and he knew he needed something to drink. He struggled painfully to his feet again and gingerly worked his way to the back of the house where they had kept their water supply. He found some undamaged plastic water bottles and stuffed them into his pockets. He washed his mouth out and then took several big gulps. He searched what had been the weapons and communications room. Finding a bandoleer of loaded AK magazines, he slung it over his shoulder. As he picked up a Motorola and pressed the button to see if it was working, he heard vehicles approaching the compound.

After seeing the resident police in action, he was not about to stick around to see what other surprises the locals had in store for him. He clipped the Motorola to his belt and with great effort hurried over to the west wall where he had left the ladder. He placed the ladder against the wall and hauled himself up with great difficulty. At the top he gripped the crushed glass with his hands and lowered himself over the other side. Before he let go, he tried to push the ladder back into the yard, but his bloody, mangled hand slipped, and he fell with a crash to the ground. The explosion of pain in his leg was so great that he stifled a scream, and he writhed on the ground in agony. He rolled onto his back and lifted his midsection off the ground, trying to relieve the pain and not cry out. Then he passed out.

When he started to come to, it was still dark. He realized it was his own groaning and pain that had awakened him, and he held his breath and froze. At first, he heard nothing, and then he made out voices and strained to hear what they were saying. It was Arabic. He rolled over to his stomach and began to crawl away to the west.

He pulled himself with his hands clawing the ground and pushed with his good leg, and then passed out again. He came to and did it again, pulling, pushing, and passing out again. He lost track of how many times he did this. Eventually, as he regained consciousness he no longer cared if anyone could see him. At this point death would have been a welcome relief. By sunrise he was well out of sight of the house, and he found himself in a shallow wadi. He crawled into some brush for concealment, rolled onto his back, and passed out again.

Alex came out of it again with new pains coursing through his back and hips. He felt behind him and realized the AK-47 and the magazines were digging into his back. He moved the weapon out from under him, and his leg sounded off again. He groaned in agony. The sun was high, and he was seriously dehydrated.

He pulled a bottle of water from his pocket and tried to open it, but his hands were ripped to shreds from the crushed glass, and they were shaking too hard to grip the bottle top. He thought, *Great, I'm gonna die right here in the desert, and the bugs and buzzards get to eat my carcass after all.*

Then he heard something and froze. He reached down and slowly picked up the AK and eased the bolt back with the palm of his hand again to make sure there was a round still in the chamber. He quietly took the weapon off safe and raised it up as best he could. The noise came closer until he could make out the crunching of footsteps on the hard-packed dirt. He held his breath and tightened his grip on the AK-47. Then he heard a voice.

"Over here, I think I've got something!" It was Thor. Alex lowered the weapon, exhaled, and then passed out again.

CHAPTER 3

Home Is Where I Hang My Helmet

ALEX REGAINED CONSCIOUSNESS IN a hospital bed. He lay perfectly still, staring at the ceiling for quite some time and not understanding where he was or what had happened. All he understood was that he was alive and in a comfortable bed, so he must be safe.

He raised his hands and saw that although they were bandaged, all his fingers were there, and they worked. The tube of an IV dangled from his wrist. He felt his head with his fingertips and could tell it was fully bandaged. He tried to move his legs and found it difficult. Down at his waist he found something hard and, pushing the sheet down, saw a cast around his waist and down his left leg. At least his leg was still there. He raised his right leg up and tried to move his toes; they all worked. He lay back and breathed a sigh of relief. *I'm gonna be OK*. He fell back to sleep.

He dreamed of Linda. She was smiling at him, and he felt

wonderful and warm. She swirled in a flowing white dress, dancing on the sand with her arms outstretched and the sun shining off her beautiful, silky hair. She was laughing and happy, and so was he. He was at absolute peace. Then everything was dark, and his heart dropped before he knew why. She was suddenly screaming and calling for him. She was being dragged across the ground into an abyss by grimy, wicked, evil hands. He had to help her, but he could not get his legs to move. Then the hands were pulling him away from her, and panic gripped his soul. With her hands stretched out to him, she disappeared into a fiery hell, and he was helpless. He screamed as the hands pulled and pulled at him until he started to fall into his own abyss . . .

The medical staff burst through the door to find Alex on the floor between the bed and the wall, thrashing around and screaming bloody murder. It took several of them to restrain him, and only after they were able to drug him could they get him back into the bed.

★ ★ ★

Alex was staring out the window when the doctor entered.

"Well, good morning. You gave us quite a scare yesterday. How are you feeling?"

Alex replied, "Where am I? How'd I get here?"

The doctor said, "You're in Walter Reed Army Hospital in Washington DC, and I'm not sure exactly how you got here. I understand you were medevac'd out of Iraq through Landstuhl, Germany, and then to here."

"What happened to me?"

"Well, again, I'm not sure how it happened, but when we got you, we put your leg back together with a dynamic hip screw. Your head was patched up at the Army hospital in Baghdad."

"How long have I been here? What day is it?"

"It's December 15, and you've been here for five days. The hip injury you suffered is as painful as they come, and that surgery was no picnic, so we only started weaning you off the drugs yesterday."

"What about the man that was with me when we got hit?"

"I'm sorry, I'm afraid I don't know anything about that either. Look, I must call your company to let them know you're conscious. They'll be around shortly, and they can probably answer those questions. Do you have any family you'd like for us to call?"

"No!" Alex did not want his family to know he was hurt. "Don't let anybody else know I'm here. How long will I have to be here?" He already felt caged.

The doctor took a deep breath and sighed. "Look, I understand if you don't want your family to know what's happened to you, but don't be too anxious to bolt out of here. If you rest for a few more days and then work at it gradually, you might be able to walk again in three months or so. Take advantage of Uncle Sam's hospitality as long as he'll have you."

Alex understood what the doctor was saying. As a civilian contractor, he was lucky to be in an Army hospital and not out on the economy racking up the medical bills and wrestling with insurance companies.

"Sure, Doctor. Thanks for taking care of me. I'll try to behave."

Alex was struggling through his first meal since the last MRE he had eaten at Valhalla when Thor and two other men entered the room. Thor was clearly glad to see him awake.

"Hey, Cap, how are you feeling? You really had us worried."

Alex swallowed the rubbery green bean he'd been chewing. "I'm alright." He was afraid to ask: "Did you find Predator?"

Thor slowly shook his head. "No. We looked everywhere, and we couldn't find a trace."

Alex's chest swelled up, and he looked away from them and out the window. Suddenly he had difficulty breathing, and his head started to pound. He tried to wipe the tears from his eyes with his bandaged hands, but he could not catch them all. He pushed the dinner tray away and rolled over on his left side as much as his cast would allow, and he sobbed, wracked with grief at the loss of his friend. He felt a hand on his shoulder, trying to comfort him, and he heard the door open and close. When he was finally able to control himself, he wiped his face with the bedsheet and turned back to see only Thor remaining, perched on the edge of the bed with his head hung low.

Thor choked out, "I don't know what to say. I only wish this war had never happened and we never got involved."

"How's your sister?"

"She's been crazy with worry about you. She's the reason we found you. She tracked you like a hound dog. She refused to think you'd gotten killed by the bomb. She found the ladder, figured you'd gotten out alive, and tracked you through the desert to where we found you. She would have come here too, but she couldn't bring herself to leave our parents. She made me promise to take care of you."

Alex's first thought was to return to Iraq. If there was any chance that he could be with her, it would never happen with him in the States and her in Iraq. Her father's business was in Iraq, she would not leave him, and Alex knew there was no end of the war in sight. His only hope of being with her was to go back to Iraq. He knew he would never be able to fit back into Stateside life without her. The close call he had just been through and the potential future risk was a small price to pay to be near her. The danger paled in comparison to the frustration he knew he would suffer if he stayed here without at least trying to be with her. If she turned him down later, that would be one thing, but he had to try. He thought if he put all his effort into it, maybe he could speed up the healing process.

"Who were those guys?" he asked Thor.

"My uncles. One of them lives here and the other one runs the show in Tennessee. They wanted to meet you."

Alex thought, *Good, maybe I won't have to wait till I'm fully healed. Hopefully, they'll feel like I'm an insider and give me preferential treatment. I'll put on my game face.* He said, "Are they still out there? Ask them to come back in."

Thor opened the door and beckoned them into the room.

Alex waved his bandaged hand and said, "Hi, I'm Alex, or Cap, and I'm sorry you caught me at a bad moment there."

The older one said, "Don't you worry about that, son. After what you've been through, your manhood's not in question with us. We're all ex-Army, and we understand the trauma of losing a close friend you've been through the ringer with. I'm Bud, or Beowulf, and this is my little brother Mark, or Hugin." He pronounced it *Hyoo-gin.*

Alex raised his eyebrow, and it disappeared under his bandages. "I understand Beowulf, but Hugin?"

"Yeah, it was either that or Dwarf." Mark snickered. "Growing up with these monsters was difficult, and while they were off having fun in the Army, they sent me to college. When we figured out these call signs, I had a choice; I could either be the dwarf that brought Odin his wine, or the raven that gave him his advice. I chose the raven, Hugin."

Bud said, "And he lives up to it too. He lives here and gets our contracts and intelligence for us. He's the brains of the outfit." Bud went on, "I run the training camp in Tennessee that we send all our recruits through. Of course, you were already in-country when Odin hired you and didn't get the pleasure of our Southern hospitality, but you're welcome down there anytime."

Alex jumped on it. "Do you have any openings down there for me until I recover enough to go back?"

Thor was astounded. "Go back? You're kidding."

"No, I was only there a short time on this trip. I hardly got to see the sights." Alex expected that last comment would appeal to their machismo.

Thor really was overwhelmed, and both of his uncles raised

their eyebrows and looked at him. His shoulders sagged and his head drooped. Alex thought, *That went over like a lead balloon.* He asked, "What's wrong?"

Now it was Thor's turn. His eyes turned misty, and he said in a timid voice, "My cup is full, Cap. I can't go back. That last firefight took it all out of me. One minute those guys were alive and fine, and the next minute they were all dead and I was sure I was next. I was scared—*really* scared, sitting there on my knees, waiting to die, until you showed up. The adrenaline kept me going for a while that day, but it screwed me up, *bad.*

"I couldn't go back on the road after that. It was just too much. Every time we passed cars, trash, people, anything, I expected it to explode, and it made me constantly cringe. I couldn't focus on anything until we got the call that you disappeared. I'd already decided to come home when we got that call." He lowered his head again, and Alex saw his hands shaking. Now he knew what Linda meant when she said her brother needed her; emotional trauma and the humiliation of it had broken this strapping big man. Now Alex's bravado had shamed him further, and Alex wondered how he could help him recover some dignity. Maybe with a little honesty about his own stupidity.

"Hey, man, nobody who's been there is going to fault you for that. It happens to the best of us. Honestly, the only reason I'm thinking of going back right now is the outside chance that your sister might be interested in me." He expected them to body-slam him, but they all looked completely unsurprised and not the least bit bothered. "Otherwise I'd have different thoughts, and I expect they might be similar to yours."

Thor looked up at him, and Alex thought *that* might have worked.

"You think so?" he asked.

"Are you kidding? Really, that was way more intense than I ever expected. I saw my share of action in the Army, but nothing like this. It's totally different and a lot scarier. Hangin' out there all alone without hope of any help? Only someone who's stupid or crazy would want to do it twice." Alex puckered his lips and strummed his bandaged fingers up and down over them as he blew air and made burbling noises.

They all laughed, and Thor said, "I guess that means you fit the crazy category."

"Yeah, crazy about your sister, and that's gonna keep me sane for now."

Bud threw in, "Yeah, but if she turns you away, then you'll just be stupid *and* stuck in Iraq." The laughter became a little hardier.

They talked a while longer before the nurse told them it was time to let Alex rest. Mark asked Alex if he would like them to call his family. Alex shook his head. "No, thank you. I'd rather they not know that I was hurt."

Bud said, "Well, when they let you out of here, you are welcome to join us down in Tennessee if you like." They said their farewells and Alex was left alone.

Alex thought of Predator, and he breathed a deep sigh. He knew that if he did not have something to look forward to, he would become a basket case, so he thought of Linda and drifted off to sleep.

Within a few days the hospital had relocated Alex to a ward with six other wounded contractors. When he saw the severity of their conditions, he considered himself lucky and became more determined to recover as quickly as possible. Their injuries were mostly amputations and traumatic brain injuries from IED explosions. New generations of body armor protected the torso well, but the arms, legs, and head were still vulnerable. So, while fewer people died than would have without the armor, many more lost their appendages and suffered debilitating brain damage.

He began a physical therapy regimen that was not challenging at first, but the therapist told him to take it easy for a while so he would not cause more damage than good. Still, after each exercise he would squeeze in a few more repetitions. Soon he was spending every minute he was awake doing something to increase his strength. Even while in bed he would do isometrics and flex each muscle in his body, count to twenty, relax, and then do it again.

Thor and Mark came to see him a few times and brought him magazines and a small flask of whiskey. Most importantly, he managed to talk with Linda on the phone a couple of times. She told him that they had moved every piece of rubble at Valhalla, and while they found several other bodies, they discovered no clue of what had happened to Predator. They made a lot of small talk, but Alex did not let on how he felt about her.

After six weeks the doctors finally cut off his cast. Alex was appalled at the sight of his leg. It was gnarled and shrunken, and there was a large scar that started at his hip and ran about twelve inches down his leg. His heart sank; recovery would take some time. He set about the task of strengthening his leg and learning to walk again. Three more weeks and the doctors agreed to release him.

✳ ✳ ✳

Alex took some time to visit his daughter, Jackie. His ex-wife was suspicious, but he only told her he was on leave and would soon be returning to Iraq.

"What's wrong with your leg and why are you wearing that stupid hat?" she harped.

"I pulled a muscle in my thigh and I like this hat. I'll probably never take it off." Actually, he did not really like the hat either, but the hair on the back of his head had only now started to grow back. A collared shirt and a boonie cap were the only way he could hide the gnarly scars that covered the back of his head and ran down the nape of his neck. Alex placated his ex and gained her tolerance by giving her the lion's share of the money Odin had given him for child support. He put the rest in an account he had previously opened for his daughter's education.

Jackie was only five years old, and she was an absolute delight to be with. She loved her father no matter what, and she let him know it. He picked her up from preschool each day, and they spent the afternoons together. They took walks in the park, he pushed her on swings in playgrounds, they visited museums and the zoo, and to her delight, they ate dinner at Chuck-E-Cheese.

The time he spent with his daughter was relaxing, and when he was with her, he thought of nothing else. But when he was alone, Alex could tell that there was something wrong.

Before he picked up Jackie one day, he went to a grocery store. As he emerged from an aisle, in his peripheral he saw two Kurds wearing black ski masks and black Kevlar helmets, and holding AK-47s at the ready as they emerged from the aisles adjacent to his. He flashed back to the assault on the little shop on route Tampa. A little while later he found himself checking a head of lettuce for explosive devices; he checked it for pressure plates and tripwires and then placed it to his ear, listening for a ticking sound, before he realized what he was doing.

Several times, as he spoke with people their faces would fade from his vision and morph into the bloody faces of dead Kurds or Iraqi police. Other times, while driving, he would slip into a rage if anyone cut him off or followed too close, and he had to restrain himself from slamming his pickup truck into their cars. Once, as he drove on a two-lane road with a no-passing yellow line, he was going the speed limit when someone began tailgating him. He maintained his temper until they tried to pass him on the right shoulder, and then he lost it. He pulled over in front of them and ran them off the road. At night he dreamt of bloody and mutilated Iraqis clawing and pulling at him and pleading for help and trying to kill him. Finally, he was gripped with fear that Linda might need help and he would not be there for her. He knew he had to return to Iraq.

★ ★ ★

The company training facility was a far cry better than the one Alex had attended with his first contracting company. His first company had taken him to a hotel where they conducted their physical fitness testing in a public park; practiced driving and motorcade and convoy tactics, techniques, and procedures in the hotel parking lot and a dirt road that ran around the hotel; and did their shooting at a local indoor firing range.

At the time Alex had nothing but his Army training to compare it with, and he imagined the company was just testing them to see what they already knew, so he did not pass judgment. In hindsight, however, he understood how pathetically inadequate the training and selection really was. It reflected the care the company took to ensure the safety of its employees, which was little more than not much at all. He remembered the difference in the vehicles back in Iraq: Alex's first company gave them unarmored pickup trucks, and Odin's company had armored SUVs. It was clear to Alex that the other company really did not care who died as long as they were able to get more replacements and fill the contract. Realistic training and equipment were expensive and cut into the owner's profits.

Odin's company, on the other hand, had quite an impressive training facility and clearly pumped a large portion of their profits back into the company to ensure competent operators. Way out in the middle of nowhere Tennessee, Odin had gotten his hands on an old National Guard compound complete with administrative buildings, barracks, a mess hall, a running track with an obstacle course and a rappelling tower, a motor pool, and an extensive shooting range. The company had also made renovations of their own, constructing roads and erecting overpasses, buildings, and barricaded compounds like those that the men would encounter in Iraq. Scattered along the roads were the normal debris and obstacles one would find in Iraq, including burned-out hulks of cars, big craters in the roads such as IEDs would produce, and burn barrels to create smoke that added to the confusion and stress of training.

Of course, it was not like basic training for the Army. All of these recruits had prior military service, and most had seen combat in some sort of special operations units like Rangers, Special Forces, Seals, Force Recon, Pararescue or the like. Instead, this training was the reorientation of their old skills to service a new task: personal protection.

When Alex drove into the facility with Thor, the compound was abuzz with activity. He heard rounds being fired at the weapons range, and he saw two groups of men training: one practicing driving formations in the road ahead of them, and the other at the motor pool, practicing cross-loading their vehicles.

Thor said, "We usually only run one class at a time, but we recently landed a contract with USAID, and we're on the verge of getting another big contract. Of course, having lost an entire team at once, we need replacements, so we ramped it up to four classes this time. They won't all go over immediately, but they'll be trained up when we need them." After Alex had completed his training with his first company, it took him three months to get the call to go to Iraq. Then when they did call, on a Thursday, their only question was, "Can you leave by Saturday?"

Thor went on, "Anyway, we're pressed for trainers, and we could use your help if you're ready. Bud has a couple of ideas for you."

The course was intended to demonstrate to the new men the standards for required skills, allow them to train for a few days, and then assess their ability to perform under stress. Selection or acceptance to the program depended on not only an acceptable physical and skill level, but judgment, teamwork, and personality as well. Prima donnas seeking a reputation and jerks were not welcome. The company was looking for mature gunfighters.

Instruction started in a classroom with lists of requirements and sketches drawn on a whiteboard, after which they went outside for dry runs and practice and, finally, scenario-based practical application with role players and Simunition bullets, or paintball-like practice rounds, in their weapons. Everything the operators learned would be tested on the final day when they ran through several operations from beginning to end. Men would be sent home for various reasons throughout the four weeks of training, and inevitably one or two would finish the training only to be told that they simply were not a good fit for the company and should seek employment elsewhere.

The regimen was extensive. The first event was a physical fitness test on the very first day—because if a candidate were to fail at the end of the class because he was out of shape, all the other expensive training would have been wasted. Candidates had to be able to run two miles in no less than fifteen minutes. Immediately at the end of the run they had to pick up a 185-pound dummy and carry or drag it twenty-five yards. This simulated the ability to run a great distance to the aid of the client and after tremendous exertion still be able to physically move the client to safety.

Upper body strength was tested by doing no fewer than sixty good pushups in two minutes, and core strength was evaluated by doing no less than sixty-five sit-ups in two minutes. Extra points were awarded for better times and repetitions than the minimums on a graduated scale, and totals were tallied with all other evaluations at the end of the course to determine who would be the class honor graduate.

Weapons skills began with the 9-millimeter Glock 17 pistol, which included the basics of drawing the pistol from a hip holster and hitting the target within a certain time at various distances. For example, at the seven-yard line the candidates were expected to draw and hit the silhouette target in one and a quarter seconds or less. From the twenty-five-yard line they had four seconds to hit the center of the target twice. Drills also included reloading the pistol when it went empty, clearing a jammed weapon, shooting one-handed with the strong hand and then the weak hand, turning and shooting, moving and shooting, shooting from behind barricades, and clearing rooms and shooting in a building constructed of tires and rubber.

Shooting was also conducted at night and indoors with the lights out using night observation devices, or NODs, infrared lasers, and flashlights. Targets included paper and steel and sometimes a combination of both. Finally, the men were run through a gauntlet of obstacles and targets called a stress shoot. The stress shoot had them begin with shooting an eleven-inch-tall steel popper from fifty yards before they could advance to the next shooting position; there were doors to enter and barricades to negotiate and targets to shoot while moving, steel plate racks, steel silhouettes, paper targets with no-shoot hostages; and it had to be completed within a certain time. Everything was timed with a shot timer, and the spirit of competition and team encouragement was high.

The rifle skills with the 5.56-by-45-millimeter M4 carbine was equally as challenging. Targets were engaged from five yards to three hundred yards. The rifle stress shoot began with the candidate sitting on a 185-pound dummy. At the buzzer, and wearing his body armor, he had to beat on the dummy with all his might for forty-five seconds before he could engage his first target. When he was told "Mark!" he rolled off the dummy, pulled his pistol and, while lying on his back, fired two rounds each at three paper silhouette targets spaced out between five and ten yards away. Then he holstered the pistol, picked up his rifle, went to the prone using the dummy for cover, and fired two rounds into a paper target three hundred yards away. Then he rose to his feet and sprinted one hundred yards forward to a burned-out vehicle where he went to the prone again and from under which he fired two rounds each at two targets now two hundred yards away.

Again, he rose and sprinted one hundred yards to another ratted-out vehicle, behind which he went to a knee and fired two rounds each at three targets now one hundred yards away. At this point his round count was configured to have him run out of ammunition and required him to reload. He was given points for reloading behind cover, but if he reloaded while on the run, he could gain points by saving time. Another sprint to the fifty-yard line to a barricade, from which he had to fire at two targets from each side of the barricade, requiring him to switch hands from his strong side to his weak side in order to maximize the cover provided by the barricade. He then fired at two more targets using a hole cut in the middle of the barricade and without sticking the muzzle of the rifle through the hole.

From this point he walked or used what they called a combat glide toward the end of the range, engaging a menagerie of steel targets to his front and left and right, and running out of ammunition and reloading as he went. Finally, he would have no more ammunition for his rifle, and he was required to transition to his pistol for the final few targets. After being pumped up with adrenaline and manhandling the trigger on the rifle, the pistol, which took much more trigger control to put lead on target, was quite a challenge.

Weapons training went on to the belt-fed machine guns: the 5.56 mm M249 Squad Automatic Weapon, or SAW, and the 7.62 mm M240G, or the PIG. Everyone would also qualify on the M203 grenade launcher and the AK-47 assault rifle. All candidates also fired the company's long-range system: the M86 sniper rifle with a magnum action for 300 Winchester Magnum bullets. Those men who shot at the top of the class and had previous sniper experience were given the opportunity to stay after selection for a weeklong designated defensive marksman, or DDM, long-range precision shooting class.

Tactical driving focused on evasive driving techniques, beginning at high speeds on a track with long straightaways punctuated with blind hills and hairpin turns requiring drivers to brake and accelerate without losing control. Close-proximity driving familiarized drivers with the way Iraqis typically drove: mirror to mirror and bumper to bumper. Crash avoidance, J-turns, and controlling skidding put drivers into seemingly impossible situations from which they were expected to extract the client uninjured and the vehicle still operational. Of course, sometimes the best defense was a good offense, so drivers were also trained in ramming and pit maneuvers. Off-road driving on sand and gravel rounded out the behind-the-wheel training. Then the men went back and did it all again in armored vehicles so they could feel the different ways that the heavy vehicles handled on and off the road.

Medical training and evaluations were based on the Army's doctrine of tactical combat casualty care, or TCCC, which was developed after the 3rd Ranger Battalion took casualties in the Battle of Mogadishu in 1993. During the battle, a number of men died because they were cut off from medical evacuation for too long, and the medics and soldiers on the spot were hard pressed to treat the wounded with their existing knowledge and equipment. For those injuries that could be treated in order to prevent death, TCCC provided the basis of effective knowledge.

Close quarters combat, or CQB, was the term used for the tactics, techniques, and procedures, or TTPs, for entering and fighting in buildings. Here, the tactics took a bit of a departure from the military's doctrine. CQB for the military generally assumed that there were follow-on forces that would press the fight should the lead elements become casualties or be held up for some reason. However, the missions contracted by this company were defensive in nature in that the client typically paid the company operators to avoid a fight and break contact when trouble happened. Also, the limited number of the men committed to a client meant that the tactics used by the military would get these men killed and they would fail their client and their mission.

This CQB was a problem-solving process. At every corner or doorway or hallway, the operator was flooded with information. Very quickly he was required to process the information, recognize problems, make decisions, and take satisfactory action, and do it repeatedly without pause. The instructors described the TTPs, demonstrated the standards, and allowed the candidates to practice them repeatedly until they felt comfortable with the principles. Here, it was stressed that while there were many ways to skin a cat, there were several principles of their brand of CQB that could not be violated. A poster nailed to the front door of the 25,000-square-foot shoot house reminded them of those principles:

Basic Principles of CQB

1. Check your 6
2. Walk, don't run (don't outrun your headlights)
3. Pie off corners and doors (use your angles)
4. Quickstep through doors and around corners
5. Number one and two men move to opposite corners
6. Dig your corners and red zones (with the muzzle of your gun)
7. Collapse your sector
8. Don't flag your buddy
9. Don't shoot no-shoots
10. Security, security, security
11. Flow like water (keep moving)

Everything else is technique

The instructors explained that there were many acceptable solutions to a single problem as long as the technique worked and did not violate the principles. From three different instructors they might see three different solutions; the point was to find what worked for them and to remain flexible.

The concept of the principles began with ensuring the security of the space behind them, or checking their six, with twelve being the direction of movement. By the third step in, if the last man had not checked behind them, they had probably violated this principal. These mantras were drilled into their heads: *Keep your head on a swivel. Walk, don't run. Don't move faster than you can process information, and don't wear yourself out.*

Pie off corners and doors referred to using angles to their advantage. Rather than charging through the door or a turn in a hallway, they were to have their gun up and off safe with their finger on the trigger and, beginning diagonally from outside the door, use their angles to view small, manageable pieces of the room, or slices of the pie. Then they would take their time and move laterally and enlarge their view of the room as they cleared the space from outside. This enabled them to shoot from outside the room, or to change their mind and go another way if they saw an unmanageable situation on the other side of the threshold. If the door was closed, they were to use their non-firing hand to open the door from the non-hinged side with their gun up and ready.

Once they committed, they had to quickstep through doors and around corners. Their lives depended on their speed through the threshold, otherwise known as the "fatal funnel." Even if they received fire, they could NOT STOP IN THE FATAL FUNNEL. If they hadn't been killed yet, their only chance to live now was to press the fight. If they had a number two man, they needed to get his gun in the fight as fast as possible. If they bogged down in the fatal funnel, they *would* die. If they got through there quickly, they *might* live.

Number one man and number two man always moved to opposite corners. If there was more than one man clearing the room, whichever direction the first man through the fatal funnel chose, the second man always took the opposite direction in order to handle any threat that might now be behind the number one man.

They were to "dig," or dominate, corners and red zones, or danger zones, with the muzzle of their gun and flashlight; just looking might not give them enough time to react if a threat presented itself. If they were by themselves, entering a center-fed room, they had two corners to dig: they dominated the first corner, then spun around and checked the other corner—fast; their life depended on it.

Once in the room, they collapsed or cleared their sector of the room by sweeping the muzzle of their gun laterally from one side of the room to the other, to within a meter of their partner.

They were not to "flag" friendlies with the muzzle of their weapon in order to prevent accidentally shooting someone on their team. They kept the barrel of their gun up or down when passing over a teammate. Flagging teammates would quickly get them dismissed from the course.

Do not shoot no-shoots. The candidate should look at their hands, yes, but just because the no-shoot might have a gun did not necessarily mean they should be engaged. For instance, responding to an active shooter inside a compound, they might come storming down the hallway and enter a room. Inside that room is someone cleared and vetted by the client, who is also armed. In what posture might the client and their companion be? Probably with the barrel of their gun in the candidate's face.

The candidate had to be able to see past the gun and say, "Holster up, sir. We're here to help you." They had perhaps less than a heartbeat to make this determination. Often, men from assaulter units in the military had a difficult time refraining from shooting everyone in the heat of the moment. Any candidate who was unable to see past the gun to delineate between a real threat and a friendly was sent home.

The principle of security was always first. Before they moved, reloaded, treated their wounded buddy, or did anything, they had to establish security.

The idea of *flow like water* was to simply keep moving. Fluid movement would keep the enemy off balance and make it difficult for anyone to maneuver against the candidate.

Everything else was technique, and however a candidate decided to solve the problem, if the technique worked and he did not violate these principles, he was good to go.

After lectures and PowerPoint diagrams, instructors demonstrated the CQB techniques in a "Tape House." The Tape House was simply duct tape outlining a building with rooms and hallways on a concrete slab so the men could see the standard without obstruction and then practice with input from the instructors.

Then they went into a building they called the "Scenario House," a 25,000-square-foot building constructed simply of framing and plywood that was intended to be repeatedly destroyed and then rebuilt. Inside the Scenario House, with instructors hovering over their shoulders, the men practiced door procedures, moving down hallways, picking up rear security or checking their six, and L-shaped, T-shaped, and four-way hallway intersections. They practiced clearing rooms with one man and with two men, single rooms, and multiple rooms, picking up danger areas inside the rooms, exiting rooms, and bypassing rooms. They rehearsed near recognition signals, target discrimination, and mitigating threats. They cleared to known and unknown locations, looking for their client and extracting the client and clearing out to a safe location.

After a couple of days of this they brought in role players to act as insurgents and used Simunition ammunition. Later, when they worked on mobile TTPs, they would incorporate the Scenario House in that training as well, moving clients in and out of venues from their vehicles. At the final evaluated exercises, operations in the House would determine success or failure in the program.

The candidates were schooled and assessed in many other skills and knowledge, such as countersurveillance, predictive profiling, IED recognition, and defensive tactics or hand-to-hand combat. The hand-to-hand combat was a form of mixed martial arts tailored to gunfighters; it was all about breaking contact at close quarters and going to your gun.

Bud assigned Alex to oversee several tasks, such as arrival and departure drills from friendly lines and roadblock and barricade confrontations. Alex explained to the candidates that entry and departure at every compound was different, with one thing in common: the men manning the gates were rightfully paranoid and would shoot to kill at the least provocation. Essentially there were a few fundamentals that you just did not violate; you moved slowly and did what they told you to do without hesitation.

Other than that, one tried to give advance notice of arrivals and departures and attempted to make contact a few minutes before arriving at an entry control point, or ECP, either for entry or departure. At some locations, prior detailed coordination was mandatory in the form of a SLANT report, or a military report of status and activity. Basically, it was up to the team leader to coordinate all arrivals and departures and to understand and make sure the team members knew what was required and that everyone complied.

Alex was also specifically assigned to the shooting range to assist those instructors when his class was not in session. At first, he was concerned that if he had been required to go through this selection before he was hired, he might not have made it. But once he got on the range, he found that he was competitive with the best of them. Still, he was able to improve his shooting skills dramatically and enjoyed this time immensely.

His greatest reward on the range, however, was when one

candidate with the call sign "Scratch," whom everybody clearly liked or they would have just sent him packing, was having trouble meeting the standard with the pistol. The primary instructor asked Alex to take him off to the side and work with him.

Alex went through a shooter's troubleshooting process, watching his every move, and perceived the slightest dip of the barrel as the man pulled the trigger.

"Hey, man, you're just jerking the trigger too hard and pulling your sights off the target at the last heartbeat. Here, let's make sure your grip is really tight first. Grip the gun like it's someone you want to strangle, like your mother-in-law. Good, now I want you to aim at the target, but keep your finger off the trigger. OK, you got a good tight grip and your sights aligned?"

"Yeah."

Alex slipped his right forefinger into the trigger guard. "Good, you concentrate on your grip and keeping the sights line up. Let me pull the trigger for you." Alex started pulling the slack out of the trigger ever so slowly and said, "Grip, sights, grip, sights, sights, sights, sights." *BOOM!* The bullet struck the target in the absolute dead center.

Alex said, "Nice shot. All of your fundamentals are perfect, but you have to be smoother on your trigger pull. If you slap it or pull too fast or too hard, you pull the sights off the target, typically low and left for a right-handed shooter. Try it again. Put your finger on the trigger but don't pull the trigger."

This time Alex put his finger on top of Scratch's finger. "OK, just feel how smooth this is. Grip, sights, sights, sights, sights." *BOOM!* Again, his round hit dead center, touching his previous shot. "You feel that?"

"Yeah!" Scratch looked surprised.

Then Alex drilled him repeatedly until he felt confident. "Just tell yourself 'Grip, sights, trigger, trigger, trigger' as you shoot, and you'll think of it every time."

He took Scratch back to the firing line with the rest of the class just as they were about to start a practice qualification. Scratch's buddies gave him encouragement, but he had no problem passing the qualification this time, and the other men whooped their approval. The lead instructor gave Alex a nod, and after they were done Scratch thanked him for the lesson.

"Man. I was really worried and now I just feel good. I can't thank you enough."

To Alex, this was the epitome of job satisfaction.

Alex started his own physical training regimen before sunrise each morning, going through sets of pushups and sit-ups and then hitting the weights and running by himself through the compound. When he started feeling better, he joined the classes during their physical training and hand-to-hand combatives training. By the end of March, he was ready to go back to Iraq.

Alex flew to New York where he met several of the men he knew from the company training course who were also on their way to Iraq. Together, they flew to Paris and connected with an Air France flight to Beirut, Lebanon. In Beirut they were met by a company "facilitator," a local man paid by the company to make sure they made it through customs and to set them up in a hotel until their flight to Baghdad the next day.

That night Alex piled the furniture in his room against the door and planned an escape route out the window and down two floors to an awning, then to the road below. They were to spend only one night in Beirut, but three days later the facilitator told them that their airline finally admitted that they could not find a flight crew that was willing to fly into Baghdad. They boarded a plane bound for Amman, Jordan, instead. They spent the night in another hotel and the following morning went back to the airport to catch their flight to Baghdad.

Waiting to board in the terminal at Queen Alia International

Airport in Amman, most of the men talked and joked to relieve their nervousness. Alex just sat back and acted like he was asleep as he watched people walking past the group. Many people glared at them, and it was quite clear to Alex that most of these people understood perfectly well what they were and where they were going. As he scanned the passersby, he also absently watched a TV monitor tuned in to Al-Jazeera news. Alex spotted one particularly creepy-looking young man with a thin beard and wild eyes. The young man consciously did not look at the Americans, which to Alex seemed suspicious. Alex pictured him on a roadside near Baghdad, dialing a cell phone to set off an IED as a convoy passed by.

Watching him intently as he slipped past the TV, Alex suddenly spotted Predator's face on the screen.

"Predator!" Alex bellowed and bolted upright. The other Americans froze and watched as Alex raced across the terminal, almost knocking down the young man with the beard. His eyes were fixed on the TV as he asked loudly, "What are they saying?" He reached the monitor and heard only Arabic. He said again, even louder, "What are they saying?" He was desperate now. He turned to the shocked people sitting nearby. "What are they saying? What are they saying?"

One seated man said in English, "They tell of an American war criminal being held captive in Iraq." Alex looked at him in amazement and turned back to the TV. He reached out to the monitor as if he could touch his friend. Then the image was gone, replaced by a commentator dressed in a dishdasha and speaking with an air of righteous indignation. Alex was stunned. His friend was still alive!

Two of the other Americans came up to him.

"Hey, man, you OK? You better sit down; you just stirred up the whole airport." Alex looked around and saw that everybody was staring at him, and two policemen were heading his way with automatic weapons. Realizing that sitting in a Jordanian jail would not help, he quickly recovered his senses and returned to his seat. The police slowed, but they did not leave.

His mind raced. *What the hell is going on? How could this be? Could it be an old picture? No, why would they do that?* It would serve no purpose to splash an obscure dead contractor's picture on the news nearly six months after his death. It had to be recent; in the picture Predator had a full beard, and Alex always knew him to sport a goatee.

Alex had to find out what was going on, but their facilitator had already left, and he had no access to a phone until they landed in Baghdad. Alex was beside himself with frustration.

One of the other operators asked him, "Do you know that guy?"

"Yeah, he's my buddy, Predator." Alex looked up and realized they were all looking at him.

"No shit. We heard about him. We were told he was dead."

Alex asked, "What else were you told about him?"

One of the other men said, "Are you kidding? We heard all about your exploits. *Captain America* and his enforcer, the *Predator*."

Alex was genuinely surprised, and the expression on his face must have given it away.

"Hell yeah," added one of the others. "That's why we never joked around in your class: respect. You mean the guy on that TV was Predator?"

Alex nodded and said, "*Is* Predator. There's no reason they'd flaunt his picture unless he was still alive." Alex realized that in his desire for solitude over the last few months, he was missing an opportunity with these men. If there was anything he could do for Predator, he might require some help. He decided he needed to rectify that now.

"They don't come any better than him. He never hesitated in a fight; no matter how bad things got, you could always count on him to be there for you. He saved my ass more than once. We were in a firefight one night when a car bomb blew up, and that's the last time I saw him. He was a lot closer to it than me, and it screwed me up pretty bad. I thought for sure he was dead, and the company looked, but they found nothing. I just don't understand how this happened. Unless . . ." His brow furrowed in thought.

One of them said, "Unless what?"

"Well"—Alex closed his eyes, trying to remember—"I looked for him after the explosion, but I was hurt pretty bad and I suppose I could have missed him if he was unconscious. Maybe he was thrown further than I thought, and I just didn't look far enough. Anyway, after a while I heard Iraqis coming back, so I got the hell out of there. Now I wonder if they found him and took him away before the company got there." Alex suddenly felt bad again at the thought of having unknowingly abandoned his friend.

The others regressed into a conversation about being captured by insurgents and what they would do if they were. Alex's thoughts stayed with what happened that night; he might know who could shed some light on the disappearance of Predator.

★★★

The Royal Jordanian airliner was directly over the Baghdad International Airport when the pilot cut the power and the plane began to drop like a rock. Alex felt his stomach rise to his mouth once again, and he looked around to see the reaction from the first-timers. Big strong men grabbed their armrests with death grips until their knuckles turned white, and their faces contorted with horrific expressions.

Unbuckling his seatbelt after they landed, Alex smiled and said to the green guy next to him, "Welcome to Baghdad."

As Alex emerged from the plane, the heat hit him in the face like a furnace. Two Burmese security guards wearing khaki pants, blue polo shirts, and baseball caps with their company logo strolled up with their automatic weapons slung across their stomachs. As the passengers entered the terminal, everyone was swept with a metal detector wand and then patted down. Alex and his companions collected their bags and moved to the customs booths where they had their bags searched and then their passports stamped. A company PSD was waiting to transport them to Erbil. Alex hoped Linda would be with them, but she was not. They made their introductions and headed for the vehicles.

Alex asked the team leader, "Have you heard anything about Predator?"

"Predator? You mean the guy that was with you at Valhalla? No, just that he was killed."

"Do you have a cell phone I could borrow?"

"Sure, you can call your family back home if you want."

"Thanks." Alex dialed Odin and asked him if he had seen anything on TV or heard anything about Predator.

Odin was surprised. "No, what do you mean?" Alex told him what he saw on TV in Amman. Odin said, "No, nothing. Are you sure it was Predator?"

"Yes, I'm certain of it. I'd know him anywhere." Alex was adamant.

Odin sounded skeptical. "I haven't heard anything, but I'll make some calls and turn on Al-Jazeera to see what I can find out."

"Thanks." Alex dialed Thor back in the States and asked him the same questions; nothing. He asked Thor to see if his uncle Mark could turn up anything. Then Alex asked him, "Was there anyone at Valhalla when you arrived there that morning?"

Thor said, "Yeah, Sheikh Ali and several of his men."

They reached the vehicles, and the PSD handed out body armor and weapons. They all piled into two armored SUVs and headed out. Alex and another operator had climbed into the cargo area with all the gear. As they pulled away from the airport, Alex saw the compound he had briefly stayed at the previous year when he was running the convoys. The company had since been blacklisted from doing business in Iraq for defrauding the government, but that was in name only. They had reincorporated in a country in the Balkans and sold themselves all their old assets and were still running convoys for the US Department of Defense under the new name. He imagined the Grim Reaper hovering over the compound.

They left the airport compound at full speed, racing through traffic and out to Route Tampa. Alex never liked driving fast back in the States. But then, he never really liked heights either, and he had still made several hundred jumps out of planes and helicopters, most of them at night. He knew the danger of traveling too slow all too well, and still, he felt that the way they were traveling was excessive. The driver weaved in and out of traffic at breakneck speed, the second vehicle getting further and further behind. Alex made a mental note to not go on any missions with this driver. He was totally amped up, and Alex could not understand why.

The driver yelled obscenities and acted like he was being pursued by insurgents. Alex lay flat on his stomach and pushed his feet against the back seat, effectively wedging himself in place. The man with him followed suit. He heard an exclamation from the passengers in the front and looked to his left in time to see their vehicle sideswipe another because it failed to get out of the way fast enough. The other vehicle's side-view mirror disintegrated as they flew past. The local behind the wheel yelled and shook his fist.

Alex thought, *Great. After everything I've been through, I'm gonna get killed in a traffic accident on my first day back.* Their other vehicle was at least a mile behind them.

Suddenly, his vehicle swerved off the left side of the road and into the sand to avoid a car in front of them changing lanes. Alex thought they were going to flip over. Then the driver recovered, and the truck gripped the asphalt and flew back up onto the road, tilting to the right until it slammed broadside into the side of a large van. The other man in the back was not as tall as Alex, and with less of a foothold he bounced around in the cargo area like a pinball. The truck went back off the road again to the left and spun around in the sand a couple of times until the wheels impacted with something solid that caused the SUV to flip over in an airborne summersault. The truck landed upright on its wheels, and they came to a halt with the engine sputtering as it stalled.

The new operators had expected a leisurely drive in the countryside in an up-armored vehicle and had not chambered a round in their weapons. They all charged their weapons at the same time.

The driver gunned the engine back to life and stomped the accelerator. The wheels gouged at the ground, spinning a geyser of sand behind the truck, but the vehicle went nowhere. Alex thought, *OK, now we're stuck, and I'm sure we've succeeded in pissing off all the locals. This is not good.* However, the driver switched to four-wheel drive and pulled back up onto the road. The rest of the ride was not much better, and Alex's leg was throbbing by the time they pulled up to the compound in Erbil. Before they entered the compound, however, the driver found it necessary to stop the vehicle and walk back to a random driver behind them to chew him out for following too close. Alex wondered what he was like back in the States. *He was probably a cop.*

Alex soon discovered that the driver was terminated.

Erbil was completely different from most of the rest of Iraq. It was the heart of Kurdistan, and the Kurds really wanted the Americans to stay. For their entire thousand-year history in the region, they had been surrounded and persecuted by hostile populations. For the last thirty-five years Saddam Hussein had done his best to eradicate them altogether using helicopters, artillery, and even poison gas. Now, with the arrival of the Americans, they were mostly autonomous, and they reaped the profits from the northern oil fields and other economic advantages. Their new prosperity and safety would be in jeopardy if the Americans left. While there was no place in Iraq that was truly safe, for the most part the Kurds kept insurgents at bay and protected American interests.

On the way to the company compound, Alex saw a few Westerners walking leisurely along the road. *This might not be a bad place to work.* Another major difference was the terrain; there was more green foliage, trees, and grass than in the south. The land here undulated with hills, and mountains loomed in the distance.

A sign above the entrance to the company compound read, *Welcome to Asgard.* Alex recognized the name as the capital of the god Odin's domain. Asgard was large and sported the normal accessories of life in Iraq: a twelve-foot sandstone wall, guard towers, a large parking area full of armored vehicles, and the like.

Linda and Odin stood on the porch of a large French-style villa with several other people. Alex lingered, trying to bring his leg back to life, as the others dismounted the vehicle. As he watched Linda through the tinted windows, his mouth went very dry. He was nervous, but now he understood the feeling, and he liked it. He slid out the back of the vehicle as Odin launched into his welcoming rant. Alex fell in next to the other new men and a little behind them. Smiling at Linda, he raised his hand to his chest and wiggled his fingers in a wave just for her. She broke into a big smile, fidgeted, and grabbed the arm of a woman standing next to her, who was also looking at Alex. He figured that she must be Linda's mother, so he gave her a little wave also. She smiled back warmly.

Now that's definitely a good sign! Alex thought. He flushed and could hardly contain himself. All his muscles relaxed, and suddenly he had to pee.

Odin was saying, "So, take five, and then if you will meet us in the briefing room, we can get this show started." The men filed up the steps into the house, and Alex followed. Odin slapped the last new man on the back as he went inside, turned to Alex, and with a completely different tone of voice he said, "Son, you look a hell of a lot better than you did the last time I saw you."

He stopped himself from grabbing Alex in a bear hug and took his hand in both of his. Gone was the bone-crushing handshake Alex had felt the first time they met.

"You don't know how happy I am that you've come back to us." He started to tell Alex about his plans until his wife cleared her throat and he stopped. "Oh, I'm sorry. This is my wife, Emma. She's got a call sign, but if I tell you you'll turn to stone when you look at her." She shouldered past him, and Alex held his hand out to her.

Emma slipped right past his hand and gave him a big hug. She said into his ear, "I'm so happy to finally meet you." She let go of him, took both of his hands, and looked directly into his eyes. "I want you to know how grateful I am for what you did for my son." Her eyes started to tear, and she hugged him again. "I just don't know what I'd do if he got hurt." Then she broke off her embrace, put one fist on her hip, wagged her finger at him, and raised her voice. "And you take care of yourself here. You're lucky to be in one piece. I don't want to hear any more stories with you involved, do you hear me?"

"Yes ma'am, I'll behave myself," Alex said and almost snapped to attention.

She turned to Odin and took him by his enormous arm and said, "Come with me, dear. We have things to do." Alex got the impression that she winked at Linda as she led her husband into the house.

They stood awkwardly alone together for a long moment. Alex looked at her, not knowing what to do or say, and Linda fidgeted some more until she blurted out, "Well, aren't you going to say anything?"

"I missed you," he croaked.

She looked around quickly and then threw herself into his arms and kissed him with a passion he had never known. His head swam as she pressed against him, her arms around his neck.

Together they entered a world all their own. For those moments nothing else existed and nothing else mattered. They kissed as her tears streamed down his face. They were finally together, and they each understood what the other felt. He whispered to her, "I love you. I've loved you since the first moment I saw you."

She whispered back, "I know. I felt it then. I knew I could trust you." They kissed again, this time with even more urgency. He became intoxicated with her, her fragrance, her body, her passion. She whispered again, "And I love you, and I've missed you more than anything else in my life." Then she pushed away from him, struck him on the chest with her fist, and with tears streaming down her face she said, "You scared the hell out of me. Don't do that again. And don't leave me again. Now go inside and I'll see you later." Wiping the tears from her eyes, she turned and ran along the porch to disappear through another door.

Alex could hardly breathe.

Linda hurried up the stairs to her room before anyone saw the state she was in. She dropped onto her bed and cried. She knew she had acted in haste, but she could not bring herself to let this one get away too. He reminded her too much of Jesse.

She had met Jesse four years earlier at Fort Campbell when she was assigned to an aviation medical company of the 101st Airborne Division and her unit was attached to the 160th Special Operations Aviation Regiment that was supporting his unit, the Special Forces Operational Detachment Delta, during a training exercise.

She first saw him in a pre-mission briefing. When he entered the room, she was immediately impressed with his presence; he was tall and handsome, and he exuded confidence and competence. Despite being commanded by others, once he took over the briefing there was no question in anyone's mind who was really in charge. He clearly understood what was required of everyone, and he treated them as if they were an essential part of the team—not at all like most of the egotistical, condescending men she regularly encountered in the Army. It was quite clear to Linda that within minutes the entire room would have followed him anywhere.

She wondered if he had noticed her and did not want to risk that he had not, so she asked a dumb question when he was finished. The only time he displayed any hesitancy was when he looked directly into her eyes before responding. He recovered quickly, and with the same quirky little smile that came over Alex when he talked to her, he gave her an answer that made her feel like she was the smartest person in the room and an integral part of the team. She was sold.

He was a perfect gentleman with her and treated her with respect. They dated whenever their jobs allowed and soon were considered a couple by their friends. Months went by, and she found herself deeply in love with him. She had finally found a real man who could not only measure up to her family, but who treated her exactly the way she had always dreamt of. She wanted to marry him and live happily ever after.

Then 9/11 happened, and he disappeared without a word. As part of Delta, he had disappeared at times, but he always contacted her and came back to her as soon as he could. She had never thought that she would not see him again. This time was different. He was going to war. Months went by, and she learned nothing.

Finally, her unit was deployed to Afghanistan. After a mission one day, she was focused on reorganizing her gear on the flight line when she suddenly felt a strange sensation and heard a soft voice say, "Hey, sweetheart." She spun around and there he was, all scruffy and grinning at her with that smile. With her heart pounding, she jumped into his arms and all her emotions spilled out. They made love that night and he asked her to marry him. She was happy again, and they talked into the early hours of the morning about their future together.

Then came Operation Anaconda, and Linda's world collapsed around her.

Jesse's unit joined an attack by some 2,000 coalition forces to destroy about 200 Taliban and Al-Qaeda fighters positioned at the base of a mountain range. Jesse and his team infiltrated into the area a day before the attack began. The operation was a fiasco from the very beginning.

"Friendly fire" from an AC-130 gunship, combined with heavy enemy mortar fire, stopped the main attack in its tracks before it even entered the valley. The expected 200 enemy fighters turned out to be more like 2,000, and they were dug in throughout the adjacent mountains. The supporting attack to close off escape routes was pinned down until the coalition forces had to be evacuated, and most of the insurgents escaped to the east. Jealous coalition commanders changed satellite radio frequencies, and the men could not call for indirect fire support or medevac. Jesse's team and a few other Special Forces and SEAL teams ended up running through the mountains, trying to rescue friendly forces cut off from help and in danger of being overrun. The last anyone heard of Jesse was that he had tried to help a soldier left behind by a helicopter. The bird hastily departed from a mountaintop under heavy enemy fire before all the soldiers were on board.

Two days later, after the generals declared the operation a resounding victory, Linda found his body. He had been shot multiple times, stripped naked, mutilated, and his head was severed from his body and tossed down the side of the mountain.

Linda slipped into severe depression. She struggled through her eighteen-month tour in Afghanistan with great difficulty. Her enlistment was supposed to be over just a few months after her return to the States, but the Army extended her enlistment "indefinitely," and she was placed on deployment orders to Iraq. Despondent, she explained her feelings to an Army psychiatrist and was eventually allowed to end her enlistment. By this time, however, Iraq was in full swing, and her father had created his new business before she had the chance to talk him out of it. After some time spent in meaningless civilian life without her family, she joined them in Iraq.

She was not happy, and her family knew it. She particularly did not like being around death and suffering, but she could not bring herself to be apart from her parents. She longed for something, although she did not know what, and she certainly did not expect to find it in Iraq.

And yet now she had found it.

It was Alex. He made her feel the way she had before. He was handsome, warm, smart, and a perfect gentleman with her. And he was obviously completely taken with her. Without presumption he had powered himself into a special place with her family both by his incredible actions and the fact that he made her smile again. She had seen him in action, or the results of his action, and knew what he had done took great courage, strength, and skill, which seemed to come natural to him. Yet she had also seen his concern for others, and she liked its implications; he was the perfect balance of strength and compassion. While they were similar in many ways, Alex was not simply a substitute for Jesse. Alex was what she wanted in a man, and she easily saw herself being happy with him for the rest of her life. He had come back for her. Alex was her salvation.

Now all she had to do was talk her parents out of this crazy business so they could all go home and live in peace.

Odin explained to the new operators their business of escorting oil company workers out to the field, running a combat taxi service to and from the various airports and a courier service to Baghdad, and a big new contract with USAID (United States Agency for International Development), providing protection for some of their reconstruction and development teams. They would have all of one day to get over the jet lag, and then it was time to work. During that "downtime," they would in-process, receive their kit, zero their weapons, be assigned to a team, and conduct rehearsals. Then he turned the meeting over to Emma for administration and life support, introducing her as "Medusa."

Odin grabbed Alex by the arm and led him to the operations room. The room had several desks, and a long table with an assortment of radios and telephones and a TV tuned to an Arabic news channel with the volume turned all the way down. The walls were papered with maps. A girl who looked to be Filipino sat at a desk, typing on a computer and monitoring the radios.

Odin went through the room and onto the porch and said, "Look, I've been in touch with the hostage crisis team at the embassy in Baghdad and they haven't heard anything about Predator, but I asked the chief of our Kurdish guards to look into it for me. If there's anything there, he'll find out. Just don't get your hopes up too much."

Alex nodded and said, "The picture was him." Still, he understood Odin's skepticism, and he expected it would be shared by everyone but Alex himself. After all, it had been almost six months, and a picture did not guarantee anything. Even if he had been kidnapped, he could have been killed months ago. Why had there been no word prior to this? Kidnappers, particularly jihadist insurgents, typically found it to their advantage to advertise their captives for prestige or to recruit men or raise money. Often, they used the media to drive up the price that they could get for the captive from other groups. Why would they wait so long, and why would they not plaster the picture and videos all over the Western media?

Odin said, "I believe you, but until we get more news, there's nothing to be done. We'll do everything we can, but I'm afraid our only real option is to wait." He continued, "Until then, we have other business to tend to. These people at USAID are real pains in the butt, and specifically, one of the principals thinks he's God's gift to the world. Our contract with them wasn't his idea, and he seems to resent our presence. He'll need to be handled with patience and diplomacy, and I think you are the one for the job. I want you to be the team leader for his PSD. Alien is with him now, but he's already asked me to be replaced. If you're up to it, I'd like you to start as soon as possible."

Alex thought, *Great, I get to babysit a prima donna in a war zone,* but he said, "Sure, I'll do my best. If it's OK, I'd like to go out with the team tomorrow to warm up."

Odin was obviously pleased. "Absolutely! They should be back soon. Meanwhile, I'll hook you up with the ops manager, and you can draw your kit tonight. You can zero your weapon at first light." Odin led him to the chow hall for dinner.

They went through the serving line and sat at a long table with the operations manager, who Odin introduced as "Asgard Three, or just 'Three' for short." As they ate, Three explained the process of the missions. Each evening they received an itinerary from the client, and Three broke it down into separate missions and issued them to the teams. The team leader would then conduct a map and satellite imagery reconnaissance, check intelligence reports, coordinate any additional support he might need, brief his team, and conduct rehearsals.

As they spoke, Alien joined them. He greeted Alex with a manly hug and declared, "Hey, Wildman, it's good to see you in one piece. Welcome back."

"How are you doing?" Alex asked him.

"I'm doin' great, especially now that you're here to relieve me of the king of all asshole clients."

Alex said sarcastically, "So, y'all are stickin' it to me, huh?"

"He'll be better with you. I'm pretty sure it chaps his ass to have a black guy in charge of his life." Alien turned to Three and said, "You know we took some more fire from that same area this morning?"

Three nodded and said, "Yeah, I got the call. I reported it

to the Army, and they don't seem too concerned over a single shooter. Make sure you stay buttoned up as you pass through that area." The ballistic windows would stop most small-arms fire.

"Roger that." Alien said, shrugging and taking another mouthful of food. It was all to be expected. Nothing would change until someone "important" was killed.

They talked business as they finished the meal and went to gather Alex's gear. Then they went back to the operations room, and Three gave them the following day's mission. They pored over the maps, chose their routes, and made photocopies to brief the team. Finally, they went to the barracks, a long building running down one side of the compound. A sign hanging above the door read *Warriors Quarters*, but someone had scratched over *Warriors* and replaced it with *Slave*. They found the team in the dayroom and, after introductions, went over the next day's business. When they finished, Alien showed Alex to his room.

Once they were alone, Alien asked, "I heard you saw Predator's picture on Al-Jazeera. What do you think?"

"I think he's still alive."

Alien raised his eyebrows. "What are you going to do?"

Alex shook his head. "Well, I'm not sure yet. Odin says he put some feelers out looking for intel, and I figured I'd give that some time, but I really don't have any confidence."

As Alien departed for his own room he said, "Well, whatever you find out, let me know and we'll figure out what we can do." He hesitated at the door and looked seriously at Alex. "Hey, man, it's good to have you back."

Alex nodded. "Thanks, brother."

Alex had just stepped out of the shower when a cell phone on his nightstand began to ring. Baffled at the presence of the phone, he picked it up and said, "Hello?"

"Would you like to meet me on the front porch of the main house?" It was Linda.

His vision blurred and his heart pounded. "I can't think of anything I'd rather do. I'll be there in one minute." He raced to put on clothes and ran a comb through his new hair, thinking, *Damn, at least for once I'll be clean when I see her, and my head doesn't look like Frankenstein anymore.* His excitement grew with every step.

She was leaning against the railing, watching him, with her long, silky hair loose and a light summer dress that flowed to her knees. Alex slowed to savor this vision of absolute beauty. As he approached, she coyly stepped back into the shadows. He reached out to her and, caressing her neck with his hands, kissed her softly but fully. She slid her arms under his and around his back and pulled herself to him. They lost themselves in a long moment of passion as all their senses focused on one another. When at last they came up for air he whispered softly to her, "I must be the luckiest man on earth."

She breathed, "I'm glad you think so. I feel the same. Tell me why you came back."

"I came back for you," he sighed. "I could hardly stand it over there thinking about you. I thought about you all day and dreamt about you at night. I couldn't stand it. I had to get back here as soon as possible to see if there was any chance that you might want to be with me."

She pulled him closer to her. "I knew it was true. I just had to hear you say it." They kissed again, anxiously this time. When they released their grips on one another, she led him by the hand into the house and up to her room.

CHAPTER 4

Back into the Valley of the Shadow of Death

ALEX BEGAN TO ASSEMBLE his kit shortly after midnight.

The first thing he checked was his primary weapon, a Colt M4 lower receiver with a new flat-top Daniel Defense upper receiver and Picatinny rail system covering the barrel. The selector switch indicated safe, semi-automatic, and three-round burst. The upper receiver sported a short ten-inch barrel with a SureFire muzzle brake that would receive a suppressor. It was spotlessly clean with a light coat of oil in all the right places. It had a collapsible stock, a small foregrip on the rail system, an Aimpoint red dot optic, and an AN/PEQ laser/flashlight combination with a remote on/off switch taped to the foregrip. He checked the dials of the PEQ and found that it also had an infrared switch and IR flashlight.

He checked the batteries of the optic and the PEQ and found them both serviceable. Also attached to the rifle was a two-point adjustable sling. He could unsnap one end and attach it to the other to make it a single-point connection, allowing him faster transition from target to target in a vehicle and in buildings. If he needed both hands, the two points enabled him to work without dragging the barrel in the dirt.

He pulled the charging handle back, ensured there was no round loaded, and then allowed the bolt carrier group to slide into battery with a loud, metallic clap. Then he pushed in and pulled out the rear takedown pin and quickly field-stripped the rifle to check the working parts for serviceability. He reassembled it and performed a functions check. Finally, he put the sling over his right shoulder, across his back and under his left arm, and let the weapon hang free in front of him. Then he lifted it tight to his right pec, his left hand extended all the way to the end of the rail in a firing position. He adjusted the butt stock, and holding it up again, he whirled from side to side and transitioned it to his left shoulder. Allowing some room for his body armor, he adjusted the sling, tried it again, and thought, *This will do nicely.*

He picked up his secondary weapon, a 9-millimeter Glock 17 pistol, and pulled the slide back to check the chamber and the magazine well. He let the slide snap shut, held the gun up in both hands, and sighted down the barrel, aiming at a spot on the wall. He was satisfied that the steel white-dot night sights were centered as he took the slack out of the trigger and pulled slowly until he heard the click of the firing pin being released. Nodding in approval, he curled the fingers of his right hand over the slide and pulled it slightly back as he pulled down on the two nubs of the slide lock and pushed forward with his fingers; the gun came apart in his hands. He peered inside at the working parts, and again he found them clean and serviceable. He put the gun back together and performed a functions check.

He then emptied his kit bag onto his bed and rummaged through the contents until he found a rigger's belt, a pistol magazine pouch, two pistol holsters, and a flashlight. The flashlight was an Insight M6 with a red-laser combination that he slid onto the rail on the lower receiver of the pistol. Again, he held the pistol at the ready in both hands and switched on the flashlight with his left thumb, and a blinding light with a red dot in the center splashed across the wall of his room. *That'll work.*

He chose a KYDEX friction-retention holster that had been formed to fit the pistol with the flashlight attached and slid it and a magazine pouch onto the rigger's belt. Rooting through the pile on his bed, he found a speed magazine pouch for the M4, so he took the belt apart again and attached the M4 mag pouch just behind the pistol mag pouch on the left side and reassembled the belt again. After a couple adjustments of the belt, he put the pistol in the holster and pushed down until it snapped securely in place.

He stood facing the mirror over his sink with his legs slightly apart for good balance and his hands at his sides. Then, in a blur, his right hand moved to the pistol, and his fingers found the pistol grip and curled around the handle and gave a mighty pull. The belt popped up over his hips, and the holster, with the gun still in it, spun around to his belly button. He jerked on the handle twice more before the gun came loose and he was able to raise it up to the mirror. His image made him think of Deputy Barney Fife rather than a cool operator.

He pulled the belt off and stripped the gear from it, then threaded it all onto his own leather belt and used the belt loops on his pants to hold it all down. He tried it again and still found too much resistance. From the pile he retrieved a Leatherman tool and used the screwdriver to adjust the holster. Once again he settled in front of the mirror, and this time in one smooth, blazing-fast motion he drew the gun and pulled the trigger and knew his round would have landed on the bridge of the nose of the reflection in front of him before that ugly bastard could even blink. *Nice.* He dry fired the pistol a few more times and then turned his attention to the rest of his kit.

He collected ten 30-round M4 magazines off the bed, opened a box containing ammunition, and pulled out two types of 5.56 rounds. One was a 62-grain green tip with a steel penetrator for shooting through walls and cars; in an adrenaline rush, it might not drop a man unless it hit something vital. The other bullets were 55-grain hollow points that would drop a man quickly but not necessarily penetrate anything of greater substance. Alex loaded the magazines by alternating green tip, then hollow point. If he put the M4 selector switch on burst, three rounds would come out each time he pulled the trigger, and the target would get the best of both worlds. He repeated the process with the six 17-round Glock mags, alternating one ball round and one Hydra-Shok hollow point until the mags were full. Then he loaded both weapons, topped off the magazines, and stood the M4 next to his bed and placed the Glock on the nightstand.

His body armor consisted of the plate carrier and two level-three steel plates that would cover the golden triangle of his torso but not much else. On the front of the plate carrier were five pouches into which he stuffed eight M4 magazines with the bullets down and angled so that when he pulled one out with his left hand, he just needed to turn it over and jam it home. Then he put a Motorola radio in the last pouch and clipped the handset microphone/speaker to the left shoulder strap so he could send a message without pulling the radio out of the pouch or taking his right hand off the fire control of his weapon.

From its sheath Alex pulled an SOG dagger, all black except for the two shiny, razor-sharp edges on the seven-inch blade. He fixed it to the center of his plate carrier behind the magazine pouches so that in a TIC he could pull it out with either hand and go to work. *Nasty business.*

Next he inventoried the contents of the Individual First Aid Kit, or IFAK: a pair of shears to cut off clothing, two SOF-T tourniquets for massive bleeding of arms or legs, two packets of

Quick-Clot gauze for massive torso hemorrhaging, and vacuum-sealed gauze that worked well when you ran out of toilet paper. There was also a cricothyroidotomy, or cric, kit to establish an airway in case his face was blown off and he needed to breathe, two halo chest seals for a sucking chest wound or evisceration, a ten-gauge needle to relieve the pressure of a tension pneumothorax, and an assortment of other items, like chemlights for illumination, nitrile gloves, and alcohol wipes.

Alex attached one of the tourniquets to his plate carrier with a rubber band so that if he needed it, he would not have to open the IFAK and could administer it to himself. Finally, he attached the IFAK to the rigger's belt and made sure it would ride above his gun belt and below his plate carrier and out of the way behind him. He could pull it around to open it without having to take off any gear.

His headgear was a sand-colored Ops-Core helmet with a mount for a night observation device on the front and a weight attached to the back as a counterbalance. The SureFire light attached to the left side of the helmet operated in red, white, and infrared light and had an IR strobe light for identification by friendly forces at night, or by bad guys if they happened to have stolen some working NODs.

He opened a small black nylon case on the bed and pulled out an AN/PVS 14. While there were advantages to binocular NODs, like better depth perception, Alex preferred the monocular 14s because they did not blind both eyes when it was necessary to take them off. He attached the NODs to the front of the helmet and put the helmet on. Like usual, the helmet was tight and guaranteed to cause a headache after a while. He buckled and adjusted the straps as best he could and jiggled his head back and forth to make sure it was tight. Then he turned the light off in the room and fired up the NODs. A greenish glow appeared. Adjusting the focus, he could see clearly in the dark room. He picked up his M4 and activated the IR laser on the PEQ, and with the monocular he watched the laser's dot dance around the room, while he saw nothing with his naked eye. He flipped on the IR flashlight, and the room turned into day through the NODs and stayed black through his other eye. *Excellent.* Then he tested the IR light and strobe on his helmet.

Damn, this is too easy. All this stuff actually works.

Alex picked up two fragmentary grenades from his pile and inspected the tape around the pin. While it took time to peel the tape off in a TIC, Alex had heard of too many inadvertent detonations, so he left the tape in place. He attached the two frags to his plate carrier and a flashbang on the opposite side.

He filled his Camelbak hydration system and checked that the small GPS was working before stuffing into the pouch next to his Motorola. Now suspicious of the weight of his kit, Alex hefted the plate carrier onto his shoulders and adjusted the straps, then swung the Camelbak onto his back and ran his arms through the straps. The veins in his neck and arms pulsed as his body adjusted to the weight. He shook his head. *This is ridiculous.*

He stuffed the Camelbak and four of the M4 mags in a three-day assault bag. That would give him four mags on his plate carrier, one in the speed mag pouch on his belt, and one in the M4, four more in his go bag, and certainly dozens more in the vehicle. He would carry some water bottles in the cargo pockets of his pants. He stood up straight again. *Better. Not good, but better.* He jumped up and down and made some adjustments on the kit to keep things in place and quiet them down.

Alex spent the next several minutes packing extras into his go bag and consolidating what he would carry in his pockets: sunglasses, Peltor earmuffs, cell phone, paper, pen, map, passport, the extra M4 and Glock mags, water, and some protein bars. Finally, he set his alarm and put it on the other side of the room and flopped down on the bed and passed out.

★★★

"Trouble sleeping?" Alien snickered as he set his breakfast tray down next to Alex.

"Yeah, jet lag," Alex grumbled as he nursed his coffee.

"Uh-huh, if you say so." Alien grinned.

"Hey, man, I was up all night putting my kit together."

"Why so defensive?" Alien gave Alex a little shove on his shoulder. "You act like you're guilty of something extracurricular."

Alex was saved by the arrival of the two assistant team leaders, or ATLs, and another team member. "Hey, man, welcome back. My name's Johnny. They call me Lizard." The tall, lanky, affable Lizard grinned and stuck out a supersized hand with extra-long fingers. Alex felt like a child when his entire hand disappeared inside those fingers. Alex leaned around the table and looked at his feet. *Jesus, how does he find shoes that fit?*

Alien said, "Lizard commands our number three truck; call sign's Charlie Three. This is Julio 'Bandito'—he's our ATL and commands truck one, or Charlie One—and this is Dingo, or Derrick, our token Australian: C One driver." Alex shook hands all around. Bandito was of medium height with enormous arms and sharp eyes, and Dingo looked like a blond surfer from San Diego's East County covered with tattoos over every inch of exposed skin. Alex liked them all right away.

Flashing white teeth behind a tanned face, Dingo said, "Hey, mate, welcome aboard. You ready to get this show on the road?"

Alex looked him in the eye and said, "I am."

Bandito flopped down in a chair. "Good, then finish up; we've got a lot to do. We'll let you zero your guns and then go over our SOPs and rehearse a bit."

"We've got plenty of time," Alien said. "His Majesty's day doesn't start until late morning. We'll pull out at about zero nine thirty." They finished their breakfast, and Alex got a large cup of coffee to go.

About fifty yards behind the main house, Alex and the team came to a bulldozed culvert that served as their shooting range. The range was ten lanes wide and 100 yards deep with just enough space to do some innovative shooting drills, perhaps even mounted. Steel targets and various barricades for training were stacked off to the side. The crest of hill formed by the dirt pushed aside was lined with T-Walls for added safety of those who lived and worked directly behind the range.

Dingo raised a large red banner on a fifty-foot flagpole, signaling the range was hot.

"This is so our Kurdish friends don't think we're under attack and decide to return fire." Nobody seemed bothered by the fact that it wasn't yet 7 AM and they were fixing to wake the dead right in the middle of the city. Lizard stapled a small M4 zeroing target to a makeshift wooden target stand, which had seen better days, and then walked back to the firing line.

Alex zeroed his rifle at 25 yards. With the bullets they were using and the offset of his optic, at 7 yards he would aim slightly over one inch high to hit center mass; at 25 and again at 300 yards would be point of aim/point of impact, and between 25 and 300 he would aim a bit low; at 50 yards about one inch low; and at 200 yards, six inches low. Alex looked at a diagram torn from a military field manual and nailed to a post next to the firing line that confirmed what he already knew.

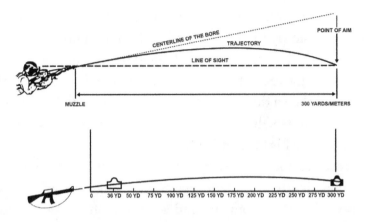

Diagram Source: US Army, Public Domain

Bandito keyed his radio. "Asgard Three, Asgard Three, this is Charlie One. We're going hot on the range."

Alex sat on a bench, put on his Peltor earmuffs, adjusted some sandbags under his M4, and turned on his optic.

"This is Asgard Three. Roger, range is hot. Call us back when you go cold."

"Roger that." Bandito set the radio down and handed Alex a mag of M4 rounds. "Plenty more where that came from. Take your time."

"Thanks." Alex dry fired his rifle a few times, getting his breathing and trigger squeeze down and his head into the game. He clicked the magazine into the well, then gave it a little tug. Holding the rifle by the fire control with his right hand, he reached up with his left and pulled the charging handle all the way back and let it go, watching the round get scooped up by the bolt carrier group and slammed home into the chamber. Then he pushed on the forward assist to ensure the bolt had gone into battery. *So far, so good.*

He rested the rifle firmly on the sandbags and adjusted the optic until the red dot was as small as it would go and still allow him to see it. Taking a deep breath and letting it out to settle his body, he sighted on the target, flipped the selector switch to semi with his right thumb, and breathed out as he squeezed the trigger slowly to the rear. *Pop* registered in his brain as the Peltors washed out the crisp, loud report of the round being fired. He brought the red dot to the same point on the target and did it again, and then a third time. He placed the weapon back on safe and set it on its side on the table, got up, called "Downrange," and walked to his target with Dingo in tow.

The three holes in the target formed a triangle with no further than one-eighth of an inch separation. Dingo remarked, "Not too bad. You could come up and left just a little." Alex nodded in agreement.

They went back to the firing line, and Alex took the caps off the adjustment knobs of his Aimpoint and used one to turn the windage knob three clicks to the right and the elevation three clicks up. Then he repeated the three-shot exercise again. This time the three holes were directly in the center of the bullseye with two of them touching and the other less than an eighth of an inch away. Dingo said, "It doesn't get any better than that."

"I'm good with that," Alex agreed.

They walked back to the line and stepped over one lane to where a human silhouette target was posted only ten meters away. Alex faced downrange, and with a flip of his right hand he cleared his cover shirt from the pistol at his hip and swiftly and smoothly drew the Glock and aimed it at the target with both hands in as tight a grip as he could manage without shaking. His focus shifted from the target to his front sight until the target was blurry and the front sight was clear, still center mass of the blurry target. Then he made sure that the very tip of the front sight was even with the tips of the rear sight and there was an equal amount of light on both sides of the front sight. He pulled the gun slightly back into his "workspace" and turned the top of it to the left. With his left hand he pinched the top rear of the slide and jerked it all the way back and let go.

With both hands, he pushed the gun out toward the target again, quickly lined up his sights, stopped breathing, and pulled the trigger as smoothly as he could until the firing pin clicked forward on an empty chamber. He charged the weapon again and repeated the dry fire four or five times. Then he holstered the Glock and did the same drill from the draw. *Slow is smooth and smooth is fast.*

When he was satisfied, he drew the gun again and aimed it at the target and pulled the trigger. This time he held the slide-lock button up with his right thumb as he charged the pistol, and the slide locked to the rear. He tilted it to the right just far enough to see the magazine well as he drew a magazine from his left hip and quickly slipped it home. He twisted the pistol to the left, charged it, pushed out toward the target, and fired two rounds with little perceptible pause. Two holes appeared in the center of the silhouette's face, barely one inch apart.

Alex then slow fired a few rounds into the head. He holstered up, then drew and fired two rounds to the chest. He did this several times until his pistol ran out of ammunition. When the gun went dry, he thumbed the magazine-release button with his right hand, ejecting the empty mag as he pulled the pistol back into his workspace while at the same time brushing his shirt out of the way with his left hand and reaching for another mag. He slipped the fresh magazine home, pressed the slide-lock button with his right thumb, rotated the pistol back as he gripped it again with both hands, and pressed it back out toward the target and fired two more rounds into the face. The whole process took no more time than a few heartbeats. Alex thought, *I gotta do better than that.*

He picked up the empty magazine, brushed it off, and switched it out with the one in his pistol, putting the full one back in the mag pouch on his left hip. This gave him one bullet in the chamber and an empty magazine. He put the gun back in its holster, looked at the target, and in a flash drew the gun and fired into the face of the target. The gun went empty with the slide locking back, he ejected the spent mag, reloaded, and fired two more rounds to the face. *Much better.* Out of the corner of his eyes he saw the team nodding approval.

Alex picked up his M4 and ran the sling over his left shoulder and under his right arm. This time he was joined by several other men who had pasted targets downrange, and they all began firing. Alex worked his M4 on semi, burst, and through a few mag-change drills, and some transitions to his pistol until he was satisfied.

As he walked back to the team room, he felt elated. *Damn, I love this shit.* Then he realized there was an upstairs veranda on the back of the main house, and Linda was standing there beside a set of French doors, watching and sipping on a cup of coffee. Alex's heart started to race, and he tried to contain himself, but he couldn't help looking at her for too long until he tripped and stumbled. He looked up again in time to see her smile as she disappeared through the door.

"Nicely done, boss. I think you really made an impression." Dingo laughed.

"More than you know." Alien's turn.

"Alright, that's enough. I feel stupid enough. Y'all don't have to make it worse."

Alien laughed, "Yes we do. That's what we're here for."

They entered the team room, and Alien told Alex to have a seat. The room was decorated with a variety of maps depicting Iraq and its cities at all scales. In the center was a whiteboard titled *Mission Brief.* When the whole team was settled, Alien cleared his throat and everyone went silent.

"You all know that Alex here has been chosen to replace me as your team leader." There were a few nods in response, but nothing betrayed an emotion one way or the other. "He's going to ride with us today and until he feels comfortable enough to take charge, so rather than just glossing through our SOPs like we normally do, I'm going to cover them in greater detail so he gets a better idea of what we do and what we expect."

He pointed at a map posted with the day's route and tapped on a red *X* marked in the city of Kirkuk. "Today we're taking the client to a house near the Kirkuk Oil Training Institute for a meet and greet and then bringing him home. A hundred *K*s down and a hundred *K*s back through Indian country."

He pointed at their compound on the big map. "We SP from Asgard at ten hundred hours and travel south on Peshawa Qazi road, then west on Koya road to the USAID compound here. We pick up the client and jump on Highway 3 all the way south to Shari Al Almas in West Kirkuk, then north on Doctor's Street to the institute. At the roundabout in front of the institute, it is my understanding that we take the first right and our venue is the first building on the left. We'll see how this works out when we get there."

He traced two alternate routes in case something went terribly wrong. The best alternative would take them nearly a hundred additional miles out of their way, but better late than dead.

He went on, "Yesterday, there were seven IEDs between here and Kirkuk that killed six and wounded eleven people, and Big Army found and destroyed an additional four IEDs along Highway 3. The method of IED employment has varied from burying them under the road to piles of trash and rocks beside the road, so look for disturbed surfaces and pretty much anything else. One car bomb detonated at the checkpoint on Highway 3 at the entrance to Erbil with four Kurdish police vaporized and a few civilian casualties.

"Also yesterday, a bit further south than our route, a mobile VBIED forced its way into a convoy and took out two coalition semis. So, they're out there driving around, looking for targets of opportunity. There was a major firefight between Big Army and insurgents in the Tapa district of Kirkuk just to the east of where we turn off Highway 3 onto Shari Al Almas. There have been so many small-arms attacks that people don't even report them anymore, and don't forget the sniper along this stretch of the highway."

Alien pointed to a section of road along the route.

"And keep in mind that there is a huge operation going on in Fallujah, and all the rats are scurrying out to all points of the country. Finally, we've met with this Iraqi contact before, but not at this venue, and we don't know the layout of the building or what to expect from his security at the new location, so be aware of what's going on around you, and sound off if you see anything suspicious. The bottom line is that there are lots of bad people out there who want us dead, and they'll use all sorts of innovative ways to make it happen."

Alien pointed to diagrams of their three cars with names in corresponding seats where each of the team members would sit.

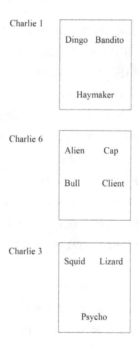

Charlie 1

Dingo Bandito

Haymaker

Charlie 6

Alien   Cap

Bull   Client

Charlie 3

Squid   Lizard

Psycho

"Vehicles will be loaded according to the diagram here, with three of us in each vehicle: driver, TC, and rear gunner in the lead and follow, and driver, TC, and package handler in the limo. The order of movement will start with C1 leading, C6, and C3 in trail. Be flexible and prepared to block roads and traffic as we move, then fall into the rear as you catch up. At high speed on the highway we'll keep about a hundred yards between vehicles and at slower speeds keep it tight to prevent other vehicles from cutting into our motorcade, but with enough room between us that one IED won't disable two vehicles. As we move, call out suspicious activity like cars following us or piles of trash and broken-down cars on the side of the road or hadji watching us while he's talking on his cell phone or, worse still, the absence of pedestrians in a normally busy area.

"If we take small-arms fire, call out contact and we'll push through and get off the X. If the limo goes down, push us off the X and then we'll cross-load or hook up to tow. If we hook up to tow, then we'll cross-load the client to another vehicle. If the limo won't be moved, then the lead lays down suppressive fire and the follow will pull up on the non-contact side of the limo, and we'll cross-load. If none of us are going anywhere, then we jack a car or evac to a hard point and call QRF. If one of the support vehicles goes down, the limo will continue to drive, and the other support vehicle will assist our downed brothers."

Alien continued by pointing below the vehicle diagram at an arrow with names in it.

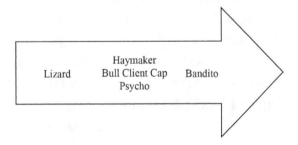

"Actions at the venue: drivers stay with the vehicles and two pax from the lead and follow dismount and move to the limo and establish security. TC in the limo opens the package door and leads the client out, with the rest of the dismount team forming a diamond around the client. ATL from the lead takes point, and C3 TC takes rear security."

Alien took a deep breath and let it out. "Of course, as we all know, a plan is only good on paper, but it gives us all a point of reference, and we've got to stay flexible and be on our game at all times." Then, for Alex's benefit: "Sometimes these folks are real anal about how many of us move around inside their buildings and we've got to collapse and expand in tight spaces like doorways and halls, but we'll do some of that when we run through rehearsals here shortly."

Alien explained supporting elements and coordinating instructions. Medevac would theoretically be provided by Big Army out of Erbil Airport or whatever forward operating base, or FOB, had birds free at the moment. He pointed out the hospitals and FOBs that were on the way. Asgard would provide a mounted quick reaction force that could be moving within minutes but might take up to an hour to reach the team, depending on how far the team was from Erbil. Big Army QRF would respond depending on availability and priority. He went over call signs and frequencies for medevac and QRF and a few other details. Finally, he asked if anyone had any questions.

Haymaker raised his hand and said, "Yeah, would you say again all after 'Good morning'?"

Dingo: "I was wondering about my raise."

Lizard: "Who's gonna win the Super Bowl this year?"

Bull: "Can I have next Tuesday off?"

Suddenly everybody was talking at the same time, and none of it had anything to do with the mission. Alien shook his head. "OK then, since there are no questions, let's move out to the vehicles and make sure the new TL's online with our basic load, and then we'll do some rehearsals."

The vehicles were three black aftermarket-armored Chevy Tahoes. The SUVs were purchased stock and then modified with armor, ballistic glass, run-flat tires, and firing ports in the doors to enable passengers to shoot outside without opening the doors, or "cracking the seal." The cargo area in the back was modified with a jump seat facing the rear of the vehicle to accommodate one man armed with a SAW or an M240 machine gun for rear security. He was responsible for keeping an eye on the following team vehicles and watching for any insurgents sneaking up behind them, and he could pop open the hatch in order to fire on a threat.

Alien showed Alex the basic load of tools and emergency equipment, like hooligans to break into a door or vehicles, tow straps, jumper cables, MREs, water, and more. Extra ammunition for the M4s, Glocks, grenade launchers, and machine guns was stowed in strategic locations throughout each of the vehicles.

"We have signal flares and smoke there between the seats, and if we need to leave a vehicle behind, you can just pop that thermite grenade and drop it in the back with the communications gear. If we put it in the front, it may just burn a hole through the floor and fall to the ground without destroying the vehicle. If you drop it in the back, at least it will take out the comms gear and the bad guys won't be able to listen to our next move." He went over the maps, GPS, and emergency food and water they carried. "Bandito is our comms guy. He'll show you the commo, and Lizard, our team medic, will go over the aid bags for you."

Bandito familiarized Alex with the radios, cell phones, a satellite phone, and the Blue Force Tracker they used to signal Big Army if they became disabled in a firefight. He pointed out, "We only initiate the BFT when we get in a TIC and can't break contact. Then"—he wiggled two fingers on each hand in air quotes—"theoretically, Big Army dedicates what assets they can to help us out."

Alex thought, *At least the hope of help does wonders for confidence and beats the hell out of the last company laughingly saying, "Don't expect any help from Big Army" just before we rolled through Shooters' Alley in unarmored vehicles.*

They mounted up and rehearsed the actions on contact that Alien had outlined in his mission brief. Then they rehearsed actions at the venue, moving the client around while protecting him from any danger, and finally, they rehearsed CQB that they might expect inside a building while dismounted. At last, it was time to roll.

Although Alien was the team leader, he chose to drive because he did not want to get too close to the principal. As he put it, "I might save him from a bullet, but I'll surely kick him in the head while I'm doing it." Alex rode shotgun so he could see everything and talk with Alien as he learned the ropes. Bull sat in the back seat on the driver's side and was responsible for the principal.

The team pulled out of the compound at about ten o'clock. As they threaded through traffic and between spot reports of potential danger, Alien explained to Alex, "Without going all the way around the city, there's only one road we can take to the USAID compound, and someone's been taking potshots at us from some bombed-out buildings. We've called it in to Big Army several times, but they can't be bothered, so we just have to make sure we button up good when we get there and hope they don't get more innovative than small arms."

Alex split his attention between his maps, the GPS, learning the new roads, and looking out for signs of danger. He was starting to get a headache when Dingo called over the radio, "Sniper zone ahead, one klick!" Alex looked up as several large buildings left of the road came into view.

Alien said, "They used to house Saddam Hussein's troops when the war started." He snickered. "Then they were shocked and awed." Alex could see that smart bombs entering through the roofs had blown out the walls and windows. There were plenty of places to hide, and at a distance of 300 meters or so from the road, with tree and scrub cover and concealed avenues of egress and clear fields of fire toward the road, it seemed a perfect sniper position.

"This is Charlie One; we have activity on the right side of the road up ahead about one klick." The radio squelched as Dingo re-keyed the microphone. "We've got us a convoy!" He paused again. "Looks like another PMC pulled off the road. They've got security out and they're signaling us to slow down."

Alien called back, "Be careful. You can slow a bit, but don't stop, and be ready for anything."

"Roger that."

The adrenaline started to rush, and Alex almost forgot about the sniper until they pulled abreast of the convoy. As they neared the other PMC, Alex saw several Mitsubishi pickup trucks with machine-gun turrets mounted in the bed and the all-too-familiar black ski masks, and he said to Alien, "At least these poor bastards have Kevlars."

Then he realized that there were no doors on the gun trucks.

"Look at these idiots running around not only in unarmored little trucks, but they took the damn doors off!" As they passed the convoy, he saw one of the trucks had overturned and a still body lay on the ground with a ripped-out throat and blood all over the head and chest. At the far end of the convoy was another dead man without a throat.

Alien said, "Damn! Sniper had a good day. Two throat shots at a moving target from at least three, four hundred meters. He's no amateur."

Alex looked back over his left shoulder at the burned-out building complex as it faded from view. "I wonder if Big Army will care now."

Alien shrugged. "Probably not. They don't even have to report contractor deaths; it's one of those mystery categories. They probably won't do anything 'til some of their own get killed."

As they passed through the city, Alex marveled at its antiquity. Erbil's history went back at least 8,000 years, to the very beginning of human civilization, and had been fought over by numerous empires, from the ancient Assyrians to the Babylonians, the Persians, the Greeks, the Mongols, the Ottomans, to the British, and now the Americans. The ancient walled citadel rose perhaps a hundred feet above the rest of the city, atop a steep hill with parapets that spoke of thousands of years of conflict. Alex was overwhelmed to think that men like Alexander the Great and Tamerlane, for better or worse, had once ridden over the same ground that he now covered. He wished he could get out and walk around.

The USAID compound reminded Alex of a country club where he was out of place and unwelcome. Men wearing suits and women in dresses sporting jewelry and makeup walked casually about and looked at the team with obvious disdain. The parking lot was full of beautiful, state-of-the-art factory-armored SUVs and Mercedes Benzes that were so clean he wondered if they were ever used.

They pulled off to the side of the lot, and Bull jumped out and briskly approached their mess hall, which looked more like an exclusive restaurant. A covered walkway adorned with flowers and potted plants led up to the entrance, a large, ornate, mahogany double door flanked by tinted glass that covered the entire front of the obviously brand-new building to protect the patrons from the blazing sun as they took their leisurely meals. To Alex it all looked out of place and excessive for a war zone.

As they dismounted to stretch, Alien said, "We're not allowed in there. Actually, we're not allowed *anywhere* in this compound except right here until it's time to go."

Bull was intercepted by an outstretched hand at the entrance of the restaurant. The man dressed as a nineteenth-century butler listened to what Bull had to say and then motioned him to stand fast and disappeared into the air-conditioning. After several minutes, the man returned, said something to Bull, and dismissed him with a wave of his hand.

Bull meandered back to the group and said, "He'll be with us 'soon enough.'"

How degrading. No wonder Alien is fed up with these people, Alex thought.

Alien said, "You risk your life to protect 'em and you'd think they'd at least offer you some of that AC out of the sun while we wait for his eminence to finish his brunch." Alien pulled out his map to show Alex where they had been and to go over again where they were going next. Alex spent some extra time looking over the area of the earlier sniper attack.

The team sprawled out in whatever shade they could find. An hour later the principal finally emerged from the air-conditioning, looking fresh and civilized in his pressed suit, immaculate white shirt, shiny dress shoes, and leather briefcase. Alex expected he had probably paid as much for his clothes as Alex had paid for his car.

Alien said to him, "This is Alex, my replacement. Alex, meet *Mr.* Jamison." Alien put all the emphasis on "Mr."

Alex held his hand out to shake, and *Mr.* Jamison handed him the briefcase and brushed past him, heading toward the vehicles. "Good, it's about time. I suppose you have some colorful call sign that I should know?"

Alex eyebrows could not have risen any higher as he said to Jamison's back, "They call me Cap."

Without even looking back over his shoulder, Jamison muttered, "Fine, *whatever.* Let's get this show on the road. I'm a busy man."

Alex shook his head and thought, *This is gonna be great fun.* Alien just smiled sarcastically.

Jamison had them drive to another part of the compound where three men, two of them armed, stood next to two large, completely stuffed duffel bags. As the team pulled alongside the men, Jamison said to the team, "Stay put."

Alex shrugged, knowing that once they left the security of this compound their roles would change. Jamison got out, and one of the men handed him a clipboard. Alex heard him say, "It's all here, sir. Four million dollars. Just the way you like it." Jamison glared at the man and scribbled something on the clipboard. The two other men struggled to lift one of the bags and heaved it onto the backseat floorboard of the SUV and did the same with the other bag. Jamison said nothing as he got back into the truck and rested his feet on two million dollars in cash. Bull gingerly arranged his feet on either side of the bag on his side of the truck.

Jamison reached over the seat and grabbed Alien's mission sheet. "You know where we're going?"

Alien said sarcastically, "Ah shore do, boss." Alex thought Alien would have preferred to say "massa" but figured that would be too direct. The team rolled out the gate, and it was all business.

They used a different route to leave the city until they were forced to get back on the road that they had traveled earlier that morning. After a short time, Dingo announced on the radio, "Sniper zone, one klick ahead."

Alien responded, "Roger that; speed up some and make sure you're buttoned up." This time the sniper would be on Alex's side of the vehicle. He made sure his firing port was closed. He scanned the buildings as they came into view and the convoy sped up. He saw daylight through some of the windows, but others were dark. He was concentrating on the dark windows when he thought he saw a flash of light. Then, suddenly, he heard a loud *thwack* on the side of the truck as a spiderweb of cracks spread across his window.

He reflexively jerked back in his seat and exclaimed, "Holy shit!" Then he keyed his mic. "Contact right, sniper in window, third floor, center building!"

Alien called into his mic, "Keep rolling! Faster!" The engine strained to capacity under all the weight, and then they were past the kill zone. Alex relaxed a little.

As he continued to scan his sector he said to Alien, "I guess that means Big Army didn't clear the area."

"Yeah, man. And this dude's got the range and lead down!" Alien glanced at his speedometer. "He must get a lot of practice. We were doin' almost eighty and he still hit us! Un-fucking-believable!"

"Yeah." Alex thought, *And if it weren't for this door, that bullet could be inside my body right now.* Alien called the contact in to Asgard Three.

✯✯✯

The road to Kirkuk took them out of the relative safety of Kurdistan and back into the cauldron of Sunni Muslim–dominated Northern Iraq. The IED pockmarks on the road soon became evident, and tension rose. Alex was amazed at the vast numbers of oil derricks pumping oil from one of the largest and oldest oilfields in the Middle East.

The city of Kirkuk itself had been largely reclaimed by the Kurds from the Arabs after Hussein's fall, but the fight was not over as the different cultures struggled violently for power. Approaching from the north, the team stayed on the highway as it skirted to the west of the city until they swung east into the city center.

Traffic became congested, and their progress slowed to a crawl. Warnings from Dingo were now constant: suspicious people, suspicious cars, piles of trash, militia with weapons, police . . . everything was a threat again. Several times they pulled into the oncoming lanes to get through traffic jams. While people clearly did not like this tactic, they were just as clearly accustomed to it, and the team managed to reach their destination with little trouble.

Five roads converged into a traffic circle. The team pulled to a halt in front of one of the buildings with the principal as close to the front door as possible. The drivers stayed in the vehicles with the engines running while the rest of the men in the first and last vehicles piled out to secure the area around the limo. The dismount team crowded around Jamison and hustled him into the building. Inside, they were immediately greeted by several Iraqis with AK-47s pointed at them from all sides. The men froze and hardly had a chance to comprehend their disadvantage before one man wearing a white dishdasha and a huge grin stepped forward and greeted Jamison.

"My dear friend Jamison, we have been expecting you. Please, have your men move your vehicles around back." He waved at the Iraqi guards. "My men will show them the way." The Iraqi security relaxed.

Jamison turned to Alex. "Do as he says. Amir is a friend of ours. I'll be fine."

Alex replied, "I'll go, but two men stay with you."

"Fine, suit yourself." Jamison waved him away and followed Amir into the interior of the building.

Alex jumped into his vehicle with one of the Iraqis, who told them to go to the next street and turn right, then right again into a narrow alley. Men watched them from the roofs. The team rolled up to two Iraqis with AK-47s standing in the street in front of an open gate, which they entered. Jamison and his buddy Amir were already waiting for them in the courtyard, and they parked where they were instructed. As Alex dismounted, four men were already pulling the two duffel bags out of the truck. Amir rubbed his hands together, still grinning.

Jamison said to Alex, "I assure you we are safe here, and I won't have need of your men for the time being. I have business to conduct." He disappeared back into the building with his buddy. The team was once again left in the heat to wait.

The Iraqi security men milled about, obviously but not intrusively keeping an eye on the Americans. Alex felt vulnerable as he sidled up to Alien. "They had the drop on us big time when we entered that building. If they had wanted to kill us, we'd be dead for sure."

"Yeah, well, wait 'til next week and they probably will try to kill you. Their good will only goes as far as their satisfaction with the last payoff."

"I thought this was about reconstruction?" Alex asked.

Alien snickered. "Only in name; it's all smoke and mirrors. Did you see any schools or hospitals or small businesses under construction on the way in? No, of course you didn't, and you won't. This payoff will find its way into a Swiss bank account, and Jamison'll be back with another one next month." Alien shook his head. "These bastards will get together on TV and talk about what great progress they're making, and the people are still without electricity, running water, jobs, food, security, or hope."

Alien gestured toward the building with a backhanded flourish. "These people are worse than Hussein. At least he gave them security and they generally had jobs. And Uncle Sam's just pumpin' 'em full of free cash." He nodded toward the Iraqi security men and said, "Tonight, these same assholes will be out planting IEDs and smokin' American soldiers."

Hours dragged by, and the courtyard grew stifling. The Iraqis offered them nothing to relieve the heat. The men had eaten their MREs and continued to wait. However uncomfortable they were, it was still better than sitting out front in the open or driving around dodging IEDs while waiting for the client's call to return. Eventually, Jamison emerged, and the team got rolling again. Alex's relief at leaving the compound was soon replaced with the familiar stress of driving through the deadly streets of Iraq.

As they skirted the border of Kurdistan and Hell on the way back to Erbil, Alex enquired, "Is there any other way back besides going through the gauntlet with that sniper again? I'm wondering when he's going to resort to IEDs to slow down his targets."

Jamison's head popped up from his papers and said, "No, there's not. I'm in a hurry to get back. Anyway, we're in an armored car and we've done it numerous times. We'll be fine."

Alex glanced at Alien, who rolled his eyes, shrugged, and said, "Anyway, Cap, we're damned if we do and damned if we don't. At this point any other route will keep us out after dark in unfriendly territory, which'll probably be more dangerous than the enemy we know."

Alex did not like it at all. He wondered what was so important to Jamison. Getting in a few rounds of golf before dark? Maybe he had a cocktail party to attend and he needed time to freshen up.

After a while Alex began to recognize his surroundings, and his body tensed and his stomach churned with butterflies. Soon, Bandito's voice on the radio announced, "Sniper zone, one klick ahead." The abandoned buildings came into view on the left. Then Bandito's voice again: "There's something in the road!" A car was stopped sideways, blocking the road.

"Go around it and push through," Alien called over the radio. On the narrow two-lane road, there was no way they could get around the car to the right. They would have to slow and go around it to the left. They were in a perfect kill zone. He braced himself and put all his attention to his sector in case something came at them from the reeds on the right.

"Shit!" Alien yelled, and Alex snapped his head around just in time to see Charlie One jerk to the right and slam into the car blocking the road. The impact launched the car into the reeds, and Charlie One spun around a few times before it came to a rolling stop in the middle of the road, facing their direction of movement.

Alien called over the radio, "Charlie One's been hit! Push through! Push through." He slowed his truck, crunched into the back end of Charlie One, and with smoking tires and screeching metal pushed the truck down the road to a stand of trees and brush that blocked the view from the buildings. "Charlie One, this is Charlie Six. Are you OK? What's going on?"

Bandito answered as they cleared the kill zone: "Driver down! Dingo's been hit! I've got the wheel." Alien stopped pushing the truck, and it rolled a little further down the road before coming to a stop.

Alex said, "I got it." He jumped out of the vehicle and ran to Charlie One. The crew pulled Dingo out on the right side. He gasped for air as Alex cut off his tactical vest and body armor and ripped open his shirt. Alex told them, "Bandito, get me the trauma kit and then check to see if the truck still works. You other two secure the area."

All three moved out quickly. Alex heard Alien calling for a medevac on his earphone as he ran his hands all over Dingo's body, looking for massive hemorrhaging—the thing that would kill him the quickest. Dingo's gasps grew shorter, and he began to thrash around wildly. *He can't breathe. He doesn't have time for a medevac. He's gonna be dead in a couple of minutes.*

Alex felt something wet on Dingo's left side and found blood bubbling out of a hole near Dingo's armpit. Bandito returned with the trauma kit.

Alex said, "Help me hold him down. He's been hit in the lung and he can't breathe." Bandito straddled Dingo's midsection and leaned forward, pinning both of his arms as Alex dumped out the contents of the aid bag. He tore open a Bolin chest seal and with one hand grabbed Dingo's shirt, wiped the wet blood off the wound site, and then placed the seal directly over the wound. Searching through the pile of medical supplies, he found a familiar red-and-brown tube that contained a ten-gauge chest decompression needle.

Alex opened the tube and pulled out the needle. With his finger on the center of Dingo's left clavicle, he felt for the space between there and the next rib, then did it again until he felt the space between the second and third ribs. He placed the point of the needle above the third rib and pressed until it popped through the sac surrounding Dingo's lungs. A liquid mist splashed his face as air from the space around Dingo's lung sputtered out through the open end of the needle. Dingo caught a small breath and then a deeper one. Finally he took in a huge lungful of air and immediately calmed down. Bandito lightened up his grip as Alex pulled the needle out, leaving the catheter in place. Alex said, "Tape," and Bandito pulled a roll out of the pile and handed it to Alex, who used it to secure the catheter.

Alex searched Dingo's chest and back again looking for an exit wound. He found one near the small of his back and applied another chest seal. Then he searched Dingo's body for any other signs of trauma that would kill him before they could get him to a hospital. He found nothing else.

Bandito said, "The truck's OK. I think he caught a bullet through the firing port. It was open."

Alien called, "Cap, Charlie Six; no medevac."

Shit, Alex thought and said to Bandito, "IV." As Alex tore away what was left of Dingo's sleeve, Bandito pulled out an IV bag of Hextend and an IV kit from the trauma bag and handed it to Alex. Alex tore open the outer cover of the fluid bag and popped off the little blue tab at one end. Then he tore open the bag that held the tube and pulled the cover off the spike. Pressing on the drip chamber, he inserted the spike into the receptacle on the drip bag and flipped the bag upside down. He handed the bag to Bandito. "Hold this, bro." He made sure the air was out of the tube and clamped it off.

Alex keyed his mic. "Roger that. How 'bout an aid station?" He tore open the kit, pulled out a large rubber band, and wrapped it around Dingo's upper arm, pulled it tight, and tucked it in on itself.

Alien came back: "Ten, fifteen mikes away." Alex found a good vein and cleaned the area with an alcohol wipe. He held the vein and stretched the skin with his left thumb, and, making sure the bevel of the needle was facing up and holding it at an angle, he pushed the needle into Dingo's arm until it slid into the vein and some blood splashed back into the needle. He pressed down on the vein with his left thumb, stopping the flow of blood, and pushed forward on the catheter until it disappeared into the vein. Pulling the needle out with his right hand, he quickly grabbed the end of the IV tube, pulled the cap off with his teeth, screwed the end into the back of the catheter, and unclamped the tube to allow the solution to flow. Bandito handed a piece of tape to Alex, who used it to secure the catheter. Then another, larger piece was used to cover the entire site, and finally he curled the tube around and taped it higher on Dingo's arm. Alex quickly scooped the medical gear back into the bag and said, "OK, let's get him out of here."

Bandito held the IV and called to the others, "Mount up!" The men picked up Dingo and put him prone in the back seat. Alex finally responded to Alien on the radio: "Roger, you better hurry. Pick me up after you drop off the client." He tossed the trauma kit back into the truck as Bandito jumped into the driver's seat.

"What?" The radio did not disguise Alien's confusion.

"I'm stayin' here. Pick me up after you drop off the client."

"*What?*"

Alex sprinted into the brush on the left side of the road as he keyed his mic again. "You better get going, and don't forget to pick me up on your way back."

The trucks roared to life and accelerated down the road.

He figured he had perhaps two hours.

★★★

Alex stopped in the cover of the brush for several minutes to adjust his senses to his new surroundings and collect his thoughts. If he was going to be forced to ride up and down this road on a regular basis, he did not want to be a duck in someone else's shooting gallery. Alex would prefer to die being proactive.

He heard no traffic and the area was remote; hopefully no

one had seen him peel away from the others. Kneeling there, his hip and leg throbbed, but they seemed to work well enough. He looked down at his bloody hands and tried to clean them with dirt.

He heard some static on his radio and turned it off. Taking off his sunglasses, he turned his baseball cap around, drank one of the two water bottles from his cargo pocket, and then buried it and the few unnecessary items from his pockets and covered it all with brush.

It had been several minutes now, and he had not been followed, so he was optimistic. He closed his eyes and visualized the maps he had seen of the area. If he moved a bit further from the road, he would come to a wadi that should offer some concealment to the back of the abandoned buildings. By that route he probably only had 500 or 600 meters to travel. He moved out slowly.

As he worked his way quietly through the brush, he caught occasional glimpses of the buildings looming closer and closer. Taking care to stay out of view of windows and the roof, he wondered what he would do when he finally got there. Eventually the wadi brought him within fifty meters behind the buildings. Staying concealed, he paused and studied the situation.

This seemed to be the business end of the facility. The three buildings were almost identical three-story structures arranged in a semicircle with an asphalt courtyard and parking lot between them. The two flanking buildings were demolished on this side, but the center building seemed largely intact with scorch marks above the windows indicating it had burned intensely. Alex imagined the occupants' surprise as the buildings blew up without warning at the beginning of the "shock and awe" bombing campaign.

He studied the center building where he had seen the flash earlier that day. The windows were all dark and there was no sign of life. Wide steps at the center and base of the building tapered up to a landing and a double door. The loading dock on the right side might offer a better entrance for him, but the angle of the building obscured his view, and he had to get closer to be sure. Several smaller outbuildings, probably for garages or storage, and piles of debris between him and the parking lot offered cover and concealment from the center building, but he would be exposed to the other buildings as he moved across the open spaces. He would like to wait until dark, but that simply was not an option. He had to do this now or not at all.

He picked his intermediate objectives, moved further to his right out of sight of the center building, and looked and listened for a moment. Then, with his M4 tucked to his shoulder, he sprinted at a low crouch as fast and quietly as he could the twenty meters or so to the side of the first garage.

Surely they heard me do that. That must've sounded like an elephant crashing through the brush. He pressed himself against the structure and tried to calm his heart rate and listen for any alarm; nothing. He picked his way through debris, past a door, and around the right side. Now he was fully exposed to the larger building on the right and expected to be shot from a window at any moment, but he continued.

He spotted his next objective: another garage-like structure. He paused, looked around and listened, then sprinted again. The door on the back of this structure was missing, and Alex slipped inside. The interior was completely empty, and he moved toward an open side door that faced his destination. From the shadows, he studied the buildings again; still nothing. He could see the loading dock now, and there was a door. He decided that would be his entry point. A large pile of debris next to the dock would offer him some cover prior to his entry.

Alex crouched, inhaled, listened, and prepared to make the final dash when there was a sudden loud *Boom!* He jerked back into the darkness and fell crashing on the floor. *Boom!* Alex got up and plastered himself to the wall and slid down to a crouch, looking out the door again. *Boom!* Then he heard the *tac-tac-tac* of more-distant gunfire and realized that the sniper was shooting at more victims coming down the road and they were returning fire.

He instinctively knew that this was his opportunity, and he didn't hesitate. He rushed toward the dock, using the gunfire to mask the noise of his movement. When he reached the debris, he jumped over several charred boards and slammed right into two small boys, who fell sprawling back against the rubble. Alex trained his weapon on them, and they threw their hands up in front of their faces. Alex realized they were no immediate threat and pointed his muzzle slightly away. Then, *Boom! Tac-tac-tac.* Alex ducked and glanced anxiously at the building and then looked back at the boys, trying to decide what to do, when one of them smiled and pointed toward the sniper, back to Alex, then motioned with his index finger like he was pulling a trigger.

Alex decided to get it over with and began to hoist himself up on the dock. The boys became animated, waving their arms and hissing, "No, no, American . . . Boom!" and pointing at the door.

Alex understood they meant that the door was booby-trapped. He lowered himself back down and looked at them. He wondered, *Why would they do this?* Then it dawned on him that these boys must be Kurdish, and the sniper was an unwelcome outsider. The boys motioned to him to follow them. Unsure of what to do now, he followed.

They swiftly threaded their way through the debris and brought him to a small broken-out window that offered access to the cellar. Alex squatted and looked inside. One of the boys touched his arm, then put his hand on the ground and smoothed out the dirt before drawing a picture. As Alex watched, a schematic of the building appeared in the dirt. The boy pointed to the window and drew an open box with a widow and then a staircase. Then he pointed at the second floor of the building and held up two fingers. Alex whispered, "Second floor."

The boy grinned and said, "Yes, second floor." Then he drew

another square, and a hallway appeared with several rooms. Finally, he drew an *X* in the center room on the road side of the building and motioned like he was shooting a rifle.

Alex thought, *X marks the spot.* He patted the boy on the arm and turned to the window, but the other boy grabbed his arm and frantically pointed back at the sketch, waving his hand. He then drew three more *X*s, one in the same room and two in an adjacent room. Alex took a deep breath and thought, *Fucking great, four shooters.* He put his hand on the boy's shoulder, smiled, and asked, "You wouldn't happen to have any extra RPGs, would you?"

The boys looked at him quizzically.

Alex pulled himself through the window and dropped to the floor. He moved into the darkest shadow for a minute, trying to adjust his eyes to the limited light and listening to the new environment. While the pictures the boys drew were sterile, the room was full of burnt, broken wood, old rusted equipment, and trash. He identified the stairwell and picked through the rubbish, and slowly, as quietly as possible, he ascended the concrete steps.

He shifted the selector switch on his M4 to three-round burst. He could pull the trigger ten times before he needed to reload. He hoped that would be enough. He thought about Predator and wished he were here now; Alex sure could use the help and encouragement. As he worked his way up to the second floor, his legs shook, his stomach went sour and churned, and he sweated profusely. His boots crunched on bits of glass and burnt wood, reverberating loudly in his ears. He felt weak, and ill, and yet he kept going.

At the second floor he pressed his back against the wall in the stairwell and listened. He heard muffled laughter and voices speaking Arabic. He exhaled with relief that he had not yet been discovered. Putting his faith in the two boys, he entered the hallway at a low crouch with his weapon trained on the two doors at the center of the corridor. All the doors were gone, and he knew he would be heard soon, so he steeled himself to charge at the first sign he was discovered. As he moved, he noticed doors adjoining each of the rooms at the center of the side walls. His mind raced. Should he sprint into the room and try to go through the connecting doors, or go to the doorway, shoot in, and then run to the next doorway via the hallway? He decided to go through the rooms using the interior doors; the sniper, or X, should be in the third room.

From the doorway just next to the first occupied room, Alex saw through to the next one, spotting furniture and partial view of one man seated in an overstuffed chair with his back to Alex. Alex slipped into the room and flattened against the left wall. Not wanting to make any noise, he wished he had taken the tape off his grenades before he got to this point—a mistake that, if he lived through this, he would never make again.

He slithered along the wall until he was next to the interior door and could hear the men talking in low tones. Sweat stung his eyes as he counted to three. At three he began to pie-off the doorway and found himself looking directly into the eyes of an unarmed Arab.

The man's eyes went wide with surprise, but in the next heartbeat he recovered and darted toward an AK-47 leaning against the sofa. Alex put three rounds square in his chest. The man crumpled straight to the ground, and Alex charged into the room as the other man fell off his chair against the wall and out of Alex's sight. Alex's next six rounds hit the chair and the wall. He fired again as he scrambled toward the window to get a better angle just as the insurgent started blindly shooting his AK on fully automatic from where he lay on the floor.

Chunks of building material erupted from the ceiling and the walls as rounds of 7.62-millimeter ammunition chewed up the room. Alex dove and rolled on the floor, clearing the furniture, and pulled the trigger twice, hitting the Arab in his legs and groin. The man screamed and lowered his weapon toward Alex. Alex sent another three rounds ripping into his chest and face. His head fell back onto the floor.

Alex came to his knees and pointed his weapon at the next door in time to see a fleeting figure dash toward the hallway. Alex fired in that direction, and the bullets went wild. He ran to the hallway door and from a low crouch brought his weapon to bear in the hallway just as the man cut loose with a burst from another AK-47. Plaster and concrete showered Alex's face as he squeezed off another three-round burst. The man jerked, spun around, and started to stagger down the hallway. Alex put three more rounds in his back, and he went down.

Alex squatted, pressing his back against the wall just outside the door, and pressed the magazine-release button on his M4 with his right index finger as he reached to his belt with his left hand and pulled out another magazine from the mag speed holster. *Boom!* The doorframe exploded in shards just above his head, and he pitched forward into the hallway as his magazine went spinning on the floor in the other direction.

The sniper had come up behind him from the first room he had entered. *Boom.* Another hole appeared in the wall. *Boom,* another *Boom.* Alex high crawled on his knees and elbows through the hallway to the room the sniper had occupied. *Boom.* The sniper was still shooting at where Alex had been. Alex came to his feet with his M4 dangling freely from the sling around his neck and sprinted through the room to try and flank the sniper. He reached for his pistol to find that it was gone.

Realizing that at this point any action was better than nothing, he drew his SOG dagger, accelerated, and charged through the connecting doorway. He slammed into the man's side like a linebacker blindsiding a quarterback with his arm back ready to pass the ball. The Dragunov sniper rifle clattered to the floor as both men sprawled to the other side of the room. The sniper was stunned, but he was not finished. He came off the ground pulling a Makarov 9-millimeter pistol from his waistband.

As quick as he was, he still had to take the weapon off safe to shoot, which gave Alex time to bury his dagger hilt deep into the man's abdomen. The Makarov fell to the floor as the sniper grabbed at the knife. Alex wrenched the seven-inch blade so it pointed up into his chest cavity, grabbed the handle with both hands, and pulled up with all his might, lifting the sniper off the ground, splitting through half his sternum, and slicing all his organs from his stomach to his throat.

Alex forced him back against the wall as blood and gore erupted from his wound. Alex pressed against him for a moment as blood bubbled from his mouth and hissed in his face, "How's *that* feel, *bitch?*"

The sniper's eyes, wide open from shock, glazed over as he died. Alex thought, *I'll be damned; you have blue eyes.* He pulled the knife out of the body and let the corpse slide down the wall to the floor. Alex wiped the knife on the dead man's clothes and put it back in its sheath. He slapped a magazine into his M4, slung the Dragunov over his shoulder, retrieved his pistol from where it had fallen out in the hallway, and moved quickly back to the stairs.

The two Kurdish boys helped him as he pulled himself through the window and would not stop touching him. They held his arms, brushed the dirt and nastiness off his clothes, patted his back repeatedly, and grinned from ear to ear. Alex shook each of them by the hand, gave them a thumbs-up, and ran back to the wadi. The boys followed. It was dark by the time Alex reached his kit and turned the radio on.

★★★

As soon as Alien figured they were in range of Alex's Motorola, he tried to raise him on the radio. "Cap, this is Charlie Six, over."

Almost immediately he heard, "Charlie Six, this is Cap, over."

"Jesus, we've been worried about you."

"Sorry, I'm good to go. Are you inbound?"

"Roger that. We'll be there in a few mikes."

"Roger. I'll be waiting. Thanks."

Alex took another swig of the warm Coca Cola the boys had produced for him and raised the bottle to them. "*Shukran.*" The boys grinned and nodded in unison.

"You are welcome, number one American!"

Alex heard Alien on the radio again: "Asgard Three, this is Charlie Six. We have contact with our wayward child." Alex heard no response. Then Alien again: "Roger that, Valkyrie. He's good to go."

Alex thought, *Holy shit, I'm in trouble now.* He saw the headlights of three vehicles approaching fast. He clicked his flashlight on and off three times, and the convoy slowed. After scanning back and forth, he stepped out of the reeds toward the road.

Alien eyeballed the Dragunov as Alex trotted out of the darkness and jumped in the passenger seat. "Trophy?"

As they accelerated down the road Alex said, "Yeah, I'm gonna give it to Dingo. Is he OK?"

"Yeah, he got hit pretty bad. The docs said right away that from the path of the bullet through his body, the round must have shredded his lung and bounced off his spine. But thanks to you he should live. They medevac'd him to the Green Zone. I expect he won't be coming back."

Alex shook his head. "Then we should mount it on the wall in Asgard, take a picture of it, and email it to him."

Alien nodded and said, "Remind me never to piss you off."

Alex peered into the darkness. Trying to pull security now was useless. "Am I in trouble?"

"Are you kidding?" Alien laughed. "Odin hit the roof and Valkyrie is fit to be tied, man. I'm glad it's you they'll focus their wrath on and not me. If you hadn't made it back, it woulda been *my* ass."

Alex shrank down in the seat and peered into the darkness. He thought, *Great, now I have to suffer through drama before I can get some sleep, and I'm so tired.*

Alien announcing his approach to the compound over the radio woke Alex out of a deep sleep. He sat up with a start. "Christ almighty, man. Why'd you let me doze off like that?"

"Can't see shit out there anyway. I figured an IED would wake you up soon enough. Anyway, that wasn't just a doze, man; you were cuttin' some serious z's." They pulled into the compound to see Odin and Asgard Three standing at the front of the house. Alex groaned.

They parked the vehicles, and as they got out, the entire rest of the team gathered to silently shake his hand, squeeze his arm, or pat him on the back. What he did was not authorized, and there would be hell to pay, but they were all very relieved and grateful.

He approached the house with a weakness in his legs similar to when he had ascended the stairs earlier. The team fell in behind him. Other teams filtered into the courtyard from all corners of the compound to witness the fireworks; the news had traveled fast.

Odin stood with his legs apart and his powerful arms folded across his massive chest, glaring down at Alex like a wrathful god.

"What have you to say for yourself?" asked Odin with a voice that would penetrate lead.

Alex, deciding drama was in order, cleared his throat and started out softly but clear for all to hear. "Odin, I have dishonored your command by taking matters into my own hands. I have risked the lives of myself and those for whom *you* are responsible, and my actions are therefore reprehensible, and I deserve to be fired."

His voice rose. "However, faced with a deadly threat to which our brothers were victim, I took the action that any worthy warrior would take." His voice began to boom, his muscles tensed, and the veins in his neck bulged. "I confronted the devil on the field of battle and vanquished him so that he will never rise again!"

He thrust the Dragunov in the air and bellowed a resounding war cry. The entire compound erupted around him as the men roared their approval with their fists and weapons raised to the sky.

The men fell silent as Alex offered the Russian-made sniper rifle up to Odin with both hands, saying in a powerful voice that carried clearly through the compound, "Great leader, please accept this trophy as my humble display of fealty, and forgive me my transgressions!"

Odin hesitated, savoring the spectacle. Then he unhurriedly reached out and grasped the sniper rifle in one large hand and took it from Alex. He turned it over with his hand and looked at it critically. He peered at Alex with a stern face and then suddenly thrust the rifle toward the sky and cut loose with a warrior's howl that reverberated off the walls of the compound. Instantly, all the men joined him in a roar that must have been heard in Baghdad.

Odin shouted, "Break out the steaks and shrimp. The drinks are on me! Tonight, we feast!" The response from the men was deafening.

Odin stepped down and grabbed Alex with one hand around his shoulder and the other still brandishing the rifle. He strode into the crowd with the men of his command swirling around, congratulating them both. Through the din, Odin pulled Alex to him with one arm and growled in his ear, "You're a piece of work. A few minutes ago, I was ready to fry your ass!"

Alex looked at him sheepishly and grinned. "Yeah, boss, and now you have a troop of men who'll follow you to hell in gasoline underwear." Odin grinned and nodded in agreement. Bandito shoved an ice-cold beer into Alex's hand and slapped him on the back repeatedly. Alien rolled his eyes and laughed.

Odin relaxed his grip on Alex and said, "Son, you're a mess. You'd better go get cleaned up. You have someone else to answer to who may not be as understanding as me."

Alex felt like a child. He said, "Yes sir."

Odin added, "And don't forget you have a mission in the morning." Alex gave him thumbs-up as he slipped away.

With a towel around his waist, Alex finished applying antibiotic to the cuts and scrapes on his body and switched off the bathroom light. Stretching his bruised shoulder and trying to rub the pain out of his throbbing hip with his other hand, he walked into his bedroom when his cell phone started to ring.

"You must be clairvoyant," he answered in a soft voice.

Linda answered a bit more sternly, "I was watching the light in your bathroom. Put your clothes on and come to my room, and don't let anyone see you." She did not wait for an answer.

Alex stared at the phone and started to feel very guilty about what he had done.

As he mentally prepared his defense, he hurriedly put on clean clothes and made his covert way to Linda's room. He tapped on the door, and as it swung open she grabbed him by the arm and pulled him into the dark room. Alex expected a torrid scolding; instead, Linda threw herself into his arms and cried uncontrollably.

With her arms locked around his neck, she kissed his face and his lips. He felt her tears run down his face and tasted them as she kissed him. Her body convulsed with her sobs, and she pressed against him in desperation. He felt so ashamed that he had made her feel this way. "I'm so sorry," he whispered. She pulled him to her bed, and they fell together in a passionate kiss as she tore at his clothes.

Afterward, as she lay savoring the feeling of being so intimate with the man she loved, she asked him, "Why?"

He said in a soft voice, "Because I was afraid that if I did not do *something*, I would never make it back here to see you again." She held him tighter and he continued, "He killed two Americans this morning, and if it hadn't been for the armor on the vehicle, he would have hit me also, and the Army still didn't do anything about it. Then he set up a broken-down vehicle as an obstacle on our way to take the client back, he hit Dingo, and I knew we had to pass through there again tonight and again tomorrow. I had a bad feeling that the next time we came through, he would use an IED to slow us down."

Linda started to cry again. "I know. I listened to your radio all day, and I had the same bad feeling. I wish I could talk my father into going home. I hate this place." Then she added, "You have things to do now, but will you come back and sleep with me tonight?"

"Yes, I would like nothing more." Alex was overwhelmed with her passion and concern for him. He kissed her gently and held her to him; he wanted to never let go.

When Alex rejoined the festivities, no one seemed to suspect he had done anything but get cleaned up. The men had all eaten, and the crowd was beginning to dissipate. Bandito shoved another cold beer into Alex's hand and slapped him on the back yet again. Odin and several of his entourage came to grill Alex about his adventure.

"Food for this warrior. He must eat and have strength for tomorrow's battle."

Someone shoved a plate piled high with steak and shrimp into Alex's hand.

Asgard Three enquired, "So, Cap, we've been speculating and wagering if there were any other insurgents with the sniper. The odds-on favorite is that he had a spotter with him. The long shot is that he was alone. Can you enlighten us? How many men were there when you took the Dragunov from the sniper?"

The men around Alex became quiet, and Odin folded his arms across his massive chest and raised one eyebrow, waiting for a response as if he knew the answer.

Alex chewed his mouthful of steak and swallowed it, and then he took a long drink from his beer, slowly lowered the bottle, and set it down. He looked around at the men as he pulled bits of steak from his teeth with his tongue. Finally, he said in a low voice, "Four."

The men were all silent as they stared at Alex. Odin's other eyebrow raised to join the first one as his face registered surprise. Only the crackle of the bonfire could be heard until one man muttered, "Holy shit!"

It was difficult for Alex to tell if they believed him or not. As the severity of what Alex said sunk in, most of the men's eyes went wide and heads started to shake from side to side incredulously, yet nobody challenged him to reconsider.

Bandito shook Asgard Three as if to wake him. "Well?"

"It's all yours," Asgard Three said absently as he reached into his pocket and pulled out a large wad of cash and handed it to Bandito.

Odin finally said, "Three, don't you have work to do?"

"Roger that, sir." He reached out and grasped Alex free hand and said, "I'm glad you're with us, Cap. See you shortly." Then he walked off toward the operations room, shaking his head.

As the men wandered off to prepare for the next day, Alex and Odin were left alone. Odin asked, "How's Linda?"

Alex choked on the last of his shrimp and coughed. After he recovered, he said, wiping his mouth, "She seems to be OK, sir."

CHAPTER 5

Taxi to Hell

SWEAT RAN DOWN ALEX'S neck and across his back as he lifted himself into a pushup position, trying to relieve the pain in his leg. Too late. Groaning as his body convulsed and stars exploded in his head, he collapsed, rolled onto his back, and surrendered.

She whispered in his ear, "I want to have your baby."

Alex pulled Linda to him and held her so that every possible inch of his body was in contact with hers. They drifted off to sleep.

"Fight and kill the disbelievers wherever you find them, take them captive, harass them, lie in wait and ambush them using every stratagem of war."

Koran 9:5

Haider checked the thermometer he had inserted into the cauldron of boiling chemical stew and turned off the gas on the Coleman stove. He knew not to overheat the mixture; the man who showed him how to do this—poor, wretched Rafee—was now blind, mute, and gasped in agony for every breath, forever tormented because he had allowed the chemicals to overheat. The toxic fumes would have killed him had Haider not arrived when he did.

Haider wondered if it would have been more merciful to allow him to die. Surely, he would go to Paradise for all his contributions to the Cause of Allah.

Doubts immediately flooded the deepest recesses of Haider's mind. He shook his head and tried to dismiss his scientific uncertainty. While he attended prayers and put on the face of a devout follower, deep in his core he questioned the veracity of religion, any religion. Still, if what the imams and the Koran said was true, then with these nagging doubts he would surely spend his afterlife in agonizing fire and eternal torment.

He did, however, completely agree with the politics of Islam; the invaders needed to be expelled at any cost. Perhaps Allah would be merciful based on his contributions to the Cause.

He placed a metal funnel into the segmented gas tank that he had modified with a separate compartment to store the mixture and still allow gas to feed fuel to the engine. He pulled the heavy mitts onto his hands, picked up the iron pot, and carefully poured the brew into the funnel. After it cooled, it would solidify, and he would then seal the opening and reattach the gas tank to the car, invisible to any inspection.

He set the first pot aside and turned to the next. He had already mixed the proper amounts of water and two simple ingredients the Americans provided for free in abundant supply: calcium nitrate fertilizer and ammonium sulfate fertilizer. Thanks to the concern of the Americans and their efforts at nation building, it was not a problem that military-grade explosives were difficult to obtain anymore; the USAID delivered these fertilizers by the truckload.

He scooped the thick white slurry off the top with a large wooden spoon and dropped it into an old oil drum. As he poured the mixture through a sieve to remove the remaining slurry, his mind wandered again. In many ways, the religious police who had shown up recently scared him far more than the Americans did, but they kept the peace. They were mostly foreigners, and he was always nervous that he might deviate from their strict interpretation of Sharia in the smallest way and incur their wrath.

He had seen them in action a few times. The woman he saw them beat and whip because she had uncovered her hair got off easy; they let her live—unlike his neighbor, who they stoned to death because her husband told them she was unfaithful to him. Haider knew his neighbor was simply tired of her and had his eye on her twelve-year-old sister. He thought sarcastically, *Now, that will be a happy marriage.*

Then there was the incident of the two men they claimed were homosexuals, both of whom lived after they were thrown off the minaret next to his house, and were then beheaded with a dull sword. The psychopath who chopped off their heads made minced meat out of them but was delighted at the mess he made. Haider panicked whenever he thought of them finding out about the intimate times he had spent with his young cousin before the war. Things were much simpler and better back then before the Americans came. He mumbled a prayer to Allah to ask for His forgiveness and to have mercy on his soul.

When he had just a thick liquid left in the pot, he placed it on the Coleman stove and ignited the burner and thought, *Too easy.* The next batch would go into the inserts he had fabricated to fit inside the car door panels.

He turned to the tools and materials spread across his table. The detonating device would have an initiator located underneath the dashboard. He had already fabricated the hidden compartment that would open when the radio and the heater switches were turned on together; a small compartment cover under the dash would drop open, exposing a fat red button that with a push would initiate the blasting cap, which would ignite the tank of ammonium nitrate concealed inside the car's dashboard, which would in turn ignite the similar tanks concealed throughout the car.

Haider figured if he listened closely, he would hear three discernable and increasingly larger explosions from the car as they daisy-chained through the vehicle: first the dash, then the front quarter panels and the door panels would probably go simultaneously, followed by the gas tank and the false undercarriage. Everything close by would be vaporized, everything within fifty meters would be destroyed, and everything within five hundred meters would feel the wrath of Allah.

Haider picked up a 5.56 mm shell casing that he had picked up on the street and wondered if the bullet it had launched had killed one of his neighbors. Now he would use it to kill Americans. He scooped up some gunpowder with a small spoon and poured it into the casing until it was almost full. Setting it upright so the propellant would not spill out, he picked up a small lightbulb. As he carefully filed off the very tip, he speculated why Westerners had conceived their foolish tradition of decorating Christmas trees with these lights.

Anyway, they were useful to him. Now he could kill them with yet another product of their own misguided vanity.

He tested the continuity with his multimeter; it still worked. Then he very carefully filled the bulb with gunpowder and sealed the hole with a thin layer of superglue. He tested the continuity again and smiled with satisfaction at the improvised detonator that he had created. Attaching the two wires from the light to the wires running from the initiator under the dash of the car, he pushed the detonator into the small hole in the tank of dry ammonium nitrate concealed inside the dash. Finally, he sealed the hole with silicon and concealed the wires using electrical tape.

The first explosion would be large enough to ensure the others detonated as well. He regretted that he would not be able to keep the big black Mercedes, but it was probably stolen anyway, and the explosion would be spectacular and very satisfying to watch.

> *"O Prophet, urge the faithful to fight. If there are twenty among you with determination, they will vanquish two hundred; if there are a hundred, then they will slaughter a thousand unbelievers, for the kafirs are a people devoid of understanding."*

Koran 8:65

Sitting in the front seat of the limo, Alex adjusted his gear to relieve the pain in his hip as the team marshalled for Alex's first mission calling the shots. Another experienced operator, Digger, took over the driver's seat in C1. Alien still drove the limo, but he had no intention of any interaction with the client.

"I'd prefer to be in another vehicle, but since you asked nicely, I'll stay with you to help you. I'm just not in any hurry to take a bullet for, or a tongue lashing from, His Majesty."

"Will you take a bullet for the rest of us?" Alex asked.

"Sure, it would be my pleasure."

"How about a tongue lashing from me?"

Alien rolled his eyes. "I'd consider it an honor."

Alex nodded. "That's good enough for me." He pushed send on his cell phone.

The phone rang once on the other end and someone answered, "JOC, Sergeant Myers."

"Hey, Sergeant Myers, this is Charlie Six. I just turned on my BFT number BVooC6."

Almost immediately, the JOC responded, "Roger that, Charlie

Six. I have your signal on the big board."

Alex went on, "I have three black Chevy Tahoes with a total of nine pax. We're gonna stop at USAID in Erbil to pick up one more pax. Then we're going to Baghdad Green Zone via Routes Tampa and Irish."

Asgard Three hurried toward the vehicle and then waited, wringing his hands excitedly until Alex was finished.

"We should begin the return run in two days, no later than fifteen hundred on Route Dover."

The JOC responded, "Roger, Charlie Six. Copy out on Tampa to Irish, back on Dover in two days, SP no later than fifteen hundred hours. Have a safe trip."

"Roger, thanks, Sergeant Myers. Talk with you later. Out."

Odin nudged his way in front of Asgard Three. "Son," he said to Alex, "you keep your mind on your mission and bring my men back here safely."

Alex thought he was being chewed out. "Yes sir, no more shenanigans. Mission first. I won't let you down."

Odin nodded. "That's good to hear because we just got news of Predator."

Alex's heart stopped beating and he held his breath.

". . . It seems he's still alive."

Alex closed his eyes and breathed deeply.

Odin continued, "I'm telling you now because Hugin told me his information is sketchy, and since you're going to the Green Zone, if you can manage, stop by the embassy annex at the Palace and talk to the State Department's Hostage Crisis Team. I already made the calls and they're expecting you. Here's their phone number and a point of contact. Call them about ten minutes out and they'll have someone meet you at the front gate."

Only with effort was Alex able to keep his senses. "Thanks, boss. I'll let you know what I find out." He took the note and Odin straightened up.

"Remember, mission first."

"Roger that, boss. I won't let you down."

"Good. Now get going and be careful out there."

Destination Baghdad, the most dangerous city on earth. At the mission brief the night before, Alex had learned that there was an average of seventy-two insurgent incidents every day in the city, not counting the random bodies that intel analysts attributed to "criminal action or sectarian violence." Between five and seven car bombs and fifteen to twenty roadside IEDs were a typical day. Gunfire was heard at all hours, and headless corpses floating down the Tigris River were a regular sight. But the first problem for Alex and the team was negotiating the most dangerous roads on earth, Route Tampa and Route Irish.

As the team pulled into the USAID compound, Alex observed three different up-armored PSD vehicles parked in front of the dining facility. He dismounted with Bull and walked up to the entrance.

"Well, if it's not John Wayne in the flesh," Jamison said mockingly as he pushed open the door. "It's a wonder you're still alive." Several other men filed out as well, including one enormously large man who instantly made Alex feel small and weak.

The big man glared at Alex and growled, "So you're the little prick that takes unnecessary risks putting your package in danger."

Alex raised his eyebrows, taken aback by the unexpected assault. Bull saved him by losing his cool and saying aggressively, "What the hell are you talking about? He saved one life outright yesterday. One of ours will see his wife and kids again because of him." He gestured to Alex. "And you can't calculate how many other lives he's saved by killing that sniper—maybe even yours." Alex looked at Bull and shook his head to say "Let it go."

The big man ignored Bull. "And I heard you were fuckin' your boss's daughter. What kind of piece of shit fucks his boss's daughter behind his back?"

Alex was shocked. "OK, you've said your peace. Now we have work to do."

Jamison said, "No more cowboy shit. If you do something like that again, I'll see to it that your company loses this contract. Do I make myself clear?"

Alex took a deep breath and said, "Perfectly."

Big man was still glaring at Alex and leaned forward and said, "Bitch, I've got your number."

"It was a pleasure to make your acquaintance," Alex said, "and I'd love to stay and chat, but we have work to do, and we really must go." He spun around and headed to the trucks. Bull snickered and followed.

He sidled up to Alex and whispered, "That roid head is the biggest prick on earth. He goes by the handle 'Iblis' and he played pro football for a few years."

Alex knew that *Iblis* was the Arabic word for "Satan," but he wondered if Bull meant steroids or hemorrhoids.

Back at the vehicles, Alien knew something had gone down; he had seen the body language, and there was a clear threat being made, but he refrained from asking in Jamison's presence.

Alex keyed the radio: "Asgard Three, Asgard Three, this is Charlie Six. Wheels up from checkpoint two."

"Charlie Six, this is Asgard Three. Roger, Charlie Papa two."

As Alex set the mic in its cradle Jamison said, "We'll go down Highway 2 and through the city to the Green Zone entry point behind the convention center. I have a four o'clock meeting at the convention center and dinner at five at the Al Rasheed Hotel."

Alien rolled his eyes. Alex said, "Sir, we'll get you there on time, but Intel says that Highway 2 is most active in the morning, and Big Army clears it for IEDs in early afternoon. Also, if we try to go through the city without an escort, we're certain to be at least detoured and make you late; worst case, the Mahdi Army will hang your burnt corpse from one of their minarets."

Jamison began to protest, but Alex cut him short. "We've already coordinated our route down Highway 1 and entry point into the Green Zone at checkpoint twelve with Big Army. If I change it now, they may well tell us not to expect any help if we get into trouble. Don't worry. We'll make sure you're not late."

Jamison's reply was terse. "You'd better."

Alex looked at the disbursement of the team. Running a tight formation as long as they were in town and in Kurdish-held territory, they would spread out between 1 and 500-meter intervals when they got on open road in Indian country. He reached for the team internal radio handset and keyed the mic.

"OK, team, let's set a good pace and make sure we reach our objective by sixteen hundred."

"Charlie One, roger."

"Charlie Three, roger."

They gunned their engines and headed out of Erbil on Makhmoor Road, which would take them the fifty miles or so southwest to Highway 1. As Alex kept his eye on his sector along the road and off to the right, he noted a difference between the general prosperity level of the Kurds who lived here and most of the rest of Iraq.

While they were in Kurdish-controlled areas, they generally followed the rules and displayed an American-flag placard when approaching a Kurdish checkpoint. The Kurds, for their part, generally took a hard look at the men as they slowed and then, satisfied that they were Americans, waved them through without stopping. Once past Kurdish areas, they would put the placard away and, if possible, blow through checkpoints without slowing down.

The ancient urban sprawl gave way to relatively fertile farms with commercial activity everywhere. Because of the Americans, people here were free to live and prosper for the first time in thirty-five years. They passed an enormous ancient cemetery covering a solitary hill that looked like a fortress or castle may once have commanded its apex. The cemetery may well have been there since the Neolithic when this was all fertile land and the cradle of modern civilization. In the fourth century BCE, Alexander the Great was a latecomer in this area. The Assyrian Empire predated Alexander by 2,000 years, and Babylon was a power a thousand years before that, and the remains of Neanderthals uncovered nearby dated as far back as 80,000 years.

Aside from cars, cell phones, and modern weapons of war, Alex conceded that not much other than the fertility of the land had changed since then.

They approached the final Kurdish checkpoint. Bandito called over the internal radio, "Charlie One, CP three."

Alex responded, "Roger."

The Kurds at the post just waved the vehicles through. They probably figured that even if these vehicles were bad news, at least they were leaving Kurdistan, and it was not worth fighting them: *Just let them go and we live another day*. Alex called over the internal, "Charlie Six, CP three."

"One, roger."

"Three, roger."

As the last vehicle passed through the checkpoint, Lizard called, "Charlie Three, CP three."

Alex responded, "Roger," and picked up another handset and keyed the mic. "Asgard Three, Asgard Three, this is Charlie Six, CP three, over."

"Charlie Six, this is Asgard Three. Roger, copy CP three."

"Roger, Charlie Six, out."

Just past the checkpoint, they reached the edge of the plateau with a dramatic escarpment extending as far to the left and right as Alex could see. Military posts and gun emplacements along the crest of the ridge stood as the Kurdish first line of defense against whoever emerged as the power in Iraq after the Americans left.

The countryside became barren desert. Only the two-lane hardball road broke the monotony. The team was spread out now, with about 500 meters between trucks. There was no other traffic to be seen.

Several miles down the road Bandito called, "CP four," and Alex saw a few buildings as they fast approached the intersection with Highway 80. They had to slow a bit to negotiate the roundabout. Most people hardly glanced at them, but one individual glared at them intently. Alex keyed the mic.

"This is Six, CP four, break." He let go of the button and then keyed it again. "Three, there's a suspicious-looking character at the right corner of the big building in a white man-dress who is very curious about us."

Lizard came back, "Roger." Moments later he called back, "Six, this is Three. CP four, roger. Hadji's on his cell phone, staring us down."

Alex keyed the mic again. "OK, gentlemen, they have our number. Pick up the pace and keep your eyes peeled."

"One, roger."

"Three, roger."

"Asgard Three, Asgard Three, this is Charlie Six; CP four, over."

"Charlie Six, this is Asgard Three; roger, copy CP four."

They chewed up the miles with no other cars on the road.

After several minutes Bandito called, "Vehicle approaching head-on." Normally, with traffic, this call would have been moot, but with no traffic, anything made the men anxious.

"Six, roger."

"Three, roger."

The sedan and Bandito's vehicle passed each other, and then moments later the sedan was zipping past Alex and then Lizard.

Alex breathed out, not realizing he had held his breath the entire time.

Minutes later Bandito called, "Village on the left."

Then, before either of the other two vehicles could acknowledge, he called again with a bit more excitement in his voice, "Pickup truck pulling out of the village—looks like it might have a mounted gun in the back!"

Alex squinted into the sun and spotted a vehicle moving from left to right toward the hardball, traveling fast and raising a billowing dust trail. Then he saw a man stand up in the bed of the truck, and it was clear that it was a "technical," or an insurgent gun truck.

"Roger, it's a technical!" Bandito was already clear, and the technical would reach the road probably as Charlie Three passed him.

"One, this is Six. Pull over and give us some covering fire. Six will push through. Three, push through." Immediately, Alex saw Charlie One slide sideways to a stop on the left side of the road, and the back hatch popped open with Haymaker earning his call sign.

The technical began firing the heavy machine gun mounted in the bed of the truck, but with the rough terrain, the rounds flew wild. Not so with Haymaker. He was on target right away. His first burst hit the front of the truck, and then he cut loose with an entire hundred-round belt. The driver took several 7.62-by-51 rounds in his torso and head, exploding his heart first and then cleaning his cranium of brain matter. The truck veered hard left and flipped in the sand, spilling the gunner, who rolled several times and tried to get up, only to be stitched from head to toe with Haymaker's bullets. The truck started to smoke from Haymaker's tracers and then burst into a column of flames as the fuel ignited.

Alex's truck sailed past Charlie One on the right, and soon Charlie Three came speeding by as Haymaker pulled the hatch shut. Lizard was blowing him kisses and called over the radio,

"Thanks, buddy. I owe ya one!"

Alex called, "Three, Six. You take point."

"Three, roger."

Looking over his shoulder, Alex saw Charlie One pulling back onto the road. "One, you OK?"

"Roger, One's up. Taking six o'clock position."

"Roger, nicely done. Give my regards to Haymaker—nice shooting—and Digger for awesome driving."

"Will do, boss."

Alex looked at Bull in the back seat. "How's it going, Bull?"

Bull smiled and said, "We're fine." He looked down and said, "You can surface now, sir." He had not so delicately stuffed Jamison as far under the seat as he could manage and made sure he stayed there by putting his boot on Jamison's head.

With effort, Jamison pulled himself back into his seat. "I hope that was really necessary."

Bull said, "Oh, yes sir, it was. If it weren't for Cap's quick thinking back there, you'd have more holes in you than a fish net, and I was giving you as much protection as possible."

Alien was hard pressed to stifle his amusement.

Alex reported the contact to Asgard Three.

Within a few more miles Lizard in Charlie Three called, "Six, Three. We're coming up on CP five and I see smoke."

"Six, roger." Alex craned to see through the haze caused by the oppressive heat. "One, you see it?"

"This is One, roger."

"This is Three. CP five, and it's a burning convoy at the bottom of the hill."

"This is Six. Roger, push through." As Alex came abreast of another escarpment, he called again on the internal net, "Six, CP five." He saw at the bottom of the hill a convoy of perhaps fifteen fuel trucks stopped alongside the road. On the road were three pickup trucks, two flipped over on their sides, and all three smoldering after having burned themselves out of fuel. Big Army HMMWVs were spread out, overlooking the convoy.

"Three, One, this is Six. Put up your VS 17 panels and American flags on the dash, slow it down, and tighten up. We don't want to scare any young soldiers with their finger on the trigger of a Mark 19"—a MK 19 being the belt-fed grenade launcher mounted on the turret of the nearest HMMWV.

"This is One, CP five."

"Roger. Asgard Three, Charlie Six; CP five."

"Charlie Six, Asgard Three. Roger, CP five."

"Six, this is Three. They want us to stop."

"Roger. Do what they say."

"Roger." Lizard rolled to a stop about a hundred yards from the nearest HMMWV. As Alex's vehicle approached, he saw the young soldier in the turret holding his hand up in a fist signaling them to stop. All three vehicles halted with about fifty yards between each vehicle.

After a few minutes, the doors of the HMMWV opened, and two soldiers in full battle array stepped out and walked unhurriedly toward Charlie Three. About twenty-five yards from the vehicle they signaled the occupants to get out. Alex called on his radio, "Stay with the truck. Just get out and let them see you, but keep the doors between you and them. Looks and smells like American army, but let's not be too hasty."

Lizard, Digger, and Haymaker opened their doors and stepped out just far enough to show that they were Americans. Lizard waved and said something to the soldiers that Alex could not hear. Then Lizard indicated that the three vehicles were together.

The soldiers seemed to consider this for a moment, and then one reached up to the radio handset at his shoulder and made a call. He listened to the response, looked at Lizard, and waved the team forward. Lizard and his crew got back in the vehicle. "Six, this is Three; we have a green light."

"Six, roger. One, we're rolling."

"One, roger."

As they came abreast of the soldiers, the troops peered through the tinted windows and waved the vehicles through one at a time. Alex could now see what had happened with the convoy. An IED had taken out the lead tanker, and the security vehicles were probably taken out by RPGs and small arms as they tried to push the rest of the convoy through the ambush. The rest of the semis were relatively untouched, while the security vehicles were shot to hell, riddled with bullet holes, and ripped apart by explosions. The burnt and mutilated corpses of the security detail lay scattered around their vehicles where they had clearly made their last stand. Bullet casings littered the road, indicating that they had put up quite a fight. As futile as it may have been, they went down like warriors.

The semi drivers had essentially set up camp, cooking their meals and tea, and were patiently waiting for the Americans to either tell them what to do or let them go. The residents of the village of Makhmur, just several hundred yards beyond the carnage, were out and intently watching everything. Alex noticed several of them talking on their cell phones. *May or may not be anything.*

"OK, Three, One, pick it up and get a good interval."

"Three, roger."

"One, Roger."

"Jesus, fuck!" Bull yelled. Alex spun around in his seat as the sour smell of vomit reached his nose, and he saw Jamison retching on the seat next to Bull. Bull pushed his head away so that what was left in his stomach hit the floor and not Bull's leg.

Alien was shaking his head as Alex keyed the mic. "Three, this is Six. Get well past this town and find a secure place to pull over with good observation. We need a pit stop."

"Three, roger."

The team rolled to a stop on high ground with a fifty-yard dispersal between vehicles. The drivers stayed in the vehicles, and the rest of the team minus Bull and Alex dismounted and assumed security around the motorcade. Alex and Bull pulled out rags and water bottles and went to work trying to scour the back seat.

As Alex finished up, he marveled at the landscape. It was roasting hot, and everything for miles was barren. Not a sound and no sign of life anywhere, only rock and dirt. Even the dirt seemed dead. Alex wondered what it was like for the Macedonian army of 40,000 marching through this wasteland on horse and on foot toward a Persian army of over 300,000.

Several miles further on, they came to the Tigris River. "Six, this is Three. CP six; Big Army is here."

"Three, Six, roger. Follow their lead. One, let's close it up a bit."

"Three, roger."

"One, roger."

They went through the same process: tightened up the dispersal of the motorcade to about fifty yards, stopped, announced themselves to a couple of poor soldiers in too much gear roasting in the sun, and were waved across the bridge. An American M1 Abrams tank with camouflage netting had dug into a hull-down fighting position near the bank of the river. A few dismounted soldiers with an M2 .50-caliber machine gun stood at the near side of the bridge. When Alex reached the far side of the bridge, he saw the same setup, but instead of the tank, there was a Bradley Infantry Fighting Vehicle. Each position faced away from the bridge, which demonstrated that the Army was not in control of anything except the bridge itself. Alex called the checkpoint in to Asgard.

Another ten miles of desolate road brought them to the intersection of Makhmoor Road and Highway 1, or MSR Tampa. Tampa was the four-lane divided highway running from Baghdad to Mosul that Alex knew well by now. From miles away, Alex saw considerable traffic on this next leg of their route.

"OK, troops, Tampa looks busy. Let's keep a visual on each other. Tighten up and spread out as needed to keep eyes on."

"Three, roger."

"One, roger."

While Big Army ran an IED-clearing operation every morning on Route Tampa, for every ten IEDs they found and neutralized, another five or six were discovered only when they detonated into the side of a vehicle. Alex was counting on the insurgents not yet having the chance to replace them.

Charlie One took the lead again as the team pulled onto the MSR and accelerated south.

They passed endless miles of baked desert dotted with occasional dilapidated buildings and villages that looked like they had been unchanged for a thousand years. Alex tried to take it all in at once, trusting his instincts to tell him when something was wrong. He focused on IED and VBIED indicators. For IEDs, of course, he looked for recently disturbed soil, piles of trash, stones, abandoned and parked vehicles or donkey carts. He also kept watch for timing markers that would tell an insurgent when a target was in the kill zone, such as odd markings on the side of the road, power line poles, advertisements . . . anything out of the ordinary.

Although at this point along their route there were few people, Alex tried to analyze their demeanor as the team passed. Again, anything extraordinary, like someone watching them and talking on a cell phone or the absence of people where he expected to see some, might tell him that trouble was brewing down the road.

For VBIEDs, Alex looked for erratic behavior, which was difficult due to the already aggressive and unpredictable nature of Iraqi drivers. Trying to spot a nervous or sweaty would-be martyr driving a suicide bomb seemed impossible until it was too late. He also looked for vehicles riding low on their shock absorbers as if weighed down with a heavy load. Because the team was maintaining as low a profile as possible, they did not wave off cars coming close to them. They could only do their best to interpret driving patterns and other ambiguous indicators to identify any threat and then take evasive action.

Nothing.

Eventually they came to the Baiji Oil Refinery, and the highway began to parallel the Tigris River. The population increased dramatically, supported by agriculture fed by the waters of the Tigris.

Still nothing.

As they approached the city of Samarra, Alex's reflected that this was another city with an incredible history of some 7,000 years.

Lizard's voice came over the radio: "Asshole coming up behind you."

In his rearview mirror Alex saw three SUVs approaching fast. His motorcade was going eighty, and this convoy was closing on him like he was sitting still. The lead vehicle bore down on Alex's truck as if they might ram him from the rear, swerving only at the last moment. As the vehicle sailed past Alex, he caught a glimpse of Iblis leaning forward over the dash and holding up his middle finger.

Alien said, "What a charming young man. I must remember to invite him over for bridge and cocktails sometime soon."

Bull let out a loud guffaw and looked over at Jamison. Alex saw the disdain in Bull's expression and craned to look behind him where the quivering Jamison was curled up in the fetal position with his eyes closed and his arms wrapped around his torso.

"Hey sir, you OK?" Alex asked.

Jamison muttered, "Leave me alone."

Alex turned back and focused on the road again as he thought, *He's not sick. I think that little prick's had it. Assuming he lives through this one, I wouldn't be surprised if this is his last trip out*. Alex shrugged at Alien and rolled his eyes.

The other motorcade disappeared from sight.

"IED, twelve o'clock!" Bandito's voice sounded over the radio.

Alex squinted into the distance as a black cloud rose over the road in front of them. "Cross the median and push through," he told Bandito.

"One, roger."

"Three, roger."

All three vehicles slowed, dropped the transmission into four-wheel drive, and crossed over the median at the same time about a hundred yards apart from each other. They roared up the other side and gunned their engines into oncoming traffic.

As they approached the IED, Alex made out that one vehicle was disabled and then saw Iblis leaning against it and firing over the hood as another one of his vehicles pulled alongside his. Iblis jumped into the open back seat and watched Alex's vehicle speed past from across the median. Alex keyed the mic.

"Stay on this side for another mile and then we'll cross back over."

"One, roger."

"Three, roger."

As Alex called the incident in to Asgard, he mused that if Iblis and his crew had not overtaken them, that IED might have hit one of his own vehicles. They continued toward Route Irish.

★★★

*"Mohammed, say to the wandering desert Arabs: 'You
shall be invited to fight against a people given to war
with mighty prowess. You shall fight them until they
surrender and submit. If you obey, Allah will grant you
a reward, but if you turn back, He will punish you with
grievous torture.'"*

Koran 48:16

Haider slapped the future martyr on the side of his head and
shouted, "No, you idiot, don't turn them both on until it's time!"
Although Haider had yet to arm the system, he wanted to be sure
that the fool who would detonate the device was certain of what
he was doing.

He glanced over his shoulder and saw Mullah Uday al-Shimarey
nodding his approval of Haider's methods. Haider thought, *Next
time I'll make it command detonated so I don't have to rely on
any more ignorant farmers to get it right.* He went over it again
with the martyr, and again, and again. When Haider felt the martyr
was ready, he left him with the mullah for last-minute tactical
instructions, a final blessing, and words of encouragement.

Twenty heavily armed men, several wearing suicide vests
that Haider had constructed, piled into two vans and two other
sedans. The two sedans pulled out of the courtyard, one in front
of the Mercedes and the other behind to ensure that the martyr
made it to their objective without incident or cold feet. The two
vans sped ahead to wait near the site of the attack. Haider got
behind the wheel of his truck, the mullah took the passenger
seat, and his two bodyguards squeezed into the small back seats.

As Haider started the engine, he considered the fastest way
to the objective where he and Mullah Uday would watch the
attack as it unfolded. The truck sped off toward the Qadisaya
Expressway—what the Americans called Route Irish.

*"O you who believe! Fight those of the unbelievers who
are near to you and let them find in you hardness."*

Koran 9:123

✫ ✫ ✫

Less than an hour later, Alex glimpsed the first suburbs of
Baghdad, a city of over seven million people. For a moment Alex
considered taking the shortest direct path to the Green Zone by
using July Fourteenth Street and entering at Assassins Gate,
but the intelligence reports from the night before insisted that
due to violence between Sunnis and Shiites, the safer path was
to continue on Route Tampa to Route Irish. Alex keyed the mic.

"One, this is Six. Stick to the plan."

"One, roger."

Route Tampa peeled off to the right and continued south.
The team tightened up the spread between vehicles and entered
the city at full throttle. At first the highway here was elevated
and offered little opportunity for an ambush, but as they pushed
deeper into the city, the MSR leveled out with the neighborhood
streets, and throngs of people and typical Iraqi urban clutter
were everywhere. The pucker factor ratcheted up significantly.
The motorcade careened and swerved through traffic for six miles
before Bandito called, "Irish coming up, a thousand meters." Alex
and Lizard responded affirmative.

The southbound exit from Route Tampa to eastbound Route
Irish was a left turn on a long, sweeping cloverleaf that passed
under the northbound lanes of Route Tampa. As the team rounded
the bend, they were forced to slow by a traffic jam entering Irish
that had been shielded from view, preventing them from taking
early evasive action.

Bandito called, "Traffic jam at the on-ramp."

Alex responded, "Roger, I see it now." He looked around for
an alternative. He keyed the mic again and said, "We don't have

a better option. See if you can pick your way around them." He broke squelch again and said, "And heads up, this is a perfect chokepoint for an ambush."

"One, roger."

"Three, copy."

The motorcade slowed to allow Bandito room to work. He called back, "Jersey barriers are making it a one-lane entrance, and there are cars all jammed in. There's no way through."

Just as Alex was about to respond, he heard an explosion behind him and twisted in his seat to see a swirling black cloud in the road as chunks of asphalt rained down on the back of his vehicle.

Lizard yelled into his handset, "Contact, rear, RPG on the overpass!"

"One, Six. Can you go through the dirt around them?"

"Roger." All three vehicles gunned their engines and swerved to the right around the traffic jam as AK-47s opened up on them from the overpass and another RPG round left its telltale trail as it zipped toward Charlie Six. Alex held his breath, but at the last possible instant the rocket must have lost one of its stabilizing fins and swerved hard to the left and slammed into a civilian car, lifting its back end off the ground and somersaulting it onto another car in a fiery explosion of high-explosive warhead and gas from the car.

As Alien sped off the road, the SUV dug all four wheels into the soft sand, sending great geysers of sand high into the air. The truck ground to a halt. He put it in reverse and tried to back out of the hole he had created, then in drive again, but only succeeded in rocking the vehicle back and forth and bogging it down further. As AK-47 rounds found their range and pelted the truck with bullets, Alex keyed the mic.

"It's Six; we're stuck. Three, we need some covering fire. One, I need you to come back and prepare to tow." Alex glanced at Bull, who had pushed Jamison facedown on the floorboard again. He said to Bull and Alien, "If this doesn't work, try a cross load; if it looks like we can't get out of this, hit the BFT, and evac to a hard point."

Bull nodded and Alien said, "Keep your head down, Cap."

As Alex opened the door, he heard Psycho open up on the bridge with his M240G. Lizard was also out and returning fire. Alex went to the back-left side of Charlie Six with his M4 pulled tight to his shoulder and looked at the bridge just in time to see the RPG gunner. Alex pulled the trigger, and Psycho must have spotted him too because the bridge parapet covering the gunner disintegrated under the 7.62 mm rounds. Alex was quite sure he hit his target, but it was superfluous because Psycho's bullets shredded his body.

Alex was looking for other targets when Charlie One backed up in front of his vehicle, the rear hatch open. Haymaker was returning fire now as well. Bandito jumped down to pull out a rolled-up tow cable, and Alex dashed to the front of his truck and connected one end to his vehicle. Bandito did the same at the rear of Charlie One.

The shooting dwindled and stopped altogether. The insurgents decided they had had enough and beat a hasty withdrawal.

Bandito banged on the back of his vehicle, and with one hand raised he signaled to Digger to move forward easy until he took up all the slack in the cable. Then he banged on the back of the vehicle again, and Digger gave it some gas. Alien gunned his engine at the same time. Charlie Six lurched forward and jumped out of the hole onto solid ground. Alex and Bandito unhooked the cable, and Bandito threw it in the back of his vehicle with Haymaker. The men mounted back up and Alex keyed the radio.

"Let's go, Three; watch out for the soft sand."

"Roger."

Alex called the contact in to Asgard, and the team found a gap in the jersey barriers and pulled onto Route Irish.

★★★

"Do not yield to the unbelievers but launch a great campaign against them with the help of the Koran."

Koran 25:52

Haider stepped out onto the rooftop and walked to the edge of the dwelling, where two lawn chairs were arranged under a large umbrella to cover them from the scorching sun. Next to each chair was a small table, each with a fresh, cold glass of orange juice and a pair of binoculars.

Mullah Uday shuffled up next to Haider with his ever-present bodyguards in tow. Haider gestured to the mullah to have a seat. Delighted, Mullah Uday seated himself and took a long drink of orange juice. He picked up the field glasses, turned them over in his hands, and noted the *Property of the U.S. Army* stamp on the underside. He nodded to Haider and said, "Nice touch. We are very pleased with your work."

Haider assumed the proper amount of humility and sat as well. He picked up the other set of binoculars, raised them to his eyes, and adjusted the focus until the southwestern entrance to the Green Zone came into focus. With one hand he pointed due east to a small building no more than 500 meters away in the middle of route Irish and said to the mullah, "Checkpoint twelve"

Haider scanned back to the west and saw the Mercedes with the two escort vehicles. He looked further west and was just able to pick out the two vans perhaps one kilometer behind the Mercedes. He said to the mullah, "Everything is in motion. We cannot fail now."

The mullah was beside himself with delight.

Haider explained, "Traffic is heavy, and it all comes to a complete standstill at the ECP while the guards check for credentials and access authority. I estimate at least forty people will die in the initial blast. That alone will make this effort successful, but with your men and the follow-on assault, the results will be spectacular."

"Yes," Mullah Uday commented. "Allah be praised; today will be a good day."

"Mohammed, fight against the disbelievers and hypocrites and be stern against them. Their dwelling will be hellfire, the most terrible fate."

Koran 66:9

★★★

Checkpoint twelve was separated into two entry lanes to the Green Zone, one for regular traffic and one for PSDs. They neared the ECP, and the team tightened their dispersal up to just a few car lengths. Alex breathed a sigh of relief.

Then two things happened. First, a flash of light from a rooftop on the north side of the road drew his attention to four men, two standing and two seated. Two of the men appeared to be looking through binoculars at the ECP. Alex's heart raced: *Not good.*

Second, a nondescript sedan slowed dramatically in front of them, forcing Alien to slam on his brakes and swerve to the left, sideswiping a black Mercedes. Rather than becoming angry at the damage to his expensive car, the driver of the Mercedes looked straight ahead and kept driving. Alex looked closer at the car and realized it was riding low for such a stout vehicle—like it had a particularly heavy load.

Alex screamed into the radio handset, "Break contact, turn around, get away from the ECP, NOW!" He slapped Alien in the arm and pointed vigorously back the way they had come. He keyed the mic again and yelled, "Turn around, turn around, go, go, go!" At this point the east and westbound lanes were separated by Jersey barriers with no way to jump the median to the other side, so all three SUVs crunched and smashed into the other vehicles, pushing them out of their way until the team was careening against traffic back the way they had come.

Jamison was screaming in Alex's ear, "What the fuck are you doing? Are you crazy? We were almost there! Stop the goddamn car and turn it around! I'm going to have you fired!" He took a breath and opened his mouth to scream again just as the shock wave from the explosion reached the car and sucked the breath out of his lungs.

As Jamison clutched his chest, Bull grabbed him by the scruff of his neck and pushed him facedown onto the floorboard again.

Lizard had taken the lead again in Charlie Three, and the motorcade was now almost bumper to bumper, swerving in and out of traffic that was mostly stopped now due to the explosion. Trying to avoid a full-on front-end collision, the team narrowly missed two vans that were still moving aggressively toward the ECP. Alex called, "Three, get off the highway as soon as you can. Let's work our way around to the north and east to Assassins Gate."

"Three, roger."

"One, copy."

Lizard took the first gap in the median and careened onto the westbound lane, moving with traffic and hurrying to put distance between them and the ECP.

★ ★ ★

"Let those who fight in Allah's Cause sell this world's life for the hereafter. To him who fights in Allah's Cause whether he is slain or victorious, We shall give him great reward."

Koran 4:74

Haider did not understand why the one motorcade panicked and turned around; everything was going perfectly. Mullah Uday, a former general in Saddam Hussein's Republican Guard, pointed at the three vehicles going the wrong way down the street and handed his phone to one of the bodyguards, Yasin Sulayman, a former lieutenant in Uday's division. The bodyguard nodded knowingly, lifted the phone to take a picture of the three SUVs speeding away, and then dialed friends who would be happy to intercept and dispatch the motorcade to a fiery afterlife. He would also arrange a final surprise for them if they were fortunate enough to reach Assassins Gate alive.

Haider went back to his binoculars just as the Mercedes pulled up to the checkpoint and an Iraqi police officer approached to check the driver's credentials. The IP walked up to the driver's window, leaned over, and then took a step back just as the car exploded. Haider saw the explosion before he heard it. Then a heartbeat later he distinctly heard the three explosions, separated by milliseconds. Everything close by disintegrated. A great plume of fire and smoke swirled high into the sky as the shock wave traveled toward Haider and the mullah and took their breath away. Mullah Uday almost fell back in his chair. Haider grinned and savored every moment of the experience. Soon debris began falling from the sky.

The two vans loaded with Holy Warriors of Allah never slowed down, and the two sedans fell in behind them as they sped into the swirling fire and smoke and rubble left by the explosion. There was no one left in any condition to contest their entry into the Green Zone. The breach was successful. The four assault vehicles crashed through several cars ripped apart by the explosion and ran over bodies strewn about. Then it was open road.

The M1 Abrams tank commander assigned to overwatch the ECP cleared his head from the concussion of the explosion as he stood up in his hatch on the turret. He saw the four vehicles emerge from the dust and fire and instinctively knew it was an insurgent attack and this was the assault force. He reached for the M2 .50-caliber machine gun mounted on his turret as he screamed into the mic on his helmet, "GUNNER, HEAT, FOUR TARGETS, LEFT TARGET FIRST!"

As the commander racked the first round of his .50 into the chamber, the gunner responded, "IDENTIFIED!"

The loader yelled, "UP!" as he slammed home the three-foot-long 120-millimeter HEAT, or high explosive anti-tank, round into the breach of the main gun.

The commander screamed, "FIRE!" and opened up on the last vehicle with the .50. The first bullet sailed over the hood of the sedan, the second round went through the engine block and buried itself in the road on the other side of the car, and the third round went through the driver's door, then the driver, then the passenger in the front seat and out through the passenger door.

The gunner yelled, "ON THE WAY!" as he pushed the red button with his thumb. The main gun rocked the tank on its chassis as it sent a supersonic warhead into the side of the first van. The van heaved into the air and ripped apart at the seams in a ball of flames, flipping over twice before it hit the ground again.

The gunner yelled, "IDENTIFIED!" again.

The loader hollered, "UP!"

"FIRE!" The commander swung the .50 over to the lead sedan this time and pressed his butterfly trigger again.

The rounds tore through the first car as the gunner yelled, "ON THE WAY!" and sent another main gun round into the second van.

Without letting go of the trigger, the commander traversed back to the last vehicle again and pulverized the men trying to get out, cutting bodies in half and disintegrating heads.

The gunner yelled, "IDENTIFIED!" The loader yelled, "UP!" and although he knew it was no longer necessary, the commander yelled, "FIRE!"

"ON THE WAY!"

BOOM! The first car shredded apart on impact.

"IDENTIFIED!" "UP!" "FIRE!" "ON THE WAY!"

BOOM! The last car sent flaming pieces and body parts fifty feet in the air.

The commander said, "Cease fire. Targets destroyed. Load HEAT. Scan for targets."

The loader said, "Up."

Haider was in shock. In a matter of seconds, all the mullah's men were gone and strewn in lifeless pieces along the road.

Mullah Uday was visibly upset also, but as he rose from his seat, he said to Haider calmly, "No matter. They are all on their way to Paradise, Insha'Allah. This mission was a success."

Then he turned to his lieutenant and said, "Find out who failed to identify that there was a tank here and have him killed . . . slowly." The lieutenant nodded and said nothing. A shiver shot up Haider's spine.

"And verily We will try you till We know those of you who strive hard in the Cause of Allah and the steadfast, and We will test your record."

Koran 47:31

The first intersection had no exit, so Lizard spun around on the entrance ramp and headed away from Route Irish, again on the wrong side of the road, swerving in and out of traffic. Alien sideswiped a car on Alex's side and disintegrated the side view mirror.

Alex looked at his GPS and map as he swayed from side to side in his seat and then keyed his mic. "Three, this is Nisour

Square comin' up. Take the first exit off the roundabout. We'll try to work our way over to Corvette Gate."

"Three, copy, first exit off the roundabout."

"One, roger."

Alex tried to raise Asgard on the radio to report the contact and their change in route, but they did not respond. He picked up his cell phone. After three rings: "Asgard Operations."

The team reached the Nisour Square roundabout and began to flow with traffic again. Alex said, "This is Charlie Six. There was an attack on checkpoint twelve just as we got there. We have to reroute. Option one is Corvette Gate; option two is Assassins Gate. We'll try to stay on main roads, but it's impossible to say for sure."

Lizard took the first exit off the roundabout and almost immediately began to slow, and called on the radio, "Major traffic jam. What do you want?"

Alex keyed his mic. "Get back up on Jinub Street and head north." He glanced at his map. "That gap in the wall to your left will take you back on Jinub."

"Three, roger."

"One, roger."

Lizard crossed over several lanes, past cars jockeying to join the traffic jam, and picked his way through a gap in the T-walls lining the road before jumping over two more lanes of traffic and up onto Jinub Street. The team accelerated down the road.

Alex noticed two cars coming back to the south on the northbound lane and keyed his mic again. "Heads up, something wrong about this." He picked up his phone again. "Ops, are you still there?"

The radio operator responded, "Yeah, Cap. Three Actual says Corvette Gate is closed. Your best bet is Assassins Gate."

Alex breathed deep. "OK, thanks. Out here."

He keyed his mic again. "OK, Corvette Gate is closed; we're heading to Assassins Gate. Break." Looking at his map, he continued, "At the next roundabout, take the Damascus Street exit. When we get to the elevated highway—that's Fourteenth July Skyway—we'll jump on that and go south to Yafa Street east; then Al Kindi Street south will get us to Assassins Gate."

Lizard called again, more urgency in his voice this time: "Roadblock ahead!"

Alex looked beyond Charlie Three and saw two sedans parked nose to nose, sideways in the road, blocking traffic. Now he knew why all the traffic had exited behind them. He looked around and saw no way to get through the barriers along the road, and he was reticent to turn around.

"Ram 'em! Push 'em outta the way!"

"Three, wilco." A wicked smile on his face, Digger slowed Charlie Three almost to a stop about twenty-five yards from the roadblock. Four men with AK-47s rose up from behind the cars and, thinking that the motorcade was stopping, began to move around their cars toward Charlie Three. Digger decided to hit the vehicle on the left. Dropping the transmission into first gear, he floored the gas pedal and braced for the impact, aiming the right front side of his truck just inside the rear wheel of the target sedan so the truck frame would take the brunt.

The insurgents began firing at Charlie Three as Lizard and Haymaker held on and prepared for the collision. Rounds impacted the windshield, making several pits and spiderweb cracks in the bullet-resistant glass. The insurgents tried to scatter out of the way, but it was too late. Charlie Three slammed into the sedan, which lifted and spun to the right with incredible violence, squashing two of the insurgents like rotten tomatoes against the other car. The two surviving insurgents sprawled to the side of the road as the motorcade accelerated past. As a parting gift, Psycho opened his hatch and sprayed them down with his machine gun, hitting one of them and motivating the other to abandon his assault rifle and scurry for cover.

What the team did not see was the surviving insurgent pulling out his cell phone and frantically dialing a number.

★★★

"Damn nice driving, Digger," Alex said over the radio. "OK, at the next roundabout the second exit will get us on Damascus Street. Then we have a right turn onto Fourteen July, then left onto Yafa, then right onto Al Kindi. How copy?"

"Three, roger. Copy Damascus to Fourteen July, to Yafa, to Al Kindi."

"One, copy the same."

"Six, roger."

Lizard came back over the net: "Six, this is Three. We may have a problem. Looks like we took some damage to the engine. We're starting to smoke."

Smoke billowed out from Charlie Three like a jet vapor trail.

"Roger, do you think you can make it?"

"No, it's gettin' worse and we're losing power." As he spoke, the engine sputtered and quit, and flames flickered out from under the hood as they rolled to a stop. "We're done. We need a ride."

Alex said, "Roger, we'll fall back and cover you. One, prepare to cross-load."

Bandito came back, "One, roger."

Alien pulled Charlie Six off the road about fifty yards behind Charlie Three and angled the truck so they could see both directions. Bull twisted around in his seat so he could watch behind them.

The crew of Charlie Three slung their assault packs on their backs, grabbed their weapons, and bailed out of the vehicle. Digger took up security at the front of the vehicle on the right side, and Haymaker went to the right rear and took a knee with his M240G at the ready. As Lizard prepared a thermite grenade, Charlie One pulled up on the right of Charlie Six. The rear door swung open and Lizard hollered, "Haymaker, go." Haymaker turned, took two steps, and dove headfirst into Charlie One. As he scrambled over the seat into the back with Psycho, Digger was right behind him, sliding over to the right side as Lizard tossed the thermite grenade into the back of Charlie Three, spun around, and dove into Charlie One. Charlie One was moving within a couple of seconds of having stopped. Charlie Six pulled out behind them and passed Charlie Three as smoke and flames began pouring from every seam on the truck. Lizard looked back and blew his truck a final kiss as the gas tank ignited and she erupted from within.

"Nicely done," Alex announced over the radio.

Alien nodded his approval. "It sure does pay to practice this stuff."

Alex looked in the back seat to see how the client was doing. He saw Jamison facedown on the floorboard with Bull's foot firmly planted on his back. Alex looked at Bull and raised his eyebrows. Bull shrugged with an innocent expression, grinned, and took his foot off Jamison and said, "There are some things I just *love* about this job."

Alex called the situation in to Asgard on his cell phone.

The roadblock ensured the team encountered no traffic on their way to Arabian Knight Square, the next roundabout. Alex keyed his mic as they neared the square. "OK, the second exit should put us on Damascus Street."

"One, roger."

They sailed through the square and past the entrance to Al-Zawra Park, made famous after the locals ate most of the animals during the American invasion, leaving the bigger, more dangerous ones to die of thirst and starve. This was a perilous section of road because the park offered endless places for insurgents to hide. He called, "Fourteen July Skyway coming up. The on-ramp should be before the overpass."

"One, roger."

They made it past the park without incident, and Bandito turned south onto the on-ramp of the skyway. Almost immediately Charlie One slowed, and Bandito called, "This's not gonna work. They have the road completely blocked off. We can't crash through this one, and there's no way around it."

Alex craned in his seat and saw T-walls in the road formed into almost a block house and IPs waving people away. The few cars there were turning around through an opening between the north and southbound lanes. "Right, follow those cars and get in the northbound lane." He added, "Be ready for anything."

"Roger."

Alex looked at his map. "Once you turn around, take the first right exit, and then one klick up turn right again on Alawi Street."

"Roger, right off this road, one klick, then right on Alawi."

"Good copy."

Bandito got turned around, and as Charlie Six was making the turn, Alex saw the IP looking hard at them and nodding as he spoke into a radio handset. Alex got the ominous feeling that they were being tracked and whoever was doing the tracking was well connected.

"Keep your eyes open. I feel like we're being herded in a certain direction."

"One, roger. Me too."

"Matter of fact, stay on this road and go back to Damascus Street. We'll take the long way around." Alex set the mic down, and Alien nodded his approval.

"One, roger; good call."

Alex really wanted to get to Shiite-controlled neighborhoods. So far, all the bad things had happened in Sunni-controlled areas. Of course, while they would all be delighted to kill Americans, he figured whatever web was trying to catch them must be Sunni, and his team would be unexpected in a Shiite neighborhood, which would increase their chances of survival. He wondered if this was how his buddies in the 3rd Ranger Battalion felt trying to get to their stranded units during the Battle of Mogadishu as they drove around the city, getting ambushed and turned around at every intersection. He knew he had to somehow be unpredictable.

Alex looked at his map again and said to Alien, "Y'know, I heard the new GPSs can give real-time bird's-eye view. We need to ask Odin to get us some."

Alien nodded. "Yeah, I know someone who's got one; he swears by it."

"Have you been all the way down Haifa Street?" Alex asked

"Yeah, but it's blocked at the Christian church there." Alien reached over and put his finger on Alex's map. "Too many suicide bombers and VBIEDs. It's a wonder there are *any* Christians left in this fucked-up country."

"I'm sure they'll remedy that soon enough. How about the river? Is there access along the bank of the river? It looks like there is here on the map."

As he turned off the skyway back onto Damascus Street, Alien considered the idea. "I really can't say, but it might be worth a try. I'm fairly sure no one would expect that."

"Then a cruise along the river it is." Alex keyed his mic. "One, this is Six. About two klicks up, this road ends. Bear to the right on Nasir Street. At the bridge find a way down to the banks of the river and we'll go south along the river and jump up on Yafa Street."

"One, copy Nasir to river to Yafa. Sounds OK. Let's see what happens."

"Six, roger."

The team passed a mosque and then what had been a large building, now reduced to rubble. There were only a few people where Alex expected multitudes, but as deep as they were into the city, their only real choice was to keep going.

Bandito bore right onto Nasir Street, and within a few blocks the bridge loomed ahead.

Alex called, "It looks like if you just stay to the right of the bridge, there's a road that leads down to the waterfront."

"Roger."

They passed through a roundabout that intersected Haifa Street, and Alex saw that Haifa was barricaded in both directions— not with Jersey barriers or T-walls like Big Army would use or provide to the Iraqi government, but with pieces of buildings, destroyed cars, and other rubble. Men dressed in random clothes, not uniforms, stood overwatching the barricades with AK-47s.

Alien saw Alex checking them out and said, "Yeah, they're people from the neighborhoods trying to protect their turf from marauders and Shiite militias. But don't feel sorry for them. They killed and ran out the people who lived here before the war."

Alex shook his head. "Nice, it's like an apocalyptic movie."

Alien laughed, "Yup, zombies and all."

Alex looked back to see how the client was doing. Jamison huddled in the corner of his seat against the door with his head below the window and his feet drawn up under him. Alex thought, *Not so high and mighty now, are you?* Bull snickered like he'd read Alex's mind.

Bandito lead the way down to the riverside and found a paved road heading south that ran along the walled-in houses along the river. Now there was not a soul in sight.

About a kilometer down, they came to a barricade in the road. Bandito called, "Nobody's home that I can see. I'm going to try to get around it."

"Six, roger."

Bandito put the truck in four-wheel drive and drove into the sand to pick his way through Jersey barriers and concertina. They passed through and continued. They drove under another bridge spanning the Tigris River, and then their road ran out. Bandito worked his way uphill through sand and brush and found another road that paralleled the river. He turned onto the paved road and picked up the pace a bit. Just when Alex spotted the Yafa Street Bridge, Bandito called, "The road is done. We can't go any further. We're in someone's neighborhood, and I don't think they like us being here."

Alex saw what Bandito was talking about; a group of young men who had been watching a TV outdoors all stopped what they were doing and sat up like bird dogs. As one, they reached down and each picked up an assault rifle.

As they stood, Alex hollered into the radio, "Reverse out! Reverse out! Follow us!" Alien slammed the truck into reverse and hit the gas. He backed up about 200 yards until Alex poked him in the arm and pointed at another road leading west away from the river and into the neighborhood. The road was barricaded with furniture and trash, but it looked like they could crash through it—if it wasn't booby-trapped. Without slowing, Alien did a ninety-degree turn, ending up with the front of the vehicle aimed at the barricade, dropped the vehicle into drive before it came to a stop, and hit the gas pedal with Bandito hot on his heels. As they crashed through the barricade, Alex cringed, but it did not blow up, and they tore into the neighborhood street.

One block further down they saw another barricade but were able to make a left turn, taking them back toward the bridge again, but they were now only one block from the group of young men who were certainly angry at the intrusion. Sure enough, as the team approached Yafa Street, the gang of locals burst from the alleyways into the street in front of them. Alex was tempted to just run them over, but this street was also barricaded at the intersection with Yafa Street, and this barricade looked to be made of more substantial material.

"Reverse out! One, you take the lead." The team again backed away with engines screaming. This time the homies began shooting. Bullets impacted Charlie Six, and the windshield took more hits. Alex had a fleeting thought as to how many more rounds it would take for the window to fail.

Bandito took the first turn and headed deeper into the neighborhood. People came out of their homes with weapons, clearly ready to defend against invaders. Bandito called, "We have another barricade, but this one looks like it has a lane through."

Alex could see it now. "Roger, try to get through."

Two men with weapons moved into the street from the side of the barricade; they had obviously been on guard there. They also obviously recognized that the two SUVs did not belong where they were and raised their weapons to fire. Alex knew they were a breath away from ending up like the Blackwater contractors in Fallujah, burned and dragged through the streets and hung from a bridge. He hollered into his mic, "Run them down! Push through!" Digger gunned his vehicle straight for the two shooters as his windshield was fractured with bullets. Both men managed to dive out of the way as Charlie One bore down on them and snaked its way through the barricade with Charlie Six right on its bumper.

Bandito started to turn left toward Assassins Gate when he saw T-walls blocking the end of the road. He hollered over the radio, "Roadblock; go right!"

Alien came out of the barricade and turned right as Charlie One turned around and fell in behind Charlie Six. They raced north up the road until they found another, larger road heading south and turned onto it toward Assassins Gate and the Green Zone. The road they chose turned out to be Haifa Street, which, once it crossed Yafa Street, became Al-Kindi Street. The ECP called Assassins Gate was at the intersection of Yafa and Al-Kindi. But it was not as simple as just crossing the street to the Green Zone. The team had to turn west on Yafa and approach the ECP on the eastbound lane.

Alex began to relax, marveling that all this had happened within a quarter mile of the Green Zone and relative safety.

As they pulled close to the serpentine barriers at the entrance of the ECP, he asked Alien, "How ya doin'?"

Alex spotted a man in the road walking toward the ECP and thought there was something odd about him.

"I'm OK, a little tired. We're running on fumes. It's a good thing we have an extra fuel tank or we'd'a never made it."

As Alien spoke, Alex was still trying to figure out what was wrong with this picture when the man suddenly turned toward them and started running, screaming as he pulled something out of the pocket of his man-jammies. Alex thought he heard "*Allahu Akbar*" as the man hit the side of the car inches away from Alex and exploded.

Alex felt the shock wave, but all the man succeeded in doing was mangling the outer skin of the truck and splattering his body all over the vehicle. Chunks of bloody, Jell-O-like substance slid down the windows.

Holy shit that was close . . . literally. Alex took a deep breath but then gagged at the renewed, horrible smell of vomit. Jamison had puked up what was left in his stomach.

Alien kept driving. Alex put the USAID PSD and American-flag placards on the dash for the guards to see. They were guided into a PSD lane, where a US soldier approached them. Alex tried to open his door, but it was stuck. Alien opened his and stuck his head over the top to talk to the soldier.

The soldier said, "Hey, man, you guys OK? That was gnarly."

Alien said, "Yeah, man. Someone shoulda told that guy about armored vehicles." He handed the soldier the USAID credentials.

"Well, y'all have a good day."

"Thanks."

✯✯✯

Alex collapsed onto the cot in the transient barracks. "Oh my God, I'm wiped out."

Alien did the same on the next cot over. "Yeah, me too. That was insane."

The rest of the guys came crashing through the wooden door that had been erected at the entrance of the oversized Air Force tent.

"Hey, Cap, that was a hell of a run. Can we do it again?" Bandito tossed an ice-cold beer on Alex's stomach. Alex groaned and rolled over, popping the top and letting the beer spew all over the floor and Alien.

"Thanks, man," Alien said as he sat up and shook his beer and opened it on Alex. "What did they say about the vehicles?"

Alex took a big swig and said through the bubbles in his throat, "No one seemed too upset about the vehicles; I think they were genuinely impressed we got here alive. They'll get us new vehicles for the ride back, but we may be going alone."

"What do you mean?"

Alex shrugged. "I think Jamison's done. He's a basket case. I think he'll claim PTSD and go home."

"Ha, I hope he gets run over by traffic in DC."

Alex said, "I knew a guy once who always bragged about how tough he was and the time he spent on a SWAT team. Well, we had a car bomb vaporize a bunch of people nearby, and we walked down to see if we could help. Of course, there was no one left alive to help, but this guy got some fresh meat on his boots from just walking around. He acted funny for a few days after that, and his boots were always wet. Then one night I found him in the latrine, scrubbing his boots, mumbling something. I asked him what he said, and he looked at me like he was crazy and said, 'It won't come off.' I said, 'What won't come off?' He said 'The blood. I can't get the blood off my shoes.' I looked at his boots and they were clean. The next day they sent him home. Jamison had the same look in his eyes."

Bandito and Lizard pulled up a couple of folding chairs and dropped a cold six-pack at the end of Alien's cot. As Alien reached for two beers and handed another one to Alex, Bandito asked,

"So, what's the plan?"

Alex said, "Well, we aren't scheduled to leave until the day after tomorrow. The motor officer at USAID said he'd have two vehicles for us tomorrow morning. I need you guys to take care of that and prep them for movement no later than noon the next day so we can get back to Erbil before dark."

Alex took another long swig of his beer and thought, *Damn, that's good after a hard day at work.* He added, "Other than that, you guys can do what you want. I don't think Jamison wants us hanging around the USAID, but they did say we could use the pool there, and there's one behind the embassy here also. You guys know about the PX, chow hall, and all that, right?"

"Yeah." Lizard nodded. "KBR puts on an awesome spread here for all the bigwigs at the State Department and visiting politicians."

"Good. Have fun, prep the vehicles, and we'll plan on a mission brief for the move at eleven hundred the day after tomorrow. I have to see someone here to find out about Predator."

Alien looked at Bandito. "Can you guys take care of Charlie Six? I want to go with Cap."

Sitting on the end of his bunk across the aisle, Bull chimed in, "I gotcha covered, brother. You go ahead." Suddenly, they heard shooting in the distance. Gradually the shooting increased until it sounded like it was coming from all around them. Then they heard a pattering noise on the top of the tent. Alex thought it had started raining.

They all picked up weapons and started for the door. Bandito opened it, pushed back the canvas flap, and looked out. "What the hell?"

Even before he stepped out, Alex could see tracers streaking across the sky. As he emerged, he saw that the entire sky was lit up with tracers. Green and red and white tracers flashed in every direction. He eased over to the side of the tent and looked behind them. They were surrounded. The sky was alive, and shooting came from 360 degrees around them as thousands of weapons were fired into the air. They were nearby and at great distance and from every type of weapon system: AK-47s, belt-fed machine guns, flares, and intermittent airbursts from some type of grenade launcher.

Alex knew that all they had to do was lower their trajectory and they would wipe out the entire Green Zone. Then a thought came to him. "Celebratory fire."

"What?" Lizard had put on a Kevlar helmet.

A soldier who had moved out of the tent with them said, "Yeah, they must have won the game."

"What game?" Lizard asked.

"The Iraqi national soccer team played some big game today. They must have won," the young soldier explained.

Alex was relieved . . . until a round smacked into the ground next to him. They all scurried back into the canvas tent.

★ ★ ★

"The unbelievers are allies. Unless you aid each other, there will be confusion and mischief. Those who accept Islam and leave their homes to fight in Allah's Cause, as well as those who give the fighters asylum, shelter, and aid—these are all believers, for them is pardon and bountiful provision in Paradise."

Koran 8:73

Mullah Uday screamed into the cell phone, "Who are these people? CIA? I want you to find them and kill them! Do you understand? I want them dead! Do not fail in this, and keep me informed!" He pushed the end button like he was pushing the initiator on a suicide bomb surrounded by nonbelievers.

Haider cringed at the mullah's wrath. No American scared him as much as the mullah did. Still, he was as perplexed by these Americans as the mullah.

This team reportedly came from the north down the Mosul highway, but there were no reports of them from Mosul. Certainly not Kirkuk. The network was too strong there; these people would have been noticed. Perhaps Erbil. They had apparently foiled attacks all along the way, killed several of the mullah's warriors, and evaded interception throughout half of Baghdad, which should have been an impossible feat. Ultimately the mullah had recreated their path through the city and would take steps to ensure that no one was able to slip through the web in the future.

The mullah's phone rang again. He snatched it up to his ear and growled, "What?" Haider heard a voice excitedly rattle away. Mullah Uday scrunched his eyebrows, pursed his lips, and nodded knowingly.

"Good...good...good. Yes, OK. This is fine work, Nosherwan. Put a generous bounty on him and make it payable when I am presented with his head. Distribute this to the entire network and have everyone look out for him. Make certain that the operations center gets all the details. Yes, you've done well. We will not forget."

Haider relaxed a bit. As fierce as the mullah was, Haider knew that he was equally generous in rewarding good, hard, and smart work.

Mullah Uday looked over at Haider with his piercing eyes. "Apparently they come from Erbil, protected by the wretched Kurds. It is expected that their leader is responsible for martyring our Chechen sniper who was doing such good work up there. He may also have overseen Sheikh Ibrahim Khalaf Ali's house that you blew up and where so many of our brothers lost their lives."

Haider's eyes went wide. His head started to spin, and he took a deep breath and leaned back as if this would help him avoid the mullah's wrath.

The mullah raised his right hand with the palm outward. "Do not worry, Haider. You have become very useful to us, and we have much work yet to accomplish."

"How many prophets fought in Allah's Cause? With them fought multitudes of godly men who were slain. They never lost heart if they met with disaster in Allah's Cause, nor did they weaken or give in. Allah loves those who are firm and steadfast."

Koran 3:146

Morning's first light revealed several holes through the top of the tent. Alex rolled over and stood up with a groan. He looked at the others and saw no blood pools, so he figured everyone was OK. He grabbed his toiletry kit and a towel and walked over to a shower tent. Alien was standing in front of a mirror, shaving.

Alex turned on a shower and said over his shoulder, "Y'know, that soccer game musta been why the streets were so empty yesterday."

Alien considered that and then said, "Yeah, but I still think someone had our number."

"Maybe."

"Really, I've been through here plenty of times, and while it's always sketchy, I've never seen anything like yesterday—too many coincidences. I got the feelin' someone was trying to corral us into a certain spot."

Alex stepped into the shower.

Alien called after him, "I think if we hadn't taken that detour, gangbangers aside, we would have had other surprises."

"Do you think there's an insider behind it? Someone who wants us killed?" Alex asked him.

Alien snorted. "No, I haven't considered that, *yet*. But I do know that insurgent surveillance can be extensive. After all, they have most of the locals on their side."

CHAPTER 6

Predator

THE US EMBASSY PROPER, where a local could go to apply for a visa or conduct other typical embassy business, was down the street in an elegant but nondescript building with a small staff. The embassy annex known simply as "the Palace" was a spacious and luxurious palace of Saddam Hussein. This was where the daily business of the former Coalition Provisional Government and now the US ambassador to Iraq, the US Department of State, and the US military's central command, or CENTCOM, was conducted.

First thing in the morning, Alex called his point of contact at the DOS and was told to wait at the main compound access-control point, or CAC, until someone could escort them into the Palace. They stowed their weapons and then wandered up to the CAC, flashing the limited-access badges that USAID had procured for them.

A big man wearing a T-shirt and ball cap with the Triple

Canopy security company logo and sporting a Glock 17 in a hip holster greeted Alien. "Hey, man. Long time no see! What've you been up to?"

Alien smiled as he shook hands. "Hey, bro. Been working PSD for USAID. This is Cap. He's the team leader. Cap, meet my old squad leader from DET 1, Jake Parsons." Alex shook Jake's hand and instantly took a liking to this jovial fellow who smiled with his eyes.

"Good to meet you." He used his left thumb to point at Alien. "Anyone who runs with this renegade is welcome in my house." He swung his hand back, indicating the Palace was "his house." "What can I do for you gentlemen?"

Alex told him, "We're here to meet with the DOS Hostage Crisis Team; they said they'll send someone here to escort us into the Palace."

"OK, no problem. Normally I'd have people wait across the street, but you guys can have a seat over there out of the way and enjoy the show." Jake pointed at some chairs along the wall. He grabbed Alien's hand again and said, "Sorry, man, I can't stay. I've got three more of these CACs and I gotta run."

"No problem, man. We'll be OK. Thanks."

Jake turned and bolted out the back door.

The Palace housed at least 4,000 people living in shipping containers, or Conex boxes, converted into living spaces behind the main building, and hosted as many as 12,000 visitors every day. By 8 AM, the Annex was an absolute zoo.

The guards working the security were primarily Peruvians with American supervisors. With their M16s at the low ready, they checked badges out on the street, and those with proper credentials could approach the CAC. Another guard checked the badges again and allowed some people with certain clearances to proceed unhindered, while others and their belongings were efficiently searched. The latter were greeted inside the CAC and told to empty their pockets and place any baggage on a conveyor belt. As those items passed through an X-ray machine, the person was routed through to a metal detector and then physically searched. Finally, their hands and pockets were swabbed, and the swab was inserted into a machine that would alert the guards if any explosive residue was present.

Adjacent to the CAC was a single-vehicle lane with a pair of delta barriers designed to trap vehicles inside and allow the guards to search the car. Guards standing well out in front the CAC first checked credentials of vehicle occupants. If the vehicle was authorized but needed to be searched, the occupants were required to dismount and routed through the main entrance of the CAC while the driver stayed with the vehicle. Once the vehicle was between the two barriers, the driver was instructed to open all compartments, doors, trunk, and the hood, and was taken into the CAC. Another guard followed and swabbed the vehicle doorknobs, the hood, the trunk, and the steering wheel. He brought the swab into the CAC to check for explosive trace. Then one of the guards inspected the undercarriage using a wheeled mirror with a long handle. Yet another guard opened the hood and visually searched the engine compartment. When they were finished and satisfied that the vehicle posed no threat, the occupants were allowed to get back into the car and proceed into the Palace grounds.

Alex watched the endless procession of people and vehicles entering and exiting the CAC. The guards dealt deftly with a menagerie of issues. From time to time they called Jake on their radio, and soon he would burst through the door to handle some sensitive issue like a lieutenant colonel who had altered the expiration date on his embassy access badge, or the brand-new female lieutenant who shot the clearing barrel three times before the guards managed to wrestle the Beretta pistol from her hands and calm her down.

By far, however, the most bizarre thing Alex saw was two

American families with three young teenage children: two blond girls and a boy. Jake asked them how they had come to Baghdad, to which one of the fathers answered, "We flew into Basra and took a taxi here."

Alex could not believe what he had heard. They were the luckiest people he had ever seen. They had traveled over 300 miles on an incredibly deadly stretch of road that Big Army had little control over. Just getting out of the airport unnoticed was lucky. The windows of the taxi must have been tinted, and the driver must have traveled as fast as he could the whole way. They were also lucky that the driver did not just take them somewhere else and sell them for someone's sport.

Jake's eyes narrowed and he asked, "But why did you come here with your family?"

The man did not seem bothered at all and innocently responded, "We wanted to show our children that the rest of the world does not live as well as we do in America so they would appreciate what we have."

Alex could not believe the ignorance, naïveté, and plain stupidity of these people. They risked their lives and the lives of their children just to teach them a lesson. Alex shuddered to think what would happen to the girls if they fell into the hands of not just insurgents but anyone, really. The men would be tortured and raped for sport, if not killed outright. The women would be raped until they died. The children would be raped and sold as sex slaves repeatedly, and if they were lucky, they would end up in someone's harem, or if not, they would be dead. These adults were idiots and had no clue of the reality of the society into which they had entered.

DOS agents came to the CAC and escorted the families away.

★★★

After what seemed like an eternity, two agents from the Hostage Crisis Team finally came to the CAC. One held his hand out to Alex and Alien.

"Hey, my name's Jeffrey. Sorry we kept you waiting so long, but we're *really* busy." Jeffrey did not bother to introduce the other man and handed Alex and Alien temporary-access badges that would get them to the interior of the building. "C'mon, I'll take you up to where we can talk." Fighting the stiffness that had settled into his hip, Alex followed Jeffrey toward the Palace. The other agent walked behind them.

The interior of the Palace showed telltale signs of what had once been opulence, but it had turned into an overcrowded barrio. The activity was like the inside of an anthill, with people scurrying in every direction at the same time. Some of the hallways had been partitioned off as office space, and people had even claimed space under the massive, sweeping staircases and in maintenance closets. They stopped off at a bathroom constructed for Saddam's attendants; what remained of the former elegance was striking. The floor was marble—not just marble tile, but a gigantic piece of solid polished marble—and the vanity was marble with marbled panels, all complemented by gilded cartouches and color-washed walls and ceiling. Even the commodes and French-style bidets in each stall were marble. The original fixtures, presumably made of valuable metal, were all gone and replaced with cheap stainless steel.

Jeffrey led them to an upper floor, past a guarded checkpoint, and into a grand room set up like an amphitheater with scores of massive TV screens streaming videos from the entire country for DOS to monitor. Men and women with headsets worked diligently at whatever was their responsibility. It all reminded Alex of the films of NASA ground control he'd seen on TV. Jeffrey stopped at one of the stations and retrieved a fat folder and a notepad from the desk.

Finally, Jeffrey took them into a small room with a placard on the door that read *Interview*, which Alex knew was just another word for interrogation. Jeffrey saw Alex looking at the placard and said, "Not to worry. We'll just have some privacy in here so we can talk without distraction." Alex got an uneasy feeling deep in his gut.

The room was small, perhaps ten by ten feet, with a stout table in the center and four small folding chairs. The table looked sturdy enough to strap someone down on. One of the walls was covered with a large mirror, and Alex wondered if there were already people on the other side, watching them and taping their conversation. Alex looked at Alien and furrowed his brow. Alien shrugged.

Jeffrey dropped the folder and notepad on the table and sat, gesturing to Alex and Alien to have a seat at the opposite side of the table. The unnamed agent remained standing at the door with his arms folded in front of him.

Alex was about to ask what they had learned about Predator when Jeffrey held up his hand.

"First let me get some information about the two of you. Can we start with your full names, social security numbers, home of record, employment?" He spun his hand in circles and scrunched his nose. "Y'know, that sort of stuff."

When Jeffrey was satisfied that he knew enough important personal details about the two, he sat back in the chair and said, "And now, tell me about the incident at . . ." He leaned forward and opened the folder and read off the address and date of the attack on Valhalla.

Alex looked at Alien again, and again he got a shrug in response. Alex said, "OK, well, it was sometime after midnight, I think—"

Jeffrey held his hand up again to stop Alex and said, "Tell me about the events leading up to the incident first."

Alex took a deep breath and said, "Where do you want me to start? I mean, I think we were surveilled for several days and attacked three times before the night Predator disappeared."

"Try starting at the beginning. I want to hear how you came to circumvent the country invitations and visa process to come to work for your current company. And I want to hear *your version* of events from when you first arrived at Sheikh Ali's house."

Alex's internal alarms were sounding off now, but they had not yet separated him from Alien. Maybe they hadn't decided if Alex and Alien were bad people or not. But then, these guys were DOS amateurs and not CIA or FBI. *Hopefully.*

It took Alex and Alien almost three hours to recount events to Agent Jeffrey's satisfaction. Jeffrey took notes, flipped back and forth in his folder, and asked questions with an intolerant tone. Finally, Jeffrey stood and moved toward the door. Alex got to his feet as if to follow when the second agent stepped threateningly forward. Alex stopped as Jeffrey spun around and sneered, "You're not goin' anywhere."

Alex said, "What's this all about? We're looking for information about Predator. He's our friend. I don't know what game you're playing or what you think we might have done. But we came here of our own free will, and we're guilty of nothing and we're not hiding anything."

As Agent Jeffrey left the room he said sarcastically over his shoulder, "We'll see about that." The other agent assumed his post at the door and glared at Alex.

Alex and Alien sat there for another twenty minutes, wondering what fate had in store for them. Alex pictured himself being sent Stateside in chains to spend the next few decades in the federal penitentiary at Fort Leavenworth.

Suddenly Agent Jeffrey burst into the room and walked over to the mirror. He tapped a knuckle and said, "Turn off the tapes and video."

A moment later two more men wearing suits walked into the room and sat across from Alex. Agent Jeffrey stood by the door with his silent partner. One of the new men exuded an aura of authority. With closely cropped hair, a hawkish face, and piercing blue eyes, he appeared to be in his mid-forties. He remained silent and just looked at Alex. The other, younger man began with an even tone: "We know everything there is to know about you."

Alex shifted his hip slightly in order to get his foot underneath him so he could spring into action. He thought, *Go figure. We haven't done anything wrong, but somehow now we're going to take the fall for something. Well, I'm not going down without a fight.* He wondered if he could fight his way out of the embassy and get away and knew that was a ridiculous idea. Still, he would try.

The younger man raised a hand. "Relax, the interrogation was only a delay tactic as we checked you out and matched your story against what we already knew."

Alex's head spun as his brain registered that statement and his body began to relax. He thought, *These bastards are playing power-trip games because they can, and it almost just cost them the lives of at least a couple of their very special agents.*

The man continued, "We think you can help us—"

Alex shook his head and cut him off. "You have a very strange way of asking for help. I'll tell you what. You tell me who this person is"—he pointed at the older man sitting across from him—"then tell me what you know about Predator, and then I'll consider helping you."

The man doing the speaking said, "That's not how it works."

The older man raised his hand to the younger man and nodded. "My name is Special Agent Kinkaid, and I am the regional security officer for the US Diplomatic Security Service in Iraq. I am terribly sorry for the inconvenience, and I apologize if you feel that you have been treated like a criminal. Your friend that you call Predator was indeed alive as of this time three days ago. After your safe house was attacked, he was taken by Sheikh Ibrahim Khalaf Ali. The images you saw of him on Al Jazeera were of him being auctioned off. Three days ago, he was sold to an unknown buyer and transferred to an unknown location."

"What are you doing about it?" Alex insisted.

"I'm afraid there is little we *can* do about it until we get some intelligence regarding his location. Once that happens, we have many options."

Alex concluded that all these guys were the same. They all had an agenda, and rather than being up front with it, they used some sort of twisted subterfuge to achieve their goal.

"That's it? I mean, do you have teams out there hunting for him? Are you actively looking for the intelligence you need?"

"Again, we do what we can within the limits of our assets and authority. We've distributed the information to units in the field. Beyond that we have to be patient and let the information come to us in the same manner as before."

"Have you '*interviewed*' Sheikh Ali, like you just did us?"

Kinkaid shook his head. "Political considerations would preclude us from doing that."

Alex's temperature rose. "But if he's the one who kidnapped Predator and he obviously knows who has him now, are you just going to give him a pass?"

Alex thought he heard a "tsk, tsk, tsk" come from under Kinkaid's breath before he responded, "The prime minister has assured us that Sheikh Ali merely kept your friend safe and nursed him back to health, after which he was forced to hand him over to insurgents. Ali claims he has no knowledge of what happened subsequently or who has him now."

Alex's anger was now palpable. "Then why the games with us?"

Kinkaid leaned forward. "When our people spoke with Ali, he mentioned you repeatedly. Clearly, he took a liking to you. We want *you* to talk to him."

Alex sat back in his chair; he was not prepared for this. But now it all made sense. Their interrogation was about determining which side he was on. His final actions with his former company and Ali's affinity toward him could easily be construed as him being sympathetic with the enemy. He breathed deep. "What do you propose?"

An hour later, with Alien in agreement, Alex told Kinkaid, "I don't like you. I *definitely* don't like your boy Jeffrey, I don't like the games you play, and I'd like to tell you to kiss my ass . . . but I'll do it for Predator."

As Alex and Alien walked back to the transient tent, Alien said, "Y'know, these guys are amateur spooks. They're likely to get us killed."

Alex nodded. "Yeah, no doubt. I'm sure they think we're just an expendable outside chance for them to get their organization on the news for heroically rescuing a hostage and furthering their careers at our expense. But if it all goes badly, they don't even have to report us as casualties because nobody's interested in dead contractors. Even if it does get out, they have plausible deniability because we're just rogue contractors acting on our own accord."

Alien shook his head. "That's definitely a rosy picture. Your optimism is encouraging."

★★★

The team was not allowed to carry their weapons inside the embassy compound, but outside, even though it was called the "Green Zone"—safe relative to the "Red Zone" of greater Baghdad—was still a dangerous place. Recently the politicians had renamed the Green Zone the International Zone, or IZ. The IZ was the legitimate home to over 20,000 Iraqi civilians, but it was estimated that up to 20,000 additional unknowns had snuck in.

Alex and Alien retrieved their pistols and headed toward the main CAC, where they saw Jake talking on his phone. Visibly disturbed, he hung up and walked over to greet Alien.

Alien asked, "What's up, man? You don't seem to be your normal happy self."

Jake said, "Yeah, this place is so fucked up it's beyond belief. I had a female interpreter who didn't show up to work today, so I sent one of the men to check on her. Apparently, the wrong people found out that she was working for us, so they cut off her head, cut open her stomach, sewed her head up inside her stomach, and dropped her body off at her mother's house."

"Let not the believers take friends or helpers from unbelievers: if any do that, then in nothing will there be help from Allah: except in the way of precaution that you may guard yourself against them. Allah warns you of his wrath, for to Allah all shall return."

Koran 3:28

The following day, after a full morning of checking their vehicles and equipment, the team started out shortly after noon. Their route this time would take them east across the Tigris River, through Shiite-dominated Baghdad to Highway 2, and then north to Erbil. If all went well, they would arrive in about five hours.

They were traveling without a client. Jamison had indeed suffered a breakdown and was currently strapped to a gurney, awaiting medevac to Germany. USAID said his replacement would arrive from the States in a week or so. Alex figured that would give him time to take care of other business.

As they departed Assassins Gate and cleared the barrier, Bandito called, "Hadj checkin' us out at 3 o'clock."

A local man had pulled a phone out of his pocket and dialed it.

"Roger, let the games begin. Be alert."

The team accelerated northeast over the Tigris River and Al Jumariyah Bridge and into Sunni/Shiite-contested Baghdad.

Despite American optimism that Sunnis and Shiites could live peacefully together and rule with a coalition government, the members of these Islamic sects were more interested in genocide. The basis for the schism between Sunni and Shiite Muslims was their disagreement over who should have succeeded as the leader of Islam after the death of their prophet, Muhammed: Sunnis believed the rightful heir was Muhammed's father-in-law, Abu Bakr, while Shiites believed the rightful heir was Muhammed's cousin and son-in-law, Ali ibn Abi Talib.

Many Iraqis, perhaps over 60 percent, were Shiite. However, the minority Sunni population had dominated the region politically and militarily for centuries, and Saddam Hussein's dictatorship completely marginalized the Shiite population for the past thirty-five years. Now, with the arrival of the Americans, the Shiites had gained control of the government and turned the tables on the Sunnis. These sentiments extended to the roots of society where neighbors killed neighbors and took control of their property. The fight was on in Baghdad for control and survival.

The good news for Alex and his team was that at this time Shiites were more interested in killing Sunnis than Americans. But of course, they would not pass up the opportunity if one presented itself.

The team crossed the bridge and made their way through a roundabout, slowing down when necessary and speeding up when possible. Vehicular and pedestrian traffic seemed thin again, probably due to the local propensity to avoid the stifling midday heat. At Tayeran Square they passed several ambulances and IP vehicles cleaning up an apparent IED attack and accelerated on toward Mohamed Al-Qasim Highway, entering the northbound lane of the highway without incident.

Within a few minutes Lizard called on the radio, "Six, this is Three. We may have a tail. Busted-up white Toyota with rusted roof's been behind us since the bridge and keeps pace with us about two hundred yards back."

Alex keyed his mic. "Six, Roger, keep an eye on him. Let us know if he closes the distance. Keep on route."

"Three, roger."

"One, copy."

To shake a tail by taking an alternate route in the city was probably more dangerous than just being aware of the possible threat and reacting if the tail became aggressive.

Then Bandito came over the radio. "Big Army dead ahead, convoy, HMMWV gun trucks and HEMTTs." He pronounced the Army transport trucks acronym as "hemmit."

Alex responded, "Roger, US Flags and VS-17s up on the dash." As the team responded, Alex considered for a moment, and then called back, "Anyone in a big hurry to get to Erbil?"

As Alien shook his head Bandito responded, "One, not particularly."

Lizard said, "Three, more interested in getting back alive."

"OK, One, fall in behind the convoy and keep a respectable distance. Three, keep an eye on our tail."

"One, roger."

"Three, roger."

Their speed slowed dramatically, but so did the pucker factor.

About halfway between Baquba and Kirkuk, the Big Army trucks pulled off the highway at the site of a civilian tractor-trailer convoy that had been ambushed. The site was completely secured by Big Army, which had apparently been there for some time. Four burned-out F-350 Ford pickup trucks lay scattered along the road, along with four semis that had clearly been ransacked. Crates of ammunition and weapons that had not been stolen were stacked. While bodies and casualties had already been taken away, Alex saw the telltale black spots and long smears of dried blood in the road where men had made their last stand. Alex looked at the crates of weapons and wondered what the insurgents had gotten away with.

As they passed the last pickup truck, Alien pointed at the bumper. "Look, it's our boys! That's Dog's truck! Holy shit."

Alex saw the half-melted Mighty Mouse sticker that had adorned the back of Dog's truck from their last company when they were running guns. He said, "Yeah, and there's four gun trucks here, so it's not likely that anyone got away." If he were still with that company, this might have been his convoy.

From there, they raced up the highway to the Erbil Governorate line and relative safety.

After the team negotiated the first Kurdish checkpoint, Lizard called, "Six, Three; our tail dropped off. I say again, the vehicle tailing us turned around at the last checkpoint."

What they did not see was a man wearing binoculars and speaking into his cell phone on the military crest of a hill overlooking the highway. Nor did they see the two nondescript sedans and the blue bongo truck that pulled out of the first village they passed to begin a tag-team surveillance of Alex and his team.

Finally, they did not see the driver of the bongo truck dial his cell phone as the team negotiated the entrance to Asgard.

★★★

Alex was sitting alone after the debrief when Odin walked in and smacked him on the back hard enough to dislocate his shoulder.

"Well, my boy, that was quite a run you made the other day. Thank you for keeping my men and the client alive. You did really good."

Alex acted like he was putting his arm back in the socket where it belonged and said, "I have a good team, sir. They've taught me well."

"Good, give credit when and where it's due, and always take all the blame for yourself. Noble. I like that. Even though you delivered Jamison to them in a basket, the director of USAID recognized you by name and highly appreciates what you've done." Odin sat down across from Alex. "Tell me what the State Department has to say."

Alex rose to close the door and then took his seat again. "They made me a proposal that I'm finding hard to refuse."

Odin raised his eyebrows. "Tell me about it."

"All they're really saying is that Predator was alive and was a prisoner of your Sheikh Ali, who sold him a few days ago. Ali pleads ignorance and has powerful political friends to back his play."

Odin grimaced. "That lying piece of shit. He convinced me he had nothing to do with it, and Predator could have been in the next room. How could I be so naïve? Go on."

"Well, they said he took a liking to me, and they want me to try to pump him for information."

"How the hell do they expect you to do that? This dude's a first-class deceiver on his own turf, and you only met him, what? Once?"

"They were hoping you would agree to go with me and appeal to him."

"HA! If I ever see him again, I'll kill him."

Alex looked at him coolly. "You can leave that to me."

Odin looked into Alex's eyes and felt a chill go up his spine. Then his eyes narrowed, and he said sternly, "You have other concerns beside yourself, Predator, and revenge. You don't need to turn assassin for Uncle Sam."

Alex knew he was talking about Linda. "Do you think I'll be much company to anyone for the rest of my life if I don't at least try to help my brother when he needs me?"

Odin drew a deep breath and let it out. "I suppose not."

"In a nutshell, you can get us an audience with Ali. If we can talk reason into him and he levels with us, we just pass that on to DOS and let them handle it. If not, then I'll take a vacation from Asgard. They'll hook me up with everything I need; you won't be involved or connected with anything that happens after that."

The smell of her hair, the taste of her breath, and the feel of her body pressed against his convinced him that he knew what heaven was like.

She breathed in his ear as she hung on to his neck, "I love you, I missed you so, and I was beyond worried about you. I can't go on like this anymore. I want to go home and start a family with you and live happily ever after."

Alex held her close and put a finger to her lips. "Linda, I can't tell you how much that means to me. Words will not do justice to my feelings for you. I love you too, like nothing else I've ever felt. I came back to this insanity because I wanted the chance to be with you."

"I know, and I'm so sorry to have brought you back here," she said. "Now I want you out. I want both of us out of here, together."

He said, "I want that too . . ."

She pulled her head back and looked into his eyes. "But?"

He took a deep breath and said, "I have one more mission to do."

He felt her body go limp. Her shoulders sagged, and her head fell to his shoulder. "It has to do with Predator, doesn't it?"

"Yes, it does."

She hugged him tighter, and he responded in kind.

"There's nothing I can say to talk you out of it, is there?"

"Do you think we can live with ourselves if you do?"

She shook her head and buried it deeper in his chest. "No, this is one of the reasons I love you. I know you won't abandon your friend."

His heart was pounding, and he wrapped his body over every inch of her.

"You have to promise me, though," she sobbed. She leaned back and looked into his eyes.

He whispered, "Anything."

"As soon as this is over, we go home, get married, and start our family."

"I promise."

As she kissed him, he tasted her tears, and he knew he would never disappoint her again.

✯✯✯

"And Allah said to the angels: 'I am with you, go and strengthen the faithful. I shall fill the hearts of the Infidels with terror. So smite them on their necks and at every bone joint.'"

Koran 8:12

Haider was excited at the prospects of his new task. This would be his most ambitious project so far—a 4,000-gallon water truck. He figured he could pack it with at least 25,000 pounds of explosives, but that was overkill. Instead, he would fabricate a container for inside the water tank and pack it with about 2,000 pounds of his special fertilizer mixture and another 2,000 pounds of C-4, shaping the container to direct the blast sideways, directly into the target. This bomb would make a spectacular explosion— more than enough to blast through the T-walls and take out the barracks at their target.

That was only a fraction of the C-4 they had procured from the raid on that convoy last night. The fools should not have been on the road after dark; no one came to their assistance.

His IEDs were a masterpiece. The first took out the first security truck, and the tractor trailers behind it stopped. When the other three security trucks came to the aid of their stricken brothers, the second set of daisy-chained IEDs obliterated the entire security detail. Mullah Uday's men simply had to mop up: cut off heads, mutilate bodies, and transfer cargo to the mullah's trucks, which had been following at a distance.

Haider marveled to think that he was literally walking in the footsteps of the Prophet Mohammed. *Peace and blessings be upon him.* He now knew what euphoria the Prophet must have felt after a successful raid on caravans traveling through the desert.

★ ★ ★

Standing outside the room, Mullah Uday nodded to his lieutenant, Yasin. Yasin stepped in and called the men to attention.

Mullah Uday left the men at the rigid position of attention as he walked around and through their ranks. He looked for physical fitness worthy of soldiers of Allah, and he looked into their eyes to measure their devotion to the Cause of Allah. He saw none wanting, and none wavered. He was pleased; 150 competent and dedicated Mujahideen should be plenty of men for blocking positions, a support team, and an assault team on their next objective.

He strode to the front of the room and told them to be seated. As one, they crossed their legs and dropped to the floor.

Mullah Uday placed his right hand over his heart and said, "Praise be to Allah, and his Prophet Mohammed."

The men in the room responded as one, "*Allahu Akbar*!"

"I am pleased that you are all here with me now in this great struggle of ours. Our next mission is one of revenge. We will strike a terrible blow against the invaders and send to hell a troop of *kafir* mercenaries who have killed too many of our brothers. The reconnaissance has already begun. Yasin will assign each of your unit commanders your tasks. Subordinate leaders will have one day to plan, coordinate actions, and disseminate orders to individuals. We will spend two days rehearsing movement to the objective, actions on the objective, and exfiltration. On the fourth day from today we will begin our infiltration. This is not meant to be a suicide mission, save for one dedicated martyr. I expect you all to return to your families five days hence."

Mullah Uday nodded to Yasin and stepped aside.

Yasin pulled away a blanket hanging on the wall to reveal a schematic map of a several-block area in Erbil centered on the compound known to the Americans as Asgard.

"Fight them and Allah will punish them by your hands, lay them low, and cover them with shame. He will help you over them."

Koran 9:14

Alex, Odin, and Haymaker came to a stop in front of Sheikh Ibrahim Khalaf Ali's compound. Fifty meters behind them, Charlie One, with Digger and Bandito in the front and Alien low in the back seat, pulled up and stopped.

After surveilling the area for a few minutes, Odin stepped out from the driver's seat, and Alex emerged from the passenger seat while Haymaker remained low and out of sight in the back seat.

Surrounded by a six-foot-high wall, the house itself was a large, modern version of a traditional Iraqi home. The bottom floor was a rectangle about 150 feet long at the front and perhaps half that length deep. It was kind of plain but obviously new and very sturdy looking. The top floor was about half the size of the first floor, surrounded by a wide veranda and a three-foot parapet. The structure on top of the house reminded Alex of the superstructure on a ship; it looked more like a fancy bunker than the second floor of a home. At each of the four corners of the top floor grew immaculately trimmed bushes—in large planters, Alex assumed—behind which he spotted movement, probably guards.

Sheikh Ali's men were ready for Alex and Odin; the front gate slowly swung open. Alex noted that it was remotely controlled and also looked very sturdy.

Inside the compound, two men in local dress and sporting AK-47s met them and indicated that they should stop where they were. Alex glimpsed two other men on the roof trying to observe them while remaining inconspicuous. The first man walked around Alex and Odin, visually inspecting them. When he was satisfied, he pointed at the Glock pistols at their right hips and gestured to a small table with a cushion on it. Both Alex and Odin pulled the pistols out of their holsters with their left hands so as not to appear threatening and set the guns down on the cushion. Satisfied, the guard motioned for them to follow. The other guard took up the rear.

The front door to the house opened before the guard reached it. Alex thought, *Cameras, and access remotely controlled.* He quickly glanced around and figured the cameras were disguised as stucco flowers carved into the building's façade.

They were led through a short hallway flanked by open doors to rooms that were elegantly furnished and decorated in traditional Arab fashion. Then they emerged into a modestly sized inner courtyard. The yard was covered but with open space between the second floor and the roof to keep the direct sun at bay and yet allow cool air to circulate. The floor was adorned with thick, richly decorated, plush handwoven rugs. Three low, ornate couches in the center of the room formed an open triangle around a short but large and heavy-looking cherrywood coffee table. The periphery of the yard was ringed with Palm Suite façade, a large Palm Suite fireplace, and decorated with large plants in elegantly painted ceramic pots. Through the façade, Alex saw several doors that must lead to private rooms, the kitchen, and whatever else the house contained. On the table was a pitcher of orange juice so cold that it dripped with moisture, three glasses, and bowls of fruits and nuts. Cool air blew down on him from vents on the walls.

Ali swept into the room in dramatic fashion with his keffiyeh billowing behind him.

"My friends, I am so glad and honored to have you visit my humble home." He rushed to Odin and gripped his hand and shook it vigorously. "I trust your family is well. You have waited entirely too long to grace my house with your noble presence." He spun around to Alex, grabbed his hand, and pulled him close and kissed both of his cheeks. "And my favored guardian angel,

Mr. Alex. I am indebted to you for your efforts to save and avenge my nephews. I am so sorry things turned out so badly. Please, please, both of you have a seat and make yourselves comfortable."

He gestured to the couches and poured them glasses of orange juice.

Alex and Odin took a seat on the edge of one couch. Ali furrowed his brow and exclaimed, "Please, don't feel you need to be formal. You are in my house. Please relax and be comfortable. I will soon have a feast fit for a king served to you."

Alex began to feel a bit overwhelmed.

Odin rose to his feet and said, "Sheikh Ali, I can't thank you enough for your hospitality, and I don't mean to be rude, but we are here on business, and we have little time to spare."

Ali shook his head. "Of course. I know. Americans—always straight to the point and seldom willing to relax and socialize. You must learn to enjoy this life; the next one may not be so pleasant and will begin all too soon."

Ali sat across from them, and Odin sat back down. Ali asked, "So, how can I be of assistance to your business efforts?"

Odin said, "We are here to ask you about our man Predator."

"Of course." His brow furrowed again. "He came to me after the attack on my property. I nursed him back to health and he was recently kidnapped."

Odin contained himself quite well. "Why didn't you tell me he was here?"

Ali looked directly at Odin and said, "He asked me not to. He said he was afraid that he would be punished for failing at his task. I owed him"—he gestured to Alex—"and Mr. Alex here, for avenging the murder of my nephews."

Alex knew he had prepared that answer.

Odin drew a breath. "Who has him? Where is he?"

Ali's eyes narrowed. "It is as I told your State Department and their soldiers: I do not know." Then his face became stern and he struck his fist on the table. "If I knew, I swear to Allah, I would take my own revenge upon them. He was my guest and I was obligated to protect him."

Alex decided that response was rehearsed as well.

"Sheikh Ali, how is it that a man of your position does not know what happens in his domain?"

Ali stood and aggressively declared, "There was a time when I knew everything that happened from here to Baghdad. But that is not so anymore. Now I have to contend with foreigners of all persuasions squeezing me from every side and at every turn!"

That outburst did not seem rehearsed.

Ali looked at Alex and went on, "I do not know who has your friend, but if I find out anything, I will be sure to let you know."

★★★

Back in the car, Alex keyed his mic. "One, Three, this is Six; how's it look?"

Lizard responded, "Six, Three. It's clear. I say again, the coast is clear."

Alex said, "Roger, prep the package for delivery."

Bandito keyed his mic. "This is One, good copy."

Odin turned his vehicle around and without hurry drove back the way they came. Charlie One fell in behind them.

As soon as they were out of sight of the house, Alex climbed into the back seat and Haymaker climbed into the front passenger seat. Alex called again, "Three, Six, how's it look?" He pulled the desert-camouflage ghillie suit up over his boots and clothes, zipped it up in the front, and flipped the hood over his head, tying it down at his neck. He put his arms through the straps of his small assault pack that would provide everything he needed for a few days if necessary.

"Six, Three; all clear, all clear."

"Six, roger."

"One, roger."

Odin reduced his speed as he took a wide right turn, placing the vehicle near the left edge of the road. The back door opened, and Alex rolled out into a wadi alongside the road. Seconds later, the ghillie suit–clad Alien rolled into the same wadi.

Bandito called on the radio, "Package delivered."

"Three, roger, I have eyes on the package. Looking good."

Odin responded, "Six, roger."

Odin and Charlie Three drove on for a few more miles and pulled off the road and parked behind an abandoned building.

About a mile from the drop-off point, Lizard lay flat on his stomach, covered with a camouflage net on the military crest of a large sand dune. For another ten minutes he continued to observe, with binoculars, the road and terrain around where the rest of the team had deposited the "packages."

When he was satisfied that the recon team had not been compromised, he keyed his handset.

"This is Three, all secure. I'm pullin' out."

Alien whispered back, "Alien, roger. We'll call on Ma Bell if we need anything."

"Three, roger. Good luck."

Lizard backed down the hill and called in his security team. They mounted up and headed back to where Odin and Charlie One waited for them, to return to Asgard and begin planning and preparation for the next phase of the operation.

After adjusting their senses to the environment, Alex and Alien slowly slithered on their stomachs to put some distance between themselves and the dirt road. They circled around the bend in the road and worked their way back toward Ali's compound. As they crawled, an assortment of desert wildlife made known their displeasure at the human invasion: a large camel spider ran across Alex's hand, which creeped him out tremendously; a desert viper burst out of the sand inches from his face and slithered away;

and some small, angry critters were biting his back over and over again. It took them the rest of the afternoon to find a culvert and drainage pipe suitable for crossing the road so that they could circle the house and observe from every possible angle. As the light faded, Alex and Alien observed their crossing site, the house at a distance, and behind them to guard against unexpected visitors. Alex decided on vantage points that he would use around the compound. Alien would stay in his current position to provide Alex with covering fire should anything go wrong.

At full dark Alex heard a dog bark in the distance, but no such alarm sounded at Ali's house, and he edged into the culvert and crossed the road. Alex was grateful that Muhammed had thought dogs were filthy beasts; there were few here to alert the locals of strangers lurking about. As Alex crawled forward he thought back to when he was still in the Army and several Iraqi children had come within twenty meters of his fighting position and proceeded to beat a little puppy to death because they knew it would bother him and he would do nothing to them. They had laughed at the mutilated puppy and at Alex. Alex wanted to shoot them, but he did not.

At his first observation point Alex determined that the security control center was the superstructure with large windows located on the roof of the house. Five guards were on duty: one was stationed at each corner of the roof and camouflaged by the potted bushes, and the fifth centered himself in the control room in front a bank of monitors that were obviously the closed-circuit TVs of the security system.

From their earlier visit, Alex knew that the interior of the house was wired with cameras and remotely controlled doors. He needed to determine if the perimeter and the roof were rigged with early-warning devices.

Between his binoculars and NODs, Alex watched the guards mill about their posts and lean against the parapet. He concluded that there were no intrusion sensors or booby traps on the roof. By 11 PM, it was clear that all the guards were sound asleep.

Alex moved from point to point on his reconnaissance of the house. Shortly after midnight he observed a large canine, maybe a jackal, move laterally in front of him and approach the compound wall. Dim lights at the corners of the exterior wall suddenly lit up, and a red light flashed in the control room on top of Ali's house. *Motion sensors.*

The jackal ran away into the dark, and Alex saw the guard in the control room stand and stretch and then walk out to a perimeter guard and speak to him quietly. The second guard went to another and woke him also. The guard from the control room walked to the parapet and peered into the dim light—the actions of a man whose sleep had been disturbed countless times for false alarms. Along with the two guards he had roused, he went back into the control room.

With their AK-47s slung over their shoulders and flashlights in hand, the two guards left the house through the front door, and as the front gate opened for them, they began a lackadaisical sweep of the perimeter. If there were cameras around the exterior of the compound, there would be no need for such a patrol. When the two guards completed their sweep, they reentered the front gate and returned to the roof. The three guards who were still awake walked out onto the roof together and smoked cigarettes before returning to their slumber. The guards never closed the door to the control room.

There was a carport covered by a flat extension of the second floor, with two pillars rising from the perimeter wall to support the roof.

A plan began to form in Alex's mind.

✴✴✴

"Prepare against them whatever arms and cavalry you can muster, that you may strike terror into the hearts of the enemies of Allah and your own enemies, and others besides them not known to you, but known to Allah. Whatever you spend in the Cause of Allah will be paid back to you in full, and no wrong will be done to you."

Koran 8:60

Haider followed Mullah Uday up the narrow stairs to the fifth floor and into a large, shadowy room. From two big holes in the wall serving as windows billowed striped burlap sacks to provide shade and break up the outline of anything within the room when viewed from outside. On the far end of the room, facing the windows and deep in the shadows, was a pair of long-range observation binoculars on a tripod, behind which a man repeatedly looked through the eyepieces, made small adjustments to the dials, and took notes on a clipboard.

Mullah Uday pointed through the windows and said, "There's your target." Haider looked at the compound about 3,000 yards away. Even at such a distance, from this vantage point he could see clearly inside the compound and discern activity as well as count vehicles and people moving to and fro.

Uday gestured toward the binoculars and told Haider, "Take a look."

Haider stepped over to the binoculars as the man taking notes backed away. He pressed his face to the eyepieces and was shocked. Aside from the fact that he now saw inside the compound in startling detail and clarity, he found himself gazing at the most beautiful woman he had ever seen. Her silky, straight dark hair reflected the light and flowed past her shoulders like shimmering waves. She wore a white blouse through which he could see her white brazier hardly obscuring her large, perfectly formed breasts. Her shirt was tucked into formfitting khaki trousers that accentuated the curves of her hips.

It had been years since he had seen anything so beautiful and revealing, "Oh my" escaped his lips, and he felt a stirring in his loins.

Mullah Uday pushed Haider aside and peered through the glass. "Oh yes, but that, my friend, is not for you. I have already promised her to Yasin first." He stepped away and told the other man, "Show him the water point."

The man referred to his notes and then turned the knob below the binoculars a few clicks to the right. When Haider looked through the binoculars again, he saw pipes sticking through the T-walls, with valves at the end for water intake and others for sewage extraction. He could also see the tops of black water tanks inside the compound. That would be Haider's target.

Uday said, "The long building adjacent to the water tanks is the barracks where the mercenary soldiers sleep. Your bomb has to be big enough to kill all of them as you create the breach."

Haider looked again and said, "That should not be a problem, but I'll increase the explosives and direct the blast toward the wall to make certain that there's nothing left of the wall or that building. Your men will be able to walk through unopposed."

Uday rubbed his hands together like a child. "Good, good. Allah be praised, our assault team is rehearsing now and should be on the way soon."

Haider asked, "How will you get them and their equipment past Kurdish security?"

"That, my friend, will not be a problem. There are plenty of locals here who helped us when we ruled this country and who, under threat of exposure, are more than willing to help us again. We already have men in the high points all around the target. Right now they are conducting surveillance like we are here.

They are also creating range cards with distances and elevations to target reference points for their machine guns and RPGs to prevent any reinforcements from arriving when we launch the attack, and to cover our withdrawal when we are finished. For the assault team, we also have American uniforms, vehicles, identification cards, and placards to help us past the checkpoints and to assist us again with extraction."

Haider looked again through the binoculars at the compound known as Asgard.

"And those who believe and emigrate and strive hard in the Cause of Allah, and those who give them sanctuary and aid—these are in truth the Believers. For them is the forgiveness of sins and provisions most generous."

Koran 8:74

Alex and Alien were led into a State Department safe house in Erbil by none other than Very Special Agent Jeffrey No-Last-Name. "There it is: everything you asked for."

Alex pulled his list out of his pocket and smoothed it open on the hood of one of two brand-new, factory up-armored Toyota Corollas. "Let's start with the weapons."

Jeffrey opened the rear door of a Corolla, and Alien reached in and extracted an M4 with an Aimpoint optic attached to the Picatinny rail.

Jeffrey said, "Ammo and mags are in the trunk."

Alien nodded as he cracked open the rifle and pulled out the bolt to look at it. He reinserted the bolt and snapped the upper receiver back in place. Then he performed a functions check, and when he was satisfied, he turned the weapon over on its side to read the serial number to Alex. He squinted and he flipped the rifle over and then back again.

"What's up with this? There's no serial number?"

Jeffrey smirked. "Yup, none of this stuff really exists . . . and neither do you."

Alien looked at him. "I guess that means if we get in a jam, you're not coming to help us out."

"Right again. And quite frankly"—he patted the trunk of a Corolla—"I hope you all die in these fine cars here."

Alien took an aggressive step toward Jeffrey and snapped, "What's your problem?"

Jeffrey recoiled and almost fell over backward.

Alien stopped. "I get it; you're awfully tough when you're in your interrogation room and you hold all the cards, but out here in the mean streets of reality, your true color shows through. You're just a weak, insecure little man who preys on other people when they're at a disadvantage. You resent the fact that you must rely on real men to do your work for you. I'll bet you fit right in back home in DC."

Agent Jeffrey recovered his balance and straightened his back. "No, that's not it at all. I've known prima donnas like you before. You think you know everything and can do anything. You're not above the law, and if you don't die soon, I'll find a reason to arrest you one of these days."

Alien laughed, "That's exactly what I would expect a hypocritical, weaselly little rat prick like you to say—claim *we're* law breakers when we're here doing *your* dirty work because *you* can't. Is this stuff you're giving us and what you're telling us to do in keeping with US law even in a combat zone? Or might *you* be doing something *you* ought to go to jail for?"

Alex had heard enough. "OK, ladies, can we get back to work?"

Alien leaned into the back seat and said, "Right, there's eight of these and eight Glock 17s." Alex heard him work the slide on a Glock and give it a functions check.

"Ho, ho, ho. What have we here?" Alien pulled two long

weapons cases out of the car. He set them on the ground and opened one.

Alex leaned over him and peered at a beautiful, brand-new, bolt-action rifle sporting a Picatinny rail along the top of the receiver. "Niiiice."

"Yeah, man, just like we asked for." Alien pulled the rifle out of the cut-to-fit foam and turned it over admiringly. "M24A3, Remington 700 cambered in .338 Lapua Magnum." Alien set the rifle down and reached back into the case. "Five mags, a bipod, a SureFire suppressor, a Leupold MK4 8.5 to 25 by 50 variable power telescope, and"—he lifted the final item out of the case—"an AN/PVS 22 universal night sight."

Alex said, "Stop it, you're getting me excited."

"Yeah, me too." Alien looked over at Jeffrey. "The serial numbers have been removed from these too."

Agent Jeffrey said, "Yeah, but that doesn't mean we don't want them back."

Alien replaced the items and opened the other case. When he was satisfied, he reached back into the car and returned with another case, smaller and fatter this time. He popped open the latches and said, "And take a look at this bad bitch." He held up a short, fat weapon with a large barrel and an enormous cylinder behind the breach. "A Milkor 40-millimeter automatic six-shot revolving grenade launcher with an M2A1 reflex sight."

After they confirmed there was plenty of ammunition, body armor, medical kits, squad radios and other essential equipment, they bid a fond farewell to Agent Jeffrey and drove the two Toyotas back to Asgard.

★★★

Alex looked at the seven men seated in front of him before he spoke. Odin and Asgard Three stood at the back of the room.

Alex took a deep breath and said, "You've each volunteered for this mission, but I have to make it perfectly clear that we will be acting entirely on our own. This operation is not sanctioned by the company, and when we roll out the gate you will no longer be employees of the company. When we return you may renegotiate your employment with Asgard Three."

Alex hesitated and then went on, "In addition, I honestly think that the agency that funded and directed our operation will disavow any knowledge of our association with them should anything go wrong. We have no support from Big Army, and our actions will likely be considered criminal in the eyes of the local coalition military commander."

He looked around and continued, "And finally, I don't expect our objective to divulge any useful information without serious *physical persuasion.*" He paused and then said, "If any of these circumstances are issues for you, no one will hold it against you if you withdraw at this time." He paused again to allow anyone who wished to leave the room time to do so. None did.

"Very well then. Our mission is to infiltrate Sheikh Ali's compound in order to find the whereabouts of Predator."

★★★

Lying on her side and resting her head on his chest, Linda slowly ran her hand across his taut stomach, through his chest hair, and finally she cupped his pectoral muscle firmly in her palm with his nipple poking between her thumb and index finger. She leaned her head over and sucked it into her mouth, kneading it with her tongue and teasing it with her teeth.

He groaned with pleasure. "You're ready for more?"

She looked up at him and breathed, 'The question is, are *you* ready for more?" She moved her hand between his legs. "Oh yeah."

She took him in her mouth, and when he was ready, she climbed on top of him and guided him gently inside her. Pinning his arms above his head, she raised herself up so her breasts were almost touching his face, and slowly moved back and forth until he was fully inside her. He could stand it no longer and wrested his arms free to cup her breasts in his hands, flicker his tongue across her nipples, and suck each in its turn.

Soon, she felt the now familiar sensation between her legs stir, and she pushed herself onto him harder and lowered herself, pressing her breasts against his chest. His mouth searched for hers. As they kissed, she rocked with more purpose until she wanted to cry out as the spasms of pleasure coursed through her body. She was still convulsing when she felt him pulse inside her, and she opened her eyes just enough to see the expression of ecstasy on his face. They lay there in that most intimate embrace, softly kissing and nuzzling each other, for quite some time.

Alex whispered in her ear, "I am *so* in love with you."

Linda smiled and whispered back, "Good, because I think I'm pregnant."

★★★

Alien snickered and said, "Hey, man, what's up with you? You look like the cat that caught the mouse."

Alex realized he couldn't wipe the smile off his face. "I got good news last night."

"You win the lottery?"

"Nope, better'n that."

Alien raised his eyebrows. "What the hell could be better than that? Let me see." He rubbed his chin and then pointed at Alex. "Oh, I get it. It has to do with a woman. You're in trouble!"

Alex shook his head. "Damn, you're good. Yeah, it has to do with a woman. Linda agreed to marry me, and after this operation we're going home. She thinks she's pregnant."

Alien whistled. "Good for you. That's awesome!" He grabbed Alex's hand and gave him a big man hug and slapped him on the back. "You're one lucky man. Getting an incredible woman and getting the hell out of here all at the same time. Let's go get Predator so we can have a bachelor's party and fight over who'll be the best man."

"Sounds good to me. But I haven't talked to the old man yet, and he might have other ideas for my future—like a funeral."

At that moment, Odin lumbered up to the vehicle before Alex could duck out of sight. "Hey, Cap. C'mere, will ya?"

They stepped out of immediate earshot. "What's up, boss?"

"First off, let's keep it at that."

Alex looked at him strangely. "Excuse me, sir?"

"Don't be doing anything stupid like calling me 'Dad.'"

Alex's eyes went wide, and he considered running away.

"Boss will do fine, for now at least."

Alex thought, *Holy crap, she told him already*, but he said, "Anything that makes you happy, boss." Alex decided to get it all out before Odin went any further. "By the way, sir, I've been meaning to ask you something."

Odin eyed him. "And what might that be?"

"Well, sir, I know you're a smart man, and while we've been trying to be discrete about things, I expect you know that Linda and I have feelings for each other. I'd prefer to say this when we have more time and I don't feel so awkward, but I love your daughter and she loves me, and I'd like your approval to ask for her hand in marriage." Alex took a step back just in case Odin decided to hit him with one of those enormous fists.

Odin looked at Alex, and suddenly everything that was hard about this warrior became soft.

"Son, you've made my daughter happy, and you've earned a place in my and my wife's hearts too. I believe you're sincere, and I believe you'll go to your grave before you let any harm come to her. We can talk about it when you come back, but for now the most important thing for you to do is retain your focus on the mission at hand. I need you to stay alive and bring my men back in one piece. If anything happens to you, my daughter may not recover."

Odin became stern again and poked his finger in Alex's chest.

"Get this done, do it well, and then take my daughter and my grandchild home."

Alex's eyes welled up, and a frog snuck into his throat. He croaked, "Yes sir, I'll be back, come hell or high water."

Odin said, "You do that," and turned and walked away.

Alex looked up at the veranda of the main house to see Linda leaning against the doorframe with a wicked smile on her face. He smiled back, looked around to make sure no one was watching him, and blew her a kiss. Linda grabbed it from midair and pressed it to her heart.

★★★

"Go forth, unarmed or heavily armed! Struggle in Allah's Cause with your possessions and your lives! That is better for you, did you but know."

Koran 9:41

Haider's special water truck slowed as it neared the Iranian border guards on the road from Piranshahr to Erbil. The driver was nervous but in fair control of his demeanor, as his partner in the passenger seat fingered the initiation device that would vaporize them all. Two Iranian guards with AK-47s at the ready approached the truck with suspicion. Suddenly, an Iranian Army officer emerged from his bunker and yelled at the two guards. They both stopped where they were. The officer walked up to the driver side of the truck and stepped up onto the running board, thrusting his head and a hand inside the cab. The driver recoiled and held up a sealed manila envelope. The officer snatched the envelope, ripped it open, and peered inside. He then smiled broadly, stuffed the envelope in his shirt, and stepped off the running board. He signaled to the guards to stand down and waved the driver to proceed through the Iranian border checkpoint toward Kurdish Iraq.

Barely a thousand feet further on, the driver entered a large, covered, bunker-like structure under which he was expected to have his truck and papers inspected. He was guided into a search pit by armed Kurdish guards and made to dismount the vehicle. The driver left another, larger envelope on the driver's seat. He was told to dismount his vehicle and was then led around the truck to open all its doors and compartments. Then the two men were escorted to a separate bunker where they were physically patted down under the watchful eye of an American soldier.

After several minutes, the two were told that they could remount their vehicle and proceed. As the driver walked toward his vehicle, he was startled by a low growl from a black devil dog staring at him with its fangs bared, snarling and salivating. The handler pulled back on the chain, and the two men scrambled into the truck and closed the doors as quickly as possible. The envelope was gone.

The driver fired up the truck and pulled out of the search pit onto Highway 3, which ran from the Iranian border to Erbil.

As evening set in, a seemingly American military convoy slowed as it neared the Kurdish checkpoint on Highway 2. A clean-shaven, blond, blue-eyed lieutenant colonel without his hat jumped out of the HMMWV leading the convoy and ran up to the guards, waving a piece of paper and sporting his military identification in a brassard on his sleeve.

"Hey, man, I've got five Hemmits and four Hummers and a hundred tired troops heading to Erbil and I'm very late." He pushed the paper into the hand of the nearest guard, who looked over his shoulder at his supervisor. Glancing at the convoy, the supervisor nodded and jerked his head to one side, indicating that they should let the convoy pass.

The officer snatched the paper back from the guard and waved his hand above his head as he ran back to the HMMWV. "Thanks, bro, you've done a great service to your nation. I won't forget you." He jumped back into his truck.

The Kurds never gave them a second look as Mullah Uday's main assault team pulled through the checkpoint and picked up speed, heading toward Erbil.

"Wherever you are death will find you, even if you are in towers strong and high!"

Koran 4:78

With their lights off and brake lights disengaged, Bull and Digger pulled the two Corollas well off the road, dismounted, and moved to high ground to overwatch their vehicles. Bull said softly into his mic, "Victors set."

Alex came back, "Roger."

Sometime later, Alien and Psycho settled on a small knoll about 500 meters behind the house. They checked their sniper systems to ensure that they had a good view of their primary targets and likely avenues of approach through which the unexpected might attempt to intervene. Alien searched for Ali's car and signs of life from within the compound. When he was satisfied that Ali was home, he keyed his mic and whispered, "Support team set, target identified."

Alex responded, "Roger." He looked at his assault team, which consisted of Bandito, Lizard, and Haymaker. He nodded and led them toward the back of Ali's compound. The wadi allowed them to move crouched over with relatively good speed.

Two hundred meters from the house, Alex paused and allowed the men to observe the house. After each of them gave him a thumbs-up, Alex crawled out of the wadi and slithered along on his stomach, edging closer to the house.

About fifty yards from the house, Alex halted and held his arms out to his sides. Bandito and Lizard came abreast of him and trained their weapons toward the house. Alex then popped an infrared chemlight, and almost immediately he heard Alien's voice in his earpiece: "Marker identified." Alex stuffed the chemlight back into its wrapper and into his pocket. He turned to Haymaker, pointed at him, and motioned toward the compound. Clad in a ghillie suit, Haymaker crawled forward by himself.

After several anxious minutes, the exterior lights came on, and the red strobe emanated from the control room. Although his view was not good, as Alex expected, the guard in the control room rousted two guards and sent them out to sweep the perimeter. The front gate opened, and the two guards meandered clockwise around the house. As they neared Haymaker, Alex fired first, and with a cough from his suppressed M4, one of the guards went down. A heartbeat later, two more coughs from Bandito and Lizard put down the second guard. The first guard started groaning, and Haymaker put another bullet in him to finish him off.

The sound of the suppressors was enough to lure the guard from the control room, who moved toward the edge of the roof. The .338 Lapua Magnum round hitting his chest made more noise than his lifeless body falling to the ground. Now the two remaining guards' sleep was disturbed by these strange, muffled noises, and they both emerged curiously from their posts only to simultaneously meet the same fate as their boss.

Alien keyed his mic. "Targets down."

Alex replied, "Moving." He rose and ran as fast but as quietly as he could toward the wall of the compound. Haymaker reached the wall and crouched with his hands cupped and fingers laced together. As Alex reached the wall, he placed his boot into Haymaker's hands, and Haymaker heaved him up so that with little effort he was on top of the wall and moving quickly toward the carport. He crouched at the carport and interlaced his fingers as Haymaker had done and lifted Bandito up to the second floor, and then Lizard, and finally Haymaker. Haymaker helped Alex up as the other two quickly searched the roof to ensure all was clear.

Alex entered the control room and proceeded down the steps into the main house. At the bottom, the team began systematically clearing rooms. Alex worried that Ali was not at home, or worse, that he might have received warning of their impending invasion and had a counterattack waiting for them. Finally, as they entered the last room, they found Ali fast asleep in a lavish four-poster bed draped with silk curtains.

Alex slung his M4 across his back and drew his Glock. He placed the barrel of the gun against Ali's temple and pulled the blankets off the bed to make sure Ali wasn't hiding a weapon under the sheets.

Ali woke with a start and cried out, but Alex pistol-whipped him in the face and snarled, "Shut up." Ali grabbed his face and cowered.

Lizard set a chair down in the middle of the room, and Bandito and Haymaker snatched Ali out of bed and tied him to the chair. Then Lizard and Haymaker left the room to establish security.

Alex keyed his mic and said, "Objective secure."

Alien responded, "Roger, all clear."

Alex sat on the edge of the bed, facing Ali. Ali's eyes were as big as saucers, and blood trickled down his face onto his immaculately white night shirt.

Alex said calmly, "I expect you to be perfectly honest with me tonight; your life depends on it."

Ali nodded.

"Where is my friend, Predator?"

Ali's eyes got bigger and he shook his head.

Alex put the pistol to Ali's knee and said, "You're not gonna get a third chance. Where is he?"

Ali squirmed and began whimpering. "For the sake of your God, I do not know where he is. Please do not hurt me."

Alex took a deep breath and let it out like he was disappointed.

He really did not want to do this. While Ali was a bad man, using this sort of force was not in Alex's nature. He thought of what Predator must have gone through and steeled himself to the task at hand. His finger took out the slack on the trigger.

Haymaker entered the room. "Hey, Cap, you gotta see this!"

Alex took another big breath, stood, and, tapping Ali on the head with the pistol, he said, "Don't go anywhere. I'll be right back."

Haymaker stepped into the room to cover Ali and said, "Both o' y'all need to go see this."

Alex and Bandito went out to the courtyard where Lizard had moved one of the ornate rugs to reveal a cellar door. Standing back with his M4 at the ready, Lizard said, "I felt the hinges as I stepped on the rug. I popped the latch and the door rose up on hydraulic arms."

"Have you been down there?"

"No, but with your flashlight you can see that it's a torture chamber."

Alex flicked the tactical flashlight on his M4 and shined it down the steps and from side to side. From where he stood, he could see steel constraints and a large, heavy wooden table. He nodded to Bandito. "Follow me." Bandito nodded back.

Alex quickly descended the steps and went left, and Bandito went right. As they cleared the room, Alex was horrified and sickened. The room was large, perhaps as large as the entire house, and it was decorated with medieval-looking devices and cages and contraptions clearly intended to inflict pain and torture. Alex thought, *Oh my God. What has Predator been put through all this time?*

Alex heard Bandito say, "Cap?"

He walked over to where Bandito stood facing a wall and stepped up beside him. What he saw horrified and sickened him. Several steel cages lined the wall, three of which bore locks and contained small children. Alex looked closer as the children peered back at him. One appeared to be a boy of perhaps ten or twelve years old, and the other two were girls of similar age, and they trembled with fear as he tried to sort things out in his mind.

He said, "Look for a key."

Alex took his cell phone from his pocket and opened a picture of Predator. He held it out to the children, and moving from one to the other he said, "Have you seen my friend?"

The boy squinted at the picture as if the light coming from it was too much for him, but he nodded and pointed to the cage next to him.

As Bandito began opening the cages, Alex looked at the cage that had once held Predator. It was no more than three cubic feet, and Alex grew weak thinking of his big friend spending months in these conditions. Then he looked around the room again and took in all the bizarre instruments of pain and torture. He walked to the large table, which seemed to be the center of activity, and considered what he was gazing at. Leather straps were bolted to the sides of the table, and the edges of it had been routed like a meat-carving table to allow the blood to drain to one side and into a bucket on the floor. Next to the table was a chair that looked like something one might see in a gynecologist's office, but this one had no padding and was also equipped with constraints and seemed to be set up for rape and torture.

He said to Bandito, "Take the children upstairs and get them some food and something to drink. Put someone on top of the house to watch the front, and let Alien know what's going on."

Up in the house, Alex walked quickly into the room and smashed Ali square in the face with his fist. Ali's nose burst open as he fell back in his chair to the ground, and Alex quickly cut his constraints and then grabbed him by his beard and dragged him through the house and down into the cellar. He hoisted Ali up onto the gynecologist's chair and strapped his arms down and then his legs up on the stirrups before Ali regained his senses.

As Ali's eyes cleared, Alex said, "First I want to thank you for clearing my conscience about being rough with you. I was thinking about waterboarding you, but now I have much quicker ideas. Next, I'll make you an offer. If you tell me where Predator is right now, I'll leave you alone and you can continue living your sick-ass life. Well? What will it be?"

Ali shook his head vigorously and cried, "I don't know where he is; I swear by Allah."

"OK, fine. Have it your way." Alex stuffed a rag in Ali's mouth. "So, this is where you *nursed* my friend back to health, huh?" He picked up a handheld tool that looked like a cross between pliers and a meat tenderizer. "What the fuck do you do to people with this?" He ripped Ali's night shirt off, revealing his manhood in the most vulnerable position. Ali's eyes went wide as Alex grabbed his balls and crushed one of them with the pliers.

Ali's screams could be heard throughout the house, but because of the rag they did not carry much further.

When Ali's screams turned to a whimper, Alex grabbed his nose with the piers and growled, "If you tell me where Predator is, I'll stop. Are you ready to talk?"

Ali couldn't breathe, and he nodded as best he could. Alex let go of Ali's nose and pulled the rag from his mouth. Ali let out a howl as he gasped for air, and Alex hit him viciously in his face.

"Stop your whining, motherfucker. Talk now or I crush your other nut."

Ten minutes later, as Alex made to leave, Ali whimpered, "Don't leave me here like this, I need medical attention."

Alex stopped, turned around slowly, raised his pistol, and shot Ali in the forehead.

"But for the Messenger of Allah and the believers who fought with him in the Cause of Allah with their possessions and in person, their reward will be all good things and everlasting happiness."

Koran 9:88

The water truck's engine sputtered and died. The driver got out of the cab and walked to the front of the truck to lift the hood. His partner yelled at him to hurry up as the Kurdish guards from the compound ambled over and watched as he tried to fix the problem. After a few minutes, he stepped down from the engine compartment and pulled out his cell phone. He shrugged helplessly at the guards, who waved at him in a dismissive fashion and returned to their post within the Asgard compound.

"Allah has established gardens for them wherein streams flow and wherein they will live forever. This is indeed the greatest triumph."

Koran 9:89

The children ran off into the darkness.

After his team rallied and was tucked away safely, well off the road and surrounded by sand dunes, Alex shared what he had learned from Ali.

"He said this Mullah Uday bought Predator fully intending to videotape cutting off his head. He gave me the exact location and told me that right now the mullah and his men are away on a special mission up north. He expects that tonight there is only a skeleton crew of old and crippled men left to guard Predator. We have a few options here. The smartest one is probably to just give this info to DOS and let them handle it—"

Alien interjected, "And let them waste time figuring it all out and eventually do nothing before Predator dies."

Alex nodded. "Yeah, that's the way I figured it too, but we're at a big disadvantage here. No good intel, no recon other than what we can determine from GPS. We'd be going in blind, and we have no authority to do this at all."

Bandito spoke: "Yeah, well, we had only tacit approval to raid Ali's house, and we've all been in these situations before. A well-planned mission followed by time-sensitive intel that requires immediate action. My vote is we go for it."

Everyone nodded approval. He said, "OK, does anyone want out?" He looked around again. "It seems we have an appointment in Samarra."

CHAPTER 7

Only the Good Die Young

THE CITY OF SAMARRA was a hotbed of sectarian violence. Although Shiite Muslims considered the city holy, at this time it was part of the Sunni Triangle and dominated by Sunni Muslims and their militias. The local Sunni militias competed for power amongst themselves as well as with the foreign Sunni newcomers, Al-Qaeda.

Tonight, however, Alex and his team encountered no Iraqi checkpoints or roadblocks as they drove into the city, and people paid little to no attention to the fact that they drove with their lights off. It seemed to Alex that the typical disenfranchised, angry young men who would normally be prowling the dark streets were otherwise engaged.

The team swung south of the Samarra Dam to avoid US Army outposts, crossed over the Tigris River on a secondary bridge, and approached the city from the south. They skirted the city, heading east along the southern perimeter road until they identified a large empty lot that their map recon had told them was an archaeological site encompassing several square kilometers and extending into the center of the city. Their objective was at the northeast corner of the dig site.

Driving with NODs, the team traveled north along the west side of the dig site until they were certain that there was no one watching them, and then they turned in to the dig site itself. They slowly and carefully worked their way through the lot until they reached what they figured was about the center. The men dismounted and established a 360-degree perimeter around the vehicles. Alien and Psycho sidled up to Alex as he observed the building that he hoped held Predator.

The compound appeared to be or had been an industrial site of some sort. It held three buildings and in typical fashion was surrounded by a five-foot-tall wall. The main building was a large two-story structure that appeared to be about 3,000 square feet on both floors. The main building was flanked on both sides by two smaller single-story buildings.

As he observed the sheer size of the buildings, Alex wondered, *How the hell are we going to clear and search the entire complex before the whole city marshals against us?* He thought again of the debacle of Mogadishu in Somalia where the entire city attacked a handful of his Ranger buddies.

From his vantage point, he saw the backs of the buildings. He scanned the compound for sentries and saw none, but that did not mean that nobody was keeping watch.

Alien patted him on the arm. Alex looked away from his optics, and Alien pointed at a structure some hundred yards behind the compound. Alex trained his optics in that direction. The structure was an unoccupied single-story building with what looked like a roof access door. Alex understood that Alien chose that spot to set up his support position. Alex nodded to Alien, and Alien and

Psycho quietly moved away. This time Psycho took his M4 and the grenade launcher and would provide Alien with security as Alien overwatched the assault team with his sniper rifle.

Alex turned his attention back to the objective. Inside the wall there appeared to be equipment and piles of product or rubbish, which would provide the team cover as they moved across the yard. The only lights came from the smaller building closest to the rear of the compound, adjacent to the dig site. That would be the place to start. He picked a spot where he figured they could go over the wall with Alien covering them.

A dog began barking not too far to the north, somewhere along the next road. A few other dogs picked up the chorus. They quieted down when someone threw something metal and yelled at them.

Alex signaled Bandito, Lizard, and Haymaker to join him. Digger and Bull would stay and secure the vehicles again. He had them observe the objective and quietly explained to them what he was thinking.

Several minutes later Alien called on the radio, "Support set. I have one tango asleep on top of the main building and another in a chair at the front gate."

Alex responded with a whisper, "Roger, wait until we're ready to enter the compound, then take 'em out."

Alien came back, "Roger, good copy."

Alex tightened the straps on his helmet, adjusted his NODs, and then gave a thumbs-up to his team. They all returned the gesture, and Alex led the way through the excavations toward the compound, moving in a diamond-shaped formation with Alex in the lead, flanked by Bandito and Lizard, and with Haymaker directly behind Alex, watching their rear, or six o'clock. They glided like ghosts through the night shadows of thousands of years of history.

It only took a few minutes for them to reach the compound

wall. The team took cover as Alex waved his arm at where he thought Alien was.

He heard Alien whisper in his earpiece, "Stand by." Then he heard the Remington cough once, then twice. Then Alien's voice again: "Targets down."

Alex turned to Haymaker and motioned to the wall. Haymaker moved to the wall and knelt on one knee with his hands cupped and fingers laced together in the same fashion he had earlier that evening. Alex stepped into Haymaker's hands and hoisted himself over the wall and dropped to the ground inside the compound. He moved away from the wall and scanned the yard with the barrel of his rifle. Clear so far. He identified a back door that he would use to try to make entry into the first building. He *hoped* it was not booby-trapped.

As he moved to the door, he observed that the hinges were visible on the right side of the door, making it an outward-opening door. He sidled up to the left of the door at a forty-five-degree angle, and with his rifle aiming at the door above the handle, weapon off safe and finger on the trigger, he waited for the signal that the others behind him were ready. He knew without looking that Bandito would be right behind him, Lizard would be securing high and right, and Haymaker would be concentrating to their left and behind them. He felt Bandito's fingers squeeze his left arm and knew they were ready to move.

Alex flicked on the infrared flashlight on his rifle, and, keeping the rifle up and his right hand on the fire control, he reached forward under the barrel of his gun and tested the door handle with his left hand. It opened. He pulled the door open, took two steps to his right so he could see as much as possible into the building, and then quickly stepped through the threshold and into a hallway. The lights came from the end of the hallway, from what appeared to be a large room at the front of the building. Alex did not slow down as he took a few steps into the hallway and quickstepped into the first room on his left, Bandito right on his heels. Alex turned to the left in the room, and Bandito went right. They scanned the empty room and turned back to the door.

Lizard and Haymaker had taken up security in the hallway past the door Alex had entered. When he and Bandito moved back into the hallway, Lizard moved to and entered the next room, which was on the right, with Haymaker hard on his heels. Alex moved past that door and secured the hallway in their direction of travel while Bandito moved with him and secured their rear. When Lizard appeared in the door, Alex moved forward to the next one and smoothly entered the open door. A quick sweep revealed another empty room.

The next door was closed with the door handle on the right side, and the hinges were not in view, which meant it would open to the inside of the room. This time Lizard and Haymaker bypassed the room to cover the part of the hallway they had not secured yet and let Alex and Bandito make entry.

Alex moved to the left of the door and felt the squeeze from Bandito. With his left hand, Alex turned the door handle and pushed it inward, took two quick steps to his right, and saw a man sitting up on a bed as if he had just woken up. As Alex stepped through the door, the man reached for an AK-47 leaning against the bed, and Alex put two rounds in his chest. He spun to the right to dig his corner of the center-fed room and saw another bed with another startled man beginning to rise; two more bullets from Alex laid him flat in the bed again. He heard the *thwak-thwak* of Bandito's suppressed M4 behind him as Bandito put a third man to rest. They scanned their sectors, quickly checked behind and under the furniture, and then turned back to the door.

As Alex exited the room, a figure holding an AK appeared at the end of the hallway, clearly silhouetting himself against the light behind him. He must have heard the noise but not realized its source, and Lizard put two rounds in his chest and dropped him like a bag of rocks. There was one more room, and Lizard moved toward it and slid through the open door with Haymaker as Alex and Bandito continued to the main room. If there was anyone left there, Alex knew they had to get to him quickly before he raised an alarm.

Alex flicked his NODs up on his helmet and scanned as much of the room as possible before he reached the end of the hallway. He entered the room, turning hard to his left while Bandito went right. Alex moved along the left side, scanning to his right until he was certain the room held no more surprises. Lizard and Haymaker entered the room.

Lizard moved left behind Alex, and Haymaker moved right. Then, after a quick glance assessing the situation, Haymaker moved back to the door where they had entered and took up rear security to ensure that no nasty surprises followed them.

Bandito signaled Alex and pointed to the center of the wall on the right side of the room. Aside from an assortment of tables and chairs in the room, hanging against the wall was a large black flag. Alex recognized the flag as the Black Standard of Mohammed. Across the top in white letters were the Arabic words for "There is no God but Allah." Under those words was a white circle with letters that spelled out "Mohammed is the Messenger of Allah." In front of the flag was video equipment mounted on a tripod. Alex looked at the floor in front of the flag and saw a large pool of dried blood. He cried out inside himself, *Please, God, do not let that be Predator's blood.*

Bandito let out a "Psst," and nodded toward the front door. Someone was coming.

The door opened, and a man stepped in while looking back over his shoulder and said something to someone else who remained outside. The man turned around and immediately sensed something was wrong. He scanned the room and his eyes went wide when he saw Alex, and he tried to unsling his weapon as Alex, Bandito, and Haymaker each put two rounds in his body.

Before the dead man hit the ground, Alex was moving toward the door. He heard the other man say something that sounded like, "Jamal?" Then he began screaming and running back toward the large building in the center of the complex. Alex came through the door and dropped him before he got there, with two rounds in his back, but the alarm had been raised.

As Alex quickly moved across the yard with his team behind him, he heard calls that sounded like questions coming from the open bay door at the front of the next building. He heard scurrying, and someone racked the bolt of a rifle. The dim light coming from the building was extinguished, and Alex dropped his NODs back to his eyes.

Alex neared the bay door and saw a figure scurrying toward the back of the warehouse; he fired two rounds and the figure went down. He rounded the corner of the bay door and turned right just as an AK-47 opened up from the center of the bay on fully automatic. Rounds splintered the doorjamb over Alex's head because of the muzzle rise caused by the automatic fire, and as he moved, he cut loose with several rounds of his own in return. The AK dropped to the ground, and the man sprawled backward as his lungs and heart quit working.

Alex moved along the right side of the bay as Bandito darted over to the left side, Lizard followed Alex, and Haymaker fell in behind Bandito. A quick search of the large room revealed that there were no other threats.

Dogs were again barking outside, and Alex heard Alien's voice: "We have nosy neighbors moving around."

Alex said back, "Roger."

Alex signaled Lizard and Haymaker to pull security as he and Bandito searched the large room. Alex was about to have them move to the last building when Bandito said, "Cap?"

The sound of his voice alerted Alex, and his heart sank. He

looked to where Bandito was standing next to a steel box that he had opened. Alex moved slowly toward him as if he were in a dream, and his legs could not function right. The box was far too small to hold his big friend.

He came abreast of Bandito and looked into the box. His heart cried out in anguish as he gazed at the pieces of what had been his friend. Predator's dirty, beaten face lay on top of the pile, with his one remaining eye staring back at Alex.

There was yelling outside. Alien came back on the radio. "Cap, they figured it out. They found the guard at the gate and everyone's running home, probably to get big guns and reinforcements."

Alex stared trancelike into the box. Bandito answered Alien, "Roger." He turned to Alex.

"Hey, man, we gotta go. And I don't think we can carry this box outta here."

Alex took a deep breath and said, "Yeah, see if you can find some gas."

As Bandito turned away, Alex pulled his phone from his pocket and turned on his white flashlight so he could get a good picture of his friend to prove that they could stop looking for him.

Screams erupted outside as Alien opened up on the locals. Bandito returned with a large gas can, and Alex poured all five gallons in the box with Predator.

"I'm sorry we can't take you with us, buddy, but at least you'll get your Viking funeral pyre." He let some of the gas run on the ground and stepped back. Lizard and Haymaker joined Alien in trying to keep the locals at bay. Alex pulled a zippo lighter out of his pocket, lit it, and tossed it toward the box. The gas ignited in a huge fireball that crawled up the wall and curved back down when it hit the ceiling.

Psycho cut loose with three rounds from the grenade launcher.

Alex yelled, "This way; there's a side door over here!"

Lizard yelled, "Haymaker, go!"

Haymaker turned and ran toward the wall, away from the front gate of the compound. When he reached the door, he threw his weight against it, and it splintered open. He sprawled to the ground outside the door and immediately jumped up and went to his right, taking a knee to cover the withdrawal of his buddies. Lizard was right behind him, and he went left and took a knee.

Alex yelled at Bandito, "Go!" Bandito fired a few more rounds in the direction of the bay door and then turned and ran out the side door. Alex followed and ran straight to the back corner of the first building they had entered, turning to cover his team as they withdrew past him. When he got to the wall, Haymaker was waiting for him with his hands cupped and launched him over the wall. Haymaker scrambled over the wall and took up point with Alex and Bandito covering their rear as they withdrew.

About halfway across the dig site Alien called, "We're pullin' out."

Alex keyed his mic. "Roger, we'll cover you." He dropped to the ground, and Bandito landed next to him. It appeared no one had pursued them past the compound. He saw Alien and Psycho sprinting toward the vehicles, and as they passed, Alex and Bandito picked up and joined their hasty withdrawal.

The vehicles punched out onto the road with the first light of predawn.

★★★

Linda's dream ended as she was thrown against the far wall in her room. Her ears were ringing wildly, and she could not breathe. As she gasped for air, she looked at the stars where her roof had been. She was confused and could not tell if she was awake or still dreaming. She tried but was unable to move. Shooting stars of red and green soared past her open roof to splash against the one remaining wall in her room. It was then she realized she wasn't dreaming, and the shooting stars were tracers. They were under attack.

She tried to scream a warning, but nothing came out of her mouth. As she finally got a little bit of air into her lungs, she looked down and realized she was covered with a large part of the wall or ceiling, which pressed down on her chest and pinned her to the floor. She struggled to lift it or push it aside without success. She panicked and screamed, "Mom! Dad! Oh God, help us, please!"

★★★

"For those who reject the true faith, I will punish them with terrible agony in this world and the Hereafter, nor will they have anyone to help."

Koran 3:56

The explosion was massive. While his efforts at directing the blast sideways were foiled by the construction limitations of the water truck, Haider had packed in more than enough explosives to demolish most of the barracks and open nearly a hundred-foot gap in the T-walls that Yasin and his men could walk through with little effort.

Machine guns opened up on Asgard from four different high points surrounding the compound. The machine guns then lifted their fire and waited for reinforcements to come to the aid of their dying American comrades. Mullah Uday had told the gunners that would take at least thirty minutes. If all went well, they would be done and gone by then.

Yasin was first to step into Asgard through the breach. He searched for targets and found none. He scrambled over the rubble and burning wreckage of the barracks as his men fanned out behind him, shooting at anything that moved.

He moved to the left through the courtyard in front of the main building, knowing that anyone who had survived such a blast would have to have significant cover between them and the explosion, like the main building. If there were survivors he could kill, he thought he would find them on the far side of the compound.

His men swarmed over the debris and up the stairs and into the front door of what was left of the main house. A substantial part of it was still standing. He saw movement in the shadows and cut loose with a burst from his AK-47. The movement stopped, and no one returned fire. Then he heard a significant fight break out inside the house. He moved toward the back of the house, shooting into the shadows as he went. He went up the back stairs and through a gap in the wall that had been a door only minutes before.

The first thing he saw was the back of a small, middle-aged woman holding an M4 and crouched down behind a counter with an Asian-looking girl. The girl turned and saw him and screamed, putting her hand out in front of her as he riddled them both with bullets and splattered their blood all over the wall. He moved past them into a hallway and came to an open door and threw himself through it as someone discharged a burst of automatic fire at him. He unloaded the rest of his magazine in the direction of that threat and succeeded in killing two more Americans. Then he changed his magazine for a fresh one, went back out the door into the hallway, and pressed toward the front of the house where he could hear the battle raging.

Yasin was amazed at what greeted his eyes as he came to the back door of the front room. The largest man he had ever seen, even bigger than himself, was in the middle of the room, pressing Yasin's men back toward the door with a pistol in one hand and a large, club-like weapon in the other. The floor was littered with the bodies of Yasin's brothers. The enormous man tore into them like a madman, slinging bodies left and right and shoving them with his sheer mass back toward the front door.

Not wanting to kill his own men, Yasin took aim and fired a single round into the man's back. The big man acted like he did not even notice. Yasin fired again, then again, and again. Finally, the big man turned, locked eyes with Yasin, and lunged toward him. Yasin dropped his selector switch to automatic again and pulled the trigger. Round after round of 7.62 ammunition slammed into the big man, and Yasin's men pressed back into the room and cut loose on him as well. Yasin was stunned that anyone could withstand such an onslaught and thought he was about to meet Allah when the big man staggered, rose up like a grizzly bear, roared something that sounded like "Valhalla!" and then fell forward on his face with a great crash. The room was suddenly quiet as a mosque as the men all stared at this massive beast.

A strange howling erupted upstairs. He looked up as one of his men appeared and called to him, "Yasin! Come quickly."

"O Prophet! Surely We have made lawful to you your wives whom you have given their dowries, and those whom your right hand possesses, and those whom Allah has given to you as prisoners of war . . . that you may be free from blame, for Allah is ever forgiving and merciful."

Koran 33:50

As Linda heard her father's death cry, her agony grew too great to bear, and she wailed helplessly.

The pressure pinning her to the floor lifted off her chest. She was hoisted up by her arms and thrown backward onto the shredded mattress that had been her bed. She tried to move and thrash her feet, but several of the men pinned her down completely. Her eyes focused on the men, and she saw their dark beards and then smelled their sour, unwashed bodies, and her stomach turned; bile rose to her throat.

Then another man entered the room, a man almost as large as her father, but dark all over like the Grim Reaper, and she knew she was going to die. His silhouette gave way to dark, close-cropped hair and beard and a face as ugly as any she had ever seen. As he moved closer, he unhitched his belt and let his pants drop to his ankles. He reached out and tore her tattered nightdress away. He grinned, revealing grotesque teeth, some of which were missing, and leaned forward and licked her face. Recoiling at his hideous breath, she twisted her head away, cried out, and bucked her torso to resist him. He leaned back and smashed her in the nose with his fist. Her blood splashed over the men who were holding her arms. They laughed.

Linda was stunned and unable to move or resist, but she could still feel as he had his men lift her legs and spread them apart, and she felt her panties ripped away. He entered her with a single thrust that ripped her insides apart. He pounded into her several times and then stiffened, and the heat of his demon seed flooded inside her. He pulled out of her and wiped his bloody member off with her nightdress.

His men laughed and loosened their grip on her, vying for who would be next. Linda suddenly found her arms free, and she reached behind her head, grabbed a shard of wood, and lunged forward, stabbing the big man in the face with it.

The big man let out a bloodcurdling yell and reeled away. His men grabbed her again and held her down. The man slowly pulled the four inches of sharp wood out of his cheek and snarled at her, and she did the only thing she could think of; she spit in his face. He wiped his face with one hand, smearing the spit with his blood as he pulled a large fighting knife from a scabbard at his hip with the other hand. He held the knife up to her face and smiled again. Linda saw in him the personification of pure evil, the devil himself.

Lifting her head up by the hair, he slashed her face deep from ear to ear, cutting her swollen nose in half horizontally so that the bottom half of her face peeled away from the top. He then threw her facedown over some wooden two-by-fours that had fallen from the roof and wedged against the remaining wall. One of his men grabbed her arms in front of her, and others grabbed her legs behind her, pinning her again, this time with her exposed bottom up in the air.

She expected to be raped again and prepared for the pain, but what she felt was far worse. She felt the blade of that big knife enter her from behind slowly. Linda took a breath in shock; she was helpless to resist. She felt the blade slice into her womb as the monster pushed it deeper and deeper. She looked down between her legs and saw her own blood streaming out onto the floor. Through the pain and fear she thought of her baby and cried out, "Noooooooo!"

She groaned as he pushed hard with one final, great effort that she felt in her chest. Mercifully, Linda finally passed out. She died less than a minute later. They left her there just like that, without removing the knife.

★ ★ ★

Alex said, "I don't get it. We have reception, and it's late enough in the morning that someone should hear the calls."

Traffic was particularly bad since they had entered the city. As they inched along Digger said, "Hey, boss, check that out."

Alex craned to see what was going on up ahead. As they worked their way further through the traffic, he finally saw that the road near Asgard was blocked and filled with police and military vehicles. They had seen the pall of smoke from some distance back, but he only now realized it was coming from Asgard. Panic overtook him, and he jumped out of the vehicle and ran down the road.

He rounded the corner and saw the enormous gap in the T-walls and the demolished barracks. He continued running toward the remains of the front gate and was turned back by Kurdish police. He ran back to the breach, squirmed his way between some American soldiers, and picked his way through the rubble and into the compound. As he stumbled through what had been the barracks, he looked up at Linda's room, and his heart felt like it would burst. The roof had been sheared off, and the entire wall on this side of the main house was gone.

He panicked and ran around the back of the house to avoid more people investigating what had happened. He vaulted up the stairs into the kitchen and stopped cold when he saw Linda's mother sprawled out on the floor with her body riddled with bullet holes. He ran down the hallway to the foot of the stairs and paused again at the sight of Odin lying on his face, surrounded by dead insurgents. He pulled himself up the demolished staircase and negotiated the hallway filled with debris. At Linda's room he froze in the doorway. Alex fell to his knees and looked away, pressing his face into the splintered doorframe and using it to hold himself up.

Anguish, horror, sorrow, guilt—they were all too shallow to describe the emotions coursing through Alex at that moment. He thought of what she must have felt as she was being brutalized. He thought of their baby. He thought that he should have been there for her when she needed him most. He heard himself groan in agony and immediately felt guilty because he knew it was selfish to feel anything. He pulled his Glock from its holster and put the barrel in his mouth.

As he took the slack out of the trigger, he heard a voice: "Don't do it, Alex."

Alien reached down and gingerly moved Alex's hand and the gun away from his mouth. He sat down next to Alex and held him as he cried like a baby.

Bandito and Haymaker slid past them and covered Linda's body with a grimy bed sheet.

As Alex cried himself out, he looked back at the form of Linda's body draped over the wood planks. After a few minutes, he forced himself to move over to her. He lifted her poor, tattered body off the wood and carried her to the shredded mattress where he laid her on her back. She was so cold and stiff. He looked at her swollen, gaping face, and the anguish renewed itself in his heart. His tears flowed down his cheeks as he pulled the knife from her body and dropped it on the floor. Then he pushed her rigid arms down by her sides and straightened out her legs so she would be more comfortable as she lay there. He kissed her forehead and whispered, "I am so sorry I was not here for you and our baby, my dearest Linda. I am so sorry."

He stayed with her until the Army investigators arrived. He could not bear to stay while they did what they had to, so he left.

✷✷✷

He found the team sitting on the back porch. Someone had found a bottle of whiskey inside that Bandito passed to Alex as he sat on the splintered wooden planks. He took a big pull from the bottle and buried his head in his knees and sobbed again. Nobody said anything.

After a few minutes something occurred to Alex and he straightened up. "You know, that son of a bitch Ali said the bastards who did that to Predator were on a 'special mission up north' last night. I wonder if this was their mission. I wonder if it was the same people."

Alien said, "It could be."

Bandito gestured wildly with his hands. "It has to be. Samarra was empty of the normal young jihadis we would've seen. How many other insurgent events went down last night with a significant number of attackers?"

Alien shook his head. "Yeah, it makes sense, but you know what that would mean?"

"What are you thinking?" Alex asked him.

"Well, if it was the same people, the coincidence would be too great."

"What do you mean?"

"Why would they risk coming here to Kurdistan to hit this

particular compound when they have far easier targets throughout the rest of the country?"

Alex understood. "Somehow, they knew we were looking for Predator and they came after us." He buried his face in his hands and shook his head in disbelief that this all might have been his fault.

Alien scrunched his brow and pursed his lips and said, "Well, that doesn't completely make sense either. Why would they bother coming all the way up here to stop us from finding Predator? They had murdered him by then anyway, and it would make more sense to just drop his body off somewhere and booby-trap it. No, the same people we were looking for specifically targeted Asgard, but it was for a different reason."

Alex looked at him. "Ali?"

"Maybe, but that still doesn't explain everything. From what you said, Ali was surprised to see us. He wasn't anticipating what we did."

Bandito offered, "Maybe they were tired of us kickin' their ass and they came here for revenge."

Alien nodded. "Now, that actually makes better sense. Unknowingly, we've been chasing them at the same time they've been chasing us."

This revelation did little to make Alex feel any better. In the end, he felt it was his actions or just his existence that had cost Linda, their baby, her parents, and so many others their lives.

Bandito asked, "So, what do we do? Tell the Army or DOS that we know who did this and where they can be found? Maybe they'll launch an operation to take these fuckers out."

Alien snorted, "I doubt it. They couldn't care less about a bunch of contractors getting slaughtered. I'll bet they won't even report the casualties other than numbers of 'civilians' killed in a suicide attack. They'll make it appear Iraqis killed more of their own. The only reason they were interested in Predator was because someone splashed his picture on Al-Jazeera and made it public, but they weren't interested enough to allocate any combat troops to the situation."

Bandito raised his hands in frustration. "OK, so what do we do?"

Haymaker looked up from the whiskey bottle. "We go kill those motherfuckers ourselves." Alex looked over at him. Haymaker's cheeks were streaked with tears and he continued, "These people were the only family I had. Outside of the Army, being here was the only time in my life I felt like I had brothers and sisters who cared for me no matter what my faults were. The men who died in those barracks were my brothers. They would have died for me if I needed them, and I want to avenge them. My best friend was in those barracks, and now he's dead. If the Army won't do it, I will."

Everyone considered what Haymaker said, and finally Bandito proclaimed, "I'm down with it."

Lizard: "Me too."

Psycho: "Count me in."

Alex looked at the men as each in turn spoke their commitment. He nodded and said, "We're going to need some serious firepower for this one."

Alien said, "I know some people who know some people."

"That sounds like it'll cost money," Alex said.

"I got that covered," said Bandito. "I know where Odin kept his operational slush fund. I'll wait till dark and see if it's still there."

Alien said, "We're going to need more than a little slush fund."

Bandito laughed. "Nothing little about Odin's slush funds. If it's there, we'll have more than enough to equip a small army. After all, that's what it was intended for."

Alex thought, *This is good. If I stay busy, I can focus on other things rather than my own self-pity.* He said, "OK, I'm going to see if I can find any maps of the area from the operations room.

Alien, if you would, contact the rear and let them know what happened here and then contact your friends of friends and see if they're still in business. Bandito, see what intel you can gather on Samarra. Lizard, you and the others gather some food and water and poke around to see what is salvageable that we might be able to use. Stay out of the way of the soldiers and police. Let's meet over by the range shack and see if we can't come up with a plan."

Alex went into the house and found the scene chaotic with soldiers and Kurdish police moving about. He squeezed through the hallway to the front room where the bodies had been removed and lined up on the ground in front of the house. Just then, two men appeared at the top of the stairs with a body bag and passed it down the shattered staircase to two other men waiting at the bottom.

Alex knew it was Linda's body. He slid down against a wall to a seated position, and the anguish overcame him again as he watched them carry her out the front door.

An Army captain approached him. "You OK, sir?"

Alex wiped his face and nodded. "Yeah, I suppose so."

"Were you here when this happened?" the captain asked him.

Alex shook his head. "No, we were on a mission out of town. We got back after it was over."

"Do you have any idea who did this?" the captain probed.

Alex looked at him. "No, do you?"

The captain shook his head. "No, we really don't at this point. Stick around in case we have any questions, OK?"

Alex said, "Sure, we'll be out back by the range."

"OK." The captain turned to walk away but then turned back and said, "I'm sorry about your people."

"Thanks," Alex choked out.

When the captain left, Alex rose to his feet and climbed the stairs. He made his way to Linda's room and stood at the door for a minute. He stepped in and pushed debris around until he found a towel. Hoping it would smell like Linda, he held it to his nose. It did not. Then he walked over to the mattress, reached down beside it, and picked up the knife. He wrapped the knife with the towel and put it in the cargo pocket of his pants.

*** ★★★ ***

After Alex had collected what maps he could find of Samarra from the operations office, he went back over to the range shack. Haymaker had brought several cases of MREs and water and was in the process of lifting the overhead cover up again from where it had fallen. Alex gave him a hand, and they braced it as best they could. Then they righted one of the tables and spread the maps out.

Digger and Psycho returned to report that the vehicles in the motor pool were largely intact, having been on the opposite side of the compound from the blast. Also, the arms room was undamaged due to its location and reinforced walls and ceiling. Alex spread their notes out on the table as well.

Haymaker said, "Check this out."

Alex looked up to see Lizard leading a group of at least a dozen Kurds their way. Lizard approach Alex and said, "These guys want to know what you have on your mind." By that statement, Alex knew that Lizard had told them nothing.

Alex narrowed his eyes and said, "What do you mean by that?"

One of the Kurds Alex had seen with Odin stepped up to Alex and held his right hand out.

"My name is Olan and I work here. I was at home with my family when this happened." He gestured behind him. "These are my men, and we are Peshmerga."

Alex took his hand and shook it. "What can I do for you, Olan?"

Olan said, "We know who you are, and we know you will not stand by and let this go unpunished. We are here to help you, and if you need more men, I can gather them."

As much as he would like help, Alex felt too many people might complicate matters and be too hard to control; he shook his head. "I don't know, Olan. It seems to me that the smartest thing for us to do is let the Army and police take care of this."

Olan seemed to have expected a rebuff and stated, "Yes, that might be smart and safe, but it will lead to nothing. It never does, and those people will be free to do this again. Look, Captain Doctor, we will pledge our loyalty to you if you will lead us against the devils that did this."

"What did you call me?" Alex asked.

Olan said, "Captain Doctor." And he gestured to one of the men standing behind him, who stepped forward. He looked vaguely familiar to Alex. "My name Adnon. My English no good, but I work with you before. You help my brother and cousin."

Alex accepted his hand and said, "Of course I remember you, Adnon. I am sorry your brother didn't make it."

Olan, whose English seemed perfect, interjected, "That's his point exactly. The way he tells it, his brother and his cousin were both as good as dead already, and you risked your life to help them anyway. And we know about how you saved Dingo. And we know you are a great fighter and leader, and so we have called you Captain Doctor."

Then he gestured to another man who stepped forward and extended his hand to Alex. Olan said, "His name is Rewan and he speaks no English, but he would like to extend his condolences and admiration. His two sons have told us many times about how you alone fought and killed the snipers who plagued us for so long." He paused and then went on, "So you see, Captain Doctor, we know who you are and how you think and what is important to you. We know you will not sit by and let this go unpunished. We insist you include us in your plans."

Alien, Lizard, and Psycho walked up just then. Alien saw Adnon and went to him and they shook hands and hugged. Alien asked, "What's up, Cap?

Alex shook his head, "These guys seem to think we've got

revenge in mind, and they want to participate." He turned to Olan. "Olan, if what you are suggesting were true, we could face serious problems with the authorities."

Olan said, "We will die before any of us say or do anything that will compromise you or your men."

"Wait one minute, please," Alex said. He gestured to the team to follow him. When they were out of earshot he asked, "What do you think?"

Alien said, "Well, I trust Adnon with my life, and I've worked with Olan before and he's an effective operator and his men follow him without question."

"Yeah, I've worked with most of these guys, and you don't get any better than them," Lizard agreed.

Haymaker nodded. "They're fearless in a fight, no doubt. And the more Iraqis they get to kill, the happier they are."

Psycho added, "Olan's pulled my bacon out of the fire more than once. He was a trusted confidant of Odin's. He's smart and I trust him."

"This is a tall order, and we sure could use the help," Alien finished.

Alex nodded and they walked back over to the Kurds. He said to Olan, "OK. We appreciate your offer, and if you like, we can start right away."

Olan grinned from ear to ear and grabbed Alex's hand. "Thank you, Captain Doctor. We will make you proud of us."

Alex had the Kurds all sit on the ground and, with the help of Olan, explained to them what they were doing in the form of a military warning order. Between the two of them, they broke the men down into teams and assigned each a task to help prepare for the mission. They dispatched four volunteers with Adnon as the team leader to go to Samarra to observe and gather intelligence.

Later, Bandito started the operations order by explaining the situation.

"The city of Samarra has about a hundred and twenty-five thousand inhabitants. Like many Iraqi cities, electricity is out more than it is on. There is an American FOB to the west of the city, but they are mostly concerned with securing the dam and not so much with what happens inside the city.

"The majority of the people in Samarra are Sunnis, but the Shiites consider it a holy city and have several shrines and mosques there. The Shiites are concentrated largely to the north and west of the city and near the Al-Askari Mosque.

"Al-Qaeda is active in the city and constantly trying to stir up problems between the Sunnis and Shiites, but the dominant force is only loosely connected to Al-Qaeda. They are called, well, I won't even try to say it in Arabic, but in English it means the Army of the Sunni People. Their leader was born in Samarra."

He pointed to one of a few pictures he had pinned on the makeshift map board.

"His name is Ibrahim Awad al-Badri, and he has recently taken to calling himself Abu Bakr Al-Baghdadi. Abu Bakr was Mohammed's uncle, and he inherited the caliphate. It seems that this man has high aspirations. It also turns out that until his recent demise, our buddy Sheikh Ali was suspected of being a prominent member of the group."

He pointed at the map. "The neighborhood we're concerned with is called Al-Jabaria I in the south-central part of the city. It encompasses a bit less than one-tenth of the city and houses approximately ten thousand people. We will focus on a one-square-kilometer section of the neighborhood. About a quarter of that is an open archeological dig site."

Haymaker mumbled, "We're gonna need more bullets."

Bandito agreed and went on, pointing at another picture, of a man in a pre-invasion Iraqi Army uniform. "The primary figure in this area is a former Republican Guard general who goes by the name Mullah Uday al-Shimarey, and this big ugly bastard here"—he pointed at a third picture—"is a former lieutenant in the Republican Guard and the mullah's right-hand man and chief enforcer, Yasin Sulayman—by all reports a very nasty fellow."

Bandito looked at his notes and picked up another picture. "That's it for the leadership, but there's one more associated character that I found most interesting." He pinned another picture up with the other three: a small, weak-looking man by comparison. "This guy's name is Haider Shawkat, an engineer by education and trade, and now he seems to be the group's chief bomb maker." Bandito pointed at the huge gap in the T-walls and the demolished barracks. "If anyone deserves to die, it's him."

Alex stepped up in front of the group. "At sunset two days from now we will conduct a raid into the neighborhood of Al-Jabaria I in the city of Samarra for the purpose of killing the leadership Bandito just outlined to you, and as many of their soldiers as possible." As far-fetched as this idea seemed to Alex, the men assembled in front of him were clearly pleased with the concept. He went on to outline a tentative plan.

"And let not the infidels think that they can outmaneuver Allah; verily they will never be able to save themselves from Allah's punishment."

Koran 8:59

While Haider had seen his wrath before, he had never seen Mullah Uday as angry as he was when they returned to Samarra. Uday raged as he pushed a stick through the smoldering embers of his warehouse.

Yasin shook his head. "No, the body is completely incinerated, and the videotape must be also."

Uday bellowed as he kicked the remains of a table into a pile of ashes.

"This is not the only bad news from last night." The sound of the unexpected voice was enough to have Uday, Yasin, and Haider freeze and look toward the front of what had been the warehouse. Al-Baghdadi stood there with his arms folded.

Barely able to mask his disdain for the man, but quite aware of his power, Uday demanded, "What do you mean?"

"What I mean, dear Uday, is that Sheikh Ali was also murdered last night."

"So what? I didn't like that little prick anyway. He was disgusting with his children. I'm glad he's dead. That's good news."

Baghdadi shook his head. "You pathetic creature. How did you ever become a general in Saddam's army? Oh yes, it was by marriage, was it not?"

Uday wanted to kill him, but restrained himself. "What are you saying? I have no time or desire for your games. Just spit it out."

"What I am saying, my good *Mullah* Uday, is that while you were out trying to kill Americans last night, those very men killed Ali in Tikrit and then came here, killed a dozen of your old men, destroyed your videotape, and burned your warehouse to the ground."

Uday was shocked. His mouth dropped open and he mumbled, "What?"

Baghdadi shook his head again. "While you were out, your intended target was here making a fool out of you."

Uday began screaming and throwing everything he could pick up.

Baghdadi let him calm down a bit.

Uday yelled at him, "Why are you still here? Go away. I have work to do. We'll be leaving tonight."

Baghdadi lost his patience and finally raised his voice. "You really are an idiot, aren't you? You don't understand this man at all, do you? You don't need to go anywhere looking for him.

He is a man of principal. Once he finds out what you did to his people, he will come looking for you. You need only to stay right here and be ready for him."

Baghdadi turned to leave, but then he stopped when he saw Haider cowering in the shadows. Haider was unsure if he should prostrate himself or not. Baghdadi looked at him and smiled.

"My dear Haider Shawkat, it is so good to finally meet you. I am a huge admirer of your work. Please come and see me when Uday is dead." He paused and stroked his beard as if deep in thought and then pointed his finger at Haider. "I expect to see you soon." He turned and strode away with his bodyguards close behind.

"Thereafter your Lord will indeed be forgiving and merciful to those who migrated after they were persecuted, waged Jihad and remained steadfast."

Koran 16:110

An hour northeast of Erbil, Alien pulled the vehicle into a small village tucked away in the mountains near the Iranian border. The first thing Alex noticed was a white Toyota Land Cruiser.

"That's not good."

Bandito leaned into the front seat. "No, it's not. Look at the placard. It's a USAID vehicle."

Alien shook his head in frustration. "Well, what do we do?"

Alex said, "We drive on as planned and get ready to cut bait." He stepped out of the car as the three trucks of their convoy ground to a stop behind him and several Kurds jumped down and fanned out to establish security.

Three men stepped out of the nearest hut and walked toward them. Alien muttered, "Oh shit, Alex, I had no idea."

Two of the men were obviously locals, but the third was none other than the giant, Ibsil.

Ibsil was grinning as he stalked up to them. "Well, well, what do we have here? They didn't tell me that the customer would be *you*." His gaze was locked on Alex.

Alien said, "What are you doing here?"

Without looking away from Alex, Ibsil said, "This is my gig, asshole, and the price just doubled."

Olan walked up and greeted the two locals.

Alex just stood there and said nothing.

Bandito said, "Hey, man, we agreed on a price on the phone. That's all we brought."

Ibsil stepped closer to Alex and said, "Then I guess you and your boy here"—he stabbed a finger into Alex's chest and pushed him back a couple of steps—"are shit outta luck. You just left me hanging there on the street in Baghdad. You didn't even stop to help."

Alex said, "We had our client. You know the rules."

"Fuck your rules. I told you before I'd have my way with you, you little prick, and that's what I'm gonna do now." He stepped forward again.

Alex dropped his right foot back and bladed his body to the big man. Iblis laughed and lashed out with a vicious side kick intended to collapse Alex's left leg, which was now forward of his center of gravity. Alex pulled his leg back quickly as he drew his pistol and pointed it at Iblis.

Alex said, "I really don't want to shoot you, but if you attack me again, I will."

After a lifetime of bullying people and getting away with it, Iblis figured Alex wasn't going to shoot him. He snarled, "You fuckin' pussy, I'm gonna cut your balls off and stuff them down your goddamn throat before I kill you, and then I'm gonna kill everything that ever meant anything to you, starting with your bitch! I'm gonna fuck the shit outta that cunt, then I'm gonna cut her throat and leave her to the buzzards!" He was raging now with saliva splashing out of his mouth as he ranted.

Alex had heard enough. Iblis was clearly not aware of what had happened to Asgard, and a rage boiled up inside Alex. "Will you really do all that?"

"AND MORE! YOU'RE GODDAMN RIGHT I WILL, YOU MOTHERFU—"

Alex thought of Jackie. *I can't have that.*

BOOM!

The 9-millimeter Hydra-Shok bullet caught the big man right on the bridge of his nose, and his brains exploded out the back of his head. His head snapped back, and his dead body collapsed straight to the ground like a rag doll.

"Jesus!" Bandito exclaimed. "I wasn't expecting that!"

Alien said calmly, "I was."

The two local men held their hands up in front of them as several other men with weapons came running out of the other huts. Alex and the other Americans moved to the vehicle for cover, but Olan stayed and held both his hands out in front of him with palms up, speaking excitedly. The other men chattered back, and then one of them turned and waved his hands toward the ground, telling the others to stand down.

Olan spoke with the two men for another minute or so as they negotiated an agreement.

Olan seemed to resolve something and moved over to Alex. "It's OK, we have worked out a deal."

Alex asked, "What deal?"

Olan smiled. "We pay them *diyya*, or blood money, for the death of the big man, and they keep his Land Cruiser and all the money from the transaction."

Alex said, "How much diyya?"

Olan said, "One hundred dollars."

Bandito whistled. "A hundred bucks and we're good to go?"

"Yes, he is a small matter," Olan said. "These men have

been supplying weapons to warring factions in Iraq and Iran for generations. He was only one source of theirs, and they did not like him anyway."

Alien snickered, "Then maybe they should pay *us* for getting rid of him."

Olan smiled again. "Perhaps, but I think it is best we accept the arrangement."

"It's a deal," Alex said.

Olan said, "Good." He turned to Bandito. "Give me a hundred dollars." He took the money from Bandito, and the four of them emerged from behind the vehicle with their weapons holstered.

They were led behind the huts to the foot of a steep hillside where the local men pulled brush away from the entrance to a man-made cavern. Once inside, Alex was amazed to find a menagerie of crates filled with weapons of every description and hundreds of boxes containing every variety of ammunition.

Alex and his men began moving what they needed to the trucks as one of the locals annotated everything.

The first weapon of note was an MK 19 fully automatic belt-fed grenade launcher with a tripod that they could mount on a vehicle. The ammunition came in cans with forty-eight rounds belted together. The weapon had devastating effect and was accurate at point targets out to 1,500 meters and area targets beyond 2 kilometers, or more than a mile. Each grenade had a kill radius of over 20 feet, a casualty radius of over 400 feet, and the system could pump out 350 rounds per minute.

But as awesome as the MK 19 was, it was still not the confidence crusher that the next weapon was. When the M134 Minigun opened up on the battlefield, it was a real game changer. Out to a thousand meters, nothing could withstand the well over four thousand 7.62-millimeter rounds per minute ripping out of the six-barreled machine gun. The gun came with batteries to power the system, four 3,200-round ammunition cans, and a tripod that could also be mounted to a vehicle.

For sheer destructive firepower that Alex was counting on to shoot through walls, demolish buildings, and reach out over four miles, the men carried out two Browning M2 .50-caliber heavy-barreled machine guns and the necessary accoutrements.

Finally, the men moved 500 pounds of C-4 plastic explosives, a spool of detonation cord, or det cord, M81 igniters, and some time fuse to the trucks. The time fuse, attached to the igniter, would give them time to get away from the ensuing explosion. The det cord, which burned—or rather, exploded—at over 7,000 meters per second, would provide the necessary heat and high pressure to ignite the C-4.

They carried the weapons to a large pit dug into the side of another hill on the far side of the village to test-fire them. The support team, led by Lizard, would operate the special weapons. Haymaker claimed the Minigun, Psycho was giddy with the idea of pounding the enemy with the MK 19, and Digger and Lizard would each operate a .50 cal.

★★★

That evening, when they returned to Asgard, Alex found that their numbers had increased substantially. The yard behind the main house was filled with Kurds who had all brought their weapons, individual gear, and vehicles. Alex became concerned that their effort might be undone with too many people and too much activity.

Adnon had also returned from Samarra. With help from Olan, Adnon explained that he had left two of his men to continue their surveillance. He told Alex that the neighborhood was alerted to something extraordinary. They had evacuated most of the families and concentrated their forces in three locations.

Alex said aloud, "They know we're coming."

Adnon and Olan nodded their agreement.

With the primary leaders crowded around the map, Adnon

went on to explain that the compound where they had found Predator was manned and fortified, but it appeared that they had made their headquarters in a madrassa, or schoolhouse, a few blocks away. Most importantly, however, he described a compound that stood in isolation in the desert, next to a cemetery to the south of the neighborhood. It appeared that they had placed the bulk of their men there as a reserve force to react to whatever they were expecting.

He described IEDs being emplaced on roads along the perimeter and main roads of the neighborhood and in the archaeological dig site. He traced his finger over back roads that seemed to be clear of IEDs and roadblocks.

Finally, he said he had seen the "general" and his lieutenant at the madrassa.

Considering this information, Alex went to work. He assigned men who had worked in their motor pool to the support team, and Olan and Lizard put them to work mounting the heavy weapons on armored Chevrolet Suburbans. The chief mechanic assured Alex that they could fabricate turrets on top of the vehicles and mount the guns in such a fashion that they could be retracted into the vehicle during movement.

Bandito and Psycho, having been Special Forces engineers, or 18Cs, took the task of building a modified car bomb and breaching explosives. They agreed on a trailer bomb that would enable them to decouple the trailer and ignite the bomb as the vehicle continued to move.

For the breaching explosive they would use a sheet of plywood cut in half and outlined with rolled C-4 and det cord. The plywood would be dotted with pegs on the side with the explosives to give it the standoff from the wall necessary to direct the blast into it. It would have a simple M81 fuse igniter with ten seconds of time fuse to set off the blast. The two halves of the plywood would then be reattached with hinges and folded together. It would be carried on someone's back with shoulder straps bolted to the frame. When it was needed, they would simply open it up, prop it against the wall, remove the safety pin from the igniter and pull the ring, get out of the way very quickly, and then they would create a four-by-eight hole through which they could enter the compound or building.

Alien, Lizard, and Olan broke the new men down into teams based on their experience and began rehearsals. The support unit would consist of four Suburbans with Lizard as the team leader. Digger, Haymaker, Psycho, and Lizard would man the weapon systems, and four Kurds were assigned to each truck, one driver and three men for security. The assault teams would be led by Alex, Alien, Bandito, and Olan, each with four Kurds with operational experience. Adnon and four other Kurds would operate the trailer bomb. Each element of the assault team would carry an M249 SAW. Finally, two vehicles would be used as ambulances, with Bull as the team leader and each vehicle with four Kurds—a driver, a man for security, and two men with medical training.

It was fully dark by the time Alex was able to practice with his new team. Fortunately, they were all experienced operators. They communicated with hand and arm signals and drilled on every situation Alex imagined they might face.

It was well after midnight when he told the men to get some sleep. He noticed that all the teams took his cue and broke up for the night. He checked on the progress of the vehicles and realized it would be quite some time before they were finished. Psycho showed him the completed trailer bomb and breaching demolitions. Finally, Alex told everyone to get some rest, and he parked himself at the maps with an MRE and considered their situation. His mind raced trying to figure out how to solve this problem as simply and effectively as possible.

CHAPTER 8

"Vengeance Is Mine," Sayeth the Lord

AS THE SUN FELL below the horizon, several construction workers left the market with their purchases, and vendors packed away their remaining produce.

The construction workers' rickety old truck and its overloaded trailer pulled out onto the main road and turned left at the first intersection. As the driver of the truck increased its speed, he ran up on the curb, and the trailer broke loose from its coupling and skidded to a halt in front of a large compound that had recently been gutted by fire. Instead of stopping, the driver continued to drive and turned left into a narrow alleyway.

The men standing guard at the compound yelled and waved at the truck as it disappeared around the corner. One of the guards had walked out into the road to get a closer look at the trailer when he saw a small smoke trail coming from the front of the trailer. He leaned around the front of the trailer and realized he was looking at a lit fuse. He had just enough time to turn around and scream in alarm before more than 400 pounds of C-4 exploded.

The blast wave brought down the compound wall and the façades of the houses on the other side of the street. A great fireball climbed a hundred feet, and the explosion rocked the city of Samarra.

From a small knoll south of the archaeological excavation site, Psycho pulled the trigger of his MK 19 and sent burst after burst of 40-millimeter grenades into the compound.

★★★

From his perch on top of the Riyadh Madrassa four blocks away, Mullah Uday was taken by surprise by the powerful explosion and fell back in his chair. As the grenades pulverized what was left of their decoy, he looked over at Yasin, who had taken cover behind the rooftop parapet. Yasin looked back at Uday and Uday said, "It has begun. Call out the brigade!"

Uday pictured the 250 men of his glorious Martyrs Brigade riding out of their hiding place and charging into the city to smash the infidel invaders.

★★★

From his position in the cemetery, Haymaker could hardly contain himself. He waited as the column left the compound and until the lead elements of the reaction force reached the intersection of the access road and the city perimeter road. He had to initiate the attack before they crossed the road and entered the city, or they would be out of his line of fire. He heard the muffled sounds of Psycho's grenade launcher pounding the city, and he was determined to not be outdone.

★★★

The commander of the lead vehicle had just reached the access road when he noticed a weird stream of red light coming from his right and slightly behind his truck. A heartbeat later the cab of his truck was ripped to shreds as he was pummeled by 7.62-millimeter rounds.

The two M2s opened up a heartbeat after Haymaker sent his first laser-like burst of death downrange. The .50-caliber machine guns raked the column from the rear to the front. White tracers of the .50s crossed over the red tracers of the minigun and back again as the guns raked back and forth over the length of the convoy.

When Lizard's gun barrel started to glow, he paused and let one of his men change the barrel for him as he reached down and pulled out the Milkor grenade launcher and fired six flares into the compound to mark the target for Psycho. Within moments Psycho had shifted his fire from his first target and was launching high-explosive grenades into the second compound. Lizard went back to work with the .50.

Alex led the assault team's motorcade through the back streets toward their objective. Adnon called on the radio, "Scimitar set."

With that call, Alex knew that Adnon and his men had worked their way to the top of a building to the northwest side of their objective to help secure the perimeter and give them supporting fire with a SAW as Alex's teams breached the building from the east. He responded, "Roger, we're one mike out."

Adnon responded, "Roger."

***

Abu Bakr Al-Baghdadi stood atop the Al Aqsa Mosque next to several men armed with RPGs. He watched as the motorcade raced past his mosque, and one of his men looked at him as if imploring him to allow them to fire on the Americans. He shook his head and said, "No. Insha'Allah. We will let Mullah Uday resolve this himself."

Olan's driver brought his vehicle to a screeching stop, and Olan's team bailed out. As he ran to the front door of the house, he heard yelling from the top of an adjacent building, and when he burst through the door, he heard the shooting begin. He and his men ran through the house and up to the top of the building as fast as they could. As he went, he turned on his infrared strobe light so Adnon and the others would be able to identify his location and not shoot him and his team. Each team leader had done likewise.

★★★

Alex and Alien's vehicles continued to the end of the road and surged across the street, sliding sideways up against the schoolhouse wall. Bandito's vehicle sailed past them to establish security at the southernmost corner of the madrassa.

Alex and his men sat tight for several moments, listening to the impact on their armored vehicles of bullets being fired at them from the rooftops across the street. They were too close to the compound wall for men inside the compound to shoot at them with any effect. When Alex heard the unmistakable chatter of Olan's SAW clearing the rooftop, the rounds hitting their vehicles stopped, and the two teams bailed out. Alex pointed at the wall, and his breacher quickly unfolded his charge, placed it against the wall, and propped it up with a long, thick stick. He took the safety pin out of the igniter and pulled the ring hard. The igniter snapped to life, and Alex and his man moved away quickly to the left, pressed against the wall, and turned their heads away.

★★★

Yasin saw the firefight on top of the buildings across the street and was screaming at his men to shoot when the SAW opened up on them from the north. The man next to him was stitched with 5.56-millimeter bullets, and one round hit the parapet in front of Yasin, splashing shards of stucco in his face and compelling him to drop as low as he could to get out of the line of fire.

He looked up and down the line and realized his men had also dropped down to protect themselves. When the breaching charge rocked the schoolhouse, he knew the Americans were making entry into the compound. He yelled at his men to rise and shoot, but the tracers from now two SAWs induced them to disregard his orders. He grabbed the closest man and physically forced him up, only to have him riddled with bullets. Another man started to rise and took two rounds in his face, blowing his brain stem all over Yasin. Yasin screamed in frustration and scurried on his hands and knees to the stairs.

★★★

Debris from the explosion was still raining down as Alex charged through the breach. As he ran, he shifted his rifle left, then right, then up, but no targets presented themselves. He made it to the building and flattened against the wall as his men caught up with him. Alien was next, and Alex pointed at a likely spot on the wall. Alien stepped aside, and his breacher placed the second charge against the wall, propped it up, and charged the igniter.

★★★

Yasin threw himself down the stairs from the roof to the second floor and sprawled at the feet of Mullah Uday. Uday was frantically yelling at him, "Where's the brigade? What's happening? How did they know to come here? What's going on?"

Yasin shook his head in confusion when he heard the second explosion. The enemy was making entry into the schoolhouse. This was all happening too fast; he had to get a grip and do something.

He saw the little engineer standing there with an AK-47 strapped awkwardly over his shoulders. Yasin grabbed the weapon and wrenched it away from Haider and pushed him out of the way. He called to his men to follow him and left Uday and Haider without a word.

★★★

Alien made entry into the empty classroom and hooked left, his number two man went right, and the rest of his team followed. Alex crossed the breach and went straight to the closed door on the far side of the room.

The door opened inward with the handle on the left side. He figured from the makeup of the building that he was about to enter a hallway, and because it was a school, he expected numerous rooms on both sides of the hall. As Alex felt the squeeze on his arm, he heard voices and pounding feet to his left.

With his M4 on burst, he pointed the barrel at the door just above the handle and reached out with his left hand, pulled the door open, and stepped through it, spinning to his left. He almost ran into three men running down the hallway, and he pulled the trigger. AK-47s opened up right next to him, and he was among the enemy as two of them fell against the wall and to the floor. The third was blasted by another AK-47 belonging to his number three man, who had followed Alex into the hallway.

More men dove into rooms further down the hallway, and Alex hooked right into the next open door. Before he made the turn, he saw the flash from the muzzle of a rifle and felt a bullet pull at the strap of his body armor. As he pulled the trigger, the muzzle of his attacker's gun rose up, sending rounds into the doorframe and ceiling above him. He spun hard right to the corner of the room and was met by the blast of another AK-47 into his chest and the sensation of being hit with a sledgehammer. He fired his weapon into the muzzle flash. Then he was on his knees, gasping for air.

His team flowed into the room, and hands grabbed him under his arms and pushed him into the corner where he collapsed. The fight raged in the hallway as Alex struggled to get a breath. He brought his hands to his chest and found three bumps lodged in his body armor just above his sternum. He struggled to his feet and pushed the hands away that tried to help him up. Finally, he was able to take some deep breaths, and sensation returned.

Alien and his team passed by the doorway, blasting their way down the hallway as they moved toward the next room.

Alex ejected his magazine and slapped a fresh one in his weapon. He stepped up to the door and nodded to his men, who readied themselves for another assault. There were only three now. Then he was out in the hallway again just as the last of Alien's team disappeared into the next room. He saw splashes of light as guns fired in Alien's room, and Alex fired down the hallway as he moved.

An AK-47 and two arms swung around the corner of the next room and fired blindly into the hallway. He fired twice at the hands, and the rifle dropped to the ground with a hand still attached. The bloody arm stump pulled back into the room. Alex fired through the wall into the room, and then he was through the doorway and shot the man again at point-blank range. The room was otherwise empty.

Alex stepped back to the door as Alien passed again, firing his rifle with his number two man blazing away with the SAW over Alien's left shoulder. Alex glanced back the way they had come and realized that Alien's entire team consisted of only him and one other man now. Alex stepped out and followed Alien.

Alien made entry into the final room before the hallway made a ninety-degree turn to the right. Alex stayed in the hallway with his weapon up and ready and sent his team to flow into the room with Alien. The room was empty, and there was a lull in the fight that Alex knew would rage again as soon as they turned that corner in the hallway. Alien emerged and fell in behind Alex. Alex signaled to the men that the first man with a SAW would strong-wall the turn in the hallway, where he would move straight to the far side of the intersection. The second man with a SAW would buttonhook, or turn hard right, at the intersection at the same time. This way they would have their greatest firepower forward and in the fight at this critical point. The men nodded their understanding and prepared to move.

The two men looked at Alex, who indicated they should move when ready. The first man took a deep breath and glided toward the intersection with his SAW up and ready. He began firing before he emerged beyond the threshold, and the number two man stepped up to the corner as both made entry at the same time. Alex was right behind the number two man and out of the corner of his eye watched the first man go down under a hail of gunfire. Then Alien was next to him, and they moved down the hallway toward an open landing and a stairwell. The bolt of Alex's M4 locked back on an empty magazine, and in the blink of an eye Alex dropped it to hang from his neck and drew his Glock and continued to fire.

The occupants had attempted to set up a hasty defensive barricade, but now there was just a pile of splintered desks and tables, beyond which freshly slaughtered bodies lay strewn among one another. As the firing dissipated, Alex holstered his pistol, retrieved his dangling rifle, and inserted a fresh magazine. He glimpsed a figure running toward the front door, grabbing the doorframe as he vaulted through it. Alex swung his weapon that way and snapped off three rounds. He heard a scream as the man disappeared into the darkness outside and two of his fingers fell to the floor.

Alex stepped over the dead men until he found one still alive. He pulled the knife he had taken from Linda's room out of his pocket, grabbed the man by his hair, and put the knife in his face. "Whose knife is this?"

The man grimaced in pain from the bullets in his stomach and looked confused. One of the Kurds repeated the question in Arabic. The man rattled off something and inclined his head up the stairs.

The Kurd said, "He says it belongs to the big man, Yasin, and he's upstairs."

★★★

Yasin and Uday now huddled behind an overturned desk about twenty meters beyond the top of the stairs. Uday began crawling down the hallway. Yasin contemptuously watched him go and turned back to the stairwell.

★★★

Alex looked at his watch and knew they were running out of time. He turned to Alien and said, "Go back the way we came and police up our men we left behind. Leave me one vehicle and take the men home."

Alien knew what Alex was thinking, and he knew he had no time to try to talk Alex out of it. He nodded and offered his hand to his friend. "Good luck, brother."

Alex gripped his hand, looked him hard in the eye, and said, "Yeah, man, you take care of yourself and get the men the hell outta here." He turned and started slowly up the stairs. Alien turned to the men and motioned to go back the way they had come. They started to resist, and Alien shook his head and forcefully told them to go. They moved tactically back down the hallway.

As Alex reached the second deck of the stairs, he heard Alien on the radio: "We're pulling out, and I need the ambulances at the breach. Continue to cover us until we're mounted up and moving." A series of "rogers" ended the call.

Alex peered through his NODs over the top of the steps and down the hall at floor level. He saw a form blocking the hallway and figured there might be someone hiding behind it. With his M4 up and ready, he took another step up the stairs. At the flash from a muzzle, he jerked his head down and heard the shot echo down the hallway. If the man's aim had been true, Alex wouldn't have had time to jerk his head in any direction.

He took a breath and stepped up, firing. His rounds ate up the table, and an AK-47 fell over the top of the barricade and clattered to the floor. A man rolled out from behind the desk and tried to retrieve the rifle. Alex put three more rounds in his torso, and the man stopped where he was and rolled over on his back. Alex walked up to him while searching the hallway for more targets. When he saw none, he looked down at the man and realized he was enormous.

Alex knelt on one knee beside him and pulled the knife from his pocket. The big man groaned and looked at Alex as Alex held the knife up to his face. "This is yours, isn't it?"

The man groaned again and tried to roll over.

Alex said calmly, "Oh no you don't. You're not going anywhere before we finish our conversation." Alex rolled him back over.

"You're probably not going to feel this, but it's going to make me feel so much better." Alex held the knife up and then slowly moved it between the man's legs. The big man struggled, but he had lost his strength and was fading fast. Alex hit him in the face with the hilt of the knife and then let his M4 hang from the strap around his neck. He grabbed the man by the throat with his left hand and put his left knee to the man's stomach, and with his right hand he cut open the big man's pants with the knife. Then Alex leaned over and took hold of the man's genitals with one hand and pulled them as he ran the razor edge of the knife along the base and sliced it off, castrating him penis and all.

The big man closed his eyes and screamed.

Alex held the parts up to the big man's face and said, "Oh, you did feel that, didn't you? Good."

Yasin opened his eyes and groaned as he looked at his own bloody manhood dangling in front of his face.

Alex then pried open the big man's jaws with the knife and stuffed his bloody balls and penis into his mouth. Then, with both hands, Alex raised the knife up high and brought it down as hard as he could, stabbing him right in the forehead. The sharp, heavy blade went completely through his skull and pinned his head to the floor.

Alex heard a panicked scuffling and raised his head to see a man scurrying to the end of the hallway, looking back just as he turned the corner.

Alex snatched his rifle up, but he was too late to take a shot. As he got to his feet and ran after the man he thought, *It's the general.*

Uday ran to the far end of the school as fast as his feet would carry him. What he had just seen he would never have believed possible. The way the American had brutally killed Yasin shocked him. He had never believed that another man could best the giant Yasin, yet the American had made it seem like an afterthought. Where the hell was the brigade? Why had they not come like he envisioned? He had to get away. He would go to Al-Baghdadi at the mosque; he would be safe there. Then he would plot his revenge.

He burst out of the door and ran to his car. Thanking Allah that he'd had the foresight to leave the keys on the dash, he fumbled for them and jammed them into the ignition. The sedan fired up right away, and he peeled out, spinning the car around in the dirt toward the front gate.

Alex fired his weapon at the car as it careened away to the left, and then he immediately turned right and ran back down the side of the building and out through the breach. Alien was already gone, and there was one DOS sedan still there. He ran his hand over the windshield wipers and grabbed the key, jumped into the car, and fired it up. He hit the gas hard, and with wheels spinning, the armored sedan shot forward and into the intersection a heartbeat after Uday sped past.

Alex fishtailed hard left behind his quarry and urged his car forward. The two cars raced down the street for several blocks toward the Al-Aqsa Mosque. At the end of the road in front of the mosque, Uday turned hard left and Alex closed the gap. One block down Uday turned hard right, and Alex caught his back-right quarter panel and hit the gas. Uday's car spun around and ground to a halt as the engine stalled. Alex rammed the car with his and kept pushing Uday's vehicle until he pinned it with a great crash against a wall across the street from the mosque.

Uday was stunned and unable to move. Alex opened his door and stepped out of his car. As he walked up to Uday's car, he drew his pistol. Uday looked up at him and raised his hands in surrender as Alex pointed the gun at his face and fired several rounds from the Glock. The Hydra-Shok bullets went through Uday's hands and into his face, and the back of his head burst apart with grisly shards of brain and bone.

Alex looked for a moment to be certain that he was dead. When he saw the brain matter dripping from Uday's head, Alex was satisfied that the job was done. He turned and walked calmly back to his car.

★★★

Al-Baghdadi watched from his perch on top of the mosque and was also satisfied that his competitor was eliminated. He allowed the American to depart unmolested.

★★★

East of Samarra, Alex had just turned on to Highway 1 and was running north when he was assaulted by the most blinding light he had ever witnessed. The light throbbed and assaulted his senses and made it impossible to see or think or do anything but apply the brakes. His vehicle skidded to a stop. He knew he had to get out, but when he opened the door, he felt himself being lifted out of the car and thrown down on the ground, crushing the breath from his lungs. As he gasped for air, he thought he was dreaming, but when his vision cleared, he realized he was being restrained on the ground, and the barrels of several weapons were pointed at his face.

He was forcibly flipped over on his stomach, and handcuffs dug into his wrists. Then he felt shackles clamped around his ankles and something connected the two; he was trussed up like a cow in a rodeo.

Gradually, as his senses returned, he heard voices speaking over him, in English. He was flipped over again on his back. He struggled against the discomfort of his restraints and the pain in his hip.

A familiar voice told him, "Relax and you'll be OK."

Alex looked up and saw Special Agent Jeffrey gloating over him.

"I told you I'd bring you down."

Alex said, "What are you doing?"

Jeffrey laughed, "What do you think? I'm arresting you."

"For what? Murder?"

"Murder? No, *nobody* gives a shit about the people you've killed. You've done us a favor, and I couldn't convict you for that here anyway. I'm arresting you for stealing that car from us." He gestured toward the smashed-up Corolla.

"What are you talking about? You gave me that car."

Jeffrey smiled. "If you can prove that in court, you can get out of jail free. The way I see it, you have our vehicle without authorization. See you in federal prison, asshole."

Alex laid his head back on the ground and thought, *Go figure.*

EPILOGUE

"Believers, when you go abroad to fight wars in Allah's Cause, discriminate carefully, and say not to anyone who greets you: 'You are not a believer!' coveting the chance profits of this life so you may despoil him. With Allah are plenteous spoils and booty."

Koran 4:94

AS HAIDER STOOD ON the balcony overlooking the courtyard, he rubbed his left hand and felt for the missing fingers he had lost so long ago. He could still feel the nerves at the fingertips that were no longer there. But life had been good to him after all; while so many others had died, he was truly blessed. The Americans had left, and the caliphate had taken over.

He now had several wives, and although he had to beat them from time to time, he loved them all equally. They had borne him almost two dozen children, and he had plenty of money to provide all of them with all the comforts they could possibly want in this life. He was now the primary imam of a very specialized madrassa, and he no longer questioned the veracity of Islam or his devotion to Allah's Cause.

Next to him stood the charismatic figure of the venerable caliph of the Islamic State, Abu Bakr al-Baghdadi. The caliph reached out and placed his hand on Haider's shoulder, looking at him with affection as he addressed the students and faculty of Haider's bomb-making school. Haider in turn glanced over his other shoulder and smiled at his two most promising and favorite students, from Dearborn, Michigan, who would soon return to the United States. He knew that no matter if it took the faithful another 1,400 years, they would succeed.

"Fight them until there are no non-Muslims and all in the world submit to Allah alone."

Koran 8:39

GLOSSARY

AAR: after action review

ASAP: as soon as possible

ASL: alternate supply route

BFT: Blue Force Tracker, a GPS device friendly forces use to signal an emergency, particularly an attack or ambush

BIAP: Baghdad International Airport

Big Army: US Army

Bobtail: the tractor part of a tractor trailer

Break: military radio jargon that indicates the caller is not finished with what he must say, but will interrupt the transmission for tactical reasons or just to collect his thoughts

C-4 or Composition C-4 or Plastic Explosive: a malleable, clay-like chemical explosive composition that is very stable and takes extreme heat and shock to detonate; a preferred military explosive

CAC: compound access control point; like ECP or entry control point

Call Sign: code name for operators, generally does not change, often assigned by others on the team—not always flattering

Chinook: military heavy lift helicopter

CPA or Coalition Provisional Authority: the post-invasion transitional governing body in Iraq from April 2003 until June 2004

Commo, Comms: short for communications, can refer to the equipment or the use of equipment

Concertina: coiled razor wire for fencing or obstacles

Copy: military radio jargon for "I understand" or "I heard," often followed by the recipient repeating the message that was sent, to ensure accuracy

CP: checkpoint, Charlie Papa
  1. a point plotted on a map to mark progress
  2. a barrier where access is controlled

CQB: close quarters battle (combat) or fighting in buildings

Cross-Load: term for abandoning a downed vehicle for one that works

Daisy Chain: multiple IEDs wired together to detonate sequentially or simultaneously

DET 1 or Detachment One: created in 2003 as a separate special operations force for the Marine Corps to test its integration into the military's Special Operations Command, or SOCOM; DET 1 was the predecessor of the Marine Special Operations Command, or MARSOC.

Det Cord, Detonation Cord: thin plastic tube filled with PETN (pentaerythritol tetranitrate) explosive that explodes at four miles per second; used to ignite other explosives, bombs, IEDs, etc.

Delta Barrier: high-security hydraulic barricades that lie flat on the pavement and with the push of a button pop up to block vehicular traffic

DFAC: dining facility, AKA mess hall, chow hall, roach coach

Dishdasha: a long-sleeved ankle-length garment that looks

like a robe that Arab men wear across the Middle East, North Africa, and Southern Asia; also becoming fashionable now in Washington DC, Detroit, Dallas, New York, LA, St. Louis, San Francisco, Chicago, Boston, etc.

DOS: US Department of State

DOD: US Department of Defense

ECP: entry control point; a compound access control point, usually checks access against records or badges; typically searches people and vehicles entering the compound; intended to be the first line of defense for a compound during an attack

Erbil, Iraq (also spelled Arbil or Irbil): capital of Iraqi Kurdistan

FOB, or Forward Operating Base: a secure military base established to support combat operations

Ghillie Suit: camouflage clothing designed to match an environment, often enhanced with local foliage or debris

Green on Blue: refers to host-country allied soldiers who turn on US soldiers when they are vulnerable

Green Zone: ten square kilometers in the center of Baghdad surrounded by T-walls, housing the coalition countries' embassies and the Iraqi Transitional Government; formally named the International Zone or IZ

Hadj or Hadji: English slang term referring to an Arab male

Hesco: a wire-mesh bastion filled with dirt that creates a significant barrier, used as a fence or a protective blast wall

HMMWV: High Mobility Multi Wheeled Vehicle, pronounced "Humvee" or called "Hummer," the tactical vehicle that replaced the Jeep; at first they were unarmored, and then they were armored with after-market kits, and finally they were up-armored in the factory.

HEMTT: Heavy Expanded Mobility Tactical Truck, pronounced "Hemmit"; the modern version of the old "deuce-and-a-half" and five-ton military transport vehicles; eight-wheel drive, 15.2-liter, 515 horsepower diesel engines; can be fully armored and configured for a wide range of transport purposes: water, fuel, cargo, troops, etc.

IED: improvised explosive device; any makeshift destructive device; may be military ordinance used in a manner not originally intended or may be homemade. May be command detonated, typically using car or garage door openers, cell phones, electric wires, or may be initiated by the victim with trip wires, pressure plates, or magnetic devices. May be disguised in all manner of ways, from inserting it into dead animals to placing it under piles of garbage to digging a hole dug in the road and covering it up with asphalt, etc.

ING: Iraqi National Guard

Intel, Intelligence: information regarding a situation gathered from every source possible

IP: Iraqi Police

Insha'Allah: Arabic for "God willing" or "If God wills"

J-turn: a 180-degree turn to the rear; while traveling in reverse, the driver whips the steering wheel hard left or right and about halfway through the turn drops the transmission to drive and hits the gas and straightens up the steering wheel.

Kafir: the actual word used in the Koran for "unbeliever," "infidel," or anyone other than a Muslim. Translation is like "dirt," but really means lower than low—like lower than the shit that sits on the ground

Kevlar: a bullet-resistant fabric

Klick: kilometer

Magazine, Mag: ammunition-feeding device that holds the bullets for automatic weapons; can be rapidly removed when empty and replaced with another full one for sustained shooting

Man-dress: see dishdasha

Man-jammies: pajama-like clothing for men; popular throughout the Arab and Muslim world, particularly Afghanistan and Pakistan and increasingly in Western Europe and America

Mike or Mic, Handset: radio microphone

Mike: Army radio jargon for minute

MK 19 or Mark 19: American 40 mm belt-fed grenade launcher; can fire up to sixty grenades per minute; can hit targets almost a mile away

MM: millimeter; one millimeter is one-thousandth of a meter, used here to measure the diameter of a projectile; a 5.56 mm bullet is slightly larger than a caliber .223; a 7.62 mm round is the same diameter as a caliber .308; the M1 Abrams tank fires a 120 mm round.

MRE: Meal Ready to Eat, individual field rations used when dining facilities are not available; damn delicious if you're starving to death; constipation is assured.

MSR: main supply route

NOD, Night Observation Device, or Night Vision Device (NVD): can be strapped to the head or mounted on a helmet or attached to a weapon; magnifies ambient light in shades of green to enable the user to see in near darkness

Out: military radio jargon terminating a conversation or message

Over: military radio jargon requesting a response to a transmission

Pillar, A, B, or C Pillar: the vertical metal support between windows; the A pillar is between the windshield and the front-seat window

PMC: private military company

Pax: military jargon for personnel or passengers

PKM: Russian-made 7.62x54 mm belt-fed machine gun, effective at about three-quarters of a mile, capable of sending bullets over two miles away

PM: program manager

PSD: personal security detail, bodyguard

Peshmerga: Kurdish militia; *pesh* means "one who confronts" and *merga* means "death," so "one who confronts death"

Pucker Factor: the involuntary tightening of sphincter muscles that happens when the human body fears for its life; a phenomenon like "scared shitless"

Roger: military radio jargon indicating affirmation; "Yes," "I hear you," "understood," etc.

RPG: rocket-propelled grenade

RPK: Russian-made 7.62x39 mm, belt/drum/magazine-fed machine gun, effective at about half a mile, capable of distances of just under two miles

Semi: tractor trailer

Simunition: a training bullet made of plastic and filled with chalk; upon impact leaves a mark at the point of impact

SLANT, SLANT Report, or SLANTREP: a military report that provides the identification, purpose, and number of personnel and equipment

SOPs: standard operating procedures; instructions that guide solutions for common tasks

SVIED: suicide-vest improvised explosive device

SP: start point; used to indicate the location where a mission begins

Tango: military jargon for terrorist

Technical: a homemade or improvised fighting vehicle, usually a pickup truck, often with a machine gun or some other weapon mounted in the bed

TIC: troops in contact with the enemy, i.e. a firefight

TTPs: Tactics, techniques, and procedures are like SOPs; they are instructions for actions a unit and personnel should take under anticipated situations.

Triangle of Death: a Sunni-dominated area south of Baghdad. The first chapter of this book takes place north of Baghdad in the Sunni Triangle, but for the purpose of drama the author chose to use the name Triangle of Death as the title of the chapter.

T-Wall: a twelve to twenty-foot-high section of concrete like a Jersey barrier commonly seen at American road construction sites; manufactured with rebar and often reinforced with a plastic coating like Rhino Lining to contain fragmentation, the barriers are put in place with a crane and connected to create a blast-protective wall often topped with razor wire.

Up-Armor: armored vehicle

USAID: US Agency for International Development

VBIED: vehicle-borne improvised explosive device, usually pronounced v-bid

Victor: military jargon for vehicle

VS-17 Panel: visual signal panel; one side is fluorescent red and the other side is fluorescent orange; completely unfolded it is about 24x70 inches.

WARNORD, Warning Order: a formal alert of an upcoming mission that contains enough information for elements to begin preparing for the event

Wilco: military radio jargon for "I will comply."

CPSIA information can be obtained
at www.ICGtesting.com
Printed in the USA
BVHW071156180521
607630BV00003B/172